Nothing Can Bring Back the Hour

Pamela Dean

iUniverse, Inc.
Bloomington

Nothing Can Bring Back the Hour

iUniverse books may be ordered through booksellers or by contacting:

iUniverse
1663 Liberty Drive
Bloomington, IN 47403
www.iuniverse.com
1-800-Authors (1-800-288-4677)

ISBN: 978-1-4620-0549-9 (sc)
ISBN: 978-1-4620-0550-5 (hc)
ISBN: 978-1-4620-0551-2 (ebk)

Library of Congress Control Number: 2011904121

Printed in the United States of America

iUniverse rev. date: 10/11/2011

Dedication

For my family, who smiles upon me in any light,
my love and gratitude

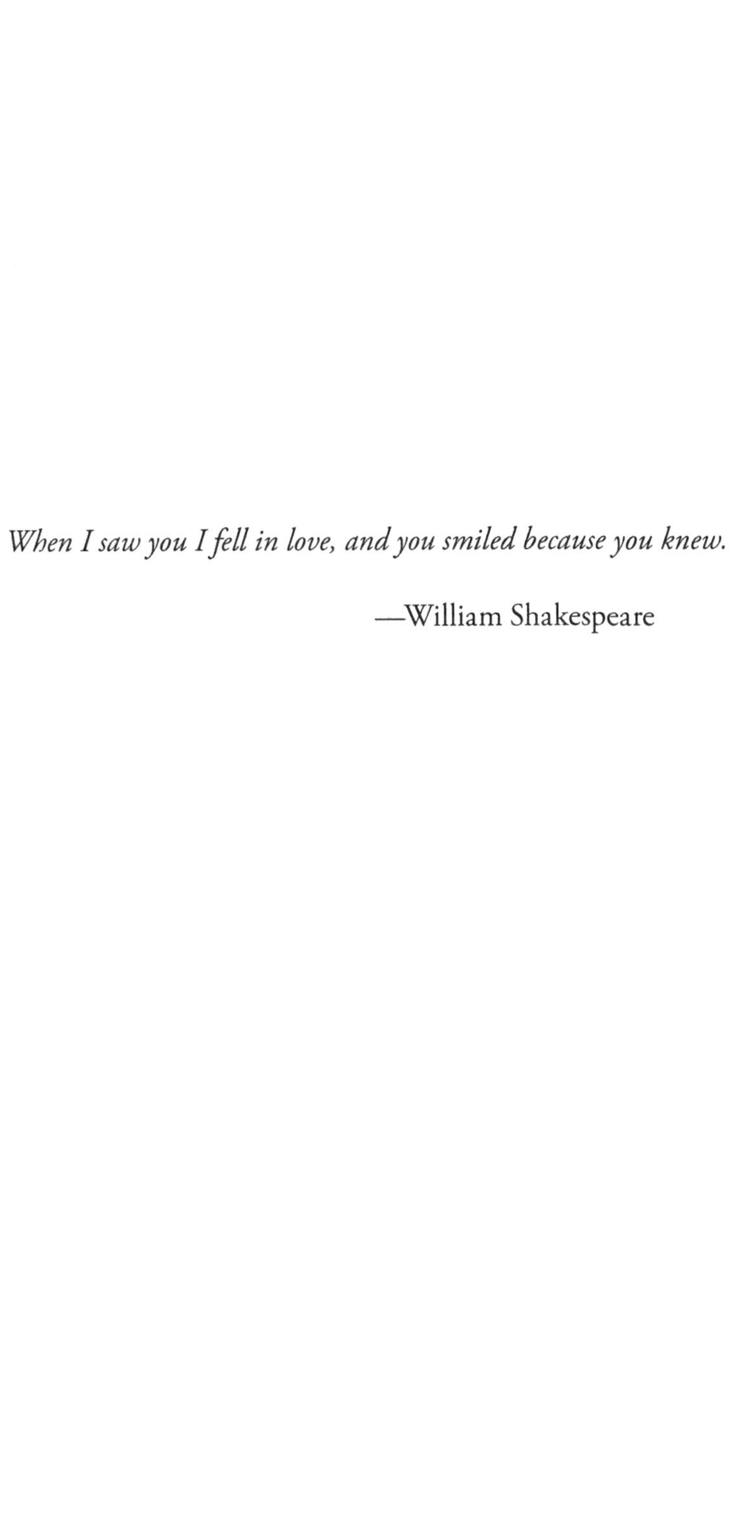

When I saw you I fell in love, and you smiled because you knew.

—William Shakespeare

It is all still so clear to me
As if it were yesterday
My body may reflect the march of time
But my soul is ageless
Age and time do not erase that which is imprinted on the heart
It finds its spot and lies seemingly dormant
It crouches and waits for its moment
Without warning, it springs forth
In the middle of some otherwise insignificant moment
A smell, a song . . . it triggers
Vivid images fill me and carry me to that place
It sometimes visits me in the middle of the night
In my dreams I am young
I feel the joy and the stinging in my heart because of him
And the echoes grow louder

I remember sixteen
The Beatles were all the rage
U.S. soldiers continued to die in Vietnam
The Rolling Stones performed on the Ed Sullivan Show
Martin Luther King moved his crusade to Chicago
And I fell in love with Buck Kendall

Acknowledgements

The writer holds the pen, creates the characters, and tells the story. But she cannot complete the job alone. Without the scrutinizing and loving eyes of my editors, the words would lack form. I was most fortunate to have three editors who not only excel in their craft but who are special people in my life. Thanks to my friend and DTA partner, Debra Talcott, who graciously said, "Yes, it would be an honor to edit your book." Endless thanks to Harriet Wolbrink, my friend, teacher-partner, and touchstone, who, after reading only the first page said, "You have to let me edit your book." I could not have managed without your loving and perceptive eyes falling upon my words. And to Jessica Dean, my daughter and my inspiration, without whose deadlines and threefold editing jobs I would not have arrived at this place, my heartfelt thanks and love—you held me up.

For the cover art inspiration, I thank my son, Geoffrey Dean, whose thoughtful interpretation of the text gradually transformed into the vision I was searching for. Your gentle spirit is reflected in your work; your painstaking efforts, the icing on the cake.

To my husband and business partner, Eric, thank you for your unconditional support and endless patience. The smile in your eyes, the one meant for only me, has been my companion and my comfort.

Part One

1964-1967

One

Looking in the mirror was not my favorite thing to do. But my grandmother insisted that I was in the "budding stages" and would bloom just fine. "I see beauty awakening, Samantha. Be patient, il mio inamorato." *My sweetheart.* "These things take time," she claimed. Easy for her to say.

In addition to my physical dissatisfaction, I was a bit of a prude. I didn't swear, wouldn't take a puff of a cigarette if you blackmailed me, and walked away when my peers told dirty jokes, which pretty much sealed my reputation. At fourteen I had never had a date or kissed a boy. When the in-crowd had the infamous "boy-girl parties," I wasn't invited. I was a good student, obeyed my parents and teachers, and followed all the doctrines of the Holy Catholic Church. So you see what I mean.

About halfway through my ninth grade year at Pioneer Public, the school I had been attending since kindergarten, Brian Determan appeared. His father, a wealthy and prestigious businessman, decided that it was time for a simpler life, so he abandoned his hectic schedule in Boston and moved the family to Carlson. Brian was the best-looking thing I had ever laid eyes on. In his presence, girls forgot how to talk. Sounds would come out of their mouths, but they weren't words, trust me. Oddly enough, he didn't seem to notice their mindless behavior. I figured he was used to it.

Brian sat next to me in both homeroom and science. I quickly discovered that while he was perfect on the outside, he possessed one unattractive flaw: he swore like a trooper. I had never been witness to such unabashed cussing. Intimidated by his good looks, I had not yet said a word to him. But one day his foul mouth just became too much.

He had just slammed the top of his desk down in anger, inadvertently jamming his finger. "God damn it! Jesus, that hurts!" He shook his hand as if to release the pain.

"You swear too much, Brian." Yes, these were my first words to the ninth-grade heartthrob. After his immediate preoccupation with his finger, he must have realized that I had spoken.

"What did you say?"

"I said you swear too much. Every time you speak, you seem to say something you shouldn't. It doesn't sound good. And girls don't like it." I'll never forget the look on his face. Somewhere between shock and admiration. I wasn't sure which route he'd take, so I readied myself for his response.

"You think I swear too much?" His fascination grew.

"Yes, you do. And it's always about God. Don't blame Him for your problems. Plus, it's a sin to take the Lord's name in vain."

And there it was! The nuns were using me as their medium again.

Brian laughed. "You're right! I do say *goddamn* and *Jesus Christ* a lot."

"See, you're doing it again."

More laughter, wonderful and infectious. "No. I wasn't swearing. I was demonstrating."

"But you still swore."

"You're a piece of work, Sam. Are you Catholic?"

"What gave you your first clue?"

"The 'taking the Lord's name in vain' thing. Who told you that?"

"Well, everybody knows that!" *Is he stupid?* "And my grandmother lives by it."

"So you never swear." He looked incredulous.

"No."

"Ever?"

"No."

"Not even when you're really pissed? Or don't you get pissed either?"

"Of course I do!" My indignation stood up for me.

"Do which? Get pissed or swear?"

"Get mad. I get mad like everybody else. I just don't swear." Keep in mind, my corruption was just around the corner.

"Why? 'Cuz of the Catholic thing?"

"What do you mean 'the Catholic thing'? It's a religion."

"I know. It's just not mine."

"What's yours? Hedonism?"

"Ouch! You are something! You just spit out whatever's on your mind, don't you?"

"Not always. But I've been sitting next to you for three weeks now, and I hear everything you say."

His amusement traveled from down deep, and he laughed heartily for a long time. "Well, I certainly am glad I have you sitting next to me to keep me on the straight and narrow. Now, Sam, this job won't be easy, but please don't give up on me, okay? You're dealing with ingrained habits here."

"I can tell."

And so the friendship began. Brian was my first male friend. I counseled him on how to behave around the girls he liked, since he didn't have a clue. He was grateful for the pointers and constantly told me that I was the best girl he knew and that someday some guy would be goddamn lucky to have me.

Amen.

Two

After my graduation from Pioneer Public, summer stood as the roadblock between life as I knew it and the life I longed for: high school. I was finally going to attend Carlson High School as a sophomore, and I couldn't wait. Kids from the Catholic schools were already there, having entered as freshmen, and they were experiencing everything I dreamt about. Soon, it would be my turn, and I was aching for it.

It was a Tuesday night, a seductive summer evening, uncharacteristically balmy for Carlson. Carolyn Jones and I were walking home on our usual route from Pioneer Public, where we had played an impromptu game of softball with some kids hanging around the park behind the school. Carolyn was one of those girls who jumped friendships—she'd leave you in the dust in a heartbeat if somebody better came along. I had been the victim of her ship-jumping a couple of times, until I finally wised up and served her some of her own medicine.

Carolyn and I were discussing our upcoming sophomore year and how we couldn't wait to be a part of the high school crowd. And, as usual, she pressed me about Brian. She couldn't believe we were just friends. I held the envious position of being the girl closest to him, and, therefore, the person everyone interrogated about his status. It was exhausting.

"Are you sure you don't like him and are just afraid he'll shoot you down?" Subtle girl.

"I'm sure."

"Well, I don't believe you. If you think you have any kind of a chance with him, you better make your move now. 'Cuz when he gets to the high school, girls are gonna be swarming him."

"I told you, Carolyn, we're just friends. Now drop it. Please!"

She continued to jabber away about how good-looking Brian was, despite my halt in the conversation. I was relieved that we would soon be parting ways. Eventually, we rounded the corner onto her street, and I noticed a boy on a bike in the distance. The rider picked up speed and headed in our direction. As the bike drew closer, I recognized Buck Kendall.

I studied him as he shifted his body to pick up speed. Leaning forward, he dropped his head while his eyes held the street in front of him. As he gained momentum, his body swayed in perfect rhythm with his ten-speed. There was a graceful determination about his movements, a bird cutting through the air toward its prey. Deliberate and unfaltering, he knew exactly what he was doing. He shifted his body with ease as he drew nearer. He waved casually. From that distance, I could detect just the edge of a smile. I remember thinking he looked different from the last time I had seen him: older, cuter—definitely cuter. There was an intensity about him that I hadn't noticed before. He had a mature presence and struck me as more serious than most boys his age.

I stared.

Before that evening, I had not paid much attention to him because I had a crush on his older brother, Greg—like every other girl my age. Whenever I saw Buck, he was aimlessly cruising around on his bike by himself or accompanied by Larry Polanski. Now there was some twisted piece of work. Okay, he had certain redeemable qualities, but I could never figure out why those two hung out. Night and day.

I had basically dismissed Buck as Greg's younger brother. Besides, sophomores didn't date freshman. However, one thing I did remember was hearing everyone talk about how smart he was. He would eventually score obscenely high on the ACTs and SATs. People said he was a genius. As far as I knew, he had never had a girlfriend. He was somewhat of a loner, withdrawn and aloof, unlike his gregarious brother.

He stopped when he reached us and stood comfortably, legs balancing the red bike in a slow rocking motion, arms hanging casually by his side. He smiled at both of us, but directed his attention to Carolyn first.

"Hey, Carolyn. What's up?"

She beamed and flipped her long tresses over her shoulder. Her body gained the signature momentum of the flattered female, and she transformed under the spell of his charm, a charm I had not noticed before. Where had I been?

I stood, watching him talk effortlessly with Carolyn, never really hearing anything he said. There was just his voice—deep, slow, mesmerizing—and his body, leaning against the bike. I was suddenly aware that my heart was pounding. I shifted position and took a deep breath. It didn't help.

When he laughed, the corners of his eyes crinkled. After a few minutes, he turned to me.

"Hi, Sam." His gaze was direct. A few strands of hair, the color of dark honey, fell over his eye. He smiled again, and my heart stopped.

God help me. And he knows my name!

Our eyes locked, and I was incapable of turning away. As I stared, I realized he was beautiful. His face was strong and slender, with grooved cheeks that gave way to dimples when he smiled. His lips were full; and his eyes, clearly his best feature, were a variegated mix of hazel and brown. They peeked out from dark, hooded brows, absorbing everything. His body was lean, and he held himself with a slight air of arrogance mixed with a bashful reserve. His brooding handsomeness was undeniable.

Experiencing Buck up close was different from watching him riding by on his bike—and the difference was startling.

"So how you doing?" He waited.

I finally realized I hadn't responded. "Hi, Buck." It was a blurt. And that was it. I shifted position again and stepped on a trailing sneaker tie, which slowly unraveled as I moved. I hoped he wouldn't notice.

He did. His smile grew with alarming assuredness.

Those eyes.

I shifted position a third time, and the lace loosened completely. He switched his attention to my feet. "Your sneaker is untied."

"Oh, yeah. It is." I was useless.

"Want me to tie it for you?"

Is he serious? His expression said he was. I continued to squirm.

"No, that's okay. These Keds always do that. Thanks, anyway." I looked down at my foot, for lack of another place to rest my eyes, and heard myself emit some stupid giggle completely foreign to my usual noises. Instead of shutting up, I continued, as if some twinkie had invaded my body. "I'll get it in a minute. It's just these stupid ties. They're too long." I prayed he would ride away before I had to bend over to tie the laces. Not the image I wanted to plant in his head. Plus, it would be just like me to fall flat on my face. I was frozen in position.

"So where are you going?" he asked me.

His focus did not waver. He drank me in and left me weak. If that wasn't disquieting enough, I was still locked in place because of my sneaker. So I tried to look cool without moving an inch. I think he was on to me. But he was polite and said nothing about my obvious embarrassment. He simply waited for me to respond as he shook a meandering strand of hair from his forehead.

Mercy!

"Home." I couldn't think of a thing to say.

"I saw you at the park the other day." His words stopped me cold.

"What?" Shock invaded my body.

"In the park, playing softball. You were with a bunch of kids, and my brother was pitching."

"Oh. Sorry. I didn't see you." And I *was* sorry.

He nodded, the line of his jaw clenched. His discomfort made him more appealing. I started to sweat, and I don't sweat pretty. Perspiration on some girls looks dewy and seductive. On me it looks like sweat.

Like divine intervention, Carolyn began chattering away again. Normally she irritated me with her need to control conversations involving boys. But at that moment, I could have kissed her. So I stood there while she babbled, one eye on my sneaker. Words would not rescue me.

"Well, I guess I better get going, or I'll be in big trouble with Jane."

"Who's Jane?" asked Carolyn.

"My mom," he smirked.

My heart sank. I knew our encounter had reached its end without my ever having made an impression. At least not the kind of impression I wanted to make. He pushed off. His bike picked up speed. Then he lowered his head and turned back toward me.

"See you around, Sam."

When he said my name, my stomach did backflips. My response came in the form of a smile, which I hoped he detected in the distance. I watched his bike fade as he peddled down the street. I stood there, pathetic. I wanted to yell: *Stop! Come back. I promise I'll do better this time.* He disappeared around the corner. I bent over and tied my sneaker.

Carolyn suspected nothing. Self-absorbed girls miss a lot. We finished the short walk to her house, all the while she yapped away about how cute Buck was. While standing on the sidewalk leading to her front door, a light illuminated her living room where her mother was peeking out the picture window.

"There's your mom," I told her.

"I see her! She always does that. Like I don't know it's time to come in. She's so annoying."

"Well, I have to go anyway. It's starting to get dark."

"Did you see how pretty his eyes are? And did you notice his cute, little flirtatious smile?"

I noticed.

I nodded my response. "See you, Carolyn."

"Call me tomorrow. I want to know what you're wearin' the first day of school."

Three

Night descended. I started counting stars—but before I knew it, I couldn't keep up with them. I walked down West Main Street, passing Pioneer Public. I smiled as the majesty of the old brick building towered over me. My eyes fell to the kindergarten windows, decorated with pictures of trees and cut-outs of letters and numbers. Ten years in that building. I turned onto Benton Street, following the familiar path.

Buck Kendall was in my head. One brief encounter exploded inside me, sending images of his body straddling the 10-speed, his soulful eyes, the crevices that grew in his cheeks when he smiled. And his voice, the sound that gripped me and lifted me with its rich tones and laughter.

Sam.

I swung around. No one was there. I stood, scanning the area in hopes that no one had witnessed my quirky behavior.

Thank God!

I picked up my pace.

As I approached my front porch, I could see the television flickering through the sheers that were drawn across the picture window. I knew my parents would be waiting up for me in the living room. When I entered, I found my dad half asleep in the corner chair, head tilted sideways, resting on his hand. Mom was stretched out on the couch in her white chenille robe, wave holders pinching her hair into position.

"Hi, honey."

"Hi, Mom."

"Have fun?"

"Yes." I leaned over to kiss her. She smelled like Johnson's Baby Powder.

"I'm going upstairs to take a bath and wash my hair. I'll come back to say good night."

"Okay, but don't wake your sister. And if your brother's light is still on, tell him I said to stop reading and go to sleep. He has a game in the morning."

I climbed the stairs and peered under my brother's door for a trace of light. Mom was right.

"Ryan, Mom said to turn off the light and go to sleep."

"Knock much?"

"Sorry, I'm just telling you what Mom said."

"I have to finish this chapter."

"What are you reading?"

"*The Yearling*, if it's any of your business."

I let it go. "Night, Ryan."

"Night. Close the door."

After my bath I retreated to the small bedroom I shared with my sister. I mechanically placed huge rollers in my hair, tightly fastening each one with bobby pins at both ends. I covered my head with a ruffled roller cap to keep everything in place. Then down the stairs to kiss my parents good night.

"I'll tuck you in when Dad and I come up." She kept one eye on the television as she spoke. Lucille Ball was sucking down another spoonful of Vitaminamejamin or whatever the heck she called it. She chuckled at the red head's antics, even though she'd seen that episode before. Dad snorted audibly.

"Nick! You're snoring. Shake 'em, Sam."

"I'm awake, I'm awake," he muttered and then fell back into a snore.

"Okay, Sam. I'll be up in a few minutes. Your dad's had it."

I crawled into the lower bunk, tossing back the pink spread. The sheets smelled like outside. Mom hung them on the line when the weather was good. I pressed the cotton to my nose, inhaling the freshness again. The shutters on the windows were open, and a breeze skimmed the length of my body. I lay on my back, staring at the bottom of my six-year-old sister's bunk. I could hear her breathing. An approaching train rumbled down the tracks in the distance. I turned toward the window to listen. The steady humming from Junction Street usually quieted me. Like the patter of rain, the rumble of trains lulled me to sleep. As a child, I'd fight to stay awake just so I could lose myself in those sounds a little longer. But always, in fading moments, I lost the battle to the repetitive cadence of the soothing rhythms. On this night, however, I lay wide-eyed, my heart thumping in my chest because of a chance meeting. Had I not been in that exact place at that exact moment, the events of my life would have unfolded differently. I was a prisoner, captured by the beautiful face of a golden-haired boy.

Four

September 1965. I made it! I was officially a high school student. And the early morning adjustment was a breeze.

The school was overcrowded and growing. My classes were bigger than at Pioneer, and each one contained a different mix of kids. I met new people every day. I joined the yearbook staff and began attending student council meetings. There were dozens of clubs, and I wanted to be a part of everything. I had a new life.

Among the popular people in my classes was Shelly Porterfield. I had heard a lot about her, and she was definitely as pretty as everyone reported. There was no question why all the boys were after her. Like all of the students who attended Catholic schools, Shelly came to Carlson for her freshman year, so she was already established. As a newcomer, I felt tentative about meeting people like her.

One day after school I was heading home with Mary Mathis. Mary and I had struck up a friendship at Pioneer. She wasn't part of the in-crowd there either, so we were a perfect match for a while. Shelly was standing in front of the school with Darlene Bailey and Patty Benson. All three had attended St. Patrick's Academy together. Patty's mother was in the same Bunko club and bowling league as mine, so we already knew each other. Bunko and bowling were the big cultural entertainment in Carlson.

"Hi, Sam!" Patty spotted me and beckoned me to join them.

Mary stiffened. "Listen, Sam, I'll talk with you later." Part of Mary's social problem was she refused to take the initiative to meet new people.

"I'll only be a minute. You should walk over there with me and say hello."

"Not interested." She smiled briefly and walked away. I headed toward Patty, a slight twinge of guilt biting me.

"Hi, Patty."

"How are you, Sam?" Patty smiled broadly. "I haven't seen you in a while. So—how do you like high school life so far?"

"I really like it. I'm meeting a lot of new people." I avoided eye contact with Shelly, intimidated by her presence and the stories that preceded her, but to my surprise, she piped in.

"That's a cute outfit you're wearing. I like the pleated skirt. Where did you buy it?" She spoke as if she'd always known me, a level of privilege in her voice. Nonetheless, I felt flattered.

"My grandmother made it. Thanks."

"Really? She made it?" She scrutinized me with a trained eye. "It's different than anything I've seen."

"She makes most of my clothes."

"You're lucky. It's real cute. Maybe I could borrow it sometime." I could feel my expression change because I didn't even know her. Considering our only link was mutual friends, her remark was presumptuous.

"Sure, I guess," I fumbled, her spell cast upon me.

"You're in my English class, aren't you?" Shelly continued.

"Yes," I beamed. She made me feel as if I needed her approval.

"Yeah, I noticed you the other day," she added. "Your hair's cute."

"Thanks."

"And you did good when you talked about that poem about the trees."

You did good. I twitched.

"Joyce Kilmer. That's one of my favorite poems."

"Maybe tomorrow we can exchange phone numbers in class." I never had a chance to answer. "Look! There's Greg Kendall. He's so cute."

"And taken," Darlene clarified.

"For now." Shelly, fluffed her hair as she spoke. "Greg! Come over here for a second."

He changed directions and walked over to our group.

"Ladies. What's going on?" He smiled genuinely, flashing perfect teeth.

"You were going to pass right by, weren't you? Too cool to talk to us?" Her flirtation flipped on like a wall switch.

He shook his head, embarrassed. "No."

"So, whatcha doin'?"

"Heading to football practice. But I have to meet my brother first to get something from him. Did you see him anywhere?"

"Buck?" asked Shelly. Hearing his name unraveled me.

"Yeah." He searched the area.

"No. So how's Sharon?" Shelly pushed on.

Greg lit up. "She's good. Thanks for asking. How's Larry?"

Her face soured. "I'm mad at him."

"Oh," he replied politely. "Well, I'm sure you'll work it out, Shelly. You always do."

"Maybe." She looked bored.

Shelly and Larry had been together since they met at St. Patrick's Academy. Everybody knew Larry. He was big and burly and, most of the time, stared through vacant eyes. Encasing him within the confines of a Catholic uniform was an oxymoron. Larry was famous for two things: his stalwart worship of Shelly and his willingness to try anything in the face of convention. His antics were legendary. I often wondered if that was what drew Shelly to him.

"There's your brother," Shelly announced. "Buck! Over here."

I couldn't move. He approached us. I think I stopped breathing for a minute.

"Hey, little brother. I've been looking for you. Mom said to get the key from you."

Buck slid his hand from his pocket. "Here you go." The sun settled on him, highlighting the threads of gold and bronze in his hair.

"You know everybody here, right?" Greg spoke with the ease of an experienced emcee and the grace of gentleman. He had a talent for making everyone comfortable.

"No. Not everybody." Then he turned to me. "Hi, Sam."

"Hi."

So gorgeous.

"So you know Sam." Greg proceeded with introductions while I suffered through standing so close to Buck that I could almost touch him. I don't know how many minutes elapsed before he spoke again.

"Well, gotta go." Then he looked at me again. "See you, Sam."

"Bye." I willed myself not to look back as he walked away. My face felt numb.

Shelly eyed me suspiciously. "You know Buck?"

"Not really. I just talked to him once this summer." My mouth dried up.

"Does your brother have a girlfriend, Greg?" she continued.

"Nope. He's a free man," kidded Greg.

"Free man!" repeated Darlene. "You say that as if you wish you were. You know you love being with Sharon."

"True, true," he grinned. "Well, ladies, gotta get to practice. Later."

Our circle huddled inward. "So Sam, wanna walk home with us?" Darlene had a trustworthy smile and happy eyes. When she spoke, her short hair bobbed around as if it had a mind of its own. It struck me that Shelly and she were an odd pairing of friends. I guessed that Shelly's allure had seduced Darlene too.

"Sure, thanks."

"You coming with us, Shel?"

"I have to wait for Larry," pouted Shelly, whose demeanor had wilted after Greg's departure.

"Okay. Well, I'll talk to you later then," Darlene replied indifferently, and we headed toward the railroad tracks on Junction Street.

"Don't forget!" Shelly shot back. "I need help with the math homework."

"I know." The expression on Darlene's face didn't change, despite Shelly's demanding tone.

"Don't forget!" she shouted again as we neared the tracks. Then she dismissed us, searching impatiently for Larry.

Five

"Each friend represents a world in us . . .

—Anais Nin

Most friendships form without intention. A gesture, a word, a laugh at the same moment—and the seed is planted. There isn't always logic to what draws us. Sometimes it just happens.

One thing led to another, and Shelly and I were borrowing each other's clothes. I was tickled to be hanging out with the popular Shelly Porterfield. Better yet, Darlene and I rolled into a comfortable routine, walking home from school most days. Conversation with Darlene was effortless. Yes, high school was improving my life.

Enter Annie.

We were sitting at the sewing machines in home economics class. Mrs. Peterson was coaching us on the zigzag stitch, hovering as she circulated among the whirring Kenmores.

"Stupid machine," Annie grumbled. "Why do I even have to take this dumb class? I'm not going to be a homemaker."

I decided to extend my assistance, for whatever it was worth. "Are you having trouble?"

She continued staring down the needle. "Trouble? I still haven't mastered the straight stitch." She made me smile. Annie had a delivery unlike anyone I had ever met.

Mrs. Peterson passed by again. "Be sure you don't pucker the material now, ladies. That would not be good," she sang.

"Oh, no. That would be a travesty," mumbled Annie.

"Remember," continued Mrs. Peterson, "if you get in trouble with a pucker, your 3-step zigzag is the solution!" Her hands were waving through the air.

"Does she think she's conducting at the Met?" I could see Annie's frustration escalating.

"Soon you'll be running circles around button holes and stitching appliqués!" delighted Peterson. Then Annie stepped full force on her pedal, and Mrs. Peterson halted. "Miss Avery! You're giving it too much gas!"

"Here she comes," I warned.

"Whatever are you . . . oh, dear!" Mrs. Peterson stared at Annie's fabric and stitch work. "Oh, dear, dear, dear."

"You can say that again," replied Annie. "I'm just not cut out for this stuff, Mrs. Peterson. Why don't you let me oil these machines instead?" The entire row of girls broke into muffled giggles.

When the bell rang, Annie turned toward me for the first time. "Hey, thanks. I didn't mean to be rude. This class just bums me out. I feel like a dipstick every time I sit in front of this stupid machine."

"I know what you mean. I never used a sewing machine before this class either."

"What's your name?" asked Annie.

"Samantha DeSantis. Most people call me Sam."

"Sam. Groovy," she nodded. "Annie Avery. Good to meet you."

"Good to meet you too."

"Come on, let's flee this scene before Peterson comes back to talk to me. I can't take anymore." I followed as she headed toward the door. "Escape at last. What class you goin' to, Sam?"

"Biology."

"I'll walk upstairs with you. You going to the game this Saturday?" she asked.

"I am."

"Who with?" She asked me questions as if she'd always known me.

"Darlene Bailey and Shelly Porterfield. Do you know them?"

"Everybody knows Porterfield. Darlene's a good kid."

"Would you like to go with us Saturday? We're meeting at my house."

She halted in front of Room 213. "That's my class. This is where we split."

I interpreted her comment as a "no" and a "good-bye." "Well, it was nice meeting you, Annie. Guess I'll see you in class."

"Saturday's cool. I'll meet you at the game." And she walked into her classroom.

Annie was one of a kind.

As unlikely as it was, Annie became a part of the foursome that gradually functioned as a unit. Thanks to my new acquaintances, my social life blossomed. We went to school dances and football games together, rotated after-school gabfests at one another's houses, and connected on the telephone most evenings. Shelly and I shopped every Saturday, followed by a visit to Ed's Diner in downtown Carlson for their famous fries with gravy. Darlene and I attempted to perfect our sewing skills under the tutelage of my grandmother, the master. We made more jokes than progress, but my time with Darlene was cleansing. Annie and I discussed our philosophies on life, arguing whose was better, while we ate junk food. Unlike my days at Pioneer, I was invited to all the cool parties. Brian Determan and I formed a pact that when one of us didn't have a date for an event, we'd go together. And, as luck would have it, Brian was perpetually in between relationships, and

I was dependably available. By second semester, I felt as if I had always attended CHS, and, happily, this odd mix of girls became my closest friends, my framework of support.

And my grandmother proved to be right: I *was* blooming.

Six

Gretta Payton knew everybody and everybody's business. She was famous for her parties: a mob of teenagers, loud music, and minimal supervision. Gretta's parents were liberals. They trusted her and extended the honor system. They were present for the beginning of the party, when kids were pouring through the kitchen door, and then they'd excuse themselves, wish everyone a good evening, and announce the exact moment at which they'd return. Droves of kids migrated to Gretta's house, even those who weren't invited. Word spreads fast in high school, and plans change just as quickly. Gretta let everybody in.

One Saturday night, the usual crowd showed up. I was standing near the snack table with Annie. Darlene and Shelly were in the "other room," better known as the "make-out room," where the established couples spent the majority of the evening locked in embrace. Mick Jagger was whining about not getting any satisfaction. I don't think he was the only one.

"God this pizza is good," Annie said, biting into a piece.

"I know. I am so hungry. I didn't eat dinner so I could fit into these jeans."

"You spaz!" she laughed. "Why didn't you wear something comfortable? Like these." She pointed to her pants."

"I don't wear hippie pants. And don't call me a spaz."

She shot back. "They're not hippie pants! They're loose and you can eat more," she grinned.

"You're a trip, Annie."

She laughed uproariously and shoved another piece of pizza in her mouth. I loved Annie. Our friendship had tightened quickly. We were yukking it up, when her expression changed. "Sam, here comes Greg."

Greg Kendall walked in, looking fairly dejected. Rumor had it that Sharon had broken up with him again. Apparently, she decided they should take another break and sort out their feelings. Their intermittent break-ups were always her idea, and, without fail, Greg took her back every time. I always thought he deserved someone who truly appreciated him, didn't take him for granted. He was smart and sweet and considerate, the kind of guy every mother wants her daughter to marry. He came from a good family and had wonderful manners. My mother said manners were your calling card, so I appreciated his good breeding. Before he met Sharon, he used to play softball with a bunch of us at Pioneer. We started talking to each other, and I must admit I was slightly enamored. Sometimes he'd offer me a ride home on the crossbar of his bike, where I could smell the remnants of his Old Spice as it escaped into the wind. Yet I could never bring myself to look back at him as we rode because our faces were too close. I thought things were going fairly well and hoped that he might actually ask me out. Then he met Sharon Krammer. He was a goner the first time he witnessed her perky little cheerleading techniques at fall try-outs. She hurled her body into the air, flinging back her arms to meet her knees. Quite skilled and provocative, I must say. They made her captain. I didn't make the squad. But I did a heck of a job on yearbook write-ups and made elaborate speeches at student council meetings. Proud moments. Anyway, that arch of Sharon's obviously made an unforgettable impression on Greg. So any romantic notions he might have had about me slipped quietly away.

Greg was making his way around Gretta's dining room, saying hello to everyone. He approached Annie and me, mid-conversation, and I barely had time to scarf down my third piece of pizza.

"Hi, Sam," he looked tired. "Have you seen my brother here tonight?"

Annie spit out part of her cherry Coke. "Excuse me. I gotta wipe off my shirt." Subtlety wasn't Annie's strong suit. As she walked away, she mouthed, "Right on! He's here." I tried not to look at her.

"No. Is he here?" A wave of electric shocks shot through my body.

"Yeah. I want to make sure he has a ride home." He surveyed the room. The Mamas and Papas were singing "California Dreamin,'" and someone turned up the volume.

"I love this song!" screamed Greta as she threw her arms around her flavor of the month. "Dance with me, Jeff!"

Greg turned back toward me, realizing he hadn't made any real effort toward conversation. "So how are you, Sam?"

"Good." I wanted to ask the same of him, but I knew. Everyone knew.

"Do you like being at the high school?"

"Yeah. It's fun. I've met a lot of new people."

He nodded while glancing sideways. "Oh, there's Buck. Kendall! Over here!" At the sound of Greg's voice, Buck made his way toward us.

My heart catapulted into my mouth. He seemed to move in slow motion. I didn't know where to look. Finally, he reached us. "Hi, Sam." The voice. I already knew it.

When I looked up, his eyes danced. "Hi."

"Haven't seen you in a while. Just at the games and in the halls and stuff."

"I know. Passing ships in the night, huh?"

Passing ships in the night? What's wrong with me?

He laughed. Thank God for his good manners. Then he turned to Greg. "So what's happening, brother? You doin' okay?"

"Yeah, I'm good." Greg was scanning the room again, clearly preoccupied. "There's Porterfield. I'm gonna go talk to her for a minute. Be right back. See you, Sam." His smile was strained.

Buck watched his brother cross the room and shook his head disapprovingly. "He's going over there to find out about Sharon."

"I heard they broke up."

"Again," he emphasized. "I don't know why he puts up with it. Well, enough with that. What's going on with you, Sam?" He returned fully to our conversation, but his sultry expression interfered with my ability to maintain eye contact.

"Well, I'm on student council."

"I know. I see you at the meetings."

"You do?"

He nodded. "Yeah. I sit in the back most of the time."

"Yeah, I know. Also, I'm on the yearbook, so that keeps me busy."

"The yearbook." His eyebrows shot upward. "Photography or writing?"

"A little of both."

"Nifty."

The music slowed down, and kids began pairing up. I fidgeted with the cross that hung from the chain around my neck.

Where's Annie?

"Good tune. Gerry and the Pacemakers," he said.

The room filled with dancing couples, some whispering secrets, some fastened in a wordless embrace. He looked at me as if he were going to say something. For a second I thought he might ask me to dance. Just then Greg's voice sailed across the room.

"Buck! I'm bookin' now. You comin'?"

"That's my ride. Guess I'd better get going. See you, Sam."

"Yeah, see you Buck."

I watched him walk toward the door. I would have been better off if we'd never talked. The ache in my heart devoured me.

Seven

May 1966

My friendship with Shelly developed unintentionally. At first, I was in awe of her and couldn't believe she had chosen me as her friend. Then I began to wonder—was it me or the clothes she wanted to borrow? Gradually, the rose color through which I had initially viewed her faded, her superficial side and judgmental attitude emerging more frequently. She had a penchant for tossing out brutal comments as if she had the right. I decided that her behavior stemmed from some basic insecurity, so I mostly let her insensitive remarks go. But sometimes it was just too much. Regardless, there was something that drew me to her. Underneath the veneer lay a vulnerable soul.

On this particular day, our after-school routine took us to her house. "We have to do something special for your birthday, Sam." She kicked the screen door shut with the back of her foot, threw her books on the dining room table, and proceeded under the archway that led to the small kitchen. I followed, setting my books on the Formica countertop, and slid onto one of the stools. A piece of cracked vinyl bit me.

Shelly's house held a certain charm. Filled with alcoves, faded tapestries, and well-worn furniture, the rooms had seen a lot of life. A week after their honeymoon in Niagara Falls, Shelly's parents moved in. The house was cozy and affordable, and Mrs. Porterfield fell in love with it the moment she saw it. This was the place where they would live out their days.

"After all, you're turning sixteen, and that's a big birthday. So we have to plan a party."

"Thanks, Shel."

Shelly tossed back her auburn hair and bit into her Twinkie. She kicked off her penny loafers as she adjusted the radio to 88.9, the station that always played the newest Beatles' songs. The DJ was all hyped up that Bob Dylan's *Blonde on Blonde* and the Beach Boys' *Pet Sounds* albums were released on the same day.

"Big deal. So they were released on the same day. What's the problem?" I asked the radio.

"What'd you say?" asked Shelly.

"The DJ is going on about how the new Beach Boys' album is being released on the same day as Dylan's."

"Who cares! I don't even like Dylan."

"What are you talking about, Shelly? Everybody likes Dylan. Did you know his song 'Like a Rolling Stone' started as a short story? That's impressive."

"Don't care about that either. We have to talk about who to fix you up with for your party. You need to have a boyfriend. You've never had a real boyfriend, have you?"

"You know I haven't."

The DJ finally stopped talking, and Paul McCartney's and John Lennon's harmonious voices filled the room.

I'm a loser.

I'm a looooser.

And I'm not what I appear to be.

"Some days I agree," I said to the crooners.

"Agree to what?" Shelly was stooped over, peering into the refrigerator.

"Nothing. I was talking to myself."

"You do that a lot. There's nothing good to eat. Shoot! I thought there was some leftover chicken and dumplings! Joey must have gotten his hands on it. Sorry, Sam. I know how you love my mother's dumplings."

"I'll live. I should lose five pounds anyway."

"Yeah, that's a good idea."

My expression must have reflected my recognition that she might not be talking about her own ample hips.

"What?" she demanded.

I decided it wasn't worth it. "Nothing."

"You're disappointed about the dumplings, huh? Admit it."

"Admitted."

Mrs. Porterfield was a great cook. I can still see her standing in the floral wallpapered kitchen in her housedress and apron, dicing celery and carrots and tossing them into the bubbling pot of chicken. The smell drove me crazy. "Want a taste, Samantha?" she'd say. And I'd rush toward the pot and her big smile. But at the moment I was somewhat preoccupied by the boyfriend conversation, so the dumplings didn't hold their usual allure.

"Yeah, five pounds will make you feel better about yourself."

Too much!

"Shelly, I only weigh 125."

"Yeah, but how tall are you?"

"Five feet four."

"That's why you should weigh less. I'm five-five and a half."

"And what do you weigh?"

"I never divulge that number."

Meanwhile, her protruding backside was clearly ammunition for a justified comeback. However, in the name of friendship, I kept my mouth shut. Instead, I sat silently and watched her spread out her finds on the counter: boiled ham, Kraft cheese slices, rye bread, kosher pickles, Hostess cupcakes, and more Twinkies. Then she plopped down on the stool beside me.

"Okay, let's find you a boyfriend."

"Just like that?"

"Uh-huh."

"What are you going to do, wiggle your nose like Elizabeth Montgomery and poof? I mean, who do you think you can get?"

"Who do you want?" You'd think I'd asked her to pass the salt. She took another bite of her Twinkie while she stacked ham and cheese on rye.

Who do you want? It was that simple for her. But we weren't talking about finding a boyfriend for Shelly. We were talking about Samantha DeSantis, mildly attractive in a quiet sort of not-yet-discovered way. A bud partially opened, waiting for that full ray of sunshine. And let's face it, a girl that people barely noticed next to her mesmerizing companion.

"Who do you think would go out with me?"

"Sam! Stop! Kids like you. You're getting popular now. Boys want to go out with you."

"What boys?"

"Lots of boys look at you in the halls at school."

"When? I want to walk by them tomorrow and see for myself. Will you point them out?"

Shelly laughed. "You're so funny. Everybody thinks you're a good kid too."

"How do you know that? Have you taken a poll recently?"

"No. I read it in the slam books."

A word about slam books. They were ordinary notebooks in which we wrote the names of selected classmates in CAPITAL LETTERS across the top of the page. These notebooks were circulated so everyone could write about each person listed. As cruel as I considered them to be, making it into the slam books was a very cool thing. I can remember the pivotal day when James Garvey passed a slam book back to me in math class. Poor James wasn't given the honor of writing in it. It was reserved for the "chosen ones." Teenagers can be so crummy to each other.

"Would you pass this back to Sam?" But don't sign it. Talk about ego busters.

I thought I was just supposed to add my words of praise about all these cool people until I opened to a page with my name boldly written in red ink: SAMANTHA DESANTIS. My mouth fell open as I stared at the page. It was at that moment I knew I had finally arrived. Praise Jesus! Then I realized there was writing on the page.

They dared to send it to me when people had already written about me? What gall!

I'd heard about how brutal the comments could be, so I braced myself as I read:

Good kid

Funny!

Kinda pretty

Kinda? Oh thank you very much!

I was at the same time flattered and contemplating wiping out the "kinda." But erasable ink wasn't available then, so my course was clear. I read on.

Not so bad. So this is what they think of me. No death threats.

Then came the word that would curse me for life:

CUTE

Cute? Dogs are cute, for God's sake!

Cute was boring! And clearly hanging on the bottom rung of the ladder of adulations. What about striking? Unforgettable? All right, I may be pushing it, but that word seriously got on my nerves.

* * *

"Whose slam books?" I demanded.

"I don't know." She was more interested in the ham and cheese.

"What did they say?"

"I told you. That you're a good kid. Oh, yeah—and cute. People write that about you a lot." I unwrapped a cupcake and shoved it in my mouth. "So who do you want? I've got a piece of paper. Give me three choices. Go."

I stared in partial admiration and partial disbelief. "Let's see, I'll take one blond about 6'2", not too heavy on the brawn, one raven-haired, blue-eyed athlete, and one . . ."

"Samantha, get serious!" Shelly twirled her pencil impatiently and glared at me. "Names, I said. Give me names!"

"You're serious. Just pick people?" *Unbelievable!* "What if these names I give you don't match up with their owners' ideas of the perfect woman?"

"What are you talking about?"

"I'm talking about rejection. I can see it all now. You just keep going down the list until it becomes a pity date."

"What?"

"Rejection. I know you've never experienced it, but it isn't you we're setting up." I bit into my fingernail.

"Stop doing that! You'll wreck your nails." She grabbed my hand and inspected it. "You need polish. Now give me the names!"

"Fine! Eric Genovese, Bobby Esposito, and Buck Kendall in ascending order." All spit out in one fell swoop.

"In what order?" She stared at me. Maybe it was my faster-than-the-speed-of-light response that threw her.

"Least favorite, middle choice, most desired. Like him a little, like him a lot, will jump him during half time at the football game in hopes of scoring." I never knew when to stop.

"I get it! But what was that last name you gave me? The one you would hump on the football field?"

"I didn't say hump! I said *jump*!"

"Same thing," she added.

"It is not." I defended. "There's a definite distinction."

"Don't shirk the issue by saying stupid things again!"

My defenses were down, so I responded in the only way I knew how.

"It's *skirt* the issue, Shelly. You *skirt* the issue, and you *shirk* your responsibilities." God, I hate it when people get those expressions wrong. And she *always* did.

"You said Buck Kendall, didn't you?" I nodded. Then she smirked. "I see."

"You see what?"

"You like Buck Kendall."

"I'm still hungry." I grabbed another cupcake.

"Admit it!"

I was beginning to feel uncomfortable, like someone had turned the high beams on me in the interrogation room.

"Just tell us the truth, Miss DeSantis? Do you like Buck Kendall? You can't hide from the law."

"Yes, I like him."

"But he's younger than you. And he's Greg's brother. What about your crush on Greg before he started going steady with Sharon?"

"Nothing came of that, as we all know."

"Buck Kendall, eh?"

"You asked me who I wanted. I gave you three names. Let's hope someone on the hit list is in the line of fire."

"Why don't you ever talk normal? And don't avoid this issue. You like Buck Kendall, and you never told me. Why didn't you ever tell me?"

"I don't know." Shelly looked put off for only a second. Then she fluffed her hair and finished the sandwich. Vanity and sustenance. I felt less guilty.

"And, by the way, how long has this been going on?" She stared, awaiting my response.

"Awhile."

Her face registered shock. "Not since the beginning of the school year!"

I studied the mallard ducks that decorated the counter. "Are these new?"

"Please tell me you haven't liked him for that long?" Her horrified expression reflected the difference between the two of us. Shelly was not the kind of girl to hold back when she wanted something. I could see that she could not fathom how I operated.

"Kinda." I licked the remaining traces of chocolate cake from my fingers, leaving no sign in even the smallest crevices of my palm.

"Oh, my God! Why didn't you say something?" she persisted.

"Where would it have gotten me if I had told you?"

"You might have snagged him quicker. I have connections. You want Buck Kendall? I'll get you Buck Kendall." She spoke with the authority of an army sergeant. Suddenly I loved her, impropriety and all! "I'll talk to Larry tonight. He still hangs around with Buck from St. Patrick's days. I'll see what I can set up. He's calling around seven, I think. After he finishes playing basketball with Scott. Then he'll stop at Tony's for a pizza and double chocolate malt. And he wonders why he's gaining weight. He'll probably get home around seven and call me after that. So it won't actually be seven, but around then. Then I'll make him call Buck. After he talks to Buck, he'll call me and I'll let you know what Buck says." The girl could talk—even to herself.

As the one-sided conversation continued, I realized my fate was in the hands of Larry Polanski, whose communication skills consisted of a limited vocabulary and a variety of surprisingly creative grunts, some of which I was beginning to understand.

God help me.

Suddenly I was perspiring as I imagined the whole testosterone conversation: "Hey, Buck." Grunt. "Samantha DeSantis has the hots for you. I'm not shittin' you. She told Shelly she wants your body. Seriously. No shit." Grunt. "Want her?" Grunt. Grunt.

"I need something else to nosh on."

"Nosh," she repeated. "You're the only person I know who uses that word." She refocused on her notes. "Forget food for a minute. This is important."

"Okay."

"So, I'll call you after I talk to Larry and tell you what Buck said. Now, if he doesn't want to be with you . . ." she trailed off, referring to her list.

If he doesn't want to be with you. Punched in the guts.

"You got any more of those pickles? The garlic kind."

"We need a back-up plan in case Buck says no. And he might, you know. You are older than him." Again with the age!

"Older than *he*." Correcting my friends had become a bad habit. I worked overtime on Shelly.

"What?"

"It's older that *he*, not older than him. Nominative case."

"Stop correcting me! It's so annoying."

"Sorry, sometimes I just can't help myself." She had no idea.

"Listen, Sam, this is your birthday party. You have to be with somebody. And you should stop eating those pickles. Your breath will stink. Look at all those garlic pieces floating in the bottle. Close the fridge, and come here."

My despair at the possible loss of the boy I never had, the boy who inhabited the majority of my recent dreams, mounted by the second. Shelly was back to her list.

"So if Buck says no, we'll go for choice number two . . ." she paused.

"That's the middle one, Shel." I pointed to the name on her list.

"Screw you, Sam! You're a pain in the ass."

"I'm just kidding."

"So we'll ask Bobby Esposito if Buck turns you down." Without skipping a beat. "Isn't Bobby in our social studies class?"

"Indeed he is."

"He's really funny. Remember he kept making all those funny comments when we were talking about religions. What was it he said about the acidic Jews?"

"Hasidic Jews! They're not fruit." I shook my head.

"He's kinda cute. Okay. Now that's settled. Let's plan the party. Categories." She wrote as she spoke. "Guests' names. We have to have the same number of boys as girls 'cause it's always a disaster when it doesn't match. Food. Everybody can bring something. Music. What records, Sam? Definitely the Beatles." I nodded to her good taste. "And we're not playing *My Name Is Barbara* at this party. So don't even think about it!"

Barbara might be my idol, but I was certainly savvy enough to recognize that my love of Streisand should be reserved for the privacy of my own home. Silent indignation was her punishment.

"What's your favorite Beatles' song, Sam? We'll make sure we play it lots of times. And the Rolling Stones." Suddenly she was inspired. "I know!" she shouted. "We'll get Ben to organize the music! He has every possible 45 record and tons of albums." Shelly looked pleased with herself.

"Ben! Are you crazy?"

"What? You love Ben. Everybody loves Ben. And he knows the name of every song and singer in the world."

"He likes Country and Western. He likes Hank Williams, for God's sake! He gave me the *Orange Blossom Special* for my birthday last year. Said if I didn't like it, he'd just keep it. I never even heard of the *Orange Blossom Special.*" I was now talking to myself. "Come to think of it, I never did see that record again after that night. Smart guy, that Ben." I chuckled at the memory of my friend's gift.

Now, Sam, Ben said, you have to open your mind to other artists. I really think you'll love this. Just give it a chance."

I sat there smiling.

"It's Ben! No one else knows music like him. Plus he's so funny." She kept on writing.

"I agree. He *is* funny."

She jumped up at my words. "You should like him!"

"I do like him. He's my friend."

"I mean like a boyfriend."

"Shelly, let me explain something to you. You can't just make yourself have those kinds of feelings for a person. It's either there, or it's not."

"But Ben's so great. And he doesn't have a girlfriend."

"Agreed. But, that's not the way it works. Besides, he likes me as a friend too. We have a perfect relationship. I don't want to ruin it."

"Fine." She was momentarily deflated. "Okay, room division. How should we do that?" She was on her feet, examining the arrangement of her parents' living room and the optimum design for make-out opportunities. On and on she went, planning every detail. I sat in silent contemplation.

What if he says yes?

I slipped away, dreaming about the possibility of being with choice number three, in ascending order.

Eight

Waiting and wondering. Prison. Not knowing is so much worse than dealing with the truth. Once you know the truth, you can move forward. But waiting? Limbo.

I was standing in front of the school, waiting for Shelly. Again. The weather was odd: one minute the sky was overcast, and the next—the sun was peeking through. I couldn't tell if it was going to rain or not. *A June rain. That could be fun,* I thought. I was checking out the sky when I heard her unmistakable shriek.

"He said yes!" Shelly jumped around, filled with accomplishment.

"What?"

"Buck! He said yes. He wants to be with you at your party!" She shook me. "Sam, aren't you happy?"

"When did you find out?"

"I just saw Larry in the parking lot."

"Are you sure Larry gave him the right name?"

"Yes!" Then she literally sang: "And I think he likes you." I looked around to see if anyone was watching us. "You should have seen him, Sam," she continued. "He was sitting in the back seat with Stan. So Larry got out of the car to talk to me, and Buck and Stan just sat there waiting for him. He's kind of shy." Giggle. "He did this cute little nod thing and waved to me. You know, he has a really nice smile." Her body was charged. "Then Larry started talking about the party, and Buck's face got all red. I didn't say anything so he wouldn't feel embarrassed. But Larry laughed really loud and pushed Buck's shoulder. Then he did that thing he does, you know 'Ahhhhhhh, Buck!' You know, that annoying fog horn noise he makes."

I knew.

"Poor Buck looked really embarrassed, but happy at the same time. I think he likes you, Sam. Larry's such a jerk sometimes. Come on. Let's go."

On the way to Shelly's house, her excitement grew with each word. I was in a stupor. Every time she mentioned Buck's name my stomach flipped, but she was so involved in relating the news, she never noticed. She rambled on about Buck's embarrassment. It was obvious that she was proud of her role as matchmaker.

"He turned all red when I asked him if he was looking forward to the party. Kind of like you did, Sam, when you told me he was first on your list. You know, he's really cute. I don't think I ever noticed it before. He is actually kind of gorgeous. Good taste."

Kind of gorgeous? Red alert! How can a person be *kind* of gorgeous? Kind of cute, yes. But *kind* of gorgeous? Miles apart.

We finally arrived at her house. "Come in. I'll fix us a snack."

"I'll come in, but I'm not really hungry."

She wheeled around. "What do you mean you're not hungry? You're always hungry. My mom made her chicken and rice casserole last night."

Still lost in thought, I followed her into the house like a trained dog.

"So what do you say?" She threw her books on the counter.

"No thanks."

She regarded me quizzically for a moment. Suddenly, her eyes popped open. "Oh! You can't eat 'cause of Buck, huh?"

I felt as if I had walked on stage naked and everyone was looking at me.

"No, that's not why," I protested too vehemently. "I'm just not hungry." I pulled out one of the dining room chairs and sat down.

"Why you sittin' there? You never sit there."

"I don't know."

"He sure is cute. He's got those eyes. Did you ever notice?"

I've noticed!

"What color are they exactly?" Her head was in the refrigerator. "He looked really shy when I told him that he was your number-one choice for the party."

I found my voice. "You said that? I can't believe you said that!"

"But Sam, I'm telling you, he likes you 'cause Larry told me he said yes right away. And it was the way he looked when Larry said your name, which he kept repeating. Even Stan was smiling at Buck. Larry's such a jerk. Aren't you happy? Don't you think this is good, Sam? Everything is going according to plan. So what are you going to wear to the party?"

A prisoner of my own thoughts and temporarily silenced by the increased pounding in my chest, I failed to respond. But Shelly didn't seem to need me anymore. She was off, organizing the party that would change my life.

Nine

For the next week, I floated about in a euphoric state. I lived happily in my imagination as I considered the wondrous possibilities of the night of June 10. In this dreamlike space, I am the producer and director. I have the power to cut any scene that doesn't meet my expectations, and I can replay the scenes, again and again. I sometimes prefer this fanciful life to reality. I have often wandered there, both willfully and subconsciously, daydreaming to gratifying distraction. The downside is the humiliation of being caught there. In those first confused moments of reentry, I find myself completely disoriented.

Preoccupation was my constant companion. My fantasies were great because I was still in a good place. Nothing had happened between us yet, except that he had agreed to come to my party. Something inside told me there was a connection between us. I felt it the night we first met. I felt it every time he passed me in the halls. I even felt it when he sat in the back of the room at student council meetings. The energy in the air changed when he was around.

My fear was that I would run into him before the big event and freeze up. One day, while pulling books out of my locker and picking up the contents that had spilled on the floor, I turned and there he was. The Gods never seemed to be looking in my direction. He was walking down the hall with his friend, Stan Murray. His eyes pierced me. I was immobilized. He said something to Stan and then disappeared around the corner. The dull pain I had been tempering surfaced. June 10 couldn't arrive fast enough.

The next day during Miss Adams' history class, I had a hard time concentrating, which was odd because the woman was a living riot. Even though history was not my favorite subject, the first fifteen minutes of Miss Adams' classes were hilarious.

"Well, hello," she'd say with a deadpan face, as if she were surprised that we actually showed up. "Glad to see you could all make it." She strung out her words in long syllables, which hung in the air. "Now let's see the homework." Invariably, she'd turn to Ben, her straight man. "Yes, Mr. Joseph, there was homework, so just allow me to save you from yourself. Whilst we all simply tremble, trying to hold back our unbridled delight at your clever remarks, we do have an agenda." And with a great flourish she'd say something like, "But, go ahead, Mr. Joseph. I can see that you are just chomping at the bit to have the floor, despite my cautionary words."

On this day Ben stood up for effect. "Why, thank you, Miss Adams. My question is might you be teaching the lesson yourself today? You know how much we all love your stories."

"Indeed I do, Mr. Joseph. They are quite remarkable stories if I do say so myself. Nonetheless, Miss Kellogg is, as you well know, your current student teacher, and she will be delivering today's lecture."

"Well, I am sorely disappointed to learn that you won't be enlightening us with your knowledge today, Miss Adams. But I am most certain we will all enjoy Miss Kellogg."

Their shtick brightened our day.

And then there was Miss Kellogg. God help her. The poor woman was without personality, style, or a clue. She was freakishly tall and abundantly endowed in the buttocks area. At the age of twenty-two, she still wore braces. Because of her metal mouth, she sprayed every time she said secession.

"So, when the Confederate schtates threatened the Northern schtates with se-SPIT-session . . ."

Nobody wanted to sit in the front row. Whenever she spit, everyone turned crimson with suppressed laughter. I willed myself not to laugh or be a part of the humiliation. I am, after all, a decent human being, not to mention a pathetically frightened Catholic. I tried to control myself for the sake of my eternal redemption. We really didn't want to ruin her life either, but she wasn't making things easy. To add insult to injury, she had the habit of leaning against the blackboard as she lectured, and when she turned around, her ill-fitting dress was covered with chalk stains, highlighting her ample behind.

When her student teaching stint halted after only four weeks, Miss Adams very politely told us to throw out our notes and forget everything the student teacher had taught us because it was not accurate. No words of condemnation, just the facts. It was all wrong. So Miss Adams started over in her unique style, and we learned every detail of the War Between the States and loved it, even those of us who thought history was as exciting as watching grass grow.

On that particular morning, I was trying desperately to pay attention. Taking notes usually does it for me. I write and write, attempting to catch every detail, no matter how small. I lose myself in the rhythm of the words, the roll of the pen. I close out everything but the sound of her voice and the lines and lines of text growing on the page. The teacher is speaking only to me.

"Pssst." Annie broke my stride. "Look who just walked in." Buck was handing a folder to Miss Adams.

"Hi, Buck," crooned Shelly.

He glanced briefly from Miss Adams to Shelly, melting every female in the room with his bashful smile.

"Ooh, Buck. Watch out. She's making her move," warned Bobby Esposito.

When Buck's face began to redden, Miss Adams announced, "Don't worry about her, son. She says that to all the boys. She's no threat. You won't need a body guard to walk you home."

The class broke up, and suddenly Shelly was the one wearing red. She shot a look at Bobby. "Bobby, that's mean!" she whined.

Buck walked out the door, and I wondered what he was thinking as my classmates continued to laugh.

The bell rang.

"What's wrong with you?" I scolded. "Why did you do that? You embarrassed him."

Students were filling the halls, rushing by one another to make it to second period on time. Every boy who passed us glanced at Shelly.

"I was just trying to get his attention so he'd see you." She maintained a hurt pout while scanning both the north and south ends of the corridor.

"Now he probably won't want to come to the party."

"Why wouldn't he want to come? You're just paranoid 'cause you like him so much."

Chad Bellusco walked in front of us. Shelly picked up her pace.

"Hi, Chad," she sang.

"Hey, Shelly." Chad was an upperclassman whom Shelly had targeted.

"He has a girlfriend," I chided after he entered study hall.

"So what. All's fair in war and love."

"Love and war."

"Same thing."

* * *

That night I played out the long-awaited evening, practicing every possible scenario and talking to myself in the room I shared with Lucy. Unbeknownst to me, Lucy was standing outside the bedroom door and overheard my one-sided conversation. Curiosity and her mop of curly, red hair sprang through the doorway. Her eyes scanned the room. Then she stared at me, brow furrowed and hands on hips.

"Sammy, I hope you know there's nobody in here. Why are you talking to yourself again, Sammy?" She loved repeating my name, a habit she'd formed as a toddler.

"I'm just practicing some lines that I have to learn for school."

I was relieved that it was only my little sister and not my parents who had caught me talking to myself. Then I would have felt like a real fool. She shook her head and walked out.

I was consumed. Dozens of times I changed my mind about the outfit I should wear to celebrate sixteen. Despite lengthy fashion consultations with Shelly, who offered expert advice and had been seriously successful in the wardrobe-for-the-right-occasion category, I decided on a pair of light blue jeans and a navy blue and white striped, short-sleeved sweater. Simple.

All systems were *go* for the party. Now I just had to wait.

Nine more days.

Ten

Anticipation . . . is keepin' me waitin'

—Carly Simon

Shelly's bedroom was a mess. Yesterday's cast-aside outfits padded the floor; mismatched shoes were flung amongst notebooks, wet towels, oversized rollers, and old copies of *Seventeen* magazine.

Annie and I flopped on Shelly's very pink bed to talk last-minute party details. She made me laugh every time I was with her. There was an odd purity about her—probably because she was so comfortable in her own skin. She said what was on her mind, regardless of popular opinion, and never fell victim to the critical remarks of others. I admired Annie for many reasons.

"So, Sam, just think, in one short week you might be kissing the man of your dreams. Ooh, the long-awaited day. 'I'm finally touching the lips of the dreamy Buck Kendall.'"

"Stop mocking me, Annie." I threw one of Shelly's many heart-shaped pillows at her.

"Been practicing at home?"

"Practicing?" I could feel my face heating up.

"I know you practice, Sam. You haven't had that much experience."

Shelly waltzed into the room. "She kissed Greg last summer when we played Spin the Bottle in her backyard. That counts for something. Anything's got to help her." She dumped the snacks on the bed. Then she picked up her comb and walked to the mirror where she began teasing her hair and sectioning it off for pigtails.

"That's true. But she only kissed him once, right?" Annie asked Shelly.

"Yes, just once. Behind her sister's kiddie pool."

"Behind what?"

"The kiddie pool. Sam's mom hangs it over the clothesline after she cleans it out. It's a perfect spot to kiss. No one can see you."

"Then how do you know it wasn't more than once?" Annie replied smugly.

"Cause they weren't gone that long, and I know Sam."

"You two *do* realize I'm still in the room."

"We do," answered Annie.

"We don't want you to act like a novice when you're finally with Buck," announced Shelly.

I swung my head around, but Annie beat me to the punch.

"Did you just say *novice*, Porterfield?" asked Annie.

"Yeah. So?" Her nonchalance was impressive.

"So? That's a pretty big word you just spit out there, partner." I gave her my "atta-girl" smile.

Her mirror double responded as she fastened the second rubber band around her other pigtail. "And I suppose you think you're the only person who can use big words, Samantha?"

"And I suppose you think you're the only person who knows how to kiss, Shelly," I shot back.

"Touché," announced Annie. "I love this stuff."

"By the way, how do you know I don't have raw talent?" I added.

"Raw talent. Score!" Annie patted me on the back. "You are one cool chick, Sam."

"Don't call me chick."

"It's not about raw talent." Shelly clarified. "It's about learning how to do it right so they come back for more. So they can't stop thinking about how good it was."

"And you've perfected this technique?" I challenged.

"Pretty close. Ask Larry."

"I'll take your word for it." Somehow, the idea of listening to Larry's version of their nights in the back of his '62 Impala didn't thrill me.

"Okay, ladies. As much as I love this exciting banter, my time is limited. I still have to do math homework. Let's get the show on the road," announced Annie.

"Annie's right. We're here to make sure everything is all set for your party, Sam. Just think, soon you'll be with Buck. We want everything to be perfect."

"What if he doesn't show?" My worst fear.

"DeSantis, you're starting to bug me with this sappy, defeatist attitude. He'll show. Now pass the Nestle's chocolate," ordered Annie.

"I'll go get my lists downstairs. And some Pepsi and chips and onion dip. Be right back."

"Right on. More food!" shouted Annie enthusiastically. "Okay, DeSantis, let's talk about these doubts you're having. Sit here." She patted the spot beside her on Shelly's bed, propped up the pillows, and leaned back. "Ouch! What the hell!"

"What's the matter?" I asked her.

Annie fiddled with the largest heart-shaped pillow behind her. "Something's poking me!" She stuck her hand behind the pillow and pulled out a box.

"What's that?"

"OH MY GOD!!" Annie yelled.

"What?"

"Sam, you'll never believe this!" Annie held out a box containing a plastic bust enhancer. I was speechless. "Freakin' A! Look at this thing!" Annie yanked the apparatus out of the box and posed like the model in the infamous build-a-better-bustline photo. We all but died. Apparently Shelly had ordered the no-fail gismo from the back pages of *Seventeen.* It came with a money-back guarantee. "This is serious blackmail material, Sam!" Mischief swam in her eyes.

"Shut up! What if she hears us? Put it back, Annie. Hurry up! She's coming."

"You're a downer, DeSantis."

"Annie! Hurry!"

Unable to stuff the thing back into the box in time, we had no choice but to confront Shelly when she walked into the room.

"Hey, Shel, when did you get this?" Annie feigned innocence.

Now this interrogation was definitely not fair because Shelly was taken completely off guard. I don't like to put people on the spot when their defenses are down, and hers were definitely deflated. Sometimes, however, she acted so surly and superior that our inquisition seemed justified. I must confess that we delighted a bit in watching her squirm. There she stood, totally exposed and vulnerable, growing visibly flustered but trying her best to respond as if this were no big deal. Now let me just tell you that our discovery was a *very* big deal. Today, everybody goes out and gets a little silicone here and a lot of liposuction there. Nobody cares. But in the '60s, you took what you were dealt, which was why this little device startled Annie and me.

"Oh, *that.* I was going to show you guys so we could all try it and laugh about it. Wouldn't that be a blast?"

Right! She spoke as if this were an everyday purchase.

Annie and I loved sharing a good joke and considered almost anything fair game for the sake of a laugh; however, we reserved comment and tried to be sensitive to Shelly's predicament and obvious embarrassment. We let her off the hook. Afterward, Annie and I agreed that depending on how long Shelly had been using this miracle machine, the money-back guarantee might not be a bad idea.

Eleven

"Between the wish and the thing, life lies waiting."

—Proverb

I go through the motions. Eat breakfast, brush my teeth, walk to school, go to my locker. Same faces, same jokes.

First period . . .

Second . . .

Third . . .

What time is it now?

Another day. I lie in bed, awaiting the sound of the alarm clock. I hear my mother downstairs, scurrying around as she prepares breakfast. My sister stirs in the bunk above me.

"Sammy, want me to get your roller bag?" she offers as she climbs down the ladder. Her cherubic face peeks at me between the rungs as she descends.

"Sure, Luce. That would be nice. You're up early, aren't you?"

"I smell eggs. Here you go." She plops the roller bag on my bed and heads downstairs.

My mind is heavy as I dress for school.

This is going to be a long week . . . what if I run into him at school again?

"Bye, Mom!"

I head down the street. The air feels good. It already smells like summer. I stop at the bottom of the hill where a train is rumbling through. The freight cars whiz by. I feel the ground vibrate as I stare at the blur of moving letters.

What if I run into him again?

I know that running into him would be awkward. He knows I like him. My invitation was my admission. On the other hand, his acceptance could have meant a number of things.

Suppose he was just too polite to refuse?

That would be in character.

Maybe he wants to see what it's like at a party with upperclassmen.

Or maybe he was simply flattered to be invited.

Not good.

I realize the train is long gone.

School.

* * *

"Miss DeSantis, if this class is so lacking in stimulation for you, why did you take it?"

"Huh?" Laughter surrounded me. As I refocused, I realized Mr. Lewis had stopped writing on the board, chalk poised in his hand as if he had stopped mid-equation.

"Lost in thought again, eh, Miss DeSantis? Or were you contemplating another way to solve this problem?"

"No, I'm sorry, Mr. Lewis. I was just . . . I mean . . ."

"And you usually have so many clever retorts, Miss DeSantis. Wherever is your tongue?"

On the way out the door, Sal Ucci accosted me. "Damn, Samantha! What planet were you on?"

Sal and I knew each other because he was going steady with Darlene. What I liked about Sal, besides the fact that he was one of the nicest guys around, was his humility. He was gorgeous and he didn't know it. Rare breed. Darlene and he made a perfect couple, and they were crazy about each other from day one.

"I hate geometry. And Mr. Lewis always picks on me. He never liked me," I complained.

"Well, you're not doing anything to help the situation. Need a math tutor?" he teased.

"Cute, Sal. No, I don't need you to tutor me. Gotta go."

"See you, Sam. Tutor option's still open." He grinned good-naturedly and waved.

I turned the corner. Buck. Wow. Would this reaction always be so strong? He stopped abruptly and then approached tentatively.

"Hey, Sam. How are you doing?" His smile edged on illegal.

"Fine. You?"

"I'm good. What class you heading to?" Just looking at him was painful. Light blue button-down collar shirt. Freshly pressed. Expensive khakis. Heaven.

"French."

"First or second year?"

"First year. I took Latin last year."

"Nifty. The dead language," he chuckled.

No response.

"I'm heading to the library to work on a paper. Got study hall this hour." He held up the blue hall pass. "Sanderson is happy to get rid of as many kids as he can so he can sit and read his newspaper without interruption."

I smiled and nodded. "Yeah, I heard that about him."

The longest moment passed during which his light-hearted demeanor dissolved into a more vulnerable posture, and the transformation somehow calmed me.

"Well, see you on Friday?" In light of my enthusiastic conversational skills, I'm guessing he was wondering if we were still on.

"Yes . . . Friday."

"Bye, Sam."

I hurried toward the stairs, but as I headed up to Room 232, my cardigan caught on the end of the banister, tugging me backward.

"Sam! Be careful!" Darlene rushed over and grabbed my arm. "You almost went down! You scared me."

"God! I'm such a klutz. I'm glad nobody saw me but you."

"You mean like Buck?"

"You saw me talking with him, didn't you?" I smiled.

She giggled. "Yup. He's so cute."

"Let's get to class, Darlene. We're going to be tardy, and Madame doesn't take kindly to late arrivals."

"Mais oui!"

The classroom was already full. I took my assigned seat by the window and settled into the environment I loved so much. Posters covered the walls. Paris, Carcassonne, Nice, Lyon. Everything about the French fascinated me.

Someday I'll get to Paris. I'll walk down the Champs-Elysées to the Arc de Triomphe.

"Bonjour, mes eleves. Sortez vos devoirs, s'il vous plait."

The sun peeked in the window, warming my face.

Twelve

"So far everyone is coming."

The lace cloth on the dining room table was pushed back to make room for all of her lists. As she checked off each completed task, the wall clock ticked audibly. Four o'clock.

"Everyone's coming?"

"You sound surprised, Sam. Why? Everybody likes you." She continued to write as she spoke.

"Thanks."

"It's because you're sweet." Her tone was uncharacteristically genuine. "So, are you excited?"

"Yes, I really am, Shel." I glanced at the wall clock.

"Are you dying just thinking about Buck?"

"I can't actually believe that I might be with him tomorrow night."

"Why? He said he was coming."

"I know. It just doesn't seem real."

She set down her pencil and studied me a moment. "You really like him, don't you?"

I nodded and began to pack up my books. I could feel her eyes on me.

"And you haven't even talked to him that many times. How'd that happen already?"

"I don't know, but I feel it. I felt it the first time I really looked at him."

"That's unbelievable. I don't think that's ever happened to me."

Her remark took me by surprise. I always assumed that this was what happened to everyone. You see the person, and you just know. How could she have a boyfriend and not experience what I already knew?

"What happens to you?"

"I don't know. I just sort of pick out some hunky boy, and I set my sights on him. Then I see."

"See what?"

"If I like the way he kisses me."

"I already know I'll like kissing Buck."

"How could you possibly know that?" Her brow furrowed in disbelief.

"I just know. When I stand near him, I know."

"You're kidding. How?"

"My heart beats faster . . . I want to touch him." I checked the clock.

"You've got it bad, DeSantis. Well, what if you kiss him and it doesn't feel the way you imagined?"

"Oh, it will." I walked to the door and slid into my loafers.

"You're that sure?"

"Yeah."

"Well, let's practice anyway."

"Practice what? I have to go home now."

"Kissing."

"Kissing? Have you flipped your wig? I don't want to kiss you."

"Don't be a flake. Come into the living room and sit here," Shelly commanded. She started rearranging furniture.

"Why?"

"Because you have to be prepared. You don't want it to look like it's your first time."

"It's not," I defended.

"Playing Spin the Bottle doesn't count. This is your *real* first time. Now, pretend I'm Buck. What if he puts his arm around you?"

"This is silly. What time is it?" I craned to see the wall clock in the dining room.

"Stop looking at the clock. Your mother will understand. And we can do this faster if you cooperate."

She put her arm around me. "Okay, I'm Buck. Now, show me what you'll do." She meant business.

"Well, I'm not exactly sure. What should I do?" I could feel a big, stupid grin working its way out.

"Sam." The warning voice.

"Okay. I'll, umm—well, I will definitely like it."

"That's not what I mean. I already know you'll like it. But what will you DO? Show me what you'll DO!" She glared.

Maybe it was the grating emphasis she placed on the word *do* that pushed me over the edge.

"Maybe I'll jump on him. After all, I've been waiting for this moment for so long, I might lose control. You know how desperate I am for a boyfriend."

She ignored my outburst, maintaining a straight face.

"Samantha, come on. Show me what you'll DO!"

"Is there something special you DO in these situations? Enlighten me. You're the expert. And, if it weren't for you, Buck never would have considered being with me." It was my turn to glare.

"I was only trying to help, but never mind." She stood up.

"Okay, I'm sorry."

"No you're not." Now *she* was the one peering toward the clock. "Don't you have to go home now?"

"No, really. I know you're just trying to help. But this feels awkward. And sometimes your tone gets sort of pushy."

"*My* tone?"

Let it go, Sam.

"Really. I'm ready." I took a cleansing breath.

"Okay. Now watch." She relished in her role as kissing coach. "You slide down in the seat a little, like this, and kinda nestle yourself into his shoulder pocket."

"His what?"

"His shoulder pocket."

"His shoulder pocket," I repeated. "Are you kiddin' me?"

"Right here. This spot. That way your head is positioned, and you're ready in case he plants one on you. And make sure you look up at him like this." The expression on her face was indescribable. "Then blink your eyes." She batted her lustrous lashes.

Too much!

"Is this a joke? Some kind of initiation rite?"

"No! This is serious."

"Blink my eyes? He'll think I lost a contact!"

"You don't wear contacts."

God help me.

"I know that! What I mean is this is dumb!" I stood up. I always make impassioned speeches better on my feet. "I realize I have very little experience in this area. And I concede that you are the expert. You've done the make-out thing plenty of times. But, lest you forget, I, too, have kissed a boy before."

"Once!"

"Regardless. I did not hear any complaints. And there was no blinking of the eyes. This is much too contrived." My voice was fevered, my breathing erratic. Shelly stared at me without a sign of what was twirling around in that pretty head of hers.

"Too what?"

"Contrived!"

"Fine. Do you want to do this or what? This is your last chance, and I mean it."

Shelly and I definitely differed when it came to matters of the heart. I wanted things to happen naturally. The idea of planning out something as personal as a kiss seemed wrong. So I spilled my guts.

"It's just that I don't think kissing should be planned."

Her eyes popped open. "What? Of course it should!"

"But why? Why can't it just happen?"

"You're so inexperienced, Sam. That's why I'm trying to help you."

"Well, everyone is inexperienced at some point. I don't really want Buck to think that I've kissed a lot of boys. I haven't."

"That's not the point," she retaliated.

"What *is* the point?"

"The point is you should be prepared if he does kiss you because the way you kiss him back could decide if he likes you or not."

I couldn't believe what I was hearing.

Is that what it is all about?

"Well, if being a good kisser is the determiner, then the person is very shallow."

"Who cares! Do you want my help or not?"

Philosophical differences aside, I knew she was only trying to help. This was her thing, her contribution to ensure that the evening would go well with Buck. So what if she didn't have a clue how I felt or what I was trying to say half of the time. She was doing this for me. I acquiesced.

"Okay. Five minutes. Then I have to go home."

After all, she was well-versed in the art of romance, and the lesson might come in handy. So in the name of friendship, I sat down and nestled myself into her shoulder pocket.

Thirteen

June 10. Thank God. I don't think I could have survived another day.

What still gnawed at me was the idea that he might not show. That would be just the type of thing that would happen to me. Public humiliation while all my friends looked on and tried to console me. Pathetic looks behind my back. I could just imagine the conversations.

"Poor Sam. Did you hear Buck didn't show tonight?"

"No! And she's such a good kid."

"Yeah, what a bummer!"

"Sam doesn't deserve this. And on her sixteenth birthday!"

"She looks so CUTE tonight too."

"Oh, don't worry, Sam. He's only a freshman anyway. He's younger than you are."

"Have another Hostess cupcake, Sam. They're chocolate."

Oh my God! What have I gotten myself into?

The ground threatened to crack and swallow me whole.

*   *   *

6 p.m.

I ran a comb through my hair, curling the blunt ends up and over my fingers.

"Too neat. I need to mess it up a little." I shook my head, a technique I'd learned from Shelly, and reexamined my appearance. A loose strand flopped over my eye. I blew it away.

"How come this look always works for Shelly? I've watched her do it a hundred times." I tried again, leaning over and shaking my head in a circular motion. I critiqued my reflection in the mirror again. "Now I look like the Tasmanian Devil."

"Who you talking to this time, Sammy?" Lucy entered, wearing the same quizzical look she had worn the last time she caught me in a solo conversation. The kid had a way of sneaking up on me. She inspected the room suspiciously.

"Nobody, honey." I smiled. Such an adorable kid.

"Again with nobody? I don't know about you, Sammy!" She exited promptly, shaking her head.

And then sometimes not.

I returned to the mirror. "How come I didn't get my sister's red hair? Brown hair is boring. Brown hair, brown eyes. Boring! Okay, this is it." I picked up the comb and smoothed my hair to its original arrangement. One last dose of Alberto V05. A perfect flip with lasting hold. I scrutinized myself in my mirror. Insecurity stared back at me.

Fully dressed, I sprayed my neck, wrists, and ankles with Ambush, my favorite perfume, and headed out of my room. I paused at the top of the stairs. I knew my parents were sitting in the living room having cocktails with their friends, the Gardners. Now I had to descend those stairs and talk to them. No escaping the house with a simple good-bye.

Face the music, Sam.

Dead man walking. I proceeded toward the inquisition.

"Here comes Sam. She's going to Shelly Porterfield's house tonight for her sixteenth birthday party. Shelly's having it in her honor." Mom's face glowed.

Dad snapped my picture at the foot of the stairs. He had the big Nikon loaded. My dad was a photographer, an artist.

"Stand there for a minute, Sammy. Let me get another shot." He angled the camera vertically.

"Dad. You're not going to take a whole bunch of pictures now, are you?"

"Just a couple. Now smile." FLASH!

"You look nice, honey. Those jeans are flattering on you. The sweater is pretty too." Mom leaned over and whispered, "Is it a small or a medium?"

"It's a medium, Mom."

The sweater definitely showcased one of my best assets, and I didn't mind showing it off, despite local household protests. While I was never completely happy with my body, especially compared to Shelly's curvaceous figure, certain parts were to my satisfaction. This was one—or two.

"You look just swell, Sam. As usual." Bill Gardner. He always liked me. "The boys better watch out. Look at that face."

"Don't you girls wear dresses anymore? The kids these days! She's wearin' jeans to her sixteenth birthday party!" Ida Gardner and her fog horn voice. "In my day . . ."

Here we go.

" . . . we wore dresses to our coming-out parties. Nothin's the same anymore, is it Peg?"

Ida was always dependable for the editorial comment. Her whole body was in motion when she spoke. And when she shook her head in affirmation or disapproval, her hair, reminiscent of a WWII helmet, never moved an inch.

"You got a fella escorting you?" Ida inquired. The ice cubs clinked as she swirled her drink.

"No, not really."

"You mean you're going to your own sweet sixteen party alone? How's that?" Ida's face pinched into a scowl.

"The kids don't do it that way anymore, Ida. It's more relaxed now." Mom to the rescue.

Ida shook her head. "I don't know." She sipped her Scotch.

"No date?" exclaimed Bill. "A girl as pretty as you? Well, I'd escort you myself if I was your age."

"You're full of shit, Bill! She wouldn't have gone with *you*. You were a skinny candy ass." She took a hefty gulp of her Scotch. "Don't pay no attention to him, Sam."

"Ida, that's not very nice," replied Dad. "Who's going to be there, Sam?" Sweet, gentle Dad. He smiled reassuringly.

"Everybody."

"Well, Sam has to get going now." Mom escorted me toward the door, out of the line of fire.

"Wait, Sam. Stand there with your mother while I take your picture."

"Now, Dad?"

"It'll only take a minute. After all, it's your sixteenth birthday party. We have to snap this shot for the memory photos." As we did with all events.

"Now tip up your chin and smile. That's it. Peg, put your arm around Sam. Tilt your head a little more, Sam. A little more. That's good. Now hold it."

FLASH.

"Great shot. Okay. Now one more for insurance."

Heavy sigh. Mine.

FLASH.

I groaned. *I'm never going to get out of here.*

Dad had a talent for photography. As a young man, he started developing pictures in the basement of our house in his makeshift darkroom. Self-taught, he excelled at his craft with passionate persistence and eventually began shooting weddings for his friends to subsidize his modest income as a boilermaker, a trade he had learned solely to earn an income to take care of his family. Oddly enough, installing and repairing boilers in a factory was opposite from the fine-detailed and reflective work he loved as a photographer. Dad became quite good. The right shading, the right moment—it all came together in his photos. Word of his work spread, and one day he was offered fifty bucks for his first shoot. Elation!

He was so excited to have his first professional photography job. The family who hired him loved his easy manner and soft smile. They welcomed him into their circle. But he broke a rule that he vowed never to break again. When they offered their amiable photographer and his accompanying wife a celebratory drink, he accepted. After all, this was a festive occasion.

"Nick, you'd better be careful. You're working," warned my mother.

"One little drink won't hurt, Peggy."

Who knows how many drinks later, he gathered the wedding party together to take another group shot. When he raised the cumbersome apparatus to snap the picture, he smashed the equipment into his face, gashing his forehead. To the horror of the onlookers, blood streamed down his nose while he continued to frame the happy party, whose expressions now reflected a mild level of horror. Who knew if he even felt the blow as he assured everyone he was just fine. After all, alcohol is a great anesthetic.

My dad now wisely declines all celebratory cocktails until *after* the photographs have been taken.

"Okay, that's a wrap, Sam," announced Dad.

Finally. Freedom.

"Bye, everybody."

A chorus of well-wishers bid me adieu. Mom accompanied me through the sunporch to the screen door.

"Ida's had too much to drink. Don't pay any attention to her."

"It's okay, Mom."

"You look pretty, honey."

"Thanks, Mom."

"What's wrong?"

"Nothing."

"Don't tell me *nothing*. I can tell by looking at you that something is bugging you."

"I'm a little nervous."

"About what?

"I don't know. Nothing really."

Mom studied me as I spoke. "Would you like me to walk a ways with you?"

I smiled. My mother was an oxymoron. Tender, sardonic, sensitive, no-nonsense, irritating, loving. An incredible woman. I often said she could run a corporation. But she dedicated herself to her family and to Dad's photography business.

"No thanks, Mom. I can walk myself."

Mind you, it was not because I was embarrassed by being seen walking with my mom. On the contrary, I loved being with her. She was young and hip and beautiful. Most of my friends couldn't believe how young she was when they first met her. In elementary school, a classmate once asked me how old she was.

"Twenty-seven."

"You mean thirty-seven."

"No, I mean twenty-seven," I corrected. "I should know my own mother's age."

The kid's faced twisted. "That's too young to be your mom!"

I went home, distressed by my classmate's comment. Mom laughed. "Never mind, honey. I might be younger than some of the other moms, but we'll grow up together."

I've never forgotten that moment—sitting in our kitchen at the round Formica table, sharing biscotti cookies with pink frosting and sprinkles. And my mom, young and beautiful, with her long, slender neck and perfectly coiffed hair, looking like a queen.

Because of our bond, Mom was never content to let things go. She pressed on. "Tell me what you're nervous about. You look really nice. That can't be it. Don't you like your new sweater? It's blue."

"Yes, I love it. It's not the sweater." Pregnant pause. "It's Shelly, I guess." I avoided direct eye contact. My mom's eyes narrowed.

"Shelly. What about her? She's having the party for you, isn't she? That's a gracious gesture." She maintained an even tone. I was impressed.

Despite the fact that Shelly was indeed hosting the party in my honor, I knew she was not my mother's favorite person. Mothers become very protective when their children's friends, who can sometimes be hurtful, mess with their kids' feelings. My mother consistently maintained that Shelly was insincere, competitive, and manipulative. She never trusted her. Now she was defending her.

"I know she is, Mom, and I shouldn't feel this way because it is really thoughtful of her. It's just . . . well, you know how pretty she is, and all the guys love her."

"Oh, for God's sake, Sammy, forget that." Her body lost its momentary tension. "So what if she's pretty. She's not that pretty, anyway. You overestimate her looks. There are probably other reasons the boys like her, but let's not get into that."

I shot her a look, wondering why she'd made that remark. She quickly rerouted the conversation.

"You are every bit as pretty as Shelly Porterfield." A mother's eyes.

I snorted aloud. "Mom! Are you nuts? She's beautiful. And everyone thinks so."

"Listen, Samantha. Don't waste another moment fretting about that. And don't place too much emphasis on appearance. Personality counts much more. The way a person *is* has more to do with appeal than looks. Have you ever noticed those pretty boys on the commercials? Handsome, right? Perfect hair, perfect teeth, bronzed, and gorgeous. You look at them and think they're something. Then they open their mouths. Need I say more?"

She was on a roll.

"Now I'm going to tell you something, Samantha. And I don't want you to get a big head about this because there's nothing worse than somebody running around with a big ego. Self-praise stinks. You don't know it, but there's . . ." she hesitated, considering the long-term effects of her admission, " . . . there's something special about you."

I remember wondering where she was going with this. And it was seriously embarrassing me.

"You have a quieter appeal than most girls. I know you make fun of yourself, and you're always quick with a punch line." She interrupted her flow, speaking almost to herself. "Actually that's one of the things I really love about you, your wit." She smiled briefly before returning to her point. "But you're lovely, honey. You're just unaware. And that, my dear daughter, makes you all the more appealing." Closing argument delivered with the confidence of a champ. She patted my back in conclusion.

"Thanks, but you're my mother. Of course you think that."

She put her arm around my shoulder. "I know. But I'm telling you not to worry."

I smiled and pulled away. "I better go, or I'll be late for my own party." I proceeded down the sidewalk and waved back at her as I walked up the street.

"Eleven-thirty! Have fun, honey." She headed toward the archway leading back into the house. Though she sometimes frustrated the hell out of me, I was always moved by the depth and conviction of her love.

Fourteen

6:45 p.m.

Like a movie I've watched over and over, I can still see myself heading down the street and distinctly remember the way I felt walking the short 10-block route to Shelly's house. It was a good time to take a deep breath and contemplate the evening. My heart matched my pace as I crossed block after block. I was confident that Buck would show, but I wondered how much time we would actually spend together. Would he just wish me a happy birthday and hang around with everybody else?

At one point I stopped dead in the middle of Port Street, a part of me wanting to turn around, retreat to the solace of my home, and forget the whole crazy notion that Buck Kendall really wanted to be with me. True, Shelly said he had agreed to come without any apparent hesitation, but that didn't mean much.

Was he just being polite?

"The son of the president of the college. What were you thinking? You couldn't pick somebody normal. You had to go for . . ."

The sudden and insistent honking of a red Mustang brought me back to my senses. I realized I was in the middle of the road, talking to myself.

"Sorry!"

The driver, a fairly young man, shook his head disapprovingly as I scurried to the curb to move out of his path. His expression screamed, "Loser!" And if that wasn't enough, he stared me down for what felt like a full minute.

Okay. I get the point.

"Sorry!" I repeated for good measure. Then I waved kindly to the gentleman.

He shook his head one more time and flipped the bird. My mouth fell open.

"Nice guy!" I don't think he heard me. "I'm only a kid!" His wheels were already hugging the corner, and his tires squealed as he sped up the street.

"Get a grip, Sam. You don't need to get killed over your preoccupation with this party. And definitely not by that jerk. And I'm still talking to myself!" My arms flailed about.

Spurred on by my near brush with death, I attempted to pump myself up for the duration of my short walk. "Everything is going to be fine, and you are going to have a blast at your party."

Two more houses till Shelly's. I slowed down. My stomach churned.

"Must be about 6:55. Party starts at seven. Good timing. Shelly said not to arrive too early, so this is good. I'm still talking to myself! I have to lose this habit." I checked behind me to see if anyone was there. Safe.

I ran my hands down the sides of my hair and up the flip. Still stiff. I smelled my wrists to see if the scent of Ambush was alive. Check.

"Okay, Sam. You can do this."

Up Shelly's driveway.

I wonder if he's there yet.

I halted.

Voices. Laughter. Music. With newfound confidence, I proceeded toward the door. When I entered the dining room, a barrage of my girlfriends greeted me. It's always the girls who arrive first. The boys are too cool. Girls are early so they can help set up and prepare the food and join in the camaraderie. Boys just show up.

"Sam!" Shelly came running over and threw her arms around me. "You look so cute. I love your shirt. Can I borrow it some time? And your jeans make you look really skinny." Skinny was important to Shelly, so I smiled at the compliment. She leaned in, "Are you excited?"

In the background Annie was guffawing and making her mocking noises. Then the infamous chanting commenced. "Buck. Buck. Buck."

"Shut up, Annie," I tossed out good-naturedly.

"Or what?" She shot back.

"Or I'll stop putting you on the guest list for my parties."

"Big threat. I'm an unabashed crasher." She laughed.

"And I'll stop editing your compositions for Kelly's class."

Her overconfident expression dissolved. "You had to play that card, didn't you? That's below the belt, DeSantis."

Shelly interrupted our slam session. "Sam, listen to me. Larry just called and said Buck's riding over with him tonight. Scott is dropping them off, and they should be here in five minutes." She shrieked in anticipation.

My stomach rolled with the mention of his name. I had to distract myself, so I walked over to the dining room table to check out the decorations and spotted the cake.

"Oh, this is really pretty, Shelly. Who did this?"

"Darlene. She ordered it from Maria's Bakery. It's chocolate." Shelly was pleased at my obvious delight.

"Where is she?"

"In there with Sal."

I searched the living room and saw them standing by the record player, grinning at each other. They had been together for almost a year, and watching them together said it all.

"Darlene," yelled Shelly. "Come here a minute. Sam saw her cake."

Darlene came barreling in and hugged me. "You like it? It's chocolate!"

Her constant enthusiasm was infectious. "I know. I love it. Thanks."

"Are you psyched?"

"I am."

"When's Buck getting here?"

"Shelly said he's on his way." I returned my attention to the cake. "Thanks, you guys. It was really great of you to do all of this for me."

Shelly grabbed her camera. "Sit by the cake so I can take your picture before we cut into it. Right there."

Following orders, I moved to the designated chair and succumbed to the orchestration of Shelly's notion of the perfect photo. In the meantime, the party was happening around me. More friends filtered in, setting gifts on the table, hugging one another, jumping up and down at the idea of a school year nearly ending, and silently waving to me to avoid upsetting the delicate balance of the perfect photo. As I adjusted my pose to fit Shelly's specifications, I breathed in those seconds when everything good seemed to be aligned.

"Okay, Sam. This is it."

"That's what you said last time."

"Seriously. Now think of something good, and give me your best smile." She lowered the camera. "Say CHEESE."

At that precise moment, the screen door swung opened, announcing a procession of boys that culminated with Buck. His expression was tentative as he scanned the room. He looked as if he felt out of place. But when he saw me, our eyes locked, and his uncertainty melted away. Shelly snapped the picture.

"Jeez, Sam, that was a really good smile," Darlene commented, unaware that Buck had entered the room.

I wanted nothing more than to head directly over to him, but Shelly needed a couple more photos for the scrapbook, and I lost sight of him as he blended into the thicket of teenagers.

Conversation hummed all around me. An invisible barrier made sound and movement surreal. I observed the happenings as if I were on the outside looking in. At the same time I was experiencing this quasi out-of-body sensation, my friends were hugging me and wishing me happy birthday. I attempted to keep up the required conversation, which at any other time would have been effortless, but I was distracted by an urgency to know where he was. I strained to concentrate.

"Hi, Ron. Where's Denise? Is she still coming?"

"Yeah, after she finishes babysitting her cousin."

"Oh, good."

"Hey, Sam. Can you believe what Mr. Nichols did in class yesterday?'

"Yeah, he's a piece of work. Time for retirement."

"No kidding. The guy talks to himself all the time. And he never makes any sense."

Laughter. Aimless chatter. Blah, blah, blah. Then, welcomed relief. Brian.

"Sammy girl!" He folded me into his arms and kissed the top of my head. "Look at you. Sweet sixteen!" Across the room, Carolyn was scrutinizing his every movement. "So—have you talked to Buck yet?"

"Shhh . . . what if he hears you?"

He leaned down and lowered his voice. "Sammy, you invited him. He knows you like him."

"I know but . . ." His laughter stopped me.

"You're something, Sammy."

"Yeah, thanks a bunch."

"Okay, I get it. I'm going over there and talk to Andrea."

He waved playfully as he headed toward his next conquest. As I watched him walk away, I spotted Buck, talking with Shelly. She was in signature motion. I was suddenly irritated that she was monopolizing his time. I had waited too damn long for this night, and she knew it.

Get a grip, Sam. She's your friend.

I watched her flirt.

No big deal. She does that with everyone. Time to eat.

I headed for the snack table where Tommy Cortellini was wiping out the dip.

"Hey, Sam. Happy birthday!" He never changed position—just continued to scoop up the dip and shove it into his mouth.

"Thanks, Tommy."

"You should try this onion dip. It's delicious. And it's better with potato chips than with the Ritz crackers. I've tried both."

Good to know. I smiled.

There he is. So gorgeous.

Beatles' music was blaring. *I don't care too much for money—money can't buy me love.* Some kids were already dancing. I kept one eye on Buck while pretending to carry on a serious conversation with Tommy at the snack table, but clearly he was more interested in the food than in talking.

"You spilled a little dip there, Tommy." He looked down. "On the front of your shirt."

While Tommy scooped up the lost mouthful with his fingers, I perused the room again. Buck was still talking to the hostess of the evening, who periodically shook her hair in that alluring way she had perfected. As I watched them, I drifted back to Carolyn's house. He haunted me. His eyes. His voice. Would it be the same tonight?

Mid-thought, he caught my eye. Excusing himself from conversation, he made his way toward me.

Here we go.

"Happy Birthday, Sam."

"Thanks, Buck."

Oh, God, my stomach.

"So. Sixteen, huh?"

"Yup. Sixteen."

And my mouth! Where'd all my saliva go?

"Today?"

"Today, what?"

"Is today the actual day—your birthday?"

"Oh! No. It's on Sunday. June 12."

"Oh—June 12. An almost summer birthday."

"Yep," I responded as I alternately glanced between the floor and his face. He unnerved me. Then, for no apparent reason, I blurted out, "Same birthday as Anne Frank."

Now here was a fact worth noting. Was I possessed?

He looked both bewildered and amused. "Oh, yeah? Really? How do you know that?"

"I read *The Diary of Anne Frank*, and her birthday was June 12 too. I just remember, that's all."

Deep doo-doo now. This must be my alter ego talking. And she's talking historical facts with the genius here.

"So it's a famous birthday." He was still smiling, and, thankfully, still standing there.

"I guess."

A famous dead person!

"Well, happy birthday to you and Anne."

"Thanks."

This was definitely not the way I pictured things.

"You have a lot of presents here. Are you going to open all of them tonight?"

Small talk. He's bailing.

"I guess. That's probably what Shelly will want me to do."

"You look really nice tonight, Sam."

His voice was low and tender. The sound of my name, falling out of his mouth, caused goose bumps to run up my arms. I saw a flicker of something familiar in his eyes, and at that moment I had a sense that everything would be all right. Then Shelly came bounding over like an unwanted puppy, messing up your homework when your papers are all lined up.

"Hey, you two!"

The sing-song voice again.

"Hi, Shelly."

"Sam, almost everyone is here. You should probably start opening your presents and cut the cake. Everybody wants to see what you got. Buck, did you bring Sam a gift?"

I'm going to kill her.

"Yeah, it's right there," he pointed to a medium-size package with a blue bow.

How did he know I liked blue? It's a sign!

I was definitely grasping.

"I wonder what's in it," said Miss Shelly with a smile. "Well, let's get going, and we'll find out." She grabbed my hand and dragged me away. Just when we were beginning to connect.

I must make a point of discussing timing with this girl.

For the next thirty minutes, I did the guest-of-honor thing. I politely thanked everyone for the gifts and smiled for two rounds of "Happy Birthday," sung with particularly creative lyrics. I graciously rebounded from everyone's taunts, blew out the candles, cut the cake, on and on. Usually I ate this stuff up. But at that moment, all I wanted was Buck, who was now with a crowd of guys, eating cake and looking uncomfortable again. He was, after all, only one of two underclassman amongst us. A "so-what?" to me. A "big deal" to him.

Cake and ice cream out of the way, Ben cranked up the music in the living room, and kids started moving in different directions. My palms began to sweat.

Is he going to walk over here anytime soon?

He did.

"Nice gifts."

"Yeah, they are. Thanks for the candle."

"No problem."

"Blue is my favorite color."

"Glad you like it."

Silence.

I looked around as more and more of my friends drifted into the living room. The noise level soared.

"Good cake."

"Yeah. Chocolate is my favorite."

Well, he's certainly learning a lot about my favorites.

"I like this song," he said.

He likes the Beatles! Hurray!

"Yeah, me too. The Beatles are my favorite."

Again with the favorites!

"Really? So what other groups do you like?"

"Oh, the Beach Boys. Chicago. The Lettermen."

The Letterman! Tactical error.

"The Lettermen?" If I tried, I couldn't describe the expression on his face.

"Well, just a couple of their songs." My palms needed ringing out, and rational thinking had taken a nose-dive.

"Like what?"

"'When I Fall in Love.'" It was indeed my favorite of the Lettermen's songs, but let's face it, I was going down fast.

"When you fall in love, what?" He regarded me quizzically.

"No. It's the name of a song. 'When I Fall in Love' is the name of one of their best songs." My face burned.

He grinned openly. "I know. I'm sorry." He attempted to hide his amusement.

Great. Now I'm missing the humor.

"Well, they have really good harmony," I defended. I didn't want to look like a moron. "Do you like harmony?"

And who cares anyway?

"As a matter of fact, I do like harmony." More grinning.

"Well, that's good." *Why* I didn't know. Does the object of one's affection have to like harmony for the relationship to work out? Don't they say that opposites attract?

"And I really like to sing. I was in the ninth grade choir at Pioneer. Second soprano. Miss Scrimshaw chose me for Select Choir to compete in States." I was beginning to amaze myself.

"Really?"

God, he's cute.

"Really." I feigned pride.

"I didn't know you were a singer. That's neat, Sam. Congratulations on the States."

"I'm only good at harmonizing. I don't sing solo like some of the girls. You know how some people can just stand there and whip off a solo? Well, that's not me."

Nothing. My attempt at modesty had no effect.

"It was called Blue Birds."

"What was?"

"The name of the girls' singing group at Pioneer. The Blue Birds. You had to audition to get in."

"And you got in."

Hiding his amusement was becoming a chore, but he followed the line of conversation politely just the same.

What in God's name am I babbling about? This was a bad idea. What made me think this would work?

At that moment it seemed that the best thing I could do was search deep inside for courage, call up my dignity, and walk out the door. Let the poor guy off the hook.

"So, you want to go in the other room, Sam?"

About face!

And there it was. The words were just hanging in the air. The words I'd dreamed about. *Do you want to go into the other room, Sam?*

Trumpets. Swell of music.

Wait! Did he actually say it? Or was I just imagining this?

Everything passed slowly around me. The Beatles were singing "A Hard Day's Night," somebody spilled a bowl of Frito Lays, and Annie was telling another joke. Laughter surrounded her. Finally, I found my voice.

"What?"

"Do you, umm, want to go in the other room?" He nodded toward the living room, where couples were making out. His jaw was taut, the muscles along the side of his face clenched.

Buck Kendall just asked me to go into the other room.

Considering how desperately I had waited for this moment, I was oddly rooted in one position for what seemed a very long time. Why? He appeared to know what I was thinking. How? The sensation was very strange and familiar at the same time.

"Sam?" The gentleness of his voice brought me back, and I nodded. He reached for my hand and tucked it inside his as he led me through the thicket of teenagers, giggling and dancing, unaware of our intrusion, each having a private party. I could concentrate on nothing but the feel of his skin.

As we entered the room, I spotted Carla and Ted on one of the green sofas. They were locked in their usual position. The Holy Ghost couldn't fit between them. I blessed myself silently.

"Let's sit here," Buck motioned toward the small couch in front of the living room window, the very same couch on which Shelly and I had practiced kissing only yesterday afternoon. What a disaster that had been. Let's hope it wasn't an omen.

As much as I wanted to be there with him, it was very awkward at first. Neither of us said a word. I wondered how long we would sit there without contact or communication.

Now what were those moves Shelly taught me?

The scent of his Jade East distracted me.

God, he smells good.

I decided to concentrate on what other people in the room were doing so I could pick up some fast pointers and, quite frankly, distract myself from the uncomfortable silence. He still wasn't saying a word.

Is he reconsidering?

Without moving my head, I managed to glance sideways to inspect the status of Carla and Ted's activities. Everybody knew about Carla and Ted. They were hot and heavy. Yep, they were into it all right. This didn't make me feel any better. I wondered if Carla went through Shelly's make-out drills to learn all those smooth moves.

Suddenly I realized I was in over my head. For as much as I dreamed about being in this exact place with this exact boy, I was desperate for an escape route. In the true spirit of a Gemini, my mind began its two-sided, irrational dialogue, as it often did in times of desperation.

Naive Sam*: Is there an open window? Would anyone even notice if I bounded out of the room? They all look pretty busy to me. I could excuse myself to go to the bathroom, slip out discreetly, and no one would be the wiser.*

Jaded Sam: *You're the guest of honor. Wake up! They'd notice. Besides, Shelly doesn't have a window in her bathroom.*

Naive Sam*: Foiled!*

Jaded Sam: *Listen, he's probably regretting his impulsive response to Larry's invitation. Just deal with it.*

Naive Sam: *I knew it! Oh, sure, it sounds pretty cool to be the object of an upper classman's affection, but on second thought . . .*

Jaded Sam: *He's only a freshman. Get over it!*

His hand landed on my left shoulder. I stiffened.

Is this the shoulder pocket thing or the eye-batting thing?

He said nothing. My heart beat faster.

He is sitting closer to me now. He must have inched over when he wrapped his arm around me. Yes, definitely closer.

I could feel his breath.

What was it Shelly said about this part? And I made fun of her. I can certainly see the value in the lesson now. She said something about sliding down on the seat a little. Of course, that's definitely a Shelly move, and I can't quite picture myself doing that. But anything is worth a shot. Oh, I love this song! "Please don't wear red tonight . . . for red is the color that my baby wore . . ."

I was so involved with the idea of red being the color that his baby wore and imagining being so crazy about someone that you experienced physical pain when you saw somebody else wearing that same color, I lost my place. And red, for God's sake! This wasn't exactly an obscure color like puce or periwinkle or some other shade that he might not happen upon. Red? The poor guy must have been in constant pain. Between the agony of John Lennon's situation and the distraction of the escalating status of the couple beside me, who were clearly going to need their own room in a minute, I never saw it coming.

His right arm swung across my chest, and he planted his hand firmly on my left shoulder. It happened so fast that I didn't have time to think. And then he kissed me. The force of determination with which he executed his plan was somewhat akin to summoning up the nerve to dive into the lake when you know the eventual pleasure you'll derive from the cool waters simply must be preceded by the moment when you work up the nerve to plunge in.

And plunge he did!

I was slightly off balance, but within seconds I responded. The room faded. His mouth was on mine, and I tasted him for the first time. The pounding in my chest increased, reverberating up through my ears, further erasing outer-world intrusions. Our first kiss was brief, but then came another and another and another . . .

Time and space slipped away. Sounds dissolved into a dull echo. Intermittent chatter and laughter drifted through in waves until a veil of peace enveloped me. No one else was in the room. A familiarity hung between us, as if we had been in this exact place before. The soft stubble of his face brushed my skin, and I felt his hand dig into my shoulder. I squeezed the arm of his shirt into a knot. He breathed audibly. His hand slid from my shoulder to the small of my back, and we pulled closer to get inside each other's space. The smell of warm Jade East surrounded me.

It was happening so fast. So fast.

Through the supple cotton of his shirt, I felt an increased pounding. It comforted me to know we were in the same place. Suddenly I needed to see his face, to know what he was thinking. I broke away. My movement took him off guard, and he leaned back, sliding his fingers through the thickness of his hair. His cheeks flushed the way mine burned. He seemed edgy, but when

I smiled at him, the muscles in his face relaxed, the corners of his mouth spreading upward in a grateful smile. He took my hand. Something extraordinary was happening. Without words, our eyes exchanged a truth that both thrilled and frightened me. *This is real.*

"Need air?" he joked.

I was grateful for the lightness of his remark. "Do you?" I replied.

"No. I'm fine, trust me. Just making sure you're all right."

"I am definitely all right." My voice sounded different to me. Older? Softer? I couldn't put my finger on it, but I knew I had never heard it come out that way before.

We sat in silence, having interrupted the magic with our words. When he turned to me again, he studied my face thoughtfully, top to bottom, eyes hanging intimately on each feature. Time slowed as he peered inside me, probing through a place where no one had ever been. Even now, in the moments when I recall what it was like to be sixteen and experience the first tugs of love, I can still feel him looking at me that way. At times my recollection is so strong, so real—the sensation sweeps over me again and transports me back to that hour.

I knew with certainty that we were forever connected. And yet, there was still so much we had to learn about each other. But a truth, however inexplicable, rose up from the center of me: I was gone, lost inside this boy. My soul was filled with Buck Kendall.

In the kitchen crammed with teenagers, carrying on in their normal party mode, Shelly exclaimed to the captain of the football team, "Greg, look at your little brother! I didn't know he had it in him."

We no longer inhabited their universe. We moved toward each other once again . . .

Fifteen

I floated past Mrs. Biglow's house and recalled the time her brute of a dog, Smokey, had sniffed after me in an attempt to snatch the cookies from my bagged lunch. His sniffing turned into a low rumbling. Determined to stand up against his fear tactics, I walked onward.

You're not getting my mother's freshly baked chocolate chip cookies!

But suddenly he leapt up and planted his huge paws on my shoulders, almost knocking me over. My usual calm gave way to the rising fear of living the remainder of my young life minus a body part. I released the package and ran for my life. The memory must have evoked a chuckle because Buck turned to me.

"What?"

"Nothing." I smiled again. I seemed to be doing a lot of that.

His fingers were laced through mine. When he adjusted his grip, the shift caused our shoulders to brush. My eyes fell to the narrow space between us where our hands were locked together. Every now and then he turned toward me as if he were going to say something. But nothing. Whenever he smiled, the hard line of his jaw eased. Time after time, his lips separated as if to speak, but he would simply return his attention to the street and our journey home. This silence didn't bother me; it was somehow comforting.

Unlike the awkward vacuum that follows angry words, our silence was communal, and I understood it.

Tall poplars lined both sides of my block, and they waved visibly, bending and swishing like waves washing ashore. I loved the sound, and tonight it enveloped me like never before. As we neared my house, I wondered if he would acknowledge what had happened between us that evening. Or would he just say good-night, rendering me a prisoner of my own thoughts?

The light shone on the steps that led to the sunporch, carefully decorated with floral print-covered chairs and black wrought iron tables. When we got closer, I noticed a pot with velvety leaves and small flowers on the corner table by the back screen. How had I missed it?

"What are you looking at?"

"That pot on the porch. I never noticed it before. I wonder if my mom . . .

He stopped suddenly, the weight of his body tugging me against him. In one fluid motion he leaned into me, and I only half saw his eyes before the length of his lashes closed over them. I wanted to keep looking at him, to watch him as he kissed me, but my lids slipped down as I lost myself. We drifted back to that place I had never been until this night. His sweet, salty scent streamed around me. In the periphery of awareness, I detected muffled sounds from the house. I was light-headed, swallowed, and never wanted to surface. Suddenly he broke away as more movement from the house reminded us of where we were. I stood trance-like.

"Guess I'd better be going." He appeared uncomfortable as he studied the sunporch, probably wondering who might appear.

"Guess so."

"I had fun tonight," he admitted. Then his eyes returned to the porch. Maybe he thought my mom was going to come running out and tell him to get the hell out and keep his filthy hands off her daughter. Possibility.

"Me too."

"Happy birthday, Sam." He looked up from the cracks in the sidewalk. "Thanks for inviting me." Then he leaned in again. A stolen kiss—too fast to savor, too strong to forget.

"I really better go before I get in trouble with your parents." He grinned as he nodded toward the house. His face lit up with amusement. "I don't want them to hate me before they even meet me."

I didn't want the night to end. Neither of us changed position for a moment. My head knew it was time for the night to be over, but my body wasn't getting the message. He reached over and brushed the top of my hand with the back of his fingers, eyes cast down as he touched me. With deliberation, he tilted his chin upward, barely moving his head, his eyes on me. The intensity made me feel strange, no longer in control. Again, he seemed on the verge of saying something important.

"See you soon, Sam."

Don't you want to tell me how you never felt like this before?

"Yes, soon."

When?

He turned and walked down our front path. When he reached the end of the long expanse of cement, he swung around in the playful manner I would come to know well.

"If I had known your actual birthday was June 12, I would have bought you an autographed copy of *The Diary of Anne Frank* instead of the candle."

"Clever!" I shouted down the path, teetering on tiptoes.

His laughter filled the air, echoing amusement.

"She's dead!" I yelled, hands cupped around my mouth.

"Oh, you *were* paying attention!" He was walking backward; then he swung around and picked up speed. His hand shot straight up in the air in his signature wave.

"Later."

Almost out of sight, he slowed down and turned to wave again. Once he passed under the branches of the old oak in front of Mr. Kent's house, I could see him no more. But from the distance came his voice.

"I promise I won't tell anybody about the Lettermen!"

What a smart ass!

Later, he told me he could hear me laughing, and I accused him of hiding behind the tree to catch my reaction. He denied it. I listened until I was sure he must have rounded the corner at the end of the block. The night quieted. I sat on the bottom step and poked at a small rock that had escaped from the yellow and orange marigold cluster on the side of the porch. Its pointed edge was chalky, so I doodled stars and hearts on the sidewalk. I wanted time to myself. I needed it not to end, this warm, consuming feeling.

My mother's voice broke my brief reverie. I scuffed away the hieroglyphics with the toe of my shoe and hopped up, walking into the house with a sense of diffused elation. My mom was on the couch, stretched out in front of the television, and I knew she'd be expecting the full report. But I wasn't ready to share yet. I needed for it to be only mine for a while.

"How was the party, honey?" Mom smiled through a sleepy haze. Dad was out cold.

"Good."

"Good?" The expression on her face said *only good*?

"Great," I added.

"That's nice," she yawned. "Oh, honey, I'm so tired. You'll have to tell me all about it in the morning."

"Deal." I was halfway up the stairs.

"So you had fun?" She was on her feet now, shaking my dad. "Nick, let's go upstairs."

The TV volume increased as a Bold detergent commercial blasted into our living room. "Now, Milly, don't be silly!" sang one housewife to the other in their mini-musical world.

"Yeah, Mom. It was fun."

"Oh, good. We'll talk in the morning," she repeated. "Try not to wake your sister. She had a hard time falling asleep tonight.

I think she might be coming down with a cold. And if your brother's light is still on . . ."

"Mom, tomorrow's Saturday. Let him read."

"Oh, yeah. You're right. I'm so tired—I can't think straight."

I knocked on Ryan's door.

"Who is it?"

"Sam."

"What do you want?"

"May I come in and say good night?"

"Sure."

He was in bed, reading as usual. "What are you reading?"

"*Gulliver's Travels.*"

"Do you like it?"

"Not as much as I liked *The Yearling*, but it's good."

"Well, night, Ryan. Sleep well."

"You too, Sam."

I started to close his door. "Was your party fun?"

His question surprised me. "Yeah. Thanks for asking."

"That's good. Well, you can close the door now."

I chuckled.

In the quiet of my room, I shed my clothes. I climbed into the bottom bunk and lay there, replaying the evening over and over in all its resplendent detail. I felt myself walking to Shelly's house, doubting the course of the evening, my stomach tightening as I entered her dining room. I caught my breath again as Buck stepped through the doorway, his face anxious. I laid my hand over my breast and felt the pounding in my chest as his smile broke the silence. I floated in disbelief as he led me to the "other room" and closed my eyes when the lushness of his lips warmed me. I brushed the back of my hand across my mouth and nose and smelled him on me. I doubted his scent would ever go away.

Lucy tossed above me and mumbled something. Sweet Lucy. She loved sharing the room with her big Sissy. She pitched once more and then settled. I listened awhile to make sure she was breathing normally.

I lay awake, frozen-eyed, comforted by the presence of my sister, who breathed and slept in my space. I could dream with her in the room, and she would never know my secrets. Once again, the late night train failed to perform its magic. I drifted periodically, but the luster of the evening gleamed through, awakening me. Until Buck, I had been a stranger to sleepless nights, blessed with the ability to place my head on the pillow and fall away instantly.

"You sleep as quiet as a little mouse," my mother used to say.

But on this night I found myself awake, trying to understand the change that had taken place in me. My sleeplessness did not disturb me. I was alive and filled with Buck and my newfound self. There would be no going back.

The sunrise, magnificent in its soundless glory, crept into my room and warmed my face. Only then did I yield to sleep as the day dawned and wrapped itself around me. A new day, the beginning of my journey, the journey that would change my life forever.

I never heard Lucy climb down the ladder from the top bunk, nor did I hear the patter of her feet as she scurried down the stairs to watch *Captain Kangaroo.* The household performed its usual functions as I slept, the sunshine and daylight my wordless companions.

Sixteen

Man's love is of man's life a part; it is woman's whole existence.

—Lord Byron

A minute is clearly not the same in every situation. Ask a parent waiting for her child to come out of surgery, as she wrings her hands and wills herself not to look at the minute hand crawling on the wall clock. Ask a soldier tiptoeing across a mine field, as he prays to God that his next step—and the one after that—will land on safe ground. Those are some long minutes. Now ask the soldier's wife how fast sixty precious seconds fly by when his leave has ended and she stands beside him at the airport, watching his chest rise and fall with every anxious breath. It's not the same. Time is relative.

Two weeks elapsed. A restlessness settled over me like a fine mist. Since the party, we had spoken only once on the telephone. Shelly explained that Buck hadn't called again because of school.

"He studies like a madman during finals, Sam."

"How do you know that?"

"Greg told me. Buck's obsessed with his grades. He plans to go to an Ivy League college. He'll call when school's out. Just wait."

Just wait.

On the first Saturday after school was finally dismissed for summer, I was walking around town with Mary Mathis simply to kill time. You wait and wait for summer, and when it shows up, you don't know what to do with all the free time. At least when you're at school, there's a good chance you'll run into one of your friends. Or Buck.

Mary and I had become friendly in ninth grade because she sat right next to me in art class. She was quirky and usually alone. She was also unusually talented. Her sketches revealed amazing depth and perspective. It was after I first commented on her drawing of Carlson's beloved lighthouse that she seemed comfortable with me. She made the lighthouse come alive, like its eyes were watching not only the waters but the town. Maybe she thought I understood a part of her that no one else did. Maybe I did.

Sadly, we had drifted since our days at Pioneer. We didn't have that much in common anymore, but I liked Mary. She was the real deal. Being a part of the in-crowd wasn't important to her. She was brilliant and made remarkable speeches about democracy and freedom of speech in history class. I always admired her insightful observations and her loyalty to causes. Her maverick attitude made her bigger in my eyes.

Most kids thought she was weird, and you know how it goes with kids like Mary. They blossom later in life when the world recognizes their worth. They are probably happier with themselves than all the rest of us who are too immersed in trying to fit in to appreciate someone outside the expected mold. Unfortunately, kids like Mary still have to endure the critical eyes of shallow peers during a fragile time of life. Mary didn't have a lot of friends, but she was always kind to me.

During our meanderings we walked by St. Patrick's Church. The sound of basketballs hitting the churchyard pavement drew my attention. When we were close enough to see what was going on, I saw Buck in the middle of a group of boys. The unexpected sight of him jolted me.

He was wearing an old, ragged short-sleeved sweatshirt and jeans. His hair was matted to his forehead. He looked happy playing basketball. His moves were polished, especially when he curled his body while jumping to dunk the ball. He scored and began sparring with one of the other boys. He looked so right in this raw state, unaware that anyone was watching him. He laughed, deep and throaty, and turned to resume play.

Then he saw me.

He stopped dead and stared at me. A smile traveled across his face, and his arm flew straight up in the air in a stiff wave, his hand stretching as high as it would reach, almost as if the higher he reached, the louder he spoke. He appeared to be on his toes, and he just stood there while basketballs sailed over his head. None of the other players missed a beat.

I waved back to him as Mary and I strolled down the street. Seeing him made me feel as if I had lost my place in the middle of a speech. Buck never said a word—just stood there watching me pass by and then returned to his game. When I heard the players' voices pick up, I glanced back and caught one more snapshot of him going in for a lay-up. I was tempted to turn around again but resisted, willing myself to hold fast to the street in front of me.

I was aware that Mary was observing me intently. "Who's that?"

"Buck Kendall."

"Kendall. Greg's brother?"

"Right."

"You know him?"

"Yes."

"He acted like he likes you. How do you know him?" Mary was puzzled.

"Well, I met him after a softball game at Pioneer Public last year."

"Last year?"

"Yes."

"That's it?"

Damn it!

"And then we were together once."

Her eyes widened. "You were? When?"

"At a party."

Her tone changed. "Whose party?"

"Umm, the party Shelly Porterfield had."

She stiffened. "For what?"

I hadn't invited Mary to the party, and I felt like crap about it. As I said, Mary and I had drifted and, to be honest, I fell prey to the high school popularity game. My friends didn't care for Mary because of her eccentricity. Whenever I was with her alone, we got along great. We appreciated each other's differences. But when she was around my other friends, awkwardness prevailed. I always hated that it had to be that way, so I decided the wisest thing was not to invite her to my party to avoid the discomfort for everyone involved. What a coward.

"Well, Shelly had a sort of sixteenth birthday party for me."

"She had a party for you?"

"Yes."

"And you didn't invite me?" Her face grew crimson as it often did with any increase in emotion.

I squirmed while at the same time admired Mary's frankness.

"Well, I didn't have it. Shelly had it."

Her expression reflected disgust. "And I suppose you had nothing to do with the guest list."

"Well, yes, but Shelly's house is small, and we had to keep it down."

"Right." Her tone said it all.

"You were on the list." What a dumb thing to say! You were on the list, but you didn't make the cut. "Honest, Mary. I just couldn't have that many people. I'm sorry."

I was.

"So who'd you cross me off for?"

"What?"

"Who'd you invite instead of me? Who made the list?"

Her candor stunned me. And she wasn't going to let me off the hook.

"Billy Jane Castanza?" she added.

"No, not exactly. I mean there wasn't one person. She was there, but not instead of you."

I wanted to turn back time. I wanted to be a better person, but I was too late.

"And you do so much with her, right, Sam?" Her face pinched with anger. "In fact, don't I remember your telling me something about how you thought she had no respect for herself because she smokes and sneaks out of her house to drink and hangs around with Hillary Jacobs, who we all know puts out for everybody."

Heavy. She had me there.

"Well, I don't know that for a fact. That's just a rumor, and you know how nasty rumors can be." Boy was I dancing.

"You're changing the subject. For somebody who says it's important to treat others fairly, you sure didn't treat me very well. I thought we were friends. I was good enough to walk home from school with you last year before we hit the big high school scene, but I guess that doesn't count. Ever since we left Pioneer, you hardly talk to me, Sam. You shouldn't treat people this way. It's not like you, and it's not right."

"I'm sorry, Mary. I screwed up. You're a better person than I."

"Don't hide behind that!"

"I mean it. You always say what's on your mind."

"Yeah, well, it's done now." Her face became stone, and an uncomfortable silence prevailed. "This is my street. I'm going home."

"I thought we were going to get a milkshake."

"I'll pass. Bye, Sam." She headed down her street.

"See you, Mary." She didn't look back.

I learned something that day. Unfortunately, it was at the expense of a friend.

* * *

He walked toward me, his hair matted to his forehead. He wiped the moisture away with his forearm. As he drew closer, his grin expanded like the Cheshire cat's. I could smell him, cologne mixed with sweat. I felt him all around me. He kept walking and walking, but he wasn't getting any closer. Then he mouthed something, but the words were inaudible.

"What? What did you say?"

Again he formed the words, but no sound came out. Nothing reached me.

He froze, his arm shot straight up into the air, and he waved. He began walking toward me again, his hand outstretched. I tried to reach him, but my legs wouldn't move fast enough.

"He acts like he really likes you. How do you know him?"

His body rose gracefully toward the net, and he sank the ball. A thunderous roar of approval filled the gym. Everyone was cheering him on. They all loved him. He smiled for the crowd as he descended, but he was looking only at me.

"He acts like he really likes you. How do you know him?" Her face was changing color.

He kept walking and walking, his hand outstretched, but he wasn't getting any closer.

"Why didn't you invite me to your party, Sam? It's not right to treat people this way."

I turned away from him and glanced over my shoulder toward Mary. A tear rolled down her cheek and stained it red.

"I thought we were friends."

She waved good-bye, leaving me the pain in her eyes. She grew smaller and smaller until she was no more.

"Come back, Mary! Please come back. I'm sorry." The pain from her eyes filled me, and I collapsed into sobs of regret. I reeled around in search of Buck, but he had faded away.

I began to tremble uncontrollably. Suddenly I was in my bed, and it was dropping through the sky.

Help me! I don't want to die. Please don't let me die!

I couldn't catch my breath.

"Wake up, Sam. You're not dying. You're dreaming."

"No! I'm falling, Dad. Look! I'm falling."

"No, you're dreaming."

"Dreaming? How did I land here?"

"Shh . . . you'll wake your sister. Come on. Go back to bed." He directed me toward my room, and only then did I realize I was standing at the top of the stairs. As the veil of disorientation slipped away, I felt mortified that my father had caught me in this defenseless state.

"You're dreaming, honey."

"But, Dad, they were right here," I insisted.

"They are gone now. Go to sleep." He kissed my forehead. "Everything will be all right. God Bless." He disappeared.

I lay there, straining to make sense of the images in my head.

Seventeen

"Sam, it's for you."

"Who is it?" I shouted down from my bedroom.

"It's Buck Kendall."

I raced down the stairs to the kitchen where my mother stood in the archway, stretching the phone cord from the wall. I could hardly believe he was calling so early on a Sunday morning. *Finally! So, he must have been happy to see me yesterday.* The image of him playing basketball was still fresh.

"Five minutes, or we'll be late for mass," Mom warned. Then she winked and left the room.

"Hello?"

"Hi, Sam. Eleven o'clock mass, huh?"

"My mom told you?"

"Yeah, you've got to leave in five minutes, or you'll be late."

"Oh, she told you that too?"

"Nah. I overheard her telling you. I already went. Jane's an early bird. Gets the clan out so we can have the rest of the day. So where were you going when I saw you yesterday?"

"Nowhere special. Just walking."

"What are you doing after church?"

"Going to my grandmother's house for dinner."

"That sounds good. So how long will you be there?"

"I'm not sure. Usually for an hour or so." I wiped the palm of my hand on the side of my skirt and switched to the other hand.

"Sam!" The warning tone carried from the front hall. "We'll wait for you in the car. Wind it up, or we'll be late." She gathered the rest of the family, and they paraded out the front door.

"Okay, be right there."

I didn't want him to hang up before some plans were laid, and it seemed as if that was the direction in which he was headed. It just took him awhile to get there.

"Well, I have to get going. Mom and church are calling."

"Okay, I'd better let you go."

I had waited too long for this phone call, so I decided to brave it.

"What are *you* doing today?"

"Not much. Cutting the lawn for my dad. Maybe playing nine holes of golf at the club with my brother."

And? And? And?

"Sounds good," I replied with all the calm I could muster.

"But I was thinking I could walk over to see you after that. If you're not doing anything."

"No, I'm not doing anything." *But waiting for you.*

"How's two o'clock?" I could hear the smile in his voice.

"Two is good."

"Okay, I'll see you then. Bye, Sam."

"Bye, Buck."

I loved saying his name.

"Samantha! There won't be any good seats left, and we'll have to sit all the way in the back. Let's go!"

St. Bartholomew's Church was spectacular for a small town house of worship. Built in the '50s, it boasted heavy pews of blonde oak with carved crosses embedded at each end, white marbled floors swirled with pink and burgundy, and stained-glass windows through which a myriad of colors cascaded upon the congregation. The pulpit from which the weekly sermons were delivered was crafted from deep green marble. The aesthetics were sometimes distracting, particularly in the middle of a traditional Latin mass. On this day I had something else to think about.

Between prayers and robotic responses, I pictured Buck walking up to my front door. What would he say? What would he be wearing? How would he act? Would he kiss me again? It felt so long since we were together. I could smell his cologne.

"Samantha!" Mom warned in her sternest whisper, "Kneel down."

Catholic mass involves a lot of standing and sitting, which has always been second nature to me. But my usual pious attentiveness was blurred by my not-so-pious preoccupation. At Mom's third prompt to pay attention, I hopped up and smiled weakly as she side-eyed me. Then she gave me "the look," which required no further explanation. My mother's look could strike the fear of God into an atheist. I did not want to be on my mother's bad side. It could take days to be in her good graces again. When she was really angry, her silence was deafening.

"Pay attention!" Another look for good measure.

Father Verducci led the Lord's prayer. The congregation joined in as one, repeating the Latin words so carefully memorized in Catechism classes.

"Pater noster, qui es in caelis, sanctificetur nomen tuum. Adveniat regnum tuum. Fiat voluntas tua, sicut in caelo et in terra . . . Amen."

I managed to behave myself like a good little Catholic for the remainder of the hour. Mercifully, mass ended, and off we drove to my nana's house.

Eighteen

All families have rituals. One of ours was to gather at my grandparents' house every Sunday after mass. When we arrived, the commotion had already begun. My dad's two brothers and their nine collective children were there. I held the coveted position of oldest grandchild on my dad's side, placing me in high esteem with the younger ones. I was also the first girl baby for a grandmother who had born three sons. She spoiled me rotten.

The little ones were running around the living room, dragging toys, clanging pots and pans, and banging on the piano keys. My grandmother let them do whatever they wanted. "What's it going to hurt?" she'd say. Then she'd break into a laugh that was bigger than she was.

After the usual greetings, including hugs and kisses dispensed to my aunts and uncles, I approached my grandfather, who always sat in his chair in front of the television.

"Hi, Papa." As I leaned down to kiss him, he adjusted the lemon ball to the other side of his mouth. My grandfather had a perpetual stash of hard candy beside him. He'd go through a bag a day while he sat for hours, reading the newspaper or watching TV. All the while my grandmother scurried around the house, the majority of her time in the kitchen.

"Hello, Sam. Did you go to mass?" inquired my grandfather.

Attending mass was a big deal in my family. Discussing it was even bigger.

"Yes. Eleven o'clock. The church was full."

"Buon. Molto buon." *Good, very good.* "Father Verducci say mass?"

"He did."

"Give a good sermon?" He popped a peppermint candy into his mouth. "Want one?"

"No, thanks, Papa."

"The sermon." He reminded, looking me squarely in the eyes.

I squirmed. Trouble. I was about to confess when my mother intervened.

"The parable about the sower and the seeds," she smiled at me, knowing she had saved me from disgrace.

"Same thing he did at our mass. We went to nine."

"That's good, Papa."

"Church was full."

"At our mass too."

"Your grandmother's in the kitchen fixin' dinner. Better go say hello. Ora vada." *Go now.*

Church dissection over, he returned his attention to the Sunday news. My grandfather wasn't much for conversation. He was content to observe rather than participate. He was the antithesis of my grandmother.

I made my way into the kitchen, my favorite place in the house. The room beckoned me with its aromas and its energy. An abundance of chairs hugged the kitchen table, which always wore two extension leaves and a freshly pressed tablecloth. Frilly white curtains cascaded around the window over the sink, framing a sill lined with ripening tomatoes, potted herbs, and a statue of the Blessed Virgin Mary. A door led to a small side porch, allowing access to both the backyard and the basement. My grandparents' backyard wasn't large, but it was home to a well-loved vegetable garden that boasted some of the biggest tomato plants in town. The basement, dark and dank, housed the family wines, an array of reds, which my dad and grandfather made every year. Tradition.

Nana stood at the stove stirring a saucepan of vanilla pudding, her whole body in motion. Her apron had trails of fresh marinara sauce.

"Hi, Nana." I planted a kiss on her cheek. She never stopped stirring. As usual, all of the burners were covered with pots of varying sizes, and pans waited on hot plates off to the side.

"Ciao, miele." *Hello, honey.* She leaned up to kiss my cheek. "Bella!" *Beautiful!* "You look so cute today. That dress looks nice on you. Did I make that?"

"Yes, remember? I bought the material in April at Woolworth's big sale."

She furrowed her brow.

"It was a Simplicity pattern. You altered it, Nana."

"I used a pattern for that one?" She stared into the pot as if to locate the memory. "Ah, yes! I remember! I did good on that one." She smiled as she admired her work. Because of my nana's talents as a seamstress, I had a better wardrobe than many of my friends.

"Sammy, get me some of those little bowls from the cupboard. This pudding is ready to go."

"Sure, Nana."

"You look happy. Something special going on?"

"Buck is coming to visit her this afternoon," announced my brother, whose presence was a secret until that moment.

I glared at him. "How do you know, Ryan?"

"I heard you talking on the phone."

"Snoop!"

"Mom sent me back into the house to make sure you were coming. She was afraid we'd be late for mass. You didn't even know I was standing there. You just kept talking." He looked smug.

"Mind your own business!"

"Buck who?" asked Nana.

"Kendall. Dr. Kendall's son," my mother offered. The look of "good catch" was on her face, and we hadn't even had an official date.

"The president of the college?"

"That's the one."

"Sammy likes him. She practices kissing in front of her mirror." Now I had to deal with Lucy.

"Lucy!" I shot her a look.

"Well, you do, Sammy. It's the truth." My humiliation continued.

Nana shook with laughter. "So that's why the cheeks are rosy." Then she pinched them.

I crossed the kitchen to fetch the pudding bowls and to separate myself from the conversation at hand. As I filled the bowls, I inspected the array of foods on the dinner table: Nana's famous browned chicken, veal cutlets in marinara sauce, pasta fagioli, tomatoes mixed with mozzarella, olive oil, and basil, breaded melanzana, crusty bread and butter, and ricotta cheesecake. My mouth watered. Nana cooked for an army, an appreciative one.

"Okay, everybody. Dinner! Come sit," directed Nana.

The family dropped what they were doing and filed into the kitchen.

"Let your grandfather sit down in his chair first, kids."

Nana began issuing orders, assigning seats. We all knew where she sat, closest to the stove, so we left that seat empty. My Uncle Danny reached for a taste of the chicken, and Nana slapped his hand. "Wait till we say grace, Daniel!"

"Sorry, Mother."

She looked around the table to make sure we were all properly seated. "Who wants to say grace?"

"I will," said my dad.

We all dropped our heads and closed our eyes.

"Bless us, O Lord, and these thy gifts, which we are about to receive from thy bounty through Christ, our Lord. Amen."

"Mangi!" announced Nana. *Eat!*

Nana began passing the food around the table. She was in her element. The noise level grew with conversation. Noise would always be my testimony to a successful gathering. Unfortunately, my normally hearty appetite didn't make its usual appearance. I checked the clock—12:30 p.m. His voice was in my head.

I was thinking I could walk over to see you, if you're not doing anything.

I checked the time again. 12:35 p.m. Time stood still.

"Eat, child. Are you sick?"

"No. I'm just not that hungry, Nana. Thanks." I put my arm around her and kissed her; she pinched my cheek again.

"I miei nipotini bella!" *My beautiful grandchild.*

"Nana, I'm your first grandchild. That's why you say that."

"Go on! It is not. Here," she handed me the veal platter. "Mangi. It's tender. Like butter. See? You don't even need a knife." She popped a bite into her mouth.

"Okay, I'll have a little."

"Somebody pass the bread." My grandfather's raspy voice was barely audible above the chatter. "Not a meal without bread."

"You want the butter, Father?" For as far back as I can remember, Nana referred to my grandfather as Father.

"Si, buon."

"Mother, the melanzana is perfect," commented Uncle Danny.

"Grazie, Daniel. It's the garlic and the sauce."

"No, Mother. It's you." His eyes twinkled when he smiled at her. Uncle Danny worshipped his mother.

The family sat around the elongated table, eating and talking over one another. Nana insisted that we taste everything. *Justa little taste*, she'd say. Every now and then I'd observe her watching us, her face round and precious, filled with the contentment she earned as our matriarch. Spending time with my family on those

Sunday afternoons was about as good as it gets. I felt genuine love from both of my uncles. The three brothers were close and looked out for each other. I'd even seen my Uncle Danny cry at the table when relating a story about one of his kids. I could always sense when his eyes were on me. He saw me as one of his own.

1:00 p.m.

"Who's ready for dessert? Sammy, help me clear."

"We'll help, Mother." My mom and my aunts moved into their usual role while the men sat back and patted their bellies.

"You kids can go play now. Take your plates to the sink." Nana directed the little ones in a procession, but not before she picked up the youngest and smothered her with kisses.

"Mother," chided my grandfather, "they're gonna spill. Too little to carry those plates."

"They gotta learn sometime, Father," she retorted.

"Andiamo!" shouted Nana to the children. "To the sink!"

During the clean-up, my grandfather and his sons retreated to the living room with the grandchildren, who never seemed to tire of running around.

1:30 p.m.

"Okay, Nana. Kitchen looks pretty good."

"You gonna go now?" She continued wiping down the counters, even though the room sparkled. Mom and my aunts were back at the kitchen table, drinking coffee and catching up.

"Yeah."

"Your parents going with you?"

"No. They have the car, and Mom said I could walk home so I can change my clothes." My mother turned toward us when she heard her name.

"But I thought that boy was coming over. You can't be there without a chaperone."

I laughed. "By the time he gets there, Mom and Dad will be home."

"Mm-hmm." She did not approve.

"Nana! What's that look? You know I'm a good girl."

My mother spoke to Nana from the table. "I told her we'd be home soon. It's okay, Mother."

"Not the point. The gentleman calls—the lady has a chaperone. Simple."

"It will be okay, Nana," I assured. "Mom and Dad will be home soon. Don't worry."

"Okay, okay." She threw her hands up in the air. "Arrivederci!" *Good-bye.*

I walked the short five blocks to my house, feeling as if the time would never elapse before I saw his face again.

Nineteen

The phone was ringing. I ran into the kitchen and grabbed the receiver from the wall.

"Hello?"

"Hi, Sam. Whatcha doin'?"

"Hi, Shel. Just got back from my grandmother's house."

"Did she make spaghetti and meatballs?" I could hear her salivating.

"Not today."

"Good. Then I don't have to think about what I missed. So, did you walk home?"

"Yeah."

"How come you didn't stop by my house?"

"I had to get back because Buck . . ."

"Buck what?" she interrupted.

"He called."

"He did!" she squealed. "Didn't I tell you?"

"Yeah."

"When?"

"This morning before church."

"Before church? Ooh, who's the eager beaver? What'd he say?"

"He asked if he could come over this afternoon."

"Thank God. So what are you going to wear?"

"I don't know."

"What do you mean you don't know? You better figure it out. I know! Wear your new navy blue shorts outfit from Harper's and show off your legs. You have good legs."

A compliment from the Queen of Fashion! Where's my diary?

"Also, it makes your waist look thinner than it actually is. Guys like small waists."

"Thanks, Shel. I'll keep that in mind." I checked the time. 1:45 p.m.

"What? I'm just tryin' to help."

"I know. Listen, I probably should get going."

"What time's he coming?"

"Two."

"Two! You should be ready by now!"

"Then let me hang up."

"Don't you want to know what *I'm* doing today?"

"If you can tell me in one minute or less."

"Larry wanted me to go to the movies, but Annie and I are going to Pioneer Park instead. I thought I might see Chad."

"Chad Bellusco?"

"Right."

Chad was the president of the upcoming senior class and very handsome. He had a steady girlfriend for two years. They seemed in love. No deterrent for Shelly. When she set her sights on someone, she usually nailed him. I had heard her talking about how cute he was before school let out for summer, but I didn't realize she had been sleuthing out his whereabouts.

"How do you know he'll be there?"

"I just know." *That* was the attitude that bugged me.

"What about Larry? You said he wanted you to go to the movies. Last I knew you two were still going steady. You know he'll follow you wherever you go."

"Don't be a downer. I'm going to break up with him anyway."

"Don't you think you ought to do it before you start going out with someone new?"

"I'm not going out with someone new. Besides, Chad's got a girlfriend."

"So you know he has a girlfriend."

"Yeah. For now."

"For now?" The girl had brass balls. "So you're just going to disregard that he has a girlfriend, who, by the way, I've heard is a really nice person, and forge ahead and possibly break them up when you don't even really know him?"

I was outraged, particularly because I was, hopefully, about to enter the same sacred sanctuary of steadies and I didn't want any backstreet Jezebel doing that to me.

"Oh, don't be such a goody-goody, Sam."

"Don't call me that. You know I hate it."

"Well, you are, and everybody knows it."

"Knows what?"

"That you're a *good* girl," she taunted.

"Well that's just swell!"

"Don't freak out. Actually, I think it's kinda ADMIRE-able.

"It's not ADMIRE-able. It's AD-mir-a-ble. And why would it be *admirable* to be a goody-goody? It's stigmatic, and I'm not!"

"Stop correcting me, and stop using stupid words! It's not a bad thing to have people think you are a good girl. Aren't you glad Buck isn't going out with you because he thinks you put out?"

"Your minute's up. I have to change."

"Call me after he leaves."

"I thought you were going to be at the park, hunting down Chad."

"I'm not hunting him down! If he happens to see me there, then fine!"

Right!

"Okay. Bye."

"Bye." Exposing her underhanded exploits made her curt.

"If he happens to see me there . . ." I muttered aloud as I pulled off my dress. I searched my closet. "This will work." I pulled on a pair of light blue culottes and a sleeveless white blouse.

The doorbell rang. My heart slowed.

"He's here!" I zoomed down the stairs, stopping abruptly at the bottom.

Breathe.

I walked through the porch to the screen door. And there he stood, on the bottom step, where he had apparently retreated after ringing the bell.

"Hi, Sam."

His smile traveled up from the bottom step, breathing on me, drugging me.

"Hi, Buck."

"So how was your grandmother's dinner?" He took his time walking up the steps. I tried to look elsewhere, but my eyes were locked on him.

"Great. As usual." He had reached the top step, and stood inches away on the other side of the screen. I felt lightheaded.

God he smells good.

"Yeah? What did you have?" Every word out of his mouth was so sexy.

"Everything imaginable. My grandmother doesn't believe in one main course."

"No?" He smiled.

"Definitely not. She cooks for an army."

"And I'll bet it's all delicious, all that Italian food."

"It is. She's a great cook."

His hand rested on the door handle. "So are you going to let me in?"

I hadn't realized he was still on the other side of the screen. He felt so close.

"Oh! I'm sorry." I pushed the door opened, and he moved closer. My strength abandoned me.

"So where are your parents?"

"Still at my grandparents' house."

"With your brother and sister?"

Oh, boy, really close now.

"Sam?"

"Huh?"

The corners of his eyes crinkled as he inched even closer. "Your brother and sister—are they with your parents?"

"I'm not sure."

"You're not sure?"

"I mean, yes, they are still there too."

Maybe if I back up a little . . .

"When are they coming home?"

Suddenly I couldn't think straight.

"I'm not sure."

Of anything. Damn!

"So do you want to hang here on the porch until they get home, or would you rather go for a walk?"

A gentleman! I love that about him.

"That would be good."

"Which? The walk or sitting here?"

"Oh, the porch is fine for now. Want some Pepsi?"

"No, thanks."

"We have all kinds of snacks if you're hungry. My mom is a great cook too."

"I'm fine. I ate before I came here."

He lowered his head to look through the porch window that peeked into the dining room.

"You have a piano in your dining room."

"Yes. Do you play?"

"I wouldn't call it playing. I just fool around with it. Do you?"

"Yeah, I took lessons for three years."

"But not anymore?"

"No. I got involved in a lot of other things, so I didn't have enough time to practice. My mom said she wasn't going to pay for lessons if I wasn't going to practice. So I quit."

"Too bad. Playing the piano is good."

"So how come you never took lessons?" The conversation began to relax me.

"I don't know. Guess I didn't want to deal with the rigidity of instruction. I just like messing around."

"Do you play other instruments?"

"Nah, I just mess around with the piano and the guitar. But no lessons. Just what I've taught myself."

Humble. I like that.

"You'll have to play for me sometime," I said.

"I think you've got that backward. You should be playing for me. You're the one who took the lessons." His eyes were soft, greener than I remembered.

"Well, I'm not that good," I admitted.

"Let me be the judge of that."

The tension in my body was dissolving.

"Okay. When my parents come home, I'll play for you. Wanna sit on the couch?"

"Sure."

He moved a pillow from between us and tossed it to the other end of the couch.

"Do you have a job for the summer, Sam?"

"Yes. I work for my dad part-time, now that he's opened his own shop. And I babysit for the people across the street. They have four daughters. They're so cute."

"You like kids?"

"I do. As long as they're not bratty. I hate bratty kids."

His mouth moved to the side in a crooked grin.

"What?" I observed his profile. The stern line of his jaw had relaxed and his dimples grew.

"Just the way you said it, that's all. I know what you mean. I hate bratty kids too."

"Don't you have a younger sister?"

"Yeah. And a younger brother. Catherine is four, and David thirteen."

"Three boys and a girl?"

"Yep. I thought it was just going to be the three of us for a while, but I guess my mom really wanted a girl." He grinned at the floor. "Catherine is the best thing that happened to our family." Then he returned his attention to me. "How old are your brother and sister?"

"Ryan is twelve. Lucy's six."

"Do you get along with them?"

I nodded. "My brother is really smart. He reads all the time, so he keeps to himself a lot. But when we're together, we get along. Most of the time. And Lucy's my little sweetie."

"Yeah?" He studied me.

"I was nine when she was born. I felt like Mom had her just for me. I spent all my time holding her. She's really attached to me."

"And you're really attached to her too."

"I am. So are you working?"

"Yeah. I have two jobs. Greg and I work on the muck a couple of days a week. It's decent money. And I caddy at the Club. That's better money."

"What do you do on the muck?"

"Get filthy digging up vegetables."

"All day?"

"Yup."

"Doesn't that get tiring?"

"Yup! But as my dad says, 'It is respectable work, son, because of the rigor of the manual hands-and-knees work.'" His imitation amused him.

"I see. And you're a caddy. Isn't it boring following the golfers around and not playing?"

"Not boring at all. Actually, I learn from those guys. They're like pros because they play so often."

"So you like to golf."

He nodded.

"And you play well?"

"Not bad. I've golfed with my dad and brothers for several years now, so I'm getting better."

"What kind of score?"

"I shot an 80 yesterday."

"Isn't that kind of low?"

He smirked, "Low is good in golf."

"So it's not the same as bowling."

I must have sounded like a jerk because he tried to suppress a smile. I felt my face grow warmer.

"No, not the same."

"Then you're pretty good."

"I do okay."

We sat in silence for a bit; then he reached over and took my hand. My shoulders tightened. So I did what I do best when I'm nervous. Babbled.

"Are you sure you don't want something to eat? We have a whole platter of freshly baked chocolate chip cookies in the kitchen. My mom made a batch this morning before church. She's always baking, and her cookies are delicious."

What is it with me and food?

"Cookies, huh? Yeah, that actually sounds good."

I leaned forward to stand up. He still had my hand and wasn't releasing. Two weeks since I was this close to him. It was killing me.

"Oh, I want one other thing."

"Sure, what?"

"A kiss."

He wasn't asking. He pulled me back. I sank into the abyss, even deeper than before.

Twenty

The first time ever I saw your face . . .
I thought the sun rose in yours eyes . . .

-Ewan MacColl

Beginnings. Food tastes better, jokes are funnier, and what might have been a boring day presents endless possibilities. Every day with Buck was the beginning. I suppose it's like that with most new couples. But to me it seemed we were the only two people in the world who looked at each other and really saw. He was in my head; I carried him with me wherever I went. No matter what the chore, there was always the promise of him when I was done. I smiled for reasons no one understood. You know when you see those people who are just happy all the time? That was me.

"Mom, is it all right if Buck and I go to the movies tonight?"

I walked into the kitchen where my mother was pulling eggs and milk from the refrigerator. She opened the yellow canisters, filled with flour and sugar, and spread her Tupperware measuring cups on the counter.

"Oh, do you have a date?" she asked.

"Yeah."

"Can you grab the vanilla out of the Lazy Susan? What are you going to see?"

"*The Sound of Music.*"

"Oh, that's a beautiful film. Julie Andrews. 'The hills are alive . . . '" Mom began singing. "Honey, hand me those two sticks of butter, will you?"

I grabbed the butter, which was rapidly morphing from a solid to a liquid. "Here you go. Anyway, then we want to go to Tony's for pizza. Is that okay?"

"Wow! This butter melted fast. As long as you're home by eleven-thirty. What time does the movie start?"

"Seven."

"Phew! It's hot in here. Turn on that fan and point it toward me, will you?" She wiped her forehead with the back of her arm. "What was I thinking, baking on a day like today?"

I smiled at her self-criticism. "You always say that, Mom."

"I know. Do you have enough money?"

"Yeah, I have babysitting money, but he's paying."

"That's sweet. But he's just a kid too. You should offer to go Dutch."

"I offered when we played miniature golf last week, but he said no."

"He has good manners. And it *is* a date, after all." She stopped stirring and regarded me more seriously. "You really like him, don't you, Sam?"

I felt exposed, as if she had been reading my diary. "Yes."

"Do you think you will keep dating?"

Now *I* was feeling the heat. "I hope so."

"Does he feel the same way?"

"So far he acts like he does. I guess we'll see."

"You're right. You'll just have to wait and see." She returned to the egg mixture and began to beat vigorously. Her face grew red.

"Well, I'm going to get ready now, Mom." It was three o'clock.

"But it's still light outside," Lucy chimed in. She was sitting on her knees at the kitchen table, putting together one of her favorite wooden puzzles. The kid didn't miss a trick.

I laughed. "Luce, do you think it has to be dark to go out with a boy?"

"It's a date, isn't it?" She looked up proudly after placing the finishing piece in its rightful spot. "There!"

I could hear my mother snickering.

"Yes," I replied, "it is a date, but that doesn't mean it has to be nighttime."

"Oh." She looked at the wall clock. "What time is your date?"

"He's picking me up at six-thirty."

"What time is it now?" she asked, continuing to study the clock.

Mom abandoned her project. A teachable moment. "Lucy, look at the little hand. What number is it on?"

Squinting in concentration, Lucy said, "The three."

"Right. Now look at the big hand."

"Why do they call them hands?" she interrupted. "They don't look like hands. They should call them arrows."

"Fine!" Mom's voice was edgy. "Then look at the big *arrow*. What number is it pointing to?"

"It is not pointing to one number. It is in the middle of two numbers."

"What numbers?" continued Mom, as she wiped her forehead again.

"The twelve and the one."

"Right. So what does that mean? Do you remember what I taught you?" pressed Mom.

Lucy nodded. "It's almost three o'clock."

"No, honey. Which way do the arrows move?"

"That way," she pointed.

"So if the arrow is going that way, and it already passed the twelve, what is the clock doing?"

"Starting over."

Mom smiled. "Toward what?"

"The next hour."

"Right! So what time is it now?"

"A little *after* three!" Lucy announced proudly.

"Good for you, honey." Mom hugged Lucy and returned to the batter.

"So, Sammy, if it's only a little after three, why are you getting ready now?"

"I have some things to do first."

"Lucy, bring the stool and come here. You can help me mix in the flour. Sam has things to do." Mom's whole body was in motion.

"Can I lick the bowl?"

"May I!" Mom corrected.

I headed up to my room, closed the door, and flopped on my bed. The air was heavier upstairs than in the kitchen, and I felt as if I couldn't breathe. I hopped up to retrieve the small fan from my closet and set it on the dresser, where it could blow directly on me. I lay there awhile, staring at the top bunk.

Do you think you will keep seeing each other?

That thought ran through my mind all the time.

* * *

Some moments crawl inside me and clench so tightly that letting go is impossible. There are times when I simply experience a hazy version of the real thing, a shallow wave of yesterday. At other times the sensation descends upon me so heavily, I cannot shake it, and I am there. I can still feel this night.

Carlson had only one movie theater, and everybody saw everybody there. Not much slipped by the people of my hometown. Sharing the personal details that belonged to others was a pastime in Carlson, not unlike many small towns. Gossip was entertaining when things were going well, but when they weren't—that was a different story. The Carlson Theater, in the heart of downtown, was a well-spring of information, spouting tales of fashion, friendship, and deception, however inconsequential. Walking through the lobby in the summertime was akin to maneuvering the halls of CHS between classes.

"Two tickets, please."

"That will be three dollars. Enjoy the show."

We made our way through the entry line, handed our tickets to the usher, and approached the concession stand.

"Want popcorn?" Buck asked.

"Sure."

"Sam!" The voice came from across the lobby.

I turned to see Darlene Bailey waving wildly, a smile lighting up her face. I waved back, and Buck turned around to see who it was.

"Hi, Buck!" Now he was the recipient of the bubbly wave.

"Hi, Darlene," he replied, almost silently, as the palm of his hand responded in kind.

Buck sensed what was going on, so he turned away to avoid embarrassment for anyone involved.

"Where do you want to sit?" He picked up the popcorn, supporting it against his chest. His free hand pressed into the small of my back, escorting me down the aisle. The touch felt electric.

"It doesn't matter."

We navigated the sloping floor of the theater house, with its heavy red carpet and floor to ceiling drapes. The seats were filling up quickly.

"This spot looks good. Is it okay with you?"

"Sure, it's fine."

We settled in the middle of a row about halfway between the stage and the exit. Safe, respectable—unlike the couples who were crammed up against the wall in the back row. Everybody knew what they were going to do when the lights went down.

I appreciated Buck's deference toward me regarding the seat choice.

"You look really nice tonight, Sam." I felt his eyes penetrate me.

"Thanks."

"Guess what today is?" he asked.

"July 10th."

"Right," he conceded. "What else?"

"Six days after the 4th of July?" This was fun. I knew perfectly well what day it was.

"Cute! Your party was a month ago today." He looked proud of himself.

"You're right. It was."

And?

"And, I just thought you should know that I remembered."

"I'm glad."

"About what? That I remembered, or that it has been a month and we're still hanging together?"

Hanging together. Not solid, but I'll take it.

"Both. I like both."

"Yeah?" His expression was almost illegal.

"Yeah," I managed.

He scooted closer, taking my hand. God I loved his touch. He leaned in closer still, his forehead touching mine. "I'm glad we're here," he said as he dropped his head, lips skimming along the side of my face. I wanted to turn into them.

Sound emanated from the big screen, and the lights dimmed.

"Movie's starting," he said. "Guess we'd better watch."

He pulled back, readjusting his position, and placed his hand on my knee. The screen lit up. Music swelled. Concentration became a monumental chore. Somehow Julie Andrews and her goatherds didn't hold the same interest as the hand on my leg. He, however, watched intently.

My thoughts drifted back to what he had said a few moments ago. *Hanging together. What was that?* Although things were going along smoothly, I was never certain of when I would see him again. I felt sure there would be a next time, but the erratic pattern irritated me. Granted, he was involved in lots of family events. Add golf, work, and friends to the mix, and his time was limited. He spent a lot of time with Stan and Larry, which intrigued me because I would have given up time with my girlfriends in a heartbeat if it meant I could be with him. But it didn't seem to work the other way around. I speculated on the differences between male and female thinking and wondered if his behavior could be attributed to the male portion of his brain—*or* if it was his choice. And I wondered if the pattern would ever change.

After the movie, kids poured onto the streets. The second show started at 9 p.m., and a line had already formed. We serpentined through the crowd and made our escape. The night was steamy.

On the way to Tony's, Buck was unusually talkative. With each conversation I learned more about him, and I liked the intimacy that came from sharing our stories. When we arrived at Tony's, the place was hopping. Not one empty stool at the counter, and every booth was jammed. Music blared from the jukebox, and a cacophony of voices filled the air. I loved Tony's.

Shelly and Larry were sitting in a booth in the back, quarreling. I wanted to bolt, go somewhere else, but Larry saw us and motioned for us to join them. Sure. He probably figured our presence would put an end to their fight.

"Hey, look who it is! You two are becoming regulars." Larry's big, goofy smile spread across his face. Shelly remained stoic.

"Sit down," he motioned to the other side of their booth.

"Nah, we don't want to disturb you two." I could tell Buck felt the negative energy too.

"You're not disturbing us, believe me. Sit down." Her tone left no room for negotiation. We slid in across from them.

"So you two look pretty cozy," Larry teased.

"Leave them alone, Larry." Shelly stared him down.

"What? I'm just saying . . . ah, here comes our pizza. Want some?"

The waitress set the pizza in the middle of the table.

"Should I bring more plates?" She winked to acknowledge our presence.

"Yeah, that would be great, Gertie," answered Larry.

"Gertie! How are you tonight?" Buck asked fondly. She was everyone's favorite waitress.

She smiled at us. "Hi kids. I'm just swell. How 'bout you two?"

"I'm fine, Gertie," I pitched in.

"Great," Buck replied.

"How's your family, Buck?" In addition to waitressing at Tony's in the evenings, Gertie cleaned houses during the day. The Kendall house was one of them, but the family was rarely there while she performed her magic.

"They're good. Thanks for asking."

"Okay, kids, I'll bring some extra plates."

"Good, 'cause there's plenty here. I always order a large with extra sausage. And I don't need to eat the whole thing anyway." Larry patted his belly proudly.

"No kidding!" Shelly spit out her words in disgust.

"Ah, come on, Shel, you know you love all of me." Larry grabbed her hand, and she yanked it away. We pretended not to notice.

The rest of our evening at Tony's was beyond awkward. In between mouthfuls of pizza, Larry tried to get Shelly to thaw out. When she stole side-glances at us, her eyes seemed to ache. I was relieved when we finally left.

"Well, that was uncomfortable!" Buck's commentary began as soon as we ducked around the corner."

"You can say that again," I added.

"Well, that was uncomfortable," he repeated.

"I didn't mean it literally." I was still looking straight ahead when it dawned on me. "You think you're clever, don't you?"

"But you're such an easy target." His irresistibility factor skyrocketed when he goofed around, so I couldn't even begin to play mad.

"Fine."

"Man! Those two are something. Glad it was them and not us in that conversation we walked into." He affirmed.

Us. I liked that.

"Yeah, Shelly didn't look too happy. I'm sure I'll hear from her tomorrow."

"I don't know why they're still together. They're not even right for each other." This admission surprised me. "But Larry's so in love with her he can't see straight. And Shelly takes advantage of that."

"You're right. She does."

"Okay, let's forget them. They're bringing us down. Look up! Millions of stars. Big Dipper!" he screamed, as if he were a kid again. He pointed as he arched to capture a wider scope of the sky. "When Greg and I were little, we used to lie on our backs in the grass at night and watch the stars pop out. It fascinated me how quickly they transformed the sky. My dad would explain that those balls of light were made of gas and that the Sun was a star too. I couldn't believe that the Sun was a star. I thought Dad was making it up. He went on to tell us that those patterns up above were groups of stars called constellations. I thought he said *complications*. So I asked him, 'Why does the sky have complications, Daddy?'"

As he spoke, his face animated in memory, I realized how much I liked this aspect of his personality. The side that noticed beauty in nature and appreciated life off the basketball court. Few boys his age were cut with this facet. Because of his family, Buck was more cultivated than most.

When we reached my house, we sat on the front steps, chatting about much of nothing. But it was the little things, the moments that others might deem insignificant, that added up to what we were. There was an intimacy in those conversations, a closeness that gradually blurred the lines of *him* and *me*.

"So, Miss DeSantis, did you have fun tonight?" His chin rested on his forearm.

"I did. And you, Mr. Kendall?"

"Very nice." He closed in, brushing my lips lightly, then retreated, leaning on his arm again. Torture.

"Maybe we ought to do this again sometime," he added playfully. I could feel his breath on my face. Already it was becoming difficult to leave him.

"Maybe," I answered. And there was that voice again! The one that was foreign until the first night we kissed. It didn't sound like me.

"Come here."

I stepped inside his charm.

Twenty-one

When you're sixteen, summer is a gift—sleeping in, waking up with the realization that you don't have homework, eating breakfast at noon, and reading whatever you want. I spent time with some of the greats that summer. I stepped into the world of Elizabeth Bennett and Mr. Darcy. Their attraction was so strong, and their plight seduced me. His pride. Her prejudice. I read faster and faster, the pace of my heart increasing with my momentum as I devoured the words and they stumbled over each obstacle. I could not wait for them to surrender to the force that was bigger than both of them. And then there were *The Great Gatsby*, *Madame Bovary*, and *A Farewell to Arms*. So much better than homework!

By August, Buck and I had rolled into a routine, and any lurking doubts about the strength of our relationship slipped away. Some days we would walk to the park and just sit on the swings and talk. Other times, when we couldn't keep our hands off each other, we would find a private spot and make out for hours.

One Saturday afternoon, we drove to the lake to meet up with a gang of friends. The day was ideal for swimming, not a cloud in the sky. We were trudging through the sand, loaded down with towels, a large blanket, and an overstuffed beach bag, when

I heard Shelly shriek. I looked up to see her running out of the water as Larry splashed her mercilessly.

"Larry! You're getting my hair all wet! Stop!"

"You're at the beach! You're sposta get wet!"

Greg and Sharon floated on inner tubes, holding hands as they breezed along. Gretta Payton was stretched out on her flat stomach, the top of her bathing suit untied to avoid the obvious line on her back. Larry ran by, chasing Shelly, and accidentally kicked up a storm of sand, which landed on Gretta and stuck to her greased body. She jerked upward, forgetting the status of the bathing suit, and her top fell off, spilling its ample contents.

"Oh, my God!" My hand went to my mouth.

"Nice rack, Gretta!" screamed Larry.

"Shut up, moron!" Gretta flattened herself on the blanket again, and Shelly slapped Larry on the back of the head.

"Stop looking!"

"Are you serious? Look at those melons!"

"Here we go," warned Buck.

That was it. Shelly marched away, nearly stepping on Ben, who sat happily strumming his guitar. "Whoa! That girl's got some temper. *'Hey, look a-yonder comin', comin' down that railroad track. It's the Orange Blossom Special, bringin' my baby back,'*" he sang.

Annie propped herself up on her elbows. "What's the matter with her?"

"Larry was looking at Gretta's boobs," said Ben, without skipping a beat from his song. "*'Well, I'm going down to Florida and get some sand in my toes . . . I'll ride that Orange Blossom Special and lose these New York blues.'*"

"What?" Annie lurched up and scanned the area like a police dog.

"The top of her bathing suit fell off. *'Talk about a-ramblin', she's the fastest train on the line . . .* '"

Annie cracked up. "Hey, Gretta! I heard you were puttin' on a show!"

"Show's over. Get your kicks from lookin' somewhere else," Gretta snapped.

"Don't get bent with me! I'm not the one lookin' at 'em! I have my own set." Annie peered down the front of her bathing suit. "And they're lookin' pretty good from here." Then she laughed as she lay back down on the blanket next to Ben, who wasn't even slightly ruffled by the drama around him.

Screams carried from the water. "Buck! Sam! Come on in. The water's great," yelled Sal. "Grab those beach balls!"

After a couple of hours of beach time, Buck and I meandered along the shore, picking up flat rocks to skim across the water. He tried to teach me the proper technique, and I finally managed to skip one.

"Holy mackerel, I did it!" I was so proud of myself that I started jumping up and down. "I can't believe it! My dad has tried to teach me to do that a hundred times, and I could never get the hang of it." When I turned around, he was looking at me with suppressed laughter.

"What?" I challenged.

"*Holy mackerel*?" He teased.

"Yeah, so?"

"I never heard you say that before. It just struck me funny, that's all." He was enjoying the moment way too much.

"Are you mocking me, Kendall?" My voice sounded parental. I approached him with the deliberation of one who meant business and was about to serve it up.

"No!" He laughed. "I'd *never* do that." Sarcasm oozed from every pore.

"Laugh your head off, pal!" I drew closer.

My joking amused him; I could always tell by the way he looked at me. So, I pressed on and picked up a small rock, pitching it at his foot like a spoiled child. When it hit, his eyes flickered. "Ouch! I can't believe you did that!"

"Oh, don't be such a baby!"

"I'm not." He was still chuckling in disbelief.

I planted my hands on my hips. "So? What are you gonna do about it?"

"I'll show you what I'm gonna do." He grabbed me and started wrestling my arms behind my back.

"Stop!" I screamed. "Stop or I'll call the beach patrol!"

Laughter forced him to release me. "You're a nut, Sam." He stood very still for a moment, holding me. Then his breath brushed the side of my face and down my neck where his lips pressed against my skin. The heat from his lips stopped me.

"I love when you make me laugh, Sam." His words were in my ear. "Come on. Let's go up there." He pointed toward the bluff.

He pulled me up the bank to a private spot under the trees. "Right over there." We sat on the grass and leaned into an old oak. He pressed against me and kissed me. It was one of those kisses that make you want to forget you're a Catholic. I started to forget. The kisses came faster. My heart beat harder. Louder. Faster. Too fast. His hand slid up the side of me. His fingers moved toward the top of my bathing suit. Sister Anastasia screamed in my ear. I clamped down my arm and broke away.

"What?" His eyes burned.

"We have to stop."

"Yeah, okay. Sorry."

We were both dazed. "You okay," I asked.

"Yeah, I'm fine." He stared at the lake.

"You sure?"

"I'm sure. I just need a minute to settle down, if you know what I mean." His eyes cast downward.

"What? Oh!" I didn't know where to look.

"You're so cute, Sam. I should be jailed for my thoughts."

"What thoughts?"

"I think the nuns would call them *impure.*"

I think you're right.

My resolve had never been tested before. Love was complicated. And I knew it wouldn't get any easier.

* * *

We sat there under the tree, watching the boats on the lake. From our vantage point, the lighthouse was framed perfectly. First built in the 1800s, our lighthouse stood steadfastly as a guardian for boats navigating the lake and river. When I was younger, my dad would walk me down to the waterfront and point out the features of this historical structure, while telling stories of the seaman who came and went on lake freighters. His voice was lusty whenever he spoke of the sea. Because of my dad, I loved the lighthouse.

Buck nudged me. "What are you thinking about?"

"The lighthouse. Dad used to walk me down here and tell me stories about it. He loves anything to do with boats and the water. He was in the Merchant Marines before he met my mom."

"Yeah, I know."

"How do you know that? I never told you."

"He had his shirt rolled up when he was working in the back yard one day. I saw the tattoo on his arm and asked him about it."

For some reason I was delighted by that admission. "I didn't know that."

"There are a lot of things you don't know, Sam." His expression taunted me.

"Like what?" I wanted to kiss him again and never stop.

"Like I know that you're a sentimental fool."

"Fool?" I objected.

"You are. You are led by your emotions. It's so obvious."

"So you think you have me all figured out."

"Yeah. As a matter of fact, I do. I figured you out the night of your party."

"You did, huh?" I felt myself squirming.

"Yeah." His voice diminished to a whisper. His words were foreplay. I was sinking again.

"How?"

"It's written all over you face, Sam. And you make wistful comments."

"*Wistful* comments?" I repeated, emphasizing his choice of words.

"Yeah." He rubbed my shoulder as he spoke.

"Are you saying I'm sappy?" I challenged.

"Not at all. You're wistful like—like pensive in a good way."

"So you think you've figured me out."

"Pretty much. You're rather transparent, you know."

"That's what my mother says."

"I miss nothing, Samantha." He leaned in for a kiss, pressing me back against the tree.

"You think you're pretty smart, don't you, Kendall?" I whispered.

"I am. Now let's go eat or I'm going to devour *you*." His restraint was impressive. He stood up, pulling me to my feet.

Not many people could respond to my sarcasm the way he did—*and* make it so sexy.

* * *

When we returned to the picnic area, the fire pits were smoking. My stomach growled at the smell of grilled hamburgers and hot dogs. Picnic baskets and coolers covered every table. Radios blared, each set to the same popular station. Paul McCartney and John Lennon sang: *"It's the dirty story of a dirty man and his clinging wife doesn't understand. The son is working for the Daily Mail, it's a steady job but he wants to be a paperback writer. Paperback writer."*

Famished, we headed toward our table. Shelly appeared to be waiting for us. She stood, posed with her hands on her hips. Her two-piece bathing suit accentuated her small waist. Without so much as a hello, she began ordering us around.

"Sam, stand over here with Buck so I can take your picture together. By this tree. Buck, put your arm around her and act like you like her."

"I *do* like her." He grinned.

SNAP!

"Good one. You look cute together. Wait right there. I want you to take my picture with Larry." Then she turned around. "Larry! Come over here!" she yelled.

I turned around in time to see him stuff the second half of a hot dog, bun and all, into his mouth.

"Coming!" Food sprayed when he spoke.

He lumbered over, releasing a disgusting burp, which only he considered entertaining. I rolled my eyes and waited patiently to take the picture.

"Larry," Buck admonished good-naturedly, "there are ladies present. Control the loud belching, please." Larry burped again.

"Larry!" Shelly whined half-heartedly. "Be good."

"I'm always good, doll." Then he manhandled her. Buck shook his head and looked at the ground while I attempted to swallow the distaste in my mouth.

"So where do you want to stand for your picture?" I asked.

The picture! I can't watch you anymore!

"Right where you and Buck stood." Shelly answered as she detached the human vacuum from her neck.

"Okay. Say cheese," I said perfunctorily.

"Wait, first tell me if I look all right in this position." Shelly turned to the side and posed.

"You look fine. Now smile."

"Wait. Do I need lipstick?"

"Shelly, we're at the beach, for God's sake! It's okay to look natural. Now smile!"

SNAP!

"Take one more in case I don't like the first one." She shook her mane of hair while I pushed back my annoyance.

"Want me to take this one, Sam?" Buck read my thoughts.

"Sure." I handed him the camera, mouthing a silent *thank you*.

"Here goes. Smile, you two."

SNAP!

"Buck!" Shelly whined. "You didn't give us any warning!"

"You didn't need any. You're both fine."

"Oh! Well, thanks anyway." She walked toward him, grabbing the camera out of his hand, and held it out to me. "Now, Sam, take one of me and Buck."

"What?" I stared her down.

"I want a picture with Buck."

"Why?"

"I am the one who got you two together. I'm proud of how well things worked out. So take our picture. Same spot." She shoved the camera into my hands.

I promptly handed it back to her. "Then you probably want all three of us in the shot," I turned to Larry. "Will you take this one?"

"I'd be delighted." He strolled over, guffawing, and pried the camera out of Shelly's hands. I could tell Larry was getting a kick out this. As much as he doted on her, he knew she was spoiled. Everyone knew. I'm sure he derived as much pleasure from seeing her ruffled as I did.

Buck stood next to me, smiling approvingly.

"Fine! Take all three of us."

We posed, with Buck between us. Shelly squeezed closer to him.

"Okay. Let's get this over with. Say whiskey."

"Larry!" More whining from Shelly.

"Just say it, Shelly. I'm hungry!"

Whiskey in unison . . . SNAP!

Larry shot the picture without further ceremony. I headed toward the picnic tables. "Okay, who wants what?"

"Wait, Buck." Shelly grabbed his hand, pulling him back to her. "One more with just us."

"Whoa, Shelly, we just took a picture together," objected Buck.

"But I want one of just the two of us. Now take the picture, Larry," she demanded. Her voice held urgency. Before I knew what was happening, Shelly had locked her hand in Buck's, tilting her head toward him in a coquettish pose. Larry snapped the picture, laughing fiendishly. Buck was simmering.

"Ooh, she got you, Buck!" More obnoxious snorting. "Porterfield, you're something, babe!" Larry wrapped his arm around her and wet her face with kisses.

I walked toward her. "What was that?"

"What?" She feigned innocence.

"You know what."

"Another picture for my album." She dismissed me, brushing past as she headed toward the table. "Come on, guys, let's eat."

One of these days . . .

Suddenly we heard the squealing of voices. Greg and Sharon came running up the hill, dripping wet. Sharon squeezed the excess water from her hair. "I need a towel! I'm freezing!" She wrapped her arms around herself and hopped around for warmth.

Buck pointed to our table, "Towels are there."

Greg was doing the same dance. "Man the water is nice, but the air is freezing." Buck tossed him a beach towel.

"Thanks, brother," said Greg good-naturedly.

Buck didn't respond.

"Hi, Sam." Sharon spoke perfunctorily as she continued to towel-dry her California blonde hair.

"Hi, Sharon."

She and I were more acquaintances than friends, and that status evolved simply because we dated brothers. She had never made any overtures toward conversation, let alone friendship, but then neither had I. I always sensed that she didn't have any use for me. Her own friends hailed from higher circles. I didn't really care because her aloofness greeted me before she did.

"That's a cute bathing suit. Where did you get it?"

"Thanks, Sharon. Actually, I bought it at Macy's."

"Macy's?" That stopped her. "There's no Macy's around here."

"Macy's in New York City," Buck pitched in matter-of-factly.

Sharon looked from Buck back to me. "When were you in New York City? Don't tell me you go there just to shop."

"No, of course not. My dad had a March of Dimes meeting there, so he took me with him."

Sharon viewed me with new eyes. "Lucky you."

"*And* she met Dr. Salk." Buck sounded like a little kid who had to share his accomplishments to garner praise. I knew his intention was to boost any envy that might be might be stirring up in Sharon's mind. He was not a fan. My eyes apparently reflected my disapproval of his comment. "What? That's something to be proud of, Sam," he added.

"Dr. Salk of the vaccine fame?" Her voice resonated with new interest.

"That's the one," Buck answered for me. His voice was flat.

"Who wants lunch?" I turned away, escaping to empty the contents of the picnic basket.

"Hi, guys. You finally got out of the water." Shelly moved toward Sharon.

"Yeah, it felt great. Your suit's cute, too, Shelly. You didn't get yours in New York, did you?" Sharon shot a side glance at me.

Nope, definitely not cut out to be friends.

"No, I'm not as lucky as Sam." Shelly stuck out her tongue at me and then returned her attention to Sharon. "Sharon, come over here under the tree. I'm taking pictures for my photo album. I wanna get one of you and Greg."

"Greg! Shelly wants a picture of us."

He was about to take a bite of his burger when she spoke. Then he looked from his hand back to Sharon and realized it was in his best interest to comply.

"Be careful she doesn't make you pose with her. She might get carried away and grab your ass," Buck warned. Greg looked perplexed.

"Buck! What if she hears you?" I pulled him toward me to put a lid on his sour mood, but I could see that he was still annoyed with Shelly and her sense of entitlement. "Just let it go."

"I'm fine," he replied as he shook off my hand.

He was petulant for the remainder of the afternoon.

* * *

Tension sat between us. He stared sullenly out the car window, seemingly memorizing the scenery that was whizzing by. This was a side of him I had not yet experienced. As I studied his stiffened profile, I felt a sense of resentment. *Why must I be subject to his ill temperament?* I had done nothing. Finally, I decided to plunge into the dark waters.

"What exactly is the matter?"

"Nothing." He continued staring.

In the rearview mirror, Greg's expression reflected a mild level of concern. Sharon, on the other hand, was oblivious. She was singing along with the radio—"The Ballad of the Green Berets" by Sergeant Barry Sadler.

"And you expect me to believe that?" I pinched him in the side, eliciting a smile. I felt a sense of relief.

"Shelly gets on my nerves. I know she's your friend, but she's really annoying and pushy." I remember thinking that he may have been the only male in Carlson who hadn't fallen under her spell. "She's manipulative. Why did she have to have a picture with *me*?"

"It was just a picture."

"Not the point."

"Well, I *will* admit that she can be annoying. She likes to have everything her way. But I don't think she really means anything by it."

"She was holding my hand when Larry took the picture!" He spit out the words in a resurgence of anger.

"Yeah, I caught that."

"It pisses me off that she thinks she can do that kind of stuff. She's got her own boyfriend." He returned to the window.

"That picture was not about her being proud of getting us together. It was about her."

"Exactly! So why do you put up with it?" He turned fully to absorb my response.

"Hard to explain. She has her good side. That's the side I like. She's my friend."

Greg lowered the volume on the car radio. Sharon grabbed his arm. "Greg! I love Herman's Hermits!" She restored the volume to its previous level and continued singing.

When I feel you put your arms around me, baby, baby, can't you hear my heartbeat?

"Hey, little brother, don't sweat it. It's just her way."

"You mean she has to have her way," corrected Buck.

"That's true. Wanna stop for an ice cream sundae?" Greg asked. I loved his timing. He intuitively did the right thing.

"That's fine," answered Buck. The tension in his face began to dissipate. "Sorry for the bad mood, Sam."

"I understand. If you were happy about the picture, *I* might be the one pouting," I added lightly, hoping to break his mood. With that he melted into the Buck I loved.

"Come here, beautiful, and give me a kiss. I haven't had one in a couple of hours."

"I can see you in the rearview mirror!"

Sharon slapped his arm. "Stop looking!"

"Watch the road, brother. This might be too much for your eyes. If you want, I can give you some pointers later."

And he was back.

"Right!" Greg picked up speed as the car hugged the curve on its way to the Ice Cream Shack. Sharon turned up the volume.

Twenty-two

Each year, for the first week of summer, I dream about school. In my dreams I am rushing to finish an assignment that I had completely forgotten, running into class late to a teacher who shakes her head reproachfully, or walking through the halls without a stitch of clothing as everyone points and laughs. I then awaken with the same horrifying thoughts. *Oh my God! I'm unprepared! I'm late! I'm naked!* When the panic dissolves into relief, I lie in bed and smile indulgently, willing myself to go back to sleep. Without fail, I cannot. Elation overpowers weariness, and I hop out of bed with an alacrity I rarely experience during the school year. For the first week, anyway. Once I adjust to my carefree schedule, I usually settle into lazier habits.

"So I had the dream again last night."

"What dream?"

"The one that I have when school first gets out. But I had it again last night, and I'm trying to figure out why."

"You have a recurrent dream when school gets out?"

"Yes, isn't that weird? And it bums me out for the rest of the day."

"What's it about?"

"It's a variation on the same theme. I'm not prepared for class or the teacher yells at me or everyone laughs at me because I'm naked."

"You're naked?"

"In the dream. When I'm walking through the halls. But sometimes I'm swimming through the streets in the dream."

"You're *swimming* through the streets?"

"Yes, they're filled with water for some reason, and everyone is swimming to school. But I'm still naked, so I stay underwater."

"Naked."

"I knew you'd focus on that part."

"Sorry. Tell me more."

"Well, the thing is, the dreams usually stop after the first week of summer. Once I relax and forget school. So it surprised me that I had the dream again last night. And I woke up with that same awful feeling, which is hard to shake because my dreams feel so real. All day I've been getting these waves of shame, like it really happened. Once I dreamed I had a fight with Annie, and I was mad at her all day. Every time I looked at her, I felt pissed. My dreams are exhausting."

"You're a complicated girl, Sam."

"Do you think I'm having that dream again because school starts in a couple of weeks and I'm thinking about classes?"

"Maybe." He was quiet for a moment. "Sam?"

"Yeah?"

"The next time you have that dream, call me. Before you wake up."

I shook my head.

"Here I am, trying to tell you about the fears and insecurities that inhabit my dreams and the effect they have on me. And all you can do is joke around."

"DeSantis," he said with deliberation, "you can't say *I* and *naked* in the same sentence and expect me not to react."

"I never should have told you," I sighed.

"But you did. Now don't you think there's an underlying message there?"

"Stop! I was simply trying to tell you how my subconscious works when I'm asleep. I dream all the time, and it drains me."

"Sorry."
We kept walking toward the park.
"Tell me what you were wearing again?"
"Honest to God, Buck!"

Twenty-three

On the last Sunday before our return to school, Buck joined my family for dinner. Of course, I had to prep all of my family, except Mom, on how to behave without embarrassing me.

Lucy and I sat on the couch in the sunporch. "Buck's coming for dinner after church today."

"I know."

"How do you know?"

"Mommy told us," she replied nonchalantly.

"She did? What did she say?"

"She said use your manners, don't ask too many questions, and don't embarrass your sister." Recited like a robot.

"Did she tell Ryan too?"

"Yes. He was there too."

"Where?"

"In the living room when Mommy called us in for a family meeting."

I hid my amusement. "A family meeting, huh?"

"Yeah, Daddy had to be there too."

"Wow." I was impressed with my mother's power. "What did Ryan think about that?"

"He didn't say too much. He just listened to Mommy and rolled his eyes a couple of times, but she didn't see him. Are you happy your boyfriend is coming to eat with us, Sammy?"

"I am, but let's not refer to him as my boyfriend when he's here, okay?"

"Why not?" she asked matter-of-factly.

"Well, it would just be better if you call him by his name."

"Why?"

"Well, we're not really official yet."

"Not official?"

"Not yet. I mean, almost. We don't go out with other people, but he hasn't actually asked me to go steady yet."

"Why?"

"I'm not sure."

"Does he have to ask you to go steady to be official?"

"Yes. Otherwise, we're just dating."

"Hmm. You think he will?"

"Yes."

"Mommy said you like him a lot."

"She did?"

"She said, 'Sam likes Buck a lot, so we want to make her feel comfortable when he has dinner with us.'" Her hands were on her hips like my mother's. "So do you?"

"Yes, I like him a lot."

"Do you love him, too, Sammy?"

Yes!

"Well, I . . . I really, really like him."

"But you don't love him?" she pressed.

"Well, Luce, I have only been going out with him since June."

"That's plenty of time. Did you kiss him yet?"

The kid had moxie. I can't imagine what expression I was wearing at that moment, having this conversation with my little sister.

"Well, yes."

"Does Mommy know this?" She was serious.

"I think she does, yes."

"Do you like to kiss him, Sammy?" For a little kid, she had some big questions.

"How about if we go upstairs and get ready for church? It's getting late."

"You didn't answer my question yet." She kept talking all the way up the stairs.

"What question was that? I thought I answered all of your questions."

"Do you like to kiss him?"

Persistent child.

"Oh, that question. Well, yes, it's pretty neat. Now let's get ready for church."

"How many times have you kissed him?"

"I don't know, Lucy." The kid was like a drill sergeant.

"I think you do."

"You think I do?" I stifled a laugh. "What makes you say that?"

"Cause you like him so much. You probably count. What are you laughing about, Sammy?"

"I'm not. And I don't count, Luce. Where did you get that idea?"

Suddenly Mom's voice came from the bottom of the staircase. "Girls, you'd better be getting dressed! We'll be late for mass!"

Saved by the boss.

The dinner went well. Everyone welcomed Buck, no one embarrassed me, and my mom's pot roast was, as usual, delizioso.

Twenty-four

"Up in the mornin' and off to school . . ."

—Chuck Berry

September 1966. My junior year at CHS was about to begin. As usual, I couldn't sleep the night before school started. Ever since elementary school, the same thing happens to me. I lie there, thinking about the first day, legs twitching and eyes wide open. It's curious, the way my psyche controls my body.

The promise of fall and school activities excited me. I looked forward to meeting the kids who would be in my classes and my new teachers. Mrs. Newton was my English 11 teacher, and everybody said she was great. I was thrilled that she was my teacher instead of McCormick, who was legendary for his dry lectures, or Fenton, who had a disquieting tic that emerged when she was irritated. And she was perpetually irritated.

As eager as I was to launch my junior year, one factor gnawed at me: split sessions. I was scheduled to attend in the morning and he, the afternoon. That took care of most of the day. In order to spend any time together during the week, we'd be studying together in the evening. Academics were a major part of his life, so I had to adjust.

Annie and I were exiting the building. It was only 12:15 p.m. It felt so odd. "Come over to my house and have lunch. We can compare schedules," said Annie.

Even though Annie's house was perpetually cluttered, it made me feel as if I belonged. Her mother was into knick-knacks. As I walked through the foyer, I glanced in the living room at the familiar faces of miniatures who smiled at me from every available space. Atop the kitchen table sat a laundry basket jammed with freshly washed clothes in need of folding. A pair of jeans was draped over a chair to finish drying. Dishes filled the sink, and the sunlight that peeked through the window above baked the remnants of food into hardened molds. A loaf of freshly baked bread and a batch of brownies sat, abandoned on top of the stove. The radio on the counter was singing a Frank Sinatra tune. Annie shook her head and turned it off. Her mother was always in the moment, and the moment often dictated her unplanned flight from the house.

"She left the radio on again. Probably ran out to the A and P to buy something for dinner. Have a seat."

I set my books on the ironing board, which stood adjacent to the table.

"Can you believe how early we have to wake up? Especially after two months of sleepin' in." Annie grabbed some chips from the bowl on the counter and pushed them toward me. "Six o'clock in the morning! It's unnatural, I tell you."

"Yeah, but it's great getting out at noon," I added.

"Total agreement on that one. These split sessions might just be okay. Toasted cheese okay with you?"

"Perfect. When they first told us about this plan last year, I thought that it was going to ruin our lives. I feel kind of sorry for the freshman and sophomores, though, having to go to school until five in the afternoon. That stinks," I added.

"Yeah, but they get to sleep in, so don't feel too sorry for them." Annie laid two pieces of bread on the counter and slapped each one with slices of Kraft cheese followed by another slice of bread, which she lathered with butter. "So who's in your classes? Anybody good?"

"Mostly a mess of kids I don't know. But Shelly's is in my music class, and we sit next to each other. Hey, Mrs. Dewey told us that the new Metropolitan Opera House opens at Lincoln Center for the Performing Arts this month."

"What does that have to do with anything?" She turned up the flame on the front burner, covering it with a large iron frying pan. In went the sandwiches, butter side down. Then she spread another coating on the top slice.

"My music teacher made a point of telling us, and I thought it was interesting."

"The classes! Who else?"

"Fine. Live in the dark. Darlene's in my science class. And lots of the boys are in my second period Algebra class: Sal, Greg, and Ben. That should be amusing. We have Miss Clark, and you know how fragile she is. I'm afraid those boys will push her over the edge."

"Yeah, but it'll be entertaining. Anyway, she's not fragile. She's loony! The woman has bats in her belfry. Hey, remember last year when Ben brought his guitar into art class and convinced Mr. Nichols that we'd all draw better if we listened to country music?" She flipped the sandwiches.

"Yeah, what a nut! He wore dark shades and sang for the whole period."

"I love Ben. He always makes me laugh."

"So who's in your classes, Annie?"

"Mostly boring people. But that's okay. I need to keep my average up if I want to go to Syracuse U. Here's your sandwich. Notice the perfect golden brown color."

"You're a better cook than you are a seamstress."

"Hey! No noise from the peanut gallery. It's lunch isn't it? Eat!" She bit into her sandwich.

"Syracuse U is a great school."

She nodded, mouth too stuffed to respond.

"I'm still hoping to go to NYU. I love The City."

"I'm well aware. Ever since your dad took you there for the first time when you were ten. Blah, blah, blah. I remember the story. But Buck won't be in NYC. What about that?"

"What do you mean?"

"Well, you two seem pretty cozy." Annie grabbed a handful of chips and washed them down with a cherry coke. "God, this stuff tastes good. Helps to wash the salt out."

"But then you eat more salt."

"Exactly. The joy of junk food. Want some chocolate?" Her toasted cheese had disappeared. "We can alternate. Chips, chocolate, pop—till we're sick." She laughed indulgently.

I shook my head as I shoved more chips in my mouth. "Why not."

"So what about Buck? Doesn't it bother you to think about going away to school and not seeing him? Leaving him behind for the younger girls?"

"We've only been together for three months, and college is two years away." Although her comment about the "younger girls" bugged me, I said nothing.

"Doesn't matter. You're made for each other. It's so obvious."

"May I have a Pepsi?" I wanted to reroute the direction of the conversation.

"Don't be so damn polite, DeSantis. Help yourself. You know where the glasses are."

I retrieved a tray of ice from the freezer and wiggled it back and forth until several cubes jumped loose and then dumped them into my glass.

"You two are good together, Sam," she said straightforwardly.

"How do you mean?"

"Just watching you together makes people smile. You look so happy. You should see yourself when you're with him, Sam. You love him, don't you?" Tenderness from Annie. A rare moment.

I poured more Pepsi into my glass.

"You don't have to answer. I can tell you do. And he loves you too. That's obvious."

"It is?" I questioned her perspective, not mine.

"Are you blind, DeSantis? People watch you together. Haven't you noticed? They want to be like you two. In love."

"You're exaggerating."

"I am not! You just don't notice because you're too busy looking at him." She stuck her finger down her throat, pretending to gag.

"Stop it, Annie!" I shoved her, almost knocking her off the chair.

"Hey, watch it! I speak the truth. You guys are pathetic."

"You love to hear yourself talk, don't you?"

"Well, yes, that's true. I do. But don't change the subject. What about the fact that you're never apart. You're goddamned joined at the hip, which is seriously starting to piss me off!"

"You're such a bad liar. You're just trying to make me feel guilty. Not gonna work. And we're not *always* together. You were just used to having me with the girls all the time because I didn't have a boyfriend."

"Well, we don't spend nearly as much quality time as we used to. And you have no idea what it's doing to my psyche." The girl should have been on stage.

"Yeah, I'm really worried about your psyche. Don't hog the chips." I pulled the bowl from in front of her, sliding it in my direction.

"So spill, DeSantis. You guys doing anything yet?" Annie was shameless.

"I can't believe you just said that!"

"Excuse me. I forgot about your strong Catholic upbringing and unflinching moral fiber. Your ever-present guardians."

Annie was Catholic, too, but the man-made rules and constraints of organized religion never interfered with her freedom of choice. She was a pretty together chick for our day.

"Don't make fun of me. It's the nuns who ruined me for life. Pass that Nestle's Crunch bar." The conversation had suddenly become uncomfortable.

She passed the candy without skipping a beat. "So he hasn't tried to cop a feel yet?"

"Annie, stop! Anyway, we haven't been together long enough for that."

"There's not a rule book that says how long you're supposed to be together before you can start doing stuff."

Silence.

"So I take it he hasn't tried anything yet. He will. But don't worry, Sammy. Stick to your guns. The boy's crazy about you. He'll respect your wishes. Well, maybe not your wishes. Your hang-ups."

"I don't have hang-ups. I have values. And I am completely comfortable with my position."

"Understood. More chocolate?"

"No thanks!" Irritation filled me, and it obviously showed.

"What's that look?"

"Nothing."

"Okay. Apparently this is not a subject you have thought much about, nor one you wish to discuss. So now you look worried. Why?"

"Why do you have to spoil things, Annie? Everything has been great so far. Why do you have to make me think about this?"

"Relax, Sam. You're naive, and I want to prepare you. All I'm saying is the time will come when he wants more. And so will you, but he'll want it first."

"Why?"

"*Why*? Foolish girl, because he's a male. Come on, Samantha, you're smart. You know the way these things go. They think with the lower half of their bodies."

"You make it sound dirty. Without feelings."

"No I don't!"

"You know what? I don't want to talk about this anymore."

"Fine. Let's change the subject then. You guys going to the Homecoming dance together, or are you going with the girls?"

"I'm going with the girls and meeting him there."

"So who do you think is going to win Homecoming queen?"

"Not a clue. Don't care much either." Small talk wasn't changing my mood, and her effort to assuage my annoyance was pointless. And she knew it.

"You would if you were running."

"Well, I'm not, am I?" I stood up. "Listen, Annie, I better go. I have a lot of homework."

"You're pissed off now, aren't you? You shouldn't be, you know. I'm just telling it like it is."

"You always do." I retrieved my books from the ironing board and headed toward the front door. She followed. "Talk to you later."

"Don't be so thin-skinned, DeSantis."

"Annie, everybody's not like you." And I left.

Twenty-five

"I only have eyes for you . . ."

—the Flamingos

Annie was right—Buck and I were one of those couples that people watched. I saw the way girls looked at us. They wanted the same thing. It can be a hard thing to watch love when you are not in it, and most girls my age were looking for just that: the perfect love—or their idea of it anyway. Even girls I didn't know told me how *perfect* we were for each other. I used to wonder—*what's perfect?* They had no idea. Girls subconsciously concoct the way love is supposed to be from watching too many romance movies, like *Doctor Zhivago*. In their eyes, anything short of that kind of undying love is not the real thing. What a let-down real life can be.

"Sam, nominations are posted for student council, and you're on the ballot." Annie met me in front of Mr. Connor's classroom. She juggled a pile of books.

"Really? I was hoping I would be. I'd love to be on the council again. Who else is nominated?"

"Sharon, Sal, Gretta, and two boys I don't know. Six of you, and they'll elect two people." She shifted her weight as she rearranged the books in her arms.

"Annie, why are you carrying so many books? You look like you're going to fall over."

"I don't want to go back to my locker after third period. I want to have time to talk to Mrs. Warren about my composition."

"So you're going to schlep those books around all morning?"

"I can handle it. The vote is tomorrow during homeroom period. Sophomore class is having their elections too. Buck's nominated for class president again."

"He is? That's great. Everybody must think he did a good job last year."

"And the posters are up for the variety show. It's scheduled for the last weekend in October. We need to come up with some skit or dance that our class can do. Oh my God! Look at what Janine Kensington is wearing! If O'Brien sees her, she's in big trouble. That chick looks easy."

"Annie, just because her skirt's short doesn't mean she's easy."

"Are you for real? She was knocked up last year."

"You don't know that for sure. That was just a rumor."

"You're too much, DeSantis. She was gone for the whole summer. And she started wearing big clothes before school got out. Remember?"

"So?"

"So these are signs. Her parents probably sent her away so she could have the baby. Her family is rich, and I'm sure they wouldn't allow their little debutante's reputation to be tarnished."

As we talked, Annie's head was on a swivel, checking out the happenings in the hall. Suddenly she waved. "Here comes Greg. Looks pretty cute in his letter jacket, doesn't he? Sure hope Krammer appreciates what she's got. Nicest guy in the junior class. Gotta go. Later, Sam."

She headed toward Greg; he stopped when he realized she was coming to talk to him. I watched them chat with ease. Annie's whole body chuckled. Greg patted her on the shoulder and moved down the hall, waving in my direction.

"Hi, Sam. I see you're nominated for student council. Congratulations."

"Thanks. Same to you for the class president. Again."

He brushed it off. "Guess so. Buck's running too."

"I saw."

"He'll find out when he gets here. He usually shows up about half an hour before his first class."

"I know."

"Of course you do." He knuckled his head. "You two seem to be getting along well."

"We are."

"That's good. He couldn't have found a better girl." Our eyes locked for a moment, and the vision of riding on the crossbar of his bike flashed before me. Funny how it goes.

"Thanks."

"See you, Sam." And he walked away.

Twenty-six

For me, autumn is a symphony of the senses. Thankfully, a landscape of radiant colors begins to consume the dry end of summer. Juicy red apples, ripe for the picking, crunch in my mouth and run down my chin. The evening scent of neighborhood bonfires fills me with a sense of well-being. Autumn is the happiest season.

The trees had already begun their transformation, their first leaves drifting to the ground. Soon the neighborhood would be blanketed in color. I buttoned my jacket and proceeded down the street. Excitement was in the air. Homecoming weekend! Everyone in Carlson loved Homecoming. The town came alive. Last year's seniors flooded home from college, parties happened everywhere, and parents lightened up with their usual curfews. Academic concentration became a chore as we watched the clock, waiting impatiently for classes to end. When the last bell finally rang on Friday, students flooded the exits, heading in all directions: home to prepare for the big night, to the gymnasium to hang banners and streamers, or to meet up with old friends who were back in town for the festivities.

I headed toward my locker.

"Hey, gorgeous." Buck walked toward me. He wore a brown sweater over a buttoned-down shirt. He looked warm and cuddly, and I wanted to fold into him.

"Hi! You're here early."

"Yeah, I came early so I could see you. Come on, I'll walk you outside. I still have time before math. Anyway, Botner loves me." His humor was lined with vanity, but he was right—Botner loved him. All of the teachers did.

We navigated the halls, which took us awhile because of the influx of students. Whenever the morning and afternoon shifts met, mob scene.

"So what time are you ladies going to the dance tonight?"

"Probably by seven-thirty. We're going to Shelly's house first for pizza. Then we're walking to the dance."

"Who's we?" His thumb rolled along the back of my hand.

"Darlene, Annie, Shelly, and I." He stepped in closer. A gust of wind blew his hair over his eyes. He shook his head to regain his vision.

"Fashionably late, eh? Making an entrance?" he teased.

I knew he was kidding, but I bristled anyway. "Not really."

"Don't give me that!" he continued. "You're big juniors now. Wait till next year. You'll own the place."

"Stop it, Buck." I stepped back. "We're having pizza first, not making an entrance." I wasn't quite sure why I was so annoyed.

"Whoa—what's that tone? Am I getting to you, DeSantis?"

I didn't answer. I stared at a passing car, cramped with girls that I knew from Pioneer Public. I waved.

He swung around to see who had caught my attention. When he turned back, he shouldered me, deliberately knocking me off balance. "What's the matter? Can't you take a little joshing?"

He sounded so stupid that he managed to coax a smile out of me.

"There it is! There's that smile." He leaned down, bringing his face up close to mine.

"Okay, knock it off." I turned away, embarrassed.

"Only if I get the first dance tonight. Then I'll knock it off. Deal?"

"Deal," I acquiesced.

"Okay, I'd better get to class now. Botner might need a little help explaining polygons to the class." He grinned. "See you later?"

"Yep, later."

He skipped up the steps, waving as he disappeared. I waited for Darlene. We had planned to go to her house for a snack. I was always starved by noon. A red Chevy cruised by with a bunch of senior girls. The windows were down, emitting overzealous voices that were singing along with Diana Ross and the Supremes. *You just keep me hangin' on.*

"Sam!" Darlene shrieked from the top step, "It's Homecoming! We're gonna have such a blast this weekend!" She scrambled down the steps and ran over to me, throwing her arms around my neck. "I'm so happy!"

"You're always happy, Darlene," I laughed. "What makes this weekend any different?"

"It's Homecoming!" She jumped around like a kid. "Come on. Let's go to my house. My mom made caramel apples. I can taste them now." She grabbed my hand and dragged me toward the railroad tracks.

"Now you're talking my language. Caramel apples.".

"Hey, did you talk to Buck? I just saw him in the hall when I was coming out."

"Yeah, I saw him. Why?"

"You know, Sam, girls are always coming up to him. You better watch that boy."

"What girls?"

"Sophomore girls in his class. 'Oh, Buck,' she mimicked, 'when's the next class meeting?' Little hussies, acting as if they don't know. Look on the bulletin board, ditz!"

"Darlene, you're a trip. I swear."

"I'm serious. If I were you, I'd be bent about those girls hanging all over him. If girls did that to Sal, I'd have a cow."

"I'm sure you would." I switched the topic. "Now tell me what you're wearing to the dance tonight."

"Okay!" A renewed sense of exuberance. "My A-line skirt, the chocolate brown plaid one, and the cable knit sweater and knee socks I bought to go with it. And my penny loafers. And . . ." She rattled on, adding more details than I had asked for. I couldn't get a word in, so I just nodded and smiled at my joyful friend. But as we stood at the railroad tracks, waiting for the train to pass, my thoughts wandered back to what Darlene had said.

You better watch that boy.

What girls?

The train finally rumbled by, and we crossed the tracks.

Twenty-seven

The lights on Shelly's front porch shone down the steps and onto the street. The television flickered through the front window. I walked up the driveway and knocked on the side door.

"It's open! Come on in. I'm in the bathroom."

I let myself in. Shelly's mother was making popcorn in the kitchen.

"Hi, Mrs. Porterfield." Her hair was filled with rollers and capped with a net, as it often was. She wore a robe and slippers.

"Hi, Sammy. You look cute tonight, honey."

With that, Shelly's head popped out of the downstairs' bathroom to check what I was wearing. If she thought I had one-upped her, she would be hiking up to her bedroom to change her outfit, lickety-split.

"That's not what you said you were wearing!" she accused.

"I changed my mind."

"Ma's right. You *do* look cute, Sam. Green is a good color on you. You hardly ever wear that color."

"Thanks." Shelly wasn't in the habit of doling out compliments, so I basked in the moment.

"I'm gonna watch some TV, girls. Make yourself at home, Sam."

"Thanks, Mrs. Porterfield." She disappeared into the front room with her buttered popcorn and root beer.

Shelly was still standing in the bathroom doorway, brush in hand. "Can I borrow it next week?" she asked. "I don't have an outfit planned for Wednesday yet. That is if the waist isn't too big on me."

And the moment was over! She disappeared inside the bathroom again. I followed, standing in the doorway. "Or the bustline," I retaliated.

She whirled around from the mirror. "That was mean, Sam!"

"Oh, and I suppose what you said to me was okay."

"It's not the same."

"How do you figure?"

"'Cause you can lose weight and have a smaller waist, but I can't grow bigger boobs."

"Gain some weight. It usually goes everywhere."

"I don't want to gain weight!"

"And I don't want to lose weight. Besides, losing weight will not change the structure of my body. I'd have to have a couple of ribs removed to do that."

"Some people do, you know."

Is she serious?

"Are you serious?"

"Yes!" she snapped.

I couldn't believe it. "Yeah, and some people get silicone implants too."

"You're so mean!"

We were going nowhere, so I changed the subject. "When is everyone else getting here?"

The cold shoulder.

"Shelly, I asked you a question. And don't pout. You started it."

She knew I was right. "Soon!" She snapped again. "Why don't you order the pizza."

This was my punishment—ordering me around. I decided to present my most amicable side and kill her with kindness.

"I can do that," I grinned. "How's pepperoni and sausage?"

"No sausage." Spoken like a true spoiled brat. "The money is by the phone. My mom's treating tonight." She talked to her reflection in the mirror.

"Wow, that's really nice of her."

I stuck my head through the archway to the living room. "Thanks for treating us, Mrs. P."

She smiled from her recliner, where she balanced the popcorn bowl on her lap. "You're welcome, Sammy. It's Homecoming weekend, after all."

"Did you order the pizza yet?" Shelly bellowed from the bathroom.

"Not yet. Want me to call right now?"

"Yeah. Call the Pizza Place. They have the best crust."

I followed orders to keep the peace. "Done!" I stuck my head into the bathroom, where she continued to primp. "It'll be here in half an hour."

"Good." I sensed a softening in her mood. "Are you meeting Buck at the dance?"

"Yes. Are you meeting Larry?"

"Well, he's going to be there, but I told him I want to hang with my friends." She blotted her lips on a tissue.

"Clue me in on the story since I must have missed it!"

"There's no story."

"Come on, Porterfield. I know you. You like having someone to dance with. Why would you tell your boyfriend you want to hang with the girls?"

"Who's saying I won't have someone to dance with? Tons of kids will be there."

"And you think you're going to dance with other boys when Larry is in the room. Are you out of your mind? He'll go ape!"

The surly tone emerged. "Well, that's his problem, isn't it?" She applied more lipstick.

"Why are you doing that? You just blotted your lips."

Her expression said *you just don't understand, do you?* "I swear, Sam, you're make-up retarded."

"Girls!" shouted Shelly's mom from the living room. We hustled to see what was going on.

"What's wrong, Ma?"

"Look at the TV. Some guy called the Zodiac killer murdered an 18-year-old girl named Cheri Jo Bates in California. It's awful!"

"Then don't watch it, Ma, if it upsets you." Shelly dismissed the news and returned to the bathroom and the mirror. If it didn't affect her life, it didn't matter.

I stared at the TV screen as the anchor reported the details of the innocent girl's slaughter. *Beaten . . . stabbed . . . multiple times . . . short-blade knife.* I felt sick.

"Dear God." Mrs. Porterfield's hand covered her mouth.

The doorbell rang, and Darlene and Annie burst into the dining room. I turned away from the horror on the television and headed toward my friends.

"Ladies," greeted Annie. "You're both looking swell this evening."

Darlene giggled at Annie's remark.

"What?" asked Annie.

"Nothing. You just crack me up sometimes," answered Darlene.

"That's her job," I added. "Right, Annie?"

"Correct, my friend. Mine is the burden of creating constant laughter to lighten the mood."

"What burden? You love to be the center of attention," I said.

"True, true. Okay, girls, let's change the subject. When's the pizza coming? I'm starved. And we have to get a move on so we can see who is crowned Homecoming queen."

"Pizza should be here soon. What do you guys want to drink?" Shelly was in the kitchen, filling the glasses with ice. "We have root beer, cream soda, and Pepsi."

"I love cream soda!" squealed Darlene.

Finally the door bell rang. "Pizza's here!" announced Shelly.

"I've got it." I grabbed the money and headed toward the door.

The remainder of that portion of the evening rolled out smoothly.

* * *

Homecoming queen was a big deal in Carlson. It was a badge that shone brightly. The Homecoming dance was sponsored by the junior class, but queen candidates were nominated from all four classes. Traditionally, the winner was a junior. However, this year she was a sophomore, Jacquelyn Livingston. Quite an upset. The badge shone brighter. Jacquelyn was cute. She had thick red hair and a flirty personality that worked in her favor. She seemed like a pretty good kid, but she had a significant flaw—an eye for other girls' boyfriends. This bad habit developed as soon as she dropped thirty pounds of baby fat, lost her braces, and straightened her hair. The contacts helped too. The lovely butterfly had shed her cocoon.

Everyone was all abuzz about Jacquelyn beating out a junior. The crowd watched intently as she received her honor. She tried to hold the crown on straight while she wiped the mascara staining her porcelain cheeks. Her current boyfriend, Skippy, escorted her to the center of the room for her victory dance. While he was not a great looker, Skippy made up for his lack of exterior draw with his comedic personality. He twirled Jacquelyn all the way from the throne to the floor.

"Look at him, waltzing out on the floor like he's the one that was crowned." Annie had that right. We all stared.

"She's a lot cuter than she used to be." Shelly's sensors were always out when it came to competition. Why she concerned herself was beyond me. She was a beautiful girl, charm and sexuality her powerful weapons.

"Yeah, didn't she used to wear thick, ugly glasses?" Annie was glued to the center court activities.

"Isn't she thinner too?" Shelly's hands slid down her own abundant hips.

"Yes, Gretta said she lost like thirty pounds." Darlene seemed pleased with herself for throwing that tidbit of information into the mix.

"Holly shit! Thirty pounds? That's a lot of blubber!" Annie was revving up, and big laughter was beginning to surround her.

"Annie, that's mean!" Darlene chuckled quietly. Nonetheless, it was clear that Darlene was entertained by Annie's wit, despite the insensitive nature of her comments.

"Seriously. What a Cinderella story!" Annie continued. "The whale transforms into a dainty, little dolphin, frolicking through the cool waters as the other fish look on."

Yep, she was on a roll. And when that happened, the line between funny and cruel blurred. Other kids gathered near Annie, which only spurred her on. Laughter was her drug.

"Ah, but will she eventually return to her former hefty self, tortoise shell glasses and all, and sink back into the deep, dark oblivion? After all, she may not be able to resist those Friday morning glazed doughnuts or Gino's double cheese meatball sandwiches forever." She turned to her admiring audience whose laughter now served as applause. "Seriously, I've seen her at the sub shop. The girl can scarf 'em down! Once a heifer, always a heifer."

Despite a few scoffs from the more sensitive females in the crowd, Annie was quite pleased with herself. It occurred to me that in spite of Annie's unique ability to make everyone laugh, she had done so at the expense of other people's feelings one too many times. I had noticed that aspect of her personality before, but I pushed it back because I liked her so much. I looked across the room at Jacquelyn, happy with her newfound glory, and suddenly the injustice was too much. Who were *we*, after all? What gave *us* the right to mock other kids? This time Annie had crossed the line. I decided to confront her. My timing couldn't have been worse.

I moved in closer, lowering my voice. "What's wrong with you, Annie? Darlene's right. You're being mean. What if someone hears you saying all this stuff? They don't understand your sense of humor like we do."

Fatal mistake. I had interrupted her flow. "What's with you, DeSantis?" She regarded me with open distain. "First, of all, I don't give a shit if someone hears me. There's so much goddamn noise in this stupid gym, no one would notice if I ripped the F-word." It would be just like her to fly in the face of convention, simply for shock value.

"Can't you just let the girl have her moment?" Annie's fans, who had now lost interest, began to disperse. Her face tensed.

"Listen to you, Miss Goody Two Shoes. Jesus! What are you, the freakin' ethics police? I was just joking. But I guess you didn't pick up on that, with your fine-tuned humor sensors. Nobody knows how to spoil a party like you, DeSantis." A viciousness inhabited her. My friends froze, and I stared at her, speechless.

Where the hell did that come from?

Annie knew my Achilles heel, so I was taken aback when she referred to me as a Goody Two Shoes. I hated that expression. Instead of retorting, as I should have, I became mute, a built-in defense mechanism that kicks in when someone verbally assaults me. My friends knew this about me. For a fleeting moment, regret flickered in Annie's eyes and in my heart. When I didn't respond, she walked away.

Awkward moments. They'll never go away. We just learn how to deal with them more gracefully over the course of time. God knows we have enough practice that you'd think we'd get good at it. But awkward moments blindside us and slap us in the face before we see the hand rising. And when in the presence of other people, especially friends, the level of discomfort grows like an ugly weed, strangling life. I stood there, naked.

"Sam—would you like . . ."

"No." I cut her off. Poor Darlene, hers eyes became saucers. Now I was the one causing the awkward moment.

I'm sorry, Darlene. But the words wouldn't come.

"I'm going out front to wait for Buck," I announced to my friends.

"Don't you think he would have found you if he was here?" Shelly never knew when to shut up.

I spun on angry heels. "Yes, Shelly, if he WERE here, he would probably have found me; therefore, I assume he has not yet arrived, and I'm going to wait for him up front, if that's all right with you?" I shouldn't have taken it out on her either. After all, these girls were not responsible for making me feel bad and stupid and somehow small.

"Well, you don't have to be such a bitch to me. I didn't do anything. Yell at your precious Annie who can get away with saying anything and end up smelling like a rose!"

I escaped into the hall and headed toward the ladies' room, wondering how all of this had happened so quickly. *Damn Annie and her lashing tongue.*

"Hey, beautiful. Where are you headed in such a hurry?" He wore a brown tweed jacket, khaki pants, and a cocky smile.

"Buck." His name fell out of my mouth as a welcomed relief. "I'm so glad you're here."

"Yeah? That's what I like to hear." When he touched me, I could feel my frustration begin to dissipate.

"What's up? You look upset."

"No. I'm good."

"Where were you headed?"

"To the ladies' room to comb my hair."

"Doesn't need combing." He grinned. "Wanna dance?"

"Yes, that's exactly what I want."

He led me back into the gym, to a little corner of the floor where it didn't matter who was around. Walking onto the floor, he turned a number of heads. I was becoming accustomed to it. And to think he never had a girlfriend. He was a well-kept secret. Thank God I found him first. I nestled into him, his arms wrapped around my waist, and my head found the small of his neck.

I exhaled.

"Are you sure everything's okay? Something happen with your girls?"

"Everything is fine." The strain of the last few minutes gradually left my body. The story wasn't worth repeating. My mood, which had been temporarily veiled in a shroud of insignificant teenage drama, was lifting. How could something so superficial cause a rift between friends? The dynamics of friendships, especially among girls, are complicated and fragile. Yet somehow that balance is different with boys. I never witnessed that drama with any of the boys I knew. When something happened with them, they simply spit out the truth, called each other assholes, and got over it. Like it never happened. Why couldn't it be that easy with girls?

Another slow song, the Beatles.

I give her all my love, that's all I do, and if you saw my love, you'd love her too . . .

"Wanna keep dancing?" he asked.

"Yes."

He pulled closer.

She gives me ev'rything, and tenderly; the kiss my lover brings, she brings to me . . .

His voice, low and sensuous, sang each word into my ear.

A love like ours could never die as long as I have you near me . . .

At certain moments, all seems right with the world. Only minutes ago I was filled with discontent, born of a few foolish words. When would I learn? You just have to let some things go.

It turned out to be a very good Homecoming weekend. Our skilled football team, the Carlton Chiefs, managed to squash our rival school, the Greenville Tigers. Everyone had a blast at Saturday night's hayride as we looped around the lake in the brisk autumn air, singing the familiar lyrics of our time. And Buck, in his ever surprising unraveling of self, became my *official* boyfriend.

And I love her . . .

Twenty-eight

I have accepted fear as a part of life—
specifically the fear of change . . .
I have gone ahead despite the pounding in
the heart that says: turn back . . .

—Erica Jong

Change can definitely be a good thing. But I had to grow into that understanding. For most of my young life, I resisted. I viewed change as a prelude to disaster. My philosophy was "leave well enough alone."

In the midst of my blossoming romance with Buck, we sold our sweet, modest homestead on North Lane and moved up on The Hill, where the bigger houses nestled themselves into their tree-lined surroundings. Sunset Terrace. Even the address was aesthetically pleasing. There on the winding street stood the coveted house my mom had been aching for. I remember countless drive-bys with her, watching her face as she gazed at her future.

"Isn't that a beautiful house, Samantha? Don't you think it's pretty, sitting there overlooking the city. Look, you can see the lighthouse on the lake from here. Your father will love that. It has so much possibility. I would just change the color of those shutters right away—to black. Black shutters on a white house, so classy. Don't you think so, honey?"

To my mom this was a dream home waiting to be redecorated and personalized and loved. For me, it was the end of life as I knew it. How could she yank me from the home where my brother and sister were born? From the house in which I had made my First Communion and my Confirmation. The house that saw big, festive Thanksgiving dinners and watched three little children descend the stairs in the dawn of so many Christmas mornings to the delight of toys and treasures under the dazzle of a tinseled tree. The house in which I turned sixteen and met Buck Kendall and spent countless hours hanging on the front porch, laughing and talking with him. How could she desert these memories? How could my parents rip my heart out of my chest in this selfish manner?

I moped, seriously irritating my mother, who was already frayed from the pressure of the move. I was obsessed with this notion that my life would change for the worse if we moved. I was sure I'd have bad luck—the malocchio, *the evil eye,* would hang over my head forever.

I was so consumed with these thoughts that even when all of the furniture was moved out of our old house, save the second-hand upright piano in the dining room, I wouldn't give up the ghost. On the very last night that the house was still ours, Buck and I sat on the barren hardwood floor in the small dining room and played cards as I soaked in the last memories the walls would offer.

"Sam, you're so sentimental. Everything is going to be okay."

"Easy for you to say. Your parents aren't making *you* move."

"Okay. Be that way. Wanna play poker now? I'm sick of Go Fish."

"Sure."

"Strip poker?" Devilish eyes peered over the top of his handful of cards.

"Nice try. Regular poker."

"Aw, you're no fun!" He tossed his cards on top of the pile on the floor.

"Yes, I am. I'm not falling for that one."

He leaned across the pile of cards, still cross-legged, and kissed me.

"Okay, back to Fish then," he said.

"I don't feel like cards anymore. You can play Solitaire if you want. I'm going to play the piano one last time."

"Samantha, it's just a house. Your new place is really nice. And the piano will be there too."

Just a house! Is he without a heart?

"It's not just a house. It's the keeper of my memories!"

"Wrong. The keeper of memories is right here." He pointed to his heart.

"I suppose," I moped. I was getting good at it.

"Come on, Sam. 'Heart and Soul.' You can play the top part."

Though he never quite convinced me that the actual house didn't matter, I was temporarily consoled. The new place grew on me in stages. At first it just seemed hollow and foreign. Then my mom arranged our furniture in a familiar set-up and performed her magic. My new bedroom was larger, and I had it all to myself. Mom let me choose any color paint I wanted. Sky blue. She made sure that she completed the paint job before we moved in so I would feel right at home. Once all of my belongings were added, posters on the walls, desk in front of the window—it felt like home again.

As it turned out, our new house had a cool walk-out basement that led to a big backyard. My parents eventually put in a swimming pool. Mom fixed up the basement with couches and chairs and a Ben Franklin stove. It became a welcoming haven for my friends and me to hang out. It was all part of Mom's plan.

I discovered I was going to survive.

Twenty-nine

Competition between friends is a tightrope walk. You do your best to proceed without faltering, but, inevitably, there is that one moment when you find yourself teetering, and that is the precise moment when you must call upon all of your discipline to avoid a nasty fall.

Each November, Carlson High School sponsored the Miss CHS formal and crowned a queen who represented the school for the next year. Every junior girl was eligible. Students would nominate their choices during homeroom period, and the five girls with the highest number of votes would make up the court.

"Excuse the interruption," boomed the voice through the public address system, "but will all teachers and students please give me your attention. The votes have been tallied for Miss CHS. Here are the names of the five girls who will be on the court to represent our school: Cecily Abbott, Darlene Bailey, Samantha DeSantis, Shelly Porterfield, and Barbie Thompson. These girls must report directly to the main office after dismissal today. Congratulations to the candidates, and thank you for your attention."

I was sitting in French class when the loud speaker spat out the names. Kids around me turned to smile their acknowledgements. I felt my face turning red.

Me? A candidate for Miss CHS? Who voted for me?

"Félicitations, Samantha," said Mrs. Chavalier as she smiled on me. *Congratulations.*

"Merci, Mme. Chavalier," I responded. *Thank you.*

"Bonne chance! Vous seriez une bonne reine," she added. *Good luck! You would be a good queen.*

"Vous êtes très aimable," I replied. *You are very kind.* Mme. Chavalier was one of the most compassionate teachers that I had the good fortune to meet.

When the bell rang, I couldn't get out of the room fast enough.

"Congratulations, Sam," said some sweet-faced girl in the hall.

"Thanks." I had no idea who she was.

I headed toward my locker, feeling as if I had stepped into someone else's body. I was unloading an armful of books when Annie slapped me on the back.

"Nice going, DeSantis! Miss CHS, eh?" She grinned from ear to ear.

"Yeah, weird, huh?"

"Not weird that you're nominated. But it's gonna be weird running against two friends. Well, actually, Darlene will be cool with the whole thing."

"Yeah, she's so self-effacing."

"Self-effacing?" She mocked.

"I want to be a writer someday. Give me a break!"

"Okay, future writer. Did you hear that the first African American was elected to the Senate?"

"What does that have to do with anything?" I had no idea where she was going with this.

"I'm going to study history when I go to college," replied my quick-witted friend. "So give *me* a break."

"Fair enough."

She reset the combination on her locker. "Anyway, the part that's going to be weird is Shelly."

"Why?"

"Are you serious? She wants this bad!"

"How do you know?"

"She already talked to me about getting nominated. The girl's got her eye on that crown. I think she might have even been politicking votes."

"She did not!"

Annie laughed at me. "You're clueless sometimes, DeSantis. Anyway, are you happy about your nomination?"

"I guess. I never even thought about it."

"That's probably why you got nominated. 'Cause you're not stuck up." Then her body language changed. "Here she comes. Prepare yourself."

I turned to see Shelly approaching. The nerves lining my stomach danced.

"So, Sam, you got nominated too," Shelly sang.

"Yeah, and Darlene too," I added.

"Aren't you happy?" She eyed me curiously.

"Sure. I just wasn't expecting it, and it feels a little weird, that's all."

"Weird? It's a big deal, Sam!"

I remember thinking that my life would turn out just fine without this nomination. On the other hand, it seemed to be a monumental event for Shelly.

"Now, we have to get Darlene and have a meeting about what we're wearing. We need to make sure no one wears the same color or style of gown." Shelly announced.

"Yeah, that would be the worst!" Shelly did not appreciate the sarcasm, so she glared. "Shel, Dalton's is the only store in town that sells formals. And they don't have that big a selection. How's that gonna work?" asked Annie, who couldn't have cared less about fashion discussions. It was the principle involved.

"We'll go to Farnsworth's in Blair City. They have tons of beautiful dresses there. And the styles are really updated. Just like in *Seventeen*." Shelly was well-versed in the demographics of shopping.

"Farnsworth's? That store is really expensive," Annie reminded her.

"Annie, this is the Miss CHS formal," she clarified, like it was the Miss America Pageant. "Besides, what do you care? You don't have to buy one."

Ouch!

"Did it ever occur to you that I might be planning to *attend* the formal? Everybody goes!"

"Well, I just meant that you don't have to go to Farnsworth's to buy your dress. The dresses here should be good enough, right?" Regardless of how she tried, nothing came out right.

Annie clamped her lips together tightly as if to hold back the tongue lashing that was trying to escape. I glanced at her as if to say—*she knows not what she says. Forgive her.* Annie nodded in quiet understanding.

"This will be fun," said Shelly, clueless to the insensitivity of her remarks. "My house after we go to the main office?"

"Sure," I agreed. I was more concerned with the repercussions that were already surfacing as a result of this competition.

"Let's go then, Sam." Shelly pranced down the hall ahead of us.

"Wait!" Annie yelled. "What? I'm not invited to your house because I'm not on the royal court with you queens?" Now this was the kind of moment when I thoroughly enjoyed Annie's sarcasm. Not malicious, just a good-natured taunting.

Shelly stopped. "Of course, Annie. We can always use your ideas." Then she spun on her heels.

I rolled my eyes at Shelly's ability to view the world through such a narrow lens.

"Well, that's just swell of you, there Miss Porterfield. May I carry the end of your royal robe?" Annie bent to the floor, pretending to pick up the train trailing behind her.

I knew this was going to be a long ordeal. And the voice from the PA system still hung in the air.

* * *

For the next couple of weeks, we ensconced ourselves in "queen" plans. Annie was right again: it was a little weird. Shelly tried to be nonchalant about winning, but I could tell she'd nail herself to a cross for the crown. And why? She was going to win anyway. She was Shelly Porterfield.

"So, Queenie," said Buck, "only two more days till the big event." He was amused by the drama.

"Don't call me Queenie." I smacked him on the shoulder. We were sitting on my Uncle Danny's couch in the front room. I was babysitting, and the kids were all asleep. Buck had just arrived.

"Why not? Shelly keeps telling me I'd better brush up on my dance steps 'cause you're going to win."

"She's just saying that. She doesn't mean it."

"How do you figure?" He walked to the TV to switch the channel.

"She knows she's going to win, but she can't very well go around saying that." Ed Sullivan's voice filled the room with details of his *really big show*.

"Since when has Shelly played by the rules?"

"She does sometimes. But *this*—her comments about brushing up your dance steps because I'm going to win—that's just what people do to appear unassuming when, in fact, they're really sure of themselves. Shelly's not the only one who does that."

"You always defend her. Do you know that?"

"She's my friend."

"Define friend."

"Stop. She's not that bad. I wouldn't be hanging around with her if she didn't have some redeeming qualities."

"For example?"

"She has a really good heart. Her actions just don't always reflect that side of her. It's because she's insecure."

"Shelly? Insecure? Wait. You just said she's one of those people who are really sure of themselves. You're contradicting yourself."

"Sure about winning Miss CHS. Because she will. Guys love her. She'll win on the male vote alone. But she's insecure about a lot of other things."

"She's done some snow job on you, DeSantis."

"She has not!" I defended. "Change the subject, will you?"

"Okay. Let's make popcorn." We headed into the kitchen, and I pulled out one of Aunt Bette's old pans. I poured a healthy amount of oil into the bottom of the pan and turned up the flame on the front burner. "Buck, would you grab the popcorn. It's in that cupboard." I dumped the kernels into the oil and placed the lid on top of the pan to contain the exploding pieces. I waited, listening for the oil to sizzle, and then began to shake the pan back and forth while the popped kernels clinked against the aluminum top. The faster it popped, the harder I shook. Buck stood next to me, observing.

"So, tell me truthfully, who do you think will win?" He pushed the subject.

I regarded him quizzically. "Have you not been listening to me at all? Unless I'm crazy, you were just participating in that conversation in there." I pointed to the living room.

"You could win."

I laughed. "You're just saying that because you're my boyfriend."

"Seriously, Sam. You could. Don't underestimate yourself."

"Popcorn's done. Grab the big bowl up there." He followed orders. "Want salt?"

"Yes. You're very clever at dodging issues, but I'm not going to let you off the hook that easily."

"Butter?"

"What's popcorn without butter?"

I retrieved a small saucepan from below me and set it on a different burner. "Grab a stick of butter from the refrig, will you, Buck?"

Once again, he followed my directive. He handed me the Land 'O Lakes, and I placed a stick in the saucepan, turning the flame on low. He moved behind me and rested his chin on my shoulder as I supervised the melting process.

"That's why I like you, Kendall. Butter is a good thing. Ask Julia Child. She puts butter in everything." I drizzled the melted liquid across the popcorn.

"I'll take your word for it on the Julia issue. But that's not why you like me," he whispered into my ear and then kissed the back of my neck. His lips were warm.

Despite weakening knees, I continued. "Pop?"

"Yep." He wrapped his arms around my waist and moved to the other side of my neck.

"Orange or root beer?"

"Root beer." He swung me around, pinning me against the counter.

"We're missing Ed."

God I love him.

"Do you really care?" His voice was low, filled with purpose.

"Lou Rawls is on tonight," I whispered back.

"You like Lou Rawls that much?" He pushed against me. I started losing my place in the conversation.

"His voice is like velvet. I love Lou," I answered.

He took my face in his hands and stared directly into my eyes. "You could win, you know."

"We're back to that? You have a one-track mind, Kendall."

"Yeah, but it's on a different track right now." Then he kissed me over and over and over. "Let's go in there," he said.

"What about the pop?" I stalled.

"Forget the pop!" He pulled me onto the couch.

"We have to be good." I heard a tremor in my voice.

"We will, Sam. We will." His hushed tones seduced me. He kissed me with a single-mindedness that consumed. I was addicted. I wanted to tell him I loved him, right then, that moment. Fear prevented me.

I love you.

His hands moved over me.

God, I love you.

"Sam, are you still okay?" He held my face in both hands.

"I . . ."

"What? You wanna stop?"

"No, but we have to be good. Promise me you'll be good."

"I promise." We saw very little of Ed Sullivan.

Thirty

My nana, genius that she was, designed my gown for the big event. Her creation had an empire waist and a train that cascaded behind me in folds of blue velvet. Nana said the movement of a gown was key. The bodice, cut from matching velvet, had a square neckline that plunged lower in the back than in the front. The bottom of the dress, a rich, creamy brocade, fell in an A-line, stopping just in time for the tips of matching velvet-covered shoes to peek out. Long white gloves twisted and puddled aimlessly as they climbed my arms, reaching above my elbows. My only jewelry was the pair of pearl earrings that my parents gave me as a graduation gift from Pioneer. Earlier that day I went to Lolita's Coiffeurs for one of their famous upsweeps. Big, loose curled piled up on the crown of my head.

"You look pretty, Sammy." Lucy's eyes widened. "Like a princess."

"Come here and give me a kiss, you." I bent over to my little sister, and Dad snapped a photo just as her arms wrapped around my neck.

"Let's have all of you ladies pose together. Three generations. Mother, move over there. Peg, stand on the other side of Sam. And, Lucy, stand in front of your mom. That's it," he said. "Now tip up your chin, girls. Good! Say cheese."

SNAP!

The doorbell rang, and Lucy ran to the foyer. "It's Buck!"

There he stood, black suit, starched white shirt, a boxed bouquet in hand. White roses with sprays of Baby's Breath and lacy greenery. A thin blue satin ribbon meandered like a hidden trail through the flowers

"Wow! Look at you." He kissed my cheek.

"And look at you."

"You are very handsome, Buckley," added Mom. Then she produced his boutonnière from the refrigerator. "Here you go, Sam. You have to pin it on Buckley's lapel." The pearl-tipped pin was in one hand, his carnation in the other.

"Don't stick me, D."

"I won't if you promise to behave yourself."

"Guess I have no choice. You're the one holding the weapon." Mom and Nana exchanged a glance and chuckled. He even charmed the old ladies.

SNAP!

"Now let's get a couple shots on the staircase," said Dad. And the orchestration began.

Pictures taken, I moved toward the closet to grab a jacket. What I didn't know was that Nana had secretly made a long evening coat to complete my ensemble. As I reached for the closet door, she presented the coat. My mouth fell open, tears springing to my eyes.

"Oh, my God, Nana!"

"Non piangere." *Don't cry.* "Your mascara will run, mia bella nipote." *My beautiful granddaughter.*

"It's perfect." I swallowed hard. "When did you make this?"

My mother, Nana's accomplice, was bursting. "In between fittings. Isn't it just lovely, Sam?" she commented as she straightened the folds in my train.

"No, no, Peg. Per l'amore de Dio! Don't straighten. It's supposed to look that way."

"Oops, sorry Marie. You're the maestro," kidded Mom.

"Get rid of that ugly jacket! Put on the coat." Nana took my arm and slid it into the sleeve as if I were five years old. Then she stood back and clasped her hands in front of her face.

"Bella!"

"Thank you, Nana." When I leaned over to kiss her, she cradled my face in both hands.

"Bella!" she repeated. I buried my face in the folds of her neck. She smelled like hot tea with honey, tapioca pudding, and fresh buttered biscuits. I breathed in her unconditional love.

"Okay, Sam. You two had better get going now," Mom reminded. "You don't want to be late." When I broke away from my grandmother, I caught my mother dabbing her eyes with a tissue. Buck smiled, embarrassed, and directed his attention to Lucy.

"What do you think of all this, Lucy?"

"I think they cry too much. And I think Sam better get going or she'll miss the dance." Thank God for the light moments.

"You're a wise one, Lucy. Ready, Sam?" He presented his arm, and I slid my hand through.

"Don't forget your purse. I tucked in your lipstick and compact—plus a couple of tissues." Mom handed me the matching brocade evening bag. "Good luck, honey. Have a wonderful time, you two.

As excited as I was for this evening to finally be here, a part of me stayed behind.

* * *

The banquet room at the Elks Club was no longer an oversized hollow room with metal chairs pushed into worn tables. It was a movie set. The band played "On the Street Where You Live," and paper murals with London cityscapes covered the bland walls. Fresh flower bundles sat in the middle of each table, and place cards reserved the candidates' seats. The reigning queen, Lucia Palazola, wore her crown for the last time. As Buck and I walked by her table, she nodded. Her expression seemed to say, *Hang in there. It's almost over.*

Shelly and Darlene were assigned to the table adjacent to mine. As we approached our prearranged spots, I noticed Sal and Darlene on the dance floor. Oblivious to everyone else in the room, they giggled as if sharing a private joke while they wore a pattern in a very small circle. Suddenly Shelly rushed over to me.

"Sam, you look so nice! I love your dress."

She was already privy to the design of my gown. We had spent hours on the telephone, discussing every detail. Of course, hers was stunning, and it cost a fortune. She had selected a unique design from Farnsworth's and had it tailored to her specifications. Her gown was form-fitting, draping longer in the back to create the allusion of a train but without the added panel attached to the dress. Less bulky and very flattering in pink silk. She wore short white gloves, trimmed with burgundy ribbon, and carried a spray of pink baby roses finished with the same burgundy ribbon. Her hair was exquisite, rolled into perfect curls everywhere, tendrils hanging down the sides and smooth bangs sweeping dramatically to the left. Tiny pink bows nestled in her curls as if they belonged there.

"You, too, Shel. Wow! It fits you perfectly."

"Thanks, Sam." She beamed.

"Have you talked to Darlene yet?" I asked.

"Just a little. She and Sal have been dancing a lot. You know them. Can't keep their hands off each other. Check out the way he's looking at her." Like the sun rose and set on her face. "They have snacks on the table in the corner if you're hungry. Me, if I eat anything now, my dress won't fit. But you look like you have room in yours," Shelly observed.

"I'm not hungry."

"Sam, wanna dance?" Buck took a hold of my gloved hand.

"Buck!" she whined. "You didn't even say hello to me."

"Sorry, Shelly. You look good." Less than convincing.

She smiled coyly as she swiveled from side to side. "Thanks, Buck." I knew he was probably thinking, *What the hell else could I say?*

I set my clutch in front of my place card and stepped onto the dance floor. The lead singer of the Don Palmer Band was crooning the lyrics to "What a Wonderful World." His rendition was not Louis Armstrong, but I enjoyed it anyway.

"How you doing, beautiful?" He had been checking my emotional status at regular intervals since we left the house.

"I'm good."

"Nervous?"

"Not really. At least not now."

"Sam!" Darlene and Sal rammed into us. "You look so pretty!" she exclaimed, louder than she should have, giddiness getting the best of her. I chuckled.

"So do you, Darlene. Look at you two! Your colors are coordinated!"

"You don't think it happened by chance, do you, Sam?" Sal was in a great mood.

"I'm thinking *no*. And you look exceptionally dashing tonight, Sal. I might have to dance with you myself."

"Please, I'm taken. And don't beg," he warned. Darlene loved it.

Dancing took my mind off the imminent announcement of the evening. Why couldn't we stay like this? No winners. No hard feelings.

I hope Shelly wins. It would be so much simpler that way.

When we returned to the table, Annie informed me that the crowning was scheduled after the next break. "They came over here to tell you, but you were dancing. You doing okay?" She was well aware of the inner turmoil plaguing me. "You look great."

"I'm good. The hall looks incredible. Who was on the decorating committee?"

"Not sure. Whoever it was did a damn decent job."

"Agreed. Where's Timmy?" Timmy was Annie's date. They had the same kind of set-up as Brian and I had before I met Buck.

"Over there. Talking to Greg and Sharon. She looks like a little sex pot in that slinky red dress, doesn't she?" I shook my head at her remark. But that was the beauty of Annie. "Where's Buck?

"Getting punch."

"Oh, yeah, I see him. He cleans up well."

"So do you, Annie. Where did you find your dress?"

"At a store where Porterfield would never shop," she guffawed. "Like the ruffles?"

"On you—yes. And the shoes."

She stuck out her foot. "Flats! Much more sensible than heels."

"I love you, Annie."

"Ditto. Oh, look. The band's returning." She leaned into me, lowering her voice. "Last set before the end of the world."

"Don't be so dramatic." But her words . . . they reminded me of a day I was trying to forget.

* * *

Shelly and I were crammed into a dressing room at Bruno's Army and Navy Store, trying on jeans.

"So, Sam, do you want to win?" She broke my concentration with her pointed question.

"I don't know. I mean it would be an honor and everything, but . . ."

"But what?" she flinched. "Those are too tight for you. Try on the other ones."

"It's weird running against friends." I unzipped the jeans and grabbed the other pair, lying on the bench.

"No it's not. It's bound to happen. We're in the *popular* group. And it'll probably happen at senior prom too, so get used to it." Her voice was edgy, and she spoke as if this were the natural order of things. Irritation seeped through me as I considered her perspective on our group's order in the universe.

I dropped the jeans from my hand. "Shelly, there are other kids who could get nominated for prom queen besides us."

"I suppose, but it's not likely." She spoke as if she were delivering an obvious truth to a child. I hated this side of her.

"Why is winning so important to you?"

"What?" she snapped into the full-length mirror.

"It's obvious that you want to win. Why does it matter so much?"

"Because it just does!" She exited the dressing room.

I picked up the jeans and followed. "Why are you so sensitive about this? You're the one who brought it up."

"Here, try on this pair. They look like you," she handed me a pair of light blue jeans.

"I already have this color." I put the jeans back on the table. "And don't change the subject." I got in her face.

"Okay, Sam. You wanna know why it's important? I'll tell you why. Because it means you're something. It means people like you and think you're special. Yes, I want to win! There!"

I was stunned. Her words were raw and sad. I wanted to tell her that you don't need other people to validate you. You have to find that yourself; otherwise, you'll never be happy. You'll always be looking to others for approval. But I knew my words would fall upon deaf ears.

"Well, I think you have a really good chance of winning," I admitted. After all, she was the most popular candidate. She was Shelly Porterfield.

She halted. Her face transformed from Mr. Hyde to Dr. Jekyll. "Really? What makes you think so?"

"Just a feeling."

"And you won't feel bad if you lose?" She was already walking toward the throne.

"No. I never even expected the nomination."

"Will you feel funny losing to *me*?"

"No, why should I? We're friends. Would you feel funny losing to Darlene? Or *me*?"

"No." She bristled slightly. "But it should be one of us. Not those other two." She picked up a blouse and held it against her while examining herself in the dusty mirror among the crowed aisles. "This is cute."

"Why not?" I pushed.

"'Cause it *should* be someone from our group. Wouldn't you rather see your friends win?"

"It doesn't really matter. It's just a small town contest." I headed toward the sweatshirts.

"Just a small town contest!" Mr. Hyde had made his return. "You have no idea what this means, do you? Of course it matters! And if that's really the way you feel, then you shouldn't win. Maybe you shouldn't even be running." As soon as the words were out of her mouth, her face flashed regret and embarrassment. I had never seen her like this.

"Shel, I didn't say that I didn't want to win. I'm flattered to be nominated, and I know it's an honor. I'm just saying it isn't the be-all, end-all."

"You don't get it, do you, Sam?" She walked away, deflated.

Our shopping excursion slid downhill, and I went home with a heavy heart, weighted down by serious questions about the difference in our view of the world.

* * *

"Samantha! Look at you!" Brian sauntered across the dance floor to our table. He lifted both of my hands in his and gave me the once over. "Belle of the ball."

"One of the belles, you mean."

He cracked up. "Hey, Buck," Brian extended his hand. "Sam looks beautiful."

Buck's eyes revealed pride. "I know. She can't help it. She always turns out this way."

I didn't know where to look.

"So what's it going to be, Buck? Is our girl going home with the crown?"

Our girl. I winced silently.

"It is my prediction that she will," replied Buck. Then he placed his arm around my shoulder with possessive defiance.

"Well, good luck, Sammy. I voted for you. I hope you win." He winked and pointed his finger at me as he departed to find his date. "Have fun, you two."

The minutes crawled. I just wanted it to be over. Then, as if reading my thoughts, a voice from the bandstand filled the room. "Will our reigning queen and the Miss CHS candidates please meet in the foyer."

My stomach lurched.

"This is it, D. Good luck." He gave me the thumbs-up.

*   *   *

The foyer felt void and cold. More waiting. Darlene giggled nervously, her cheeks flushed. Cecily shifted from foot to foot as she bit her bottom lip. Barbie stared at her gold satin shoes. Her pallor made Darlene's face seem beat red. I realized that my breathing had become erratic, and I prayed no one else could tell. Shelly smiled at Lucia Palazola, regarding her with open admiration.

The double doors opened, and Constance Wilshire sashayed through, official-looking, holding index cards in her hand. "Well, ladies, this is it! Time to crown the new Miss CHS. Are you excited?" Judging by the looks on most faces, excitement had taken a back seat to nausea. But everyone sucked it up and smiled politely. "First, congratulations to all of you. It is an honor that your classmates nominated you. And you all look beautiful tonight." She paused for effect. "Here we go, ladies! The second runner up is . . ."

Second runner-up? What! So the bottom two can flip a coin to decide who's the bigger loser? Just announce the winner, for God's sake!

High school was not a kind environment.

" . . . Darlene Bailey!" We all turned toward Darlene, who brought her hand up over her mouth. "I thought I was going to be last!" she cried happily.

"The first runner-up . . ."

Poor Barbie appeared as if she were going to keel over, and Cecily's lip threatened to bleed. Shelly, on the other hand, maintained her mannequin-like pose.

How does she do that? My face felt hot. *Let's get this show on the road! Waiting is torturous.*

" . . . is Shelly Porterfield!"

Shelly's eyes widened in disbelief. Then, instead of accepting graciously, she faced me with a robotic movement. "Sam, you won."

I stared back at her, thinking . . . *there are three of us left . . . what makes you think it's me?* In a split second, I understood her presumption: if she hadn't won, it couldn't possibly be one of these other two flunkies. And the truth spoke volumes.

"And Miss CHS is . . ."

My mouth was sandpaper.

" . . . Samantha DeSantis!"

"See, Sam, I told you." The mannequin wore a blank expression.

The other three girls charged toward me, hugging me and kissing the side of my face. Before I could process what was happening, Constance was lining us up for the procession back through the double doors. Lucia, the reigning queen, led the pack, and I, the newly elected, assumed the traditional position, bringing up the rear. As soon as we entered the hall, a barrage of cameras exploded in my face.

FLASH! FLASH! FLASH!

Light blinded me. Familiar faces appeared distorted as they gawked at the line-up of candidates, straining to see who entered last. I heard people saying my name. I saw them smiling at me. Then I spotted my parents. *When did they arrive?* Dad had his

Nikon. *Oh, no.* Mom was crying. When I saw the expression on her face, I began to cry. Faces crowded together, craning over shoulders to catch a glimpse of the pageantry. As I neared my parents, Mom stepped forward and threw her arms around me.

FLASH!

"Congratulations, honey!"

The next thing I knew, I was sitting on the throne, and Lucia placed her crown atop my curls, securing it in with the nearby bobby pins that held me together. Kids clapped and beamed all around me. Suddenly Buck was walking up the steps toward me. He lifted my hand and led me onto the dance floor. Finally, I breathed.

"So, Queenie," he whispered, "my prediction was right."

And there we were, dancing in the middle of the banquet room at the Elks Club on a Saturday night in November, rotating slowly to the music as face after face smiled on us from the sidelines. When we rounded the floor a second or third time, I saw Shelly, standing in line with the other members of the court. She held the position nearest the throne. So close. Her regal body masked its broken spirit. Our eyes locked briefly, and she smiled at me. Then she dissolved into the loss of her hope. I wanted to cry.

The tightrope felt taut. I had made it past the midpoint and was drawing nearer to the other side, safe ground in sight.

Don't look down, Sam. Don't look down.

I felt myself falter.

Thirty-one

Buck and I attended opposite sessions that year, spreading our school hours over the majority of the day and leaving very little room for much else besides homework and sleep. Nonetheless, we managed to see each other as often as possible. He would stop by my house after school, around 5:30, and we'd do homework together. Because it was the dinner hour, Mom began inviting him to eat with us. He became a permanent fixture in my home; he even had a designated chair at the kitchen table. One evening, after two helpings of Mom's spaghetti and meatballs, we decided to give her a break and offered to do the dishes. He washed; I dried.

"So how has Shelly been acting since the crowning?" His words provoked disturbing images that I had been trying to bury: the emptiness in her eyes as she stared blankly at the dance floor; the awkward way she wrapped her arms around me in congratulations; the transformation of her poise and regal carriage to a posture of defeat.

"She's fine. We don't talk about it."

"I haven't seen you with her much lately."

"She's been avoiding me." Her face flashed before me as she took her seat in history class on the Monday after the formal. No eye contact. When finally she braved it, her smile was strained.

"Are you upset?" While he held no kinship with Shelly, he was, nevertheless, concerned about my relationship with her.

"A little. But it will pass. The day we were nominated I knew there might be friction. But I never expected to win." I could feel the knot growing in my gut as I spoke. "Everything would be all right if I hadn't won. So I just don't talk about it, and neither does she."

"It wouldn't be that way if she won though. She'd probably be wearing the crown at school."

"That's not true! Don't be mean, Buck." But even as I censured his remark, I knew there was a level of truth to his words. She might not be flaunting the actual crown, but it would be sitting high on her head as she parted the crowd on her runway down the hall. I questioned how I could admit these things to myself and still maintain our friendship. A level of guilt prevailed in the admission. But, once we form these alliances, we deal with the total package, and for some strange reason, Shelly and I had an affinity that kept us together. High school friendships are sometimes odd pairings.

"Okay. I'll change the subject. Want to go bowling Friday night?"

"Bowling? I didn't know you liked to bowl."

"Bowling's okay. And you like it, too. I heard you joined the afternoon leagues at the Central Bowl last year." Smug smile. He handed me a dinner plate.

"Who told you that?"

"My informants have been assured complete anonymity. Come on, Samantha. I want to see how you look out there on the lane."

"I'm not a proficient bowler. There's nothing to see."

"You're so cute when you are embarrassed. I like that about you." He leaned over and kissed me.

"What if my mother walks in?" I protested.

"She won't. She went down to the basement to do laundry. Besides, she knows we kiss."

"Yeah, but you know my mom," I reminded.

"Stop talking." He put his soapy hands on my back.

"You're all wet. You did that on purpose!"

He looked like the Grinch, calculating his next move. "How come when I look at you, all I want to do is kiss you?"

"Finish the dishes, Kendall." I pushed him away.

"You know you want me to, DeSantis. Come here, or I'll splash dishwater all over you."

"Don't you dare."

"You know I will."

"You'll get the floor all wet. Then you'll have to deal with my mother."

"Then kiss me. And not one of those stupid pecks. Make it good."

"I thought it was always good." I leaned into him, brushed his lips, and then swatted him with the dish towel.

"You brat!" He immediately cupped dishwater in his hands, threatening to douse me.

"Okay! You win. Don't."

This time I didn't care that his wet hands were all over my back.

Lucy walked in. "Where's Mom?"

We pulled apart. "She went downstairs to do laundry, Luce."

"Okay." She headed toward the stairs. ""I saw you kissing, you know. But I won't tell Mommy." She disappeared, and we burst into laughter.

"Lucy's got chutzpah!" Buck had become very fond of my outspoken sibling. She was an old soul who seemed to understand life better than all the rest of us.

"Yeah, she's got chutzpah, all right. I'll have to have a little talk with her."

"Leave the kid alone. She's neat. Now stop kissing me and finish the dishes, will you Sam? You can't keep your hands off, can you?"

* * *

The Pin-a-thon was the only bowling alley in town. The place was jammed, half of the lanes occupied by men's leagues. Smoke hovered above them like low-hanging clouds, defining their area. Beer cans and overfilled ashtrays covered the tables behind them. Pins slammed against each other, their crashing sound carrying several lanes down. Victorious and sometimes off-colored remarks filled the air. The smell of hot dogs, fries, and popcorn blended into the mix to create a carnival-like atmosphere.

"Sam, move over to the right more. Your ball is hooking. If you keep your arm straight on your release, it will hug the side and curve toward the pocket—on the Brooklyn side."

Gutter ball.

"You turned your hand when you released. You have to hold it straight, like you're shaking hands."

"Stop telling me what to do! I hate this stupid game. I didn't used to be this bad." I plopped down on the seat next to Buck and crossed my arms like a perfect brat.

"You're not that bad. You just have to control that wicked curve of yours." He stood up. "I think it's kind of sexy." He walked past me and approached the lane.

"How can a curve ball be sexy?" I whined.

"Yours is." He smiled over his shoulder as he lifted his ball from the return.

"It always lands in the gutter!" I continued. "Isn't it time for cheeseburgers now? When are Sal and Darlene meeting us?" I didn't deal well with public humiliation.

"Patience, my dear." He moved toward his mark.

"I used to be able to do this, you know," I shouted at him. "I could make spares, and I even got a few strikes. Look at my score! It's not even 100 yet, and we're in the last frame."

"I told you, you have to control your hand when you release. Now watch the master at work."

"The master? You're conceited, Buck Kendall." I cupped my hands around my mouth. "Boo! Miss it!"

Tuning me out, he positioned the ball chest high, while he concentrated on the lane, the pins, and his approach. He stood there for what seemed like a full minute; then he went into motion. He strolled rhythmically toward the invisible line he had formed, right arm swinging back in practiced motion. He released the 15-pound, custom-made ball and stood poised as it found its way to the center pocket, right side.

SMASH! A flurry of wood.

"Yes!" He whipped around, satisfaction oozing everywhere. "Did you see that?"

Did I see that? Grrrr . . .

"I saw."

"Come on, Sam. Be happy! That was a perfect strike."

"It was. Congratulations. Great execution." I proceeded toward the lane.

"What's wrong?" he smirked.

"Nothing. I'm up. Excuse me." My face was stone.

"Hey, it's just a game."

"People always say that when they're winning. Would you say that if our positions were reversed?" I spit my words into his boastful eyes. He stifled a grin, eyes cast down at his bowling shoes.

"No smart answers now, eh?" I tried to push by him.

"You are a pistol sometimes, D."

"Only when provoked. Now move. I'm up."

"Go get 'em, tiger. Remember what I said about hugging the right side," he called out.

I shot him a dagger.

"Okay, I'll shut up. But I'm just trying to help."

I cradled the ball and stared at the pins. "St. Jude, I need you now. Please deliver me from further humiliation."

"Who you talking to, Sam?"

"Myself."

"You do that a lot," he confirmed, matter-of-factly.

"So I've been told," I muttered.

Okay, here we go. Arm straight on release, drop the ball close to the right edge, follow through.

I held my breath. As if in slow motion, I watched the ball glide from my hand onto the alley and follow the right edge of the lane, half off and threatening to commit fully to the right. Three quarters of the way down the lane, don't you know, that little son-of-a-gun began to curve toward the center, spinning wildly. Unfortunately, it passed its intended mark and rolled fearlessly toward the head pin. Disaster!

"God no," I whispered. "Split pins. I might as well lie down on the alley and die. I'm never bowling again."

I was still talking to myself when that lovely blue hunk of faux marble wiggled a dash more to the left and found the other pocket. No, it nestled into that pocket and owned those pins!

CRASH!

"Ha-Ha!! Sam, I can't believe it! You did it! Strike!" He was on his feet, applauding.

Elation! "St. Jude, I owe you one," I whispered as I looked toward the Heavens.

"That's unbelievable. All night you've been overthrowing, and then this! What the heck happened?"

I turned around, "Told ya."

Behind us, Darlene and Sal broke into applause. I swung my hand across my middle and bowed indulgently. "Thank you, my friends."

"Sammy!" screamed Darlene. "You did so good!"

"Nice going, DeSantis!" Sal added.

"Get over here, you little brat," Buck was still standing by the scoring desk. I ran over and jumped on him, wrapping my legs awkwardly around him.

"You're a nut!"

"Hey, you two, this is a public place. No PDAs." Sal was still shaking his head in disbelief.

"Come on, let's get burgers. You earned it." Then he announced, "Burgers for everyone!"

"You paying, Kendall?" Sal asked.

"If you take us to the submarine races after."

"Why not?" Sal agreed. "Dessert!"

Thirty-two

"Flowers leave some of their scent in the hand that bestows them."

—Chinese Proverb

Smells are memories, painful longings. Some smells never go away. They tug and coax until I walk in old footsteps. Just a hint of familiar fragrance transports me. I breathe it in again, and it is yesterday.

It was his scent. It hung on his clothes and lingered in the space around him. Jade East mixed with soap and his body and his mother's detergent—joined to create that special blend. And only one person had that scent.

We were walking from my house to the Theta pajama party. My hometown was an anomaly because we had high school sororities. Traditionally, such affiliations begin in college, but I was well-versed in the ways of the Greeks by the time I moved into the next academic phase of my life. High school sororities accounted for a huge part of our social life in Carlson; as well, they provided the expected level of community service and sisterhood.

This night's pajama party was held at Betsy Meyer's palatial estate on Admiralty Drive. Betsy's father owned a lucrative construction company, and, to the envy of every girl in our circle, Betsy had everything she wanted, including a family room large enough to accommodate the fifty-five non-stop talkers who made up the membership of Theta Epsilon. Our pajama parties were notorious gab fests, equipped with the latest 45s, an obscene amount of junk food, and an available telephone to call friends who weren't there. Plus Betsy's house had four bathrooms. Bonus!

Before our trek to the pajama party, Buck and I hung out with Darlene and Sal, who had become our closest buddies. We all got along famously, and as our high school years progressed, we became a recognized foursome. On this night we had been listening to records and eating popcorn at my house before we packed up to leave for the party.

"Look, it's snowing!" I spread my arms to catch one of the big flakes but erupted into a sneeze.

"Sam, you get so many head colds," Darlene commented.

"I know. It's a pain." I shoved my hands into my coat pockets in search of a clean tissue when Buck unceremoniously handed me his handkerchief. I loved using his handkerchiefs because they bore his monogram, BRK, and for some reason I got a kick out of that. When I put the cloth to my nose, I smelled his cologne.

"You sprayed this with Jade East!" I stopped in the middle of the block and threw my arms around him, burying my face into the thickness of his jacket.

"You noticed." He was pleased with himself.

"Oh, isn't that sweet!" razzed Sal. "Buck sprayed cologne on his snot rag just for Sam. How touching!"

"Shut up, Sal! It's sweet. Why don't you do stuff like that for me?"

"Come here, woman! Let me warm you up!" Sal grabbed Darlene and smothered her, their muffled laughter carrying down the street.

I remained burrowed in Buck's neck, where it was warm and comforting, yearning to stay there forever. Sal and Darlene didn't seem to mind: they were in their own world. My face was still buried in his jacket when I heard the words.

"I love you, Sam."

The words I lived for, dreamt about, just slipped out so naturally, as if he had spoken them a thousand times. I pulled back to look at his face.

"Did you hear that? Buck just told Sam he loves her!" howled Sal.

Darlene squealed. "I heard! It's about time!"

"We're witnesses, pal. You can't deny it now!" Sal continued.

"Why would I want to deny it?" Buck's face was lit up. "I love her, and I don't care who hears."

My world was spinning. "I love you, too." *And I always will.* Then he kissed me.

"Hey, you two. We're freezing here." Sal announced.

"Looks to me like you're occupied!" Buck retorted.

"Look who's talkin'!" Sal puckered his lips and started making smooching noises, "Oh, Buck, you're sooooo romantic and such a good kisser. Pucker up and kiss me."

Buck strolled over to him and planted a wet one directly on his lips. Sal's eyes opened so wide that I thought they were going to pop out of his head. Darlene and I doubled with laughter while Sal spit into the snow and wiped his face.

"That's disgusting! Don't ever kiss me like that again, Kendall." Then he paused. "Next time, no tongue!"

I loved these friends. There was a purity about the time we spent together, and their friendship marked a significant time in my life. As did this night. Our walk to Betsy's house was marked by a silence that possessed an extraordinary truth. *He loves me.* The energy changed when we looked at each other.

Our trip ended in front of Betsy's, and from where I stood on the street, I could hear music blaring from the house. "Love Potion Number Nine." I peered through the stately front windows of the Meyer's mansion, as we called it, and saw my sorority sisters dancing mindlessly in their pajamas.

"What time will you be home tomorrow?"

"Around eleven. Mom wants me to help her bake pies."

"Pies? Hmm . . ." he smiled. "Okay. I'll call you at eleven thirty, and then you can tell me when I can come over for dessert." I could feel myself grin. "What? You know I can't resist those pies."

"That's not it."

"What is it then?" he hummed seductively. My gut turned inside out. "Oh, that. Well, it's true. Has been for a long time."

"Yeah?"

"Yeah."

"You just made me wait, huh?"

"Not at all. I just needed the right moment."

"And that was it? In front of my house?" The ordinary nature of the night didn't occur to me as *a moment.*

"Yeah. There was just something . . . a feeling I had. A sense of well-being, like I never want to be without you."

"Hey, you two! Cut the mush. It's freakin' freezing out here!" reminded Sal.

With that we called it a night, and Darlene and I headed toward the front door. Suddenly Buck's voice screamed out, "padiddle!" as a car with only one headlight drove by. Then he grabbed Sal's face and smacked him on the lips again. Sal never saw it coming.

"Get off me!" Sal wiped his mouth. "What's wrong with you, Kendall?"

"You said no tongue next time. No tongue!" laughed Buck.

"Asshole! You're perverted. Does Sam know about this side of you?"

We entered the house to a barrage of noise. A group of girls came running over to the door, drunk with giddiness. "Where have you two been?"

"With Sal and Buck," sang Darlene. "And Buck told Sam he loves her!" What followed was more than I was prepared for. However, in the name of sisterhood, I put on my best face throughout the litany of congratulations and giggling commentary. All the while, delighted as I was with the events of the evening, I was dying to crawl into my sleeping bag and relive the moment—all by myself. But circumstances dictated otherwise. Finally, I broke away and slipped into my nightgown.

"Sam! Dance with us! It's Leslie Gore!" screamed a collection of voices in unison.

"She has a bad cold. Let her sleep," added Darlene. "Come on. Let's go in the other room."

"Ah, she just wants to dream about Buck," said a voice.

"You would too if you were going steady with that hunk," replied another.

"Down girl."

Their voices trailed off. Inside the sunken family room, the music revved up.

It's my party, and I'll cry if I want to,
Cry if I want to, cry if I want to.
You would cry too if it happened to you.

I curled up, ready for sleep, but my stuffed head and labored breathing prevented me from falling off. I stared out the window, exhausted but happy. A sense of peace enveloped me. I could feel the weight of my lids growing heavier with each blink as I watched the heavy snow lowering the branches of the tall pine in the front yard. It was perfect and majestic, like a Christmas tree flocked with artificial white, dispersed in just the right places. Eventually, I felt myself drifting . . . sinking into a semi-conscious blur. Then my whole body convulsed into a sneeze. Buck's handkerchief was still balled up in my hand, and when I pressed it to my face, I inhaled him.

I love you, Sam . . . I love you too . . .

"Look," said some voice, "she's smiling in her sleep."

* * *

"He told you he loves you?" We were walking to the auditorium to watch a film on urbanization and social change in the South.

"Yup!" I beamed.

"Way to go, Sammy girl." He paused slightly. "You're happy, right?"

"Brian, of course I am!"

"Good for you, Sammy. Now listen, this new level of commitment doesn't mean I'll never get to see you again, does it?"

"What are you talking about? We're friends. Of course it doesn't mean that."

"Good. It's just that," he hesitated, his eyes narrowing.

"What?"

"Sometimes I get a bad vibe from your boyfriend."

"What do you mean?"

"I can't put my finger on it. The way he looks at me when I'm around you."

His words took me by surprise. "Brian, you're imagining that. Buck thinks you're a good guy."

"How do you know?"

"I just do."

"Has he ever said anything about our friendship?"

"No, why would he?"

"He looks like the jealous type."

"Buck? You're crazy, Brian. And don't worry about our friendship," I assured. "It's solid."

"Ah, Sammy girl, I love ya. Buck's a lucky man." As we moved toward our respective seats, his eyes wandered to the row to the left of us. He leaned down and whispered in my ear. "Who's that girl with the pink sweater sitting next to Amelia?"

I glanced sideways to inspect. "Don't know."

"Well, I'm about to find out," he crooned. Then he stood upright and lit up the room with that famous grin. "Later,

Sammy!" His eyes danced as he walked toward the assigned area for his class.

I laughed. "You'll never change, Determan."

"Would you want me to?" he fired back before schmoozing with the girl walking next to him. Heads turned as he passed by. Female, of course.

Thirty-three

December 1966

"It's the most wonderful time of the year"

—Pola and Wyle

Christmastime brings out the best in people. It's not about religion. It's about the spirit of good will. People soften, and life just seems more tolerable with strings of sparkling lights.

I was browsing through the men's section at Feinstein's. Wreathes with red velvet bows decorated every display; mannequins wore holiday sweaters, strewn with tinsel; and Andy Williams' voice traveled up and down the crowded aisles. Every year the Feinsteins offered hot wassail and cookies to thank their faithful shoppers. Santa's elves doled out goodies, while Santa bounced crying children on his knee. Despite the children's objections, doting parents snapped pictures to mark the event.

Once again, I searched for the perfect gift for Buck. I wanted something to jump out at me like the wool sweater I had spotted the week before. This was our first Christmas together, and I had put a lot of thought into what I was going to give him. Gifts hold different meanings. And there were unwritten rules about these things. Don't spend too much money at this stage of the relationship. Don't buy a better gift for him than he buys for you. Don't buy something that says you want to marry him and have eight kids as soon as you graduate from high school.

I could easily pay for a decent gift with my babysitting money, which I accumulated at a steady rate, thanks to my Aunt Bette and Uncle Danny. But I didn't want just any gift, and I found myself gravitating toward the wool sweater that had stopped me. Although pricy, it was heads above the other gifts I considered. The sweater was light brown and green tweed with a V-neck. It matched the color of his eyes, and it was classy, just like him. I held it up, examining the quality and presentation it would make. I could definitely see it on him, pulled over a perfectly pressed button-down collar shirt that emitted freshly sprayed cologne. I smiled as I proceeded to the cashier.

I remember sitting on the floor next to our tree, wrapping the box in snowflake paper, topping it with fresh holly, and tying it up with a silver bow. Under the bow, I tucked a handmade card on which I had crafted a message in calligraphy. I added my package to the pile already collecting under the Scotch pine.

Christmas Eve was a huge deal in my family: big breakfast, last-minute shopping trips downtown, and festivities at Nana's house in the evening, allowing plenty of time to secure prime seats at midnight mass. After church, we'd head home, where Mom cooked homemade Italian sausage from DeLuca's, sautéed with peppers and onions. Then we'd sit by the tree, eating while we exchanged gifts.

Earlier in the day, Buck surprised me. My girlfriends convinced me that he had chosen some garish, insignificant object that I wouldn't like. At first I figured they were kidding. But each one remained so consistent in her story, I began to believe them.

"Act happy when you open it," Annie said.

"Of course I'll act happy—no matter what it is."

"Right," she replied.

"Now, Sam," directed Darlene, "be open-minded. It's the thought that counts."

"I know."

"Some people just have different taste," she added.

"Maybe you'll like it. At least it will be different, and no one else will have it," said Shelly.

"I'm sure I'll like it."

"Well, we'll see. Want a cupcake?"

My spirit wilted. I had no idea what to expect.

He walked in, smelling like the outdoors. He wore a cashmere coat and brown plaid scarf. I tasted the crisp cold of winter on his lips.

"I can only stay for about an hour. We're going over to my grandparents' house to celebrate with the rest of the family. Then we're going to mass."

"Us too. Let me hang up your coat."

"Sure. Just let me pull something out of the pocket." He produced a small package and carried it over to the tree. I could tell that he was bursting.

Okay, no matter what . . . it's the thought that counts . . .

After a suitable interval, filled with milk and cookies, he turned to me. "Want to open your present now?"

"You first." I handed him the package and picked up the Kodak camera from the coffee table.

"Wow. Nice wrap job, DeSantis. I feel bad breaking the bow." My intake of air was shallow as he lifted the lid off the box and pushed back the tissue paper. But then his smile said it all.

"Sam. This is great. Looks like you broke the bank." He draped the sweater across the front of him.

"Smile." I snapped the shot.

"Thanks, Sam." He placed the sweater back in the box. "Your turn." He handed me the package.

How bad could it be? It's so small. The girls were just giving me a hard time.

"Open it."

I pulled off the gold foil paper. When I opened the box, I caught my breath.

"Try it on."

I slipped the ring on my finger and held up my hand in admiration.

"Say something."

"I love pearls."

"I know."

A pearl ring, understated, presented in a black velvet box from Tutor Royale, our local jeweler.

"I can't believe it."

"Why?"

"The girls said . . ."

"They were messing with you."

"How do you know?"

"I talked to them about the gift. Shelly told me jewelry was a good choice. Annie said you liked pearls. And Darlene looked like she was going to cry and said you'd love it."

"I'm gonna kill them!"

"So you like it?" I detected insecurity.

"Are you kidding? I love it." I admired my hand, now bearing a part of him.

Heaven!

He smiled, pleased and relieved.

"What about you? Do you like your sweater?" I asked.

"Yeah, it's the nicest one I own."

"It is not."

"Sure it is. But admit it—you bought it because you want to make sure I look acceptable in front of your friends." He smirked.

"That's not true. I picked it because it matches your eyes."

"You think?" He wiggled his eyebrows up and down. His eyes revealed an unusual amount of green that day. "What?"

"Your eyes. They change color," I replied.

"You never noticed that before?"

"Yes, but I never said anything."

"Hazel eyes," he said. "They're unpredictable.

"But they're not really hazel. It's weird."

"Are you calling me weird?" His crooked smile made me weak.

"No. I'm just saying that your eyes are different from most people's. Mine always look brown, same shade every day. But yours—a bunch of browns and greens."

"They reflect my moods." He smiled.

"And what mood are you in today?"

"A good one.'

"So the greener, the better, huh?"

"Anybody's guess. Hey, you think we could go downstairs until I leave? Would that be okay with your mother?"

"Probably." I headed into the kitchen. "Mom, Buck and I are going to the basement. He has to leave in half an hour."

"Okay. That's just about the time the apple pie will be done. I'll wrap up a piece for you to take home, Buckley."

"Apple pie, Mrs. D?" He hummed the words.

"Apple pie, Buckley," she sang.

"Mrs. D, you make the best pie. Better than Jane's, but don't tell her." What a charmer. My mother ate it up.

"Oh, go on, Buckley! Go ahead, kids. I'll call you when the pies are done."

"Thanks, Mrs. D."

"You're welcome, Buckley." We headed toward the basement stairs.

"You are such a brown nose, Kendall!"

"No I'm not," he retorted, most unconvincingly.

"'You make the best apple pie, Mrs. D,'" I mimicked. "You could give Eddie Haskell a run for his money." Eddie Haskell, an infamous character on the television series *Leave It to Beaver,* was a suck-up, especially with his friends' parents.

"Don't compare me to him. He's annoying. And your mother *does* make the best apple pie." He hurried me down the stairs.

"Be careful! You'll knock me down."

"I'm in a hurry. We only have half an hour. Quick! To the couch."

The basement was decorated for the holidays. The only source of light came from the bulbs bubbling on the tree. The flickering cast a sleepy haze over the room. We sat on the couch under the stairs; his hands immediately dug into my back. Time never diminished the power of his touch. I have often heard people say the intensity slips away after a while. Not with us. We headed relentlessly toward the pinnacle.

He must have been thinking about this moment for a while because he went from first gear to fifth without shifting. God, he was hard to resist. Within minutes a strand of hair matted to his forehead. We wrapped around each other. I could never get close enough. Each time we were together, the battle between body and soul escalated. But my Catholic upbringing, my ever-present chaperone, kept a close eye on my soul.

"Sam, I love you so much," he breathed.

"Pie!" Lucy announced, invading our privacy.

"Whoa!" He sat up, disoriented. "Was that half an hour already?" His fingers threaded through his hair.

"I guess." I peeked up between the stairs to determine if Lucy was checking on us, then turned back to him, feeling robbed of time. "Your hair's all sweaty."

"Your face is red," he grinned. Then he touched my cheek where his stubble had grazed me. "Sorry."

"Shave more often then." I teased. I stood up, grabbing his hand. "Come on; we'd better go upstairs."

"Yeah, just a sec." He remained seated.

"Your hair's not *that* bad."

"It's not my hair I'm concerned about."

"Oh!" It took me a moment. "Again?"

"What do you mean *again*? That's how these things work."

I laughed. "I'm sorry. I didn't think . . ."

"Doesn't take much. But, hey, don't worry about me. I'll just go home and bang my head into the wall again—like I always do after we're together. Besides, I only like you for your mother's pie." He stood up. "Come on. Let's go upstairs before she runs down here with a baseball bat."

"Don't underestimate her."

Thirty-four

January 1967

Mrs. Newton's English class was my favorite of the day. Shelves of books lined her walls, creating a feeling that no other space in Carlson High could claim. Walking into her room always made me happy. I never tired of looking at her books.

We were about to read Thornton Wilder's play *Our Town*. The small hand on the wall clock moved ever so slightly—10:45 a.m. One hour and twenty minutes till we would meet on the front steps. Ten minutes to refresh my senses, absorb the deep tones of his voice, inhale him. The second hand crawled. Then Mrs. Newton began to speak, and I was all hers.

"Before we get started with our performance of *Our Town,* I want to assign your homework." Groans from the back.

"You'll live, Mr. Donaldson, believe me." She smiled at him; then her expression turned somber. "As you know the American public has been demanding that the Vietnam War be ended."

The room went dead.

"I would like you, as American citizens and the future generation, to write about your perspective on this war. Imagine yourself in it, watching comrades fall beside you, fearful of stepping on a hidden landmine, terrified of losing your life. Step into the shoes of the parent whose child has gone to war. Look through the eyes of our president, who has the weight of the world on his shoulders."

"Way to bring us down, Mrs. Newton," moaned Chad from his corner.

"'Some things we must deal with, Mr. Donaldson. So—just do it." The class broke into welcomed laughter.

As she explained the criteria for the paper, I thought about the thousands of American and Vietnamese soldiers who had already lost their lives. Of the massacres and terrorism. Of how I was able to sit safely sheltered in my classroom in Small Town USA, discussing Wilder and Anderson and Steinbeck, while innocent people awakened to die that day. None of it seemed right. Why did some people live with privilege? Were certain people destined to die? My Nana always said that the good die young and when someone young dies, it was because God needed a beautiful angel in Heaven. Were they chosen because they were better human beings than the rest of us? Or less lucky? I couldn't imagine how a mother carried on after receiving the news of her child's untimely and senseless death. Now there was the crime.

Mrs. Newton's voice drifted back in . . .

"Sam, you always do such a good job with roles like this one. Would you read it for us, please?"

"I'm sorry, what did you say, Mrs. Newton?"

"Where were you, Sam?" She smiled kindly as my classmates snickered their amusement.

I loved Mrs. Newton, and she loved me. Simple as that. She made a huge impression on my life and was partially responsible for my wanting to be a writer.

"You've got a gift, Sam," she told me after reading my first paper. "You must use what you have. Stick to what you know, and trust your instincts. It's a gift. Respect it, celebrate it, and, most of all, share it. You're too good *not* to write."

"I was just thinking about the composition topic. Sorry."

"Sure you were, Sam!" taunted Chad. His cronies egged him on.

"Oh, Chad, you came out from under your rock to join the class. How special!" I sneered. My classmates applauded my comeback.

"Touché, DeSantis. You're back in the game." He winked at me.

Mrs. Newton shook her head–she loved the banter.

"I was asking if you would read the part of Mrs. Gibbs in *Our Town,* Sam. You have a marvelous voice with intuitive inflection. And you know this character from our discussions."

"Sure, Mrs. Newton," I headed for the front of the room, the designated stage for all dramatic renderings.

"I could do it, Mrs. NEWTRON!" blurted Chad, who had a habit of changing people's names. "My voice is rather marvelous too! I guarantee my rendition will be jazzier than Sam's." The class was now an attentive audience, awaiting the next witticism.

"I have no doubt, Mr. Donaldson."

Chad smirked at me. "So what's the deal, DeSantis?"

Mrs. Newton deferred to me, so I tipped my head and waved him on. "Be my guest."

"Okay, Chad, you're on! Grab your book and come up here," announced Mrs. Newton.

"Cool! You sure, Sam?" he taunted. "I wouldn't want to upstage you or nothing."

"You're a regular blast, Chad. Can't wait to see your interpretation. It will be so much better than algebra."

"Cute, DeSantis. You hate algebra," he replied. His cronies fell on the floor.

Mrs. Newton's eyes twinkled. "Okay, kids, let the play begin!"

Thirty-five

Friday, January 20, 1967

How can something so extraordinary change? When was the moment? One grain of sand slipped down, altering the balance.

The tricky part about our relationship was the time factor. Our conflicting schedules became the silent interloper. I went to school in the morning, he, the afternoon. We were both involved in school activities, and then there was homework. Buck studied obsessively to maintain his perfect average. Me, I could live with much less. Because of our curfew, we literally had to steal time to be together. It frustrated me to wait for the weekends to spend any real time with him, but I accepted it. *Next year will be different,* I told myself.

About halfway through January, right before mid-terms, irritability settled upon him like a fine rain, saturating every pore. As I said, he had his moods, which could be very trying. I never knew when they would appear or how long they would last. His moodiness made me uneasy. He wore a shield that no one could penetrate. At times I wanted to tell him to grow up, stop being so self-indulgent. *The world doesn't revolve around you, pal.* But I started to see that this behavior was embedded in who he was, and I'm not sure he could have changed. His erratic transformations began to trouble me on a deeper level. But I always pushed back my fears. In the race between emotion and logic, emotion won, hands down.

It was Friday night. We were walking home from his league basketball game at the church. He was unusually quiet, and I detected a change in his body language. I thought maybe he wasn't happy with the way he played.

"You okay?"

"Yeah, I'm fine." His smile was wrong, more forced.

"You played well tonight."

He nodded, avoiding eye contact. We walked up the hill to my house in silence, a silence unlike any we had ever shared. A disconnect. The deafening sound that hangs in the air when you have something to say but don't know how to say it.

"So, is it my breath?"

"What?" He looked at me as if I weren't there.

"Do I have bad breath or what?"

"What are you talking about? Your breath is fine." Not the response I was going for.

"It's just that you're so quiet tonight."

"I have a lot of stuff on my mind."

"School stuff?"

"Yes." His brusqueness spoke volumes.

"Got it."

We neared my house. The picture window glowed, casting light onto the snow. The lamppost stood like a beacon, awaiting my arrival.

"Are we still going bowling with Darlene and Sal tomorrow afternoon?"

"I'm not sure." He stared straight ahead. A hand reached inside my chest and squeezed.

"What aren't you sure about?"

"If I can go."

By the time we had reached my door, I knew he wasn't coming inside. This was more than just one of his moods.

"Are you coming in?" I asked anyway.

"I'd better go." He studied the ground.

"Okay."

"Come here, Sam."

"What's wrong?" The hand in my chest gripped tighter. Before I knew what was happening, his arms imprisoned me. He stood very still as he held me.

"You know how I feel about you, right, Sam?" His warm breath vaporized, feathery circles swirling around the side of my face and dissipating into the night.

"Why are you saying this?" I summoned up strength to break free to face him, but he held tight.

"You know, right?" The insistence in his voice forced my answer.

"Yes."

"Good." His body eased slightly. "Cause someday . . . someday when . . ." His words were choked by an invisible hand on his throat.

"Someday what? You're not making any sense." Panic crept through me like an insidious disease. "Buck, what's wrong? Are you sick or something?"

"No." He held tighter.

"Then what? Someday what?" Fear constricted movement. My brain screamed *pull back, look at his face.* But I was frozen.

"What's going on?" I whispered weakly.

"Nothing."

Finally, it was he who pulled away, revealing a defeated expression. "Listen, I have to go home now. Jane will kill me if I'm late." My throat thickened when he let go of my hand. "I have a math mid-term on Monday. I need to study tomorrow."

I wanted to say, *Who gives a shit about your stupid math test? You know you're going to ace it.* But the words were stuck.

"Bye, Sam."

When he stepped away, I felt my insides collapse. I watched him walk away, his form growing fainter until he was a shadow. The wind bit my face. It felt like snow. When finally I breathed in, the cold filtered through my lungs, numbing me.

He didn't call the next day.

Sunday, January 22, 1967

He didn't call on Sunday.

I went to 9 o'clock mass.

I wore the new plaid jumper my Nana had made for me.

I ate lasagna at Nana's house after church.

I napped on her couch while my little cousins ran around the house.

I played the puzzle race with my sister when we got home. She won.

I organized my closet and found a sweater that had been lost for a month.

I helped my mother bread the veal cutlets for dinner.

I washed the dinner dishes. My brother dried.

Mom made chocolate pie for dessert.

I finished my French homework for the whole week.

I didn't talk to Shelly when she called. Mom told her I was sleeping.

I took another nap. I could hear my dog breathing beside me on the rug.

I forgot to write in my diary.

I went to bed at 8 p.m.

I heard my mother open the door to check on me. I kept my eyes closed.

Nana's rosary glistened in the light that cast in from my neighbor's lamppost.

I lay awake, staring at the blank canvass of my ceiling.

Monday, January 23, 1967
6:30 a.m.

I didn't understand what was happening? How could things be fine one day and go crazy the next? My head swam, fighting for an answer.

I walked to school in a stupor. I toyed with the idea of staying home, faking illness, but I decided avoidance was the coward's way out.

Face the music, Sam.

Part of me just wanted it to be over.

Just do it, and let me move on!

The other part held out, blaming his behavior on academic pressure. I replayed the conversation over and over, analyzing his words, the stance of his body, the look in his eyes. Something was very wrong.

"Sam, what's the matter with you? Are you sick?" Shelly's face registered concern.

"No. I'm fine."

"You don't look fine. You look like shit."

"Thanks."

"Something must be wrong. Tell me."

"There's the bell. I have to go. I'll be late for class."

"Sam!" She bellowed out as I headed in the opposite direction, "Call me after school!"

The girls' room door swung shut. A colorless face stared at me from the wall-to-wall mirror.

"I do look like shit. I can't do this. I have to get out of here," I leaned over the sink to collect myself.

A girl walked out of one of the stalls and looked around the empty room. "Are you okay?"

"Yeah, I'm fine." I didn't care what she thought about the state of my sanity.

The nurse's office smelled of unpleasant medicine and disease. I hated going in there.

"Hi, Mrs. Jacobs. I'm not feeling well."

"What's the problem?" She eyed me suspiciously.

"I just started my period, and I have bad cramps." Lies. Normally, lies bothered me, but I had to escape.

"How bad are the cramps? Can't you take something and wait it out?"

"I took Pamparin this morning, and it's not helping. Please, Mrs. Jacobs, I can go to my grandmother's house. She lives close by. You can call her." Next time the cramps hit for real, I'd just have to suck it up.

"Okay. You do look like you're not feeling so well. Here's your pass. Let your teacher know before you leave."

"I will. Thanks, Mrs. Jacobs."

"And you had better make an appointment with your doctor, Samantha. Weren't you in here for the same problem last month?" She consulted her records.

A nod of shameful affirmation. I hated this. "I have bad periods." I did. But that wasn't the point at the moment.

"See your doctor, Sam. You can't be missing school for this every month."

"I know, Mrs. Jacobs. Thanks."

7:25 a.m.

Nana's house was my sanctuary: its walls did not judge, its eyes did not scold, its heart did not preach.

"Have a cup of tea. The hot will make your cramps feel better. I put in a little whiskey. It'll relax you."

"No whiskey, Nana. I have a lot of homework to do this afternoon."

"Okay, I'll drink this one and fix another cup for you. The water's still hot." She sipped from an old porcelain teacup as she returned to the kitchen.

I pulled the afghan up over my legs and curled into the couch. The warmth of the room that normally soothed me had no effect. And I was deceiving my sweet Nana. I knew I couldn't hang on to my pretense for long: she knew me too well. Nana and I had a strong connection. My father said I had her spirit. *You remind me of my mother. You have her way about you, Sammy.*

She handed me my tea in a blue-flowered china cup, the kind she saved for special occasions. Nana always knew what to do. "You don't look so good, honey. Are you sure it's just il vostro ciclo menstral, la maledizione?" *Your menstrual cycle, The Curse.* That's what my grandmother called it. On the other hand, my mother referred to my monthly cycle as "my friend." I was in my grandmother's camp on this one.

Our eyes met, and I knew there was no point in continuing the charade. "To tell the truth, Nana, it's Buck."

Her wise little head nodded up and down. "I thought something else was going on. What's up?"

"I'm not sure." Tears welled up in my eyes, and I tried to swallow the lump that was growing in my throat. But the tears were too close to the edge, and when l looked at my nana again, they spilled out.

"It's Buck," I sobbed.

"Ah, Ah, le questioni del cuore." *Issues of the heart.* "What of him?"

"Something's wrong, and I don't know what it is. I haven't talked to him since Friday."

"Mio Dio!" *My God!* "That was only two days ago!" She chuckled, not yet grasping the gravity of the situation.

"You don't understand. I think he's going to break up with me, Nana."

"Break up with you? Oh, I don't think so. He really likes you, Sammy. I can tell by the way he acts around you, il mio amore." *My love.* Her face was tender, concerned. Even though over half a century hung between us, she was in touch with my feelings.

"I thought so too, but he was acting funny on Friday, and I haven't talked to him since then."

"Impazienza di gioventù." *Youth's impatience.* "He'll call. Maybe he has other things to do."

"No, Nana, something is really wrong."

"Ah, Sammy. Giovane amore." *Young love.* "Such a touch-and-go thing. You're only sixteen, my beauty. If he breaks up with you, you'll meet other boys, and you'll get over him."

The ache in my heart pumped through my blood, traveling to every inch of my body. "No, I won't, Nana. I love him." My head dropped into my hands, and my grandmother patted my back as I wept out my pain.

"Oh, dear Lord, you do love him, don't you?"

I spent the morning on her couch while she wore a path from the kitchen to the living room checking on me.

"Dormire ora." *Sleep now,* advised my Nana.

When I awakened, the pain had doubled. I ate some homemade chicken and meatball soup. Then I walked home.

12:05 p.m.

It was waiting for me when I walked through the door, staring at me from the credenza in the foyer. I stared back, willing it to go away. The postmark was Saturday's. The words he could not speak were in print for me to read and reread until I had to vomit.

Dear Sam,

I'm writing to explain what I did this afternoon. All last week I had been thinking how little I get to see you, and recently, with exams coming up, I am lucky if I see you once a week. I'm not talking about meeting on the school steps for ten minutes in between classes because that doesn't count. I don't think it should be like this. You go to school in the morning, and I go in the afternoon, and when the weekend rolls around, there are always the basketball games. I never know what you are doing, and you don't know what I'm doing. It shouldn't be this way.

I've reflected on how well we have always gotten along. We never had any big fights—maybe a few minor disagreements, but I don't even remember what they were about now. I only remember the good times we've shared. I'll never forget the time we spent together and the neat things we've done.

I want you to know that you didn't do anything wrong. I'm not mad at you. I just think it's time we stopped seeing each other for a while and started going out with other kids. We can always see each other at dances and games and still remain the best of friends, I hope. Maybe we could even go out again.

These last seven months we've been together have been the happiest months of my life. I hope you don't mind if I keep your picture from Miss CHS because it will always remind me of you and how sweet you are. I'd like to see you some time soon, if that's all right with you.

Well, I guess I've said enough for now. Take care of yourself and always be the good girl you are now. Okay? I hope this doesn't hurt our friendship any because I never want to lose that.

BEST OF FRIENDS ALWAYS,
BUCK

4:35 p.m.

My mother knocked on the door and found me sitting on my bed, the letter still opened in my hand.

"What's going on, honey?" Mom was the one who retrieved the mail every day. She knew about the letter. She knew what was going on. She had observed me for the last forty-eight hours.

"Buck broke up with me. And he didn't even do it in person. He wrote me a letter. A letter! And he signed it BEST OF FRIENDS ALWAYS. Isn't that the stupidest thing you've ever heard in a break-up letter? Bastard!"

My mother flinched at my choice of words but promptly let it go. I turned toward the window as tears began to spill out again.

"Sam, I'm sorry. I know how much you like him."

I stared at the kids in the yard next door. They were lying on their backs making snow angels. I could hear them laughing. I wanted to be them—released from my body and my pain.

"Sam?"

I was still looking out the window when I spoke again. "See, that's the thing, Mom. I don't just like him—I love him." Saying the words aloud made the pain dig deeper.

I could feel her studying my face. "I'm sure you think you love him now, but . . ."

I never looked up. "I don't think . . . I know."

She pressed no more because she knew too. "Is that the letter?"

"Yes!" Anger suddenly surged through me. Thank God. I preferred it to the exhaustion of despondency.

"May I read it, or is it too private?"

I thrust the letter forward. "Burn it for all I care! It's a stupid letter anyway! Just a vehicle for him to allay his guilt. Coward! He should have told me on Friday when he was acting like a jerk."

As my mother read the letter, I watched her face, attempting to decipher what was going through her head. She nodded a couple of times. I waited for her to say something, to give me her take on things.

"Well, it's a nice letter. He just seems to need some space. He refers to you as a 'good girl.' That's a compliment, you know. Maybe he's just looking for something else right now."

"I don't care what he's looking for. I hate him for making me feel this way! I hate him for acting like I was the only girl in the world and for making me fall in love with him. Then he says he wants to be with other people. 'Oh, and by the way, Sam, these have been the happiest months of my life.' He's so full of it! What a liar. I hate him for doing this to me!"

Mom sat down next to me and handed me his letter. "Is there anything I can do?"

"No." I stared straight ahead. Normally I welcomed the comfort of my mother's presence, but at that moment I needed to be alone.

"I can fix you something to eat."

"I'm not hungry."

"Want me to bring your Barbara Streisand records up from the dining room? That always puts you in a good mood."

"No. I just want to be by myself."

"Okay. I'll be downstairs if you need me." She paused at the door long enough to draw my attention to her again. "Sam, I know you can't believe this right now, but you will survive. You're strong, honey. You'll look back on this and realize that it was just a high school romance."

What? Does she really believe that malarkey? She fell in love when she was my age. But I didn't have the energy to fight. Instead, I tossed my pillow to the bottom of the bed and lay back in response. The door closed, and I heard her shuffle down the stairs. I lay there, staring at the shelf over my headboard. It held all of my favorite books. I remember how vocally Mom had objected to its placement.

"Put it on the side wall, Sam. It'll look better there."

"Actually," my dad piped in, "I agree with Sam. Above the bed."

"But she'll fill it with all of her hardcover books, and it won't be safe."

"Peg, I'll locate the studs and anchor it securely. It'll be fine."

"Well, if it falls down on her head in the middle of the night, you're to blame!"

Looking at the bookshelf, I wondered: *Maybe I'll be lucky, and the shelf will fall on me during the night, killing me instantly. If it hit while I was asleep, I probably wouldn't feel much. A painless death. But then my bloody demise would bring such grief to my parents, they wouldn't be able to carry on. Ruined lives! I can hear it all now.*

Did you hear what happened to the DeSantis girl?

Yes, smashed senseless in the safety of her own bedroom.

So tragic!

And they were such a happy family.

To add insult to injury, it would be my fault for willing such a violent end, simply to eradicate my own pain. The height of selfishness! I'd probably walk around the bowels of Hell feeling guilty for eternity.

"Damn! I wonder what level of Hell that would put me in? And I'm guessing the place would be devoid of chocolate." I sat up and grabbed my diary from my dresser.

"Enough wallowing!" I decided to focus on what irritated me most about him. So I created a list to make myself feel better.

What Pisses Me off about Buck Kendall!

1. ***His aloofness drives me crazy. Who does he think he is?***
2. ***His deliberate silences are self-indulgent. Selfish, selfish, SELFISH!***
3. ***His bad moods, which he doesn't come out of even to say hello to my parents, are beyond rude! What happened to those reputedly good manners, huh Kendall?***
4. ***Watching his jaw clench and the muscles tighten in his face is always a sure sign of a mood swing and trouble. I'm so sick of enduring his bad moods!***
5. ***He holds onto anger like a final breath. Does he think he's the only one who ever gets pissed off? HOLD YOUR BREATH TILL YOU DIE!***
6. ***He is self-absorbed. What makes him think he's so wonderful and so cute? Conceited boys are obnoxious.***
7. ***His know-it-all attitude is totally infuriating. So what if he's smart! Who gives a shit? Smart isn't everything. BE A LOSER JEOPARDY CONTESTANT, WHY DON'T YOU?***
8.

I couldn't think of anything for No. 8. Upon reviewing my list, I realized my mom was right—he was difficult, and we were entirely opposite. I hated conflict and was incapable of holding long-standing grudges. Grudges ate me up. In fact, when things bugged me, I spit out everything on my mind. Spilled it all, detail by irritating detail. If I didn't let out the poison, I would shut down. And if I ever shut down, everyone would know I was in bad shape because talking and venting are my therapy.

I closed my diary and put on the Beach Boys. Bad choice. They reminded me too much of him. "Maybe I should call Shelly or Darlene," I said aloud. "No, Shelly would only make things worse, and Darlene would be so sympathetic that I would never stop crying." I didn't know what to do with myself, and I couldn't shake his face from my head.

Six-thirty. I went to bed. I could hear my mother washing the dinner dishes all by herself.

Thirty-six

Tuesday, January 24, 1967
6 a.m.

Why am I losing sleep over you?

—Gary Puckett

"I didn't mean it. I don't know why I said those things. I'm an asshole. You know I can't live without you, D."

He was walking toward me, but he wasn't getting any closer.

"I don't want to be just friends. I could never be just friends with you, Samantha. Ever since the first time I saw you, I have been in love with you."

I reached out to touch him. He was so close, and I desperately needed to touch him. "Why did you do this? I don't understand."

"We're so young, Sam. I met you too soon."

"Too soon?"

"I have to go . . . but someday . . ." He was fading.

"Someday what?" I couldn't see him anymore, but I could still hear his voice.

"Someday, we'll be . . ."

"Sammy, wake up." Lucy was shaking me. It's time for school. Who you talking to, anyway?"

The images disoriented me. "He was just going to tell me why."

"There's nobody in here. You better get ready, or you'll be late."

I sat upright in my bed and gazed around the room to stabilize myself. "I guess I was dreaming. What are you doing up already, Luce?"

"Mommy's making fried dough with butter and sugar."

"She is? Why is she making that today?" Fried dough was reserved for special occasions.

"She said it might make you feel better." She eyes me curiously. "You're not sick, are you." Not a question.

"No."

"You feel bad because of Buck, huh?"

SLAM! Right in the gut.

"I have to get dressed now, Lucy. Thanks for waking me up."

"Okay." She proceeded toward the door, stopped, and returned to the side of the bed where she wrapped her arms around my neck. "You'll be okay, Sammy."

That put me over the edge.

Wednesday, January 25, 1967
10 a.m.

The road gets rougher
It's lonelier and tougher.
With hope you burn up,
Tomorrow he may turn up.
There's just no letup
The livelong night and day.

—Harold Arlen

I am inside the telephone booth, isolated, looking out at the rest of the world going about its usual business. A film of glass separates me from reality, blurs my vision. I exist in my own space. People are looking in at me. They are trying to talk to me. I can see their mouths forming words, but I cannot hear their sounds. They want to help me; I can tell by their expressions. But they cannot extricate me, and I'm suffocating.

I walk around the halls of Carlson in a fog. I seek circuitous routes to avoid my friends and their questions. Every now and then someone says, "Hi, Sam! How's Buck?" Their words grind broken glass into my heart.

And the walls grow thicker.

I skip student council meetings, dance committee meetings, sorority meetings. I race out the door the second the bell rings and head straight home. I complete my homework before dinner, a sure sign of mental illness. My mother's concern escalates.

Consumed. Preoccupied. Overwhelmed at the thought of having to live one more day without him.

And it owns you.

* * *

When you're down and troubled
And you need a helping hand
And nothing is going right . . .

—Carole King

Thank God for girlfriends. My life would not be the same without them. They calm me, hold me up, and heal me—even when there's nothing to fix. Girlfriends tend to one another with just the right blend of mothering and reality. They understand your tears and listen when you need them. You can repeat your stories as many times as you want; they still listen. Unlike most males I know, women are drawn to each other to fill that space that thrives only on the comfort of other women. I think men are devoid of this space. Clearly, I would not be complete without my girlfriends.

My girls saw me through the next few weeks. They made a pact that one of them would hang out with me at all times so I wasn't by myself. Darlene made a double batch of chocolate fudge, and we ate the whole thing while singing along with the Lettermen. Heaven. Shelly delivered a generous portion of her mom's beef stew and some of her best outfits—amazingly kind gesture—and we hung in my room, exchanging outfit for outfit. Annie resurrected me, regaling me with her best stories, although I'm not sure if they were for my benefit or her amusement. Regardless, she made me laugh. And their most magnanimous gesture was when they put aside their disdain for screen musicals and accompanied me to a matinee of *My Fair Lady*. I usually saw those with my mom.

God bless my girls; they tried to say all the right things, including their well-intentioned assurances that I would meet someone new.

"Sam, there are lots of boys who are dying to go out with you."

"Maybe you and Brian could start up something now. He's so gorgeous."

"Don't worry. You'll meet someone who will wipe Buck right out of your head."

What about my heart?

I lost myself in the company of others whose lives were riddled with angst. I felt Scarlett O'Hara's pain as she fought for love, only to discover that it was not in the arms of the man she had ruthlessly pursued. *Wake up!* But Rhett left her, just when she realized he was the one. My heart broke for Jake Barnes who was physically stripped of his ability to love Brett Ashley. Yet she continued to burn through him, reigniting the flame that no amount of alcohol could quench. And she, saddled with a perpetual yearning and the torture in his eyes, could find no other man to make it better. *Hemingway! Change the words. Eradicate the dull ache that is their lives.* But it was too late. So I turned to Jay Gatsby, who was incapable of moving on, his obsessive love for Daisy consuming him. *Let her go . . . she's not worth it!* He didn't listen either. No one ever does when it comes to love. I grieved for all of them. And as I did, I thought *I'm not going to be like them.*

Thirty-seven

Thursday, February 16, 1967
9:15 a.m.

"Sam, we're going to the basketball game tomorrow night, and you're coming with us," Shelly announced. She was standing in front of the first floor bulletin board, checking out the week's activities.

"I don't want to go to the game," I replied firmly.

"He won't be there."

A familiar pang coursed through me. Talking about him made his existence more present.

"How do you know that?"

"Greg said he's sick and his mother won't let him play 'cause it might make him worse."

At that moment, a couple walked by, holding hands. Whenever the boy looked at her, she giggled.

"Sam?"

"Yeah."

The girl looked at him longingly when they parted for class, but she was still smiling. My smile had gone to sleep.

"Did you hear me?" Shelly sounded like a correctional officer.

I nodded. "Are you sure, Shelly?"

"Yes! Greg told me he's been out of school with the flu or something like that. And it should be a good game. We're playing the Flames. They have some really cute boys on their team."

Who cares!

"I don't know, Shel. I think I'd rather stay in."

"Sam, you can't stay in forever. It'll be good for you to get out." I wasn't convinced. "He won't be there," she urged.

I knew she was right. I had to keep moving forward. "Okay, I'll go."

Friday, February 17, 1967
7:45 p.m.

Basketball games were a major social event in Carlson. Everyone flocked to the gym and crammed into the bleachers, huddling with friends and screaming for the Carlson Chiefs. The cheerleaders, in their red and white uniforms, shook their pom-poms at the crowd and led us in the fight song.

The game was tied. The Chiefs were having an exceptionally good season, so the fans held high hopes for another victory. After halftime, the team poured back onto the court to the roar of an appreciative crowd. Our players looked strong; they nodded to one another as if they shared a secret. Darlene stood up in the middle of the bleachers and cheered shamelessly for Sal. From within the pack of players, Sal smiled conspicuously and waved to her. The other players gave him a hard time.

I was having a decent time. Basketball was my favorite spectator sport. After my fear of running into Buck had dissipated, I got into the songs and cheers, not to mention the popcorn. The team was warming up for the second half. Ben, who happened to be the tallest player on both teams, was performing for the crowd. Everybody waited for this moment because he was hilarious. When he rolled into his Globe Trotter moves, "Sweet Georgia Brown" blared over the loud speakers, and the crowd went wild. Second only to Ben's antics were Greg's. The two, who had long been best friends, entertained the crowd for a while, and the coach allowed it to go on a bit longer than he should have. Finally the referee blew the whistle, signaling the time for the jump ball to start the third quarter. Play resumed, but neither side made any headway. With the game in a temporary stalemate, our attention drifted. Annie and I kidded Darlene about her blatant behavior with Sal during halftime.

"Holy shit!" Shelly's tone nearly jolted us out of our seats.

"Jesus! What? You scared the life out of me." Annie stood up to peer onto the court. "Did someone get hurt?"

"No." Shelly's hand went to her mouth. Then she turned to me. "Buck's here."

His name sliced into me like a knife.

"You said he was sick!" accused Annie.

"That's what Greg told me," Shelly defended.

"Where is he?" asked Darlene, searching the room.

"Right there. See him, on the end of the bench," said Shelly. They all stood up to look.

"Oh, I see him. He doesn't look sick to me," added Darlene.

"How the hell can you tell that from over here?" Annie pitched in, all the while craning to see him herself. "Yep, that's Buck!"

Jab! Jab! Jab! Bull's eye to the heart.

Sure enough, across the court sat Buck on the bench with his team. Not in uniform, he was apparently there to support the Chiefs. Pain coursed though me.

"When did he get here?" asked Annie. "I didn't see him before."

"He wasn't here before," confirmed Shelly. "He must have come during halftime."

A numbing sensation crept up my face. "I have to get out of here."

"Sam, you can't get up and walk out now. That would be the worst," advised Annie.

"She's right, Sam. Everyone will see you." Darlene regarded me with sympathetic eyes.

"I'm sorry, Sam. Greg said Buck was staying home," pleaded Shelly.

"Please stop saying his name." My head hurt. *I can't do this.*

"It's almost the fourth quarter. Just try to watch the game. That will distract you," said Annie.

On the court, it was a face-off. Point for point. Neither side was advancing. Greg looked at the clock and called for a time-out. The red and white shirts went to one side, the gold and black to the other. The cheerleaders led us in a familiar victory chant. Kids clapped and stomped their feet on the bleachers, creating a thunder that blocked out the sounds in my head. I closed my eyes.

No one heard the whistle blow, so the referees approached both sides of the gymnasium and warned the fans to keep it down. Two minutes remained on the clock. Two minutes: a lifetime. The players walked back on the court. Greg had the ball. He started dribbling and passing to waste time. He sent the ball to Sal, who passed it to Ben, who sent it back to Greg. This stalling tactic went on for a while, occasionally including other players to mix up the routine. The Carlson fans shouted their impatience.

SHOOT!

The Flames' players lost their cool. They swore at each other and at their failed attempts to steal the ball. The ref issued a warning. Greg grinned and dribbled in place, shifting the ball adeptly from hand to hand just to mess with the player who was guarding him. He wore confidence as he glanced up at the clock. The fans began to chant, picking up momentum as they cheered.

Shoot! Shoot! Shoot!

Suddenly Greg went into signature motion, rushing the hoop. As he leapt into the air, he faked it and passed the ball to Ben, who handled it like a hot potato and sent it flying back to Greg. Greg moved toward the open mouth of the net, and just as he was about to shoot, he twisted his body toward Ben and released the ball. Ben snatched it, barely moving, and dunked the ball with ease. Poetry. The whistle blew, and the Chief fans were on their feet. Hats, mittens, and empty popcorn containers flew into to the air while the team slapped one another and hauled Greg onto their shoulders. Selfless to the end, he passed off the winning ball.

I must have been holding my breath because when I exhaled, I felt a mild sense of relief.

It's over. I gotta get out of here. Now.

My friends were lost in the victory. Grateful to blend into the merging crowd, I focused on my escape, lowering my head and moving steadily along. With each step down the bleachers, I forced myself not to look around. Finally, we neared the door.

"Sam, where are you?" yelled Shelly.

"I'm right here. By the door."

"Good. Let's go, ladies," Shelly was in her orchestrating mode.

Then Darlene spoke up. "I'm waiting here for Sal."

"Darlene! You didn't tell us that," accused Shelly.

"What difference does it make?" yelled Annie above the noise. "Keep moving. If we don't get to Tony's before this crowd, we'll never get a booth."

At that point I mustered up my nerve, fearing that my words might lead to unpleasant repercussions. "Guys, I'm going to pass on the pizza." Amidst the jubilance and mayhem, our inner circle became silent.

Annie's eyebrows arched. "Really?" Then her expression softened. "You know, I don't really want pizza either. I'll walk home with you, Sam."

"Me either," agreed Shelly. For as much as she loved to make the scene and be in the limelight, she was putting me first. At that precise moment, she proved why I called her my friend.

"If you want, we can go to my house and get some food," Shelly continued.

"Right on. Let's get going then," said Annie, keeping the tempo upbeat.

We exited. Grateful for the loyalty of my friends, I breathed deeply. The cold air felt like freedom. We hurried down the steps, arm in arm, and when we reached the bottom, there he stood. Staring at me. My chest tightened.

"Let's get the hell out of here." I broke away and headed relentlessly through the parking lot.

I had the dream again that night. And like the last time and the time before, he turned and walked away.

Thirty-eight

Ten Days Later
10:05 a.m.

"The sophomore class is sponsoring a dance this Friday." Shelly turned from the bulletin board and grinned. "I love dances! We have to decide what we're wearing. My house. After school."

"I'm not going." I was resolute.

"They hell you're not!" barked Annie. "Kiddo, you have to do something else besides reading all those heavy books. Those things can bring you down."

"She's right, Sam. And how much Barbara Streisand can you listen to?"

Annie's left eyebrow nearly reached the top of her forehead. "What planet are you on, Porterfield? She listens to Babs even when she's happy. That's not gonna change."

Even when she's happy. The words hung in the air.

"Who says I'm not happy?" I defended. "I'm happy! I read because I love literature. You do remember that I am an English major." Then I faced Shelly squarely. "And I listen to Barbara because her voice is an instrument and her songs make me happy."

"Right." Shelly wasn't buying it.

"You're going to the dance, Sam. We'll be with you." Annie's face was a dare.

"Fine. See you at twelve-thirty." I walked away.

"Groovy!" yelled Annie after me. "You're one cool chick, DeSantis!"

I halted and swiveled back toward her. "Don't call me chick!"

Friday, March 3, 1967
7 p.m.

To make money for the senior prom, each class sponsored school dances. Kids flocked to the gym and danced until the lights went up. Live bands played the songs we loved. School dances defined us.

We stood in a huddle outside the gym, pulling out our money.

"Now, Sam, you're probably going to see him tonight. The sophomore class sponsored the dance," reminded Shelly.

"She knows, Porterfield," Annie chided.

"It's been over a month now. So that should help," added Shelly.

"Six weeks."

A collective set of eyes stared at me. No one knew what to say.

"You look really pretty tonight, Sam." Dependable Darlene.

We headed inside the gym. The place was packed.

"Oh my God! He's selling the tickets." Shelly. "What are the chances of that?"

"Actually, pretty high, Shel. He's class president, remember?" Annie rolled her eyes.

Shelly ignored her. "You have to give your money to him, Sam. He did this on purpose so you'd have to see him. I just know it."

Despite the time that had elapsed since the break-up, I was still fairly raw. Granted, there had been no fight between us, nor had there been any particular reason for his leaving, besides his claim that we didn't have the time to see each other often enough. *And*, he felt the need to be single and date other girls. One of the girls in my sorority, Jenny Watkins, told me that he had announced his plan to date every girl in the sophomore class now that he was free. *Knock yourself out, pal*! A week later she told me he looked lost all the time and confessed that he had made a big mistake breaking up with me. You'd think I would be elated to hear this information, but I would have been better off not knowing. I was doing fine as long as I didn't have to see him or consider his existence. Seeing him reopened the wound, which was healing at a snail's pace as it was. So I decided if I lived and breathed in a world without him, I would be fine. I went to great lengths to avoid him—it was the less painful route. And now, Jenny's words presented hope, but I simply could not deal with possibilities formed on thin ice. I would not let myself get set up.

"Sam, he's looking this way," said Shelly. "And he's holding the wheel of tickets."

"Isn't someone else selling tickets?" Darlene searched the area. "Yes! Look! Julia Davis is selling them at the other end of the table. Let's go to her."

"Good idea. Then he'll see you when we pass by. Make him suffer!" Shelly.

"Candyasses!" Annie stopped us in our tracks. "Samantha DeSantis, I will not allow you to back down. You've got the chops for this! Show him what you're made of."

I gazed from her to Buck and back. I stood on shaky ground, and they all sensed it.

"And," she continued, "if you buckle under, you have your entourage to protect you."

"Thanks for the vote of confidence," I retorted. Yet somehow, her words goaded me on.

"Just telling it like it is. So what's it gonna be?" she challenged.

"What do you think, Sam?" asked Darlene, the only one who ever gave me a break.

"Come on, Sam. Annie's right." Porterfield moved closer to her new ally.

In the long days since January 20, I had resurrected myself from a pile of broken pieces. Now, as I stood facing my army of supporters, I wondered if I had the stamina to move forward and chance destruction.

"Let's go." My conviction won.

"Ladies, we're bookin'! Let's buy our tickets from the boy who didn't know how damn good he had it," announced Annie. "Come on, Sam!"

"You look really pretty tonight, Sam. Remember that when you see him. He'll probably eat his heart out when he sees you." Darlene patted my shoulder.

We approached the ticket table.

Breathe.

"Hi, ladies," greeted Buck. His smile was genuine, his gaze unfaltering.

"Hi." The ever sweet Darlene.

"Hi, Buck," sang Shelly. Shameless hussy.

"Oh, Buck, I didn't see you there. Here, I need change for this five." The smart-ass. She sort of flung the five at him and held out her hand for change as she surveyed the room. Her treatment of him as a personal serf didn't seem to faze him. He returned the three dollars without a hint of awkwardness.

"Hi, Sam."

"Hi."

"How are you?" He slipped the money from my hand to his.

"Good. You?" His hand touched me, the sensation sinking in too deeply.

"Fine."

Why did I come here? This is too hard.

"Let's go see who's here." Shelly grabbed my arm.

"See you, Sam."

Don't say my name.

A set of bleachers held the coats, and we tossed ours onto the pile. I stuffed my mittens in the pockets so I'd know which coat was mine.

"You did good Sam. Are you all right?" Darlene asked.

I nodded. "I'm good." I wasn't.

"Okay, let's check out the action." Annie looked around the room.

I fought the urge to glance back as we blended into the sea of teens. On a make-shift stage at the far end of the gym, Billy and the Boppers were singing. The mood was easy and light, thank God. Seeing Buck had jolted me, and I couldn't shake the feeling of his touch.

Darlene regarded me with concern. "Are you okay?"

"Yeah, I'm fine." I was still experiencing an out-of-body sensation and wanted a couple of minutes to stabilize. I had managed to survive the last six weeks without him and didn't need any set-backs.

"You sure?"

She knew. "I'm sure." I smiled appreciatively.

"Want to go to the snack table and get a Pepsi?"

"Great idea." My mouth was lined with sandpaper again. I was getting used to the taste.

Suddenly Shelly was upon me.

"Sam, you're doing good so far. Now we need to find someone for you to dance with. If Buck still likes you, that'll make him jealous."

A pain shot through my gut.

"We just got here, Shelly. Leave her alone for a little while. Let her drink her Pepsi."

"But we need to make sure she looks like she's having fun, not just standing here wasting time drinking Coke."

"Pepsi," Darlene corrected.

"Who cares!" she snapped. Then she directed her words to me. "You need to have fun."

"Who says I'm not having fun?"

"Well, you sure don't look like it."

Darlene shot a reproachful glance. "Leave her alone. She doesn't need this right now. We got her out, didn't we?"

"I'm just trying to help." While her sincerity was apparent, her relentless march toward revenge overshadowed good will. "What if he asks you to dance? You gonna cave or make him suffer?"

Why is she pestering me with these questions?

"Sam, are you listening? What if he asks you to dance?"

I turned to my unremitting friend. "He won't."

"But what if he does ask?" repeated Darlene genuinely. "He keeps looking at you."

This was a mistake.

"It's time to think now, Sam!" The girl just kept pushing.

At that moment, Annie intervened. "Whoa, Shelly, working on the boot camp voice? Better pay attention, Sam. She means business." Everyone chuckled but Shelly.

"Boot camp voice? Where'd you come up with that?" She glared.

I decided to let Shelly off the hook. "She's just trying to help, Annie."

"I *am* just trying to help. Thank you, Sam! At least somebody recognizes it."

"And I appreciate it. But can't we stop thinking for a while and relax?"

"Fine." Her pout emerged. "But don't blame me if he comes over here and you're unprepared. And he might, you know. He acted like he still likes you when you bought your ticket."

Thankfully, the band interrupted:

Come on, baby
Let's do the twist

"I love Chubby Checker. Sam, dance with me." Annie pulled me onto the floor—Shelly and Darlene joined us.

"This is great exercise," said Shelly. "Good for the waist."

I didn't give a damn about her waist—or mine. I was twisting. And I kept twisting till my sides ached. Beautiful, glorious, welcoming pain to release me from myself. Mercifully, the song ended and another, less exhausting, began.

"I love this song!" Darlene jumped into the air. "Be my back-up singers!"

I lost myself in the base guitar and the spiraling sounds around me. I was a back-up singer, on stage at the Fox Theater in Motown. The crowd was going wild. *More*, they shouted. *Encore*! It felt good not to think. Just dance and sing and lose yourself and . . . "Okay, we're gonna slow it down now."

What?

The tempo dropped, and so did the lights. Everyone began pairing up, wrapping around each other. In my head I was still dancing on the stage.

Time to shift.

I readied myself to stand along the sidelines when I felt a tap on my shoulder. "Wanna dance, Sammy?" Taken aback, I swung around only to be greeted by the broad and luminous smile of my friend Brian.

"Brian! Are you ever a sight for sore eyes!" He scooped me into his arms, hugging me tightly. He made me feel safe.

"How's my best girl?"

"Pretty good. Especially now that you're here."

"I figured the old pact might come in handy tonight. We're both solo." Brian's smile eased my loneliness.

"You figured right."

"So, you gonna dance with me or what?"

He waltzed me onto the floor. I knew other people were watching, mainly because he was so good-looking, but I liked the attention anyway. It made me feel less pitiable. His voice lowered into my ear. "Did you see Buck?"

"Yes."

"Did you talk to him?"

"No, we just said hello."

"Isn't this the second time you've run into him?" Only a friend would keep track of such details. And a guy at that.

"Right. I'm impressed, Determan!"

He grinned. "Hey, I've got to look out for my best girl. So did he speak to you when you saw him last time?"

"No, he just stared, and I got out of there as quickly as I could."

"Listen, I know this is really tough on you. But hang in there, kiddo. Don't let him see that you're hurting." He pressed his lips into my ear. "I think he still likes you."

I pulled back. "Don't say that, Brian."

"Why? I do."

"I can't think that way. I just have to keep moving forward."

"Got it, doll. Whatever you say. You know, other girls would be hanging on those words. But not you, Sammy. You're something!"

I shook my head dismissively. His constant praise embarrassed me. "Thanks, Brian."

"No more talk. Let's show 'em how it's done." He tightened his grip around my waist, directing me in a graceful double turn. I loved dancing with Brian. It was so easy to follow him. Unlike most high school boys, who circled aimlessly, Brian knew the difference between a foxtrot and a waltz.

"Sammy, your Arthur Murray dance classes are paying off! We make a good team. Most of these girls can't follow for shit. Hey, how about if I walk you home? I can keep your dance card filled, and later we can stop by Tony's for a pepperoni pizza."

"That's sweet, but I came with the girls."

"So. Isn't there a rule or something that says walking home with a boy trumps the girl thing?"

"If you're an established couple," I clarified, as if I were reminding him of the rules of parliamentary procedure.

"What about friends of the opposite sex? Isn't that legal?"

"I guess good friends might supersede the girl rule."

"Supersede?" He laughed heartily. "Ah, I love you, Sammy girl. You're not like these other chicks. You're the real deal. You know what I think?"

"Not a clue."

"I think that if we're both single when we're thirty, we should get married. Fred and Ginger. We can dance our lives away. Deal?"

"Thirty, eh? You planning to be a playboy till then?" I teased.

"Maybe. What if nobody good comes along?"

"I'd say you'll have the pick of the litter. All of them." He threw his head back in amusement, which was what I was going for. "Okay, Determan. But, you'll never stay single that long. Some girl will snap you up."

The song ended. "I'm going to work the room now, Sammy. If you need me, whistle."

"I never mastered the art."

He snorted. "You're a piece of work! See you in a few."

When I returned to my friends, they were clenched together like a closed fist, chatting intently as their eyes followed Brian.

"You and Brian looked really good out there. Smooth move dancing with him." Annie patted my shoulder.

"He dances better than anyone else here. And he's soooo cute! Is he going out with anybody?" As she spoke, she tracked him like a hawk.

"Not now. He sort of liked Linda Ainsley for a while, but that didn't really work out."

"Why?"

"She got too clingy."

"I can see why. So he's available?"

Honest to God!

"Isn't Larry here, Shelly?" I reminded.

"Why?"

"Why? Because the last I knew you were still going with him."

"I love this song!" Annie burst forth. "It's the best slow song ever!" She began swaying in position as she sang along with the Beach Boys. Couples flooded the dance floor.

"Sam," Darlene tugged on my sleeve. I ignored her, irritated by Shelly's designs on my friend.

"We're probably going to break up," said Shelly off-handedly.

Her egocentric attitude put me off. "Do you have any moral guidelines whatsoever?"

"What are you talking about? I just asked if he was available. It's not like I asked you to tell him I like him or something." Harmonious voices filled the gym.

There's a world where I can go and tell my secrets to.
In my room, in my room.

"Sam," Darlene tugged more urgently this time, "I think you better . . ." Our circle was huddled tightly, the intensity of the conversation shutting out the rest of the world. Before I had a chance to respond to Darlene, I heard the voice.

"Hey, D. Dance with me?"

The talking stopped cold. I turned around. There he stood.

"Okay." Like a damn robot.

He reached for my hand, and everything else melted away. We stepped into the mix. His arm slid around my waist. *Breathe.* At first he maintained a respectful distance, the space between us forming a protective wall for which I was initially grateful. He moved me gently, subtly. Then his hand pressed into the small of my back. The room became hazy.

Do my dreaming and my scheming lie awake at night?

He drew me closer, his shirt brushing me when we turned. *What's happening?* He lowered his head, as if to speak, and I felt his skin brush my face. The warmth intoxicated me. *Breathe.*

The Beach Boys crooned louder, and when the music swelled, he pressed his hand deeper into my back. Instinctually, I tightened my arm around his neck. The heat from his face was a familiar drug.

Do my crying and my sighing laugh at yesterday?

He tucked my hand, which he had first held tentatively, into the spot between his chest and mine. Sensation further drowned out the room. He dropped his head into the base of my neck. His breath was on me. When his footing changed, so did mine. We fit together, just as we always had.

Remember what he put you through, Sam.

I thought I could feel his heart beating though his shirt. Was I imagining it?

Why did I dance with him? This is too hard.

The song ended. He stopped but did not change position. His hands were still on me, his head lowered over my shoulder. I was immobilized. Since our dance had begun, no words passed. Finally, he pulled back. His face wore repentance, eyes pleading for a second chance.

* * *

When we are in love, we often doubt that which we most believe.

—Francois de la Rochefoucauld

"You're letting him walk you home?" Shelly's words registered shock. "Are you crazy?" As I searched for my jacket in the pile of look-alikes, I worked overtime to avoid her questions.

"You are caving awfully fast, Sam." Annie shoved her hands into the pockets of her parka.

I didn't answer.

"Well, if you're going to go home with him, at least don't let him kiss you!" Shelly commanded.

I flung my scarf around the neck of my pea coat. "What are you talking about?"

"When he walks you home tonight, if he tries to kiss you or hold your hand, don't let him."

"Why?"

"'Cause it will make him want you more. He's got to pay. God, Sam, have you forgotten what he put you through? I haven't. I was there. He broke your heart!"

"I have to agree, Sam. The light inside you went out." Annie nodded toward Shelly.

Then Darlene piped in, "Let her make her own decisions. No one knows how she feels. We don't know what Buck was thinking or what just passed between them when they danced. But I'm sure Sam knows. She's always been a pretty good judge of character, and she knows Buck better than we do. Lots of people break up. It's not like he cheated on her. We have to trust Sam's judgment and support her. We're her friends. It could happen to any one of us."

Annie regarded Darlene with resignation. "When did you get so wise?"

"Guys, thanks. I'm walking home with him."

"Go for it then . . ." added Annie. "But protect your heart."

"Don't let him kiss you, Sam! And call me tonight!" Shelly. "I want a full report."

"Good luck, Sammy." Darlene smiled warmly.

*   *   *

Standing on my front steps was different that night. It was no longer pure. I wanted to close my eyes and erase the time we had spent apart. Where had we gone? Why had he interrupted our seamless dance with his doubts and desires? I wondered if we could ever be the same. Uncertainty formed a buffer between us.

"I guess I'd better go inside. It's almost eleven."

He smiled. "Curfew. I know." The words of familiarity tugged at me.

"Thanks for walking me home."

"It was good to be with you tonight, Sam." He stared at me for an awkward moment. I wondered if he felt the presence of the stranger between us. If so, he ignored him and leaned in, nearly penetrating the barrier. Fear wrestled with hope. I retreated.

"Good night."

He stepped back. "Night, Sam." He looked like the Buck I first met, and I wanted to run down the steps and throw my arms around him. Instead, I turned and walked inside.

The face of the grandfather clock was illuminated. The second hand crawled audibly, and the sound of time, with which I had become so familiar, was my sole companion in the room. I pulled back a corner of the sheers and watched him walk down the hill, hands buried deep inside his pockets, head down. The pain that had shut me down crept back into my chest.

What was I thinking?

I headed upstairs, tiptoeing by my brother's room. The lights from our neighbor's house filtered through my window, and my rosary glistened on the nightstand. I pulled down the shade and picked up the rosary, rolling my fingers over the familiar crystal beads.

"Sam?" Her voice drifted in from her bedroom.

"Yeah, Mom."

"Did you have fun tonight?"

"Yes, we had a good time."

"Come in and say good night after you brush your teeth."

When I walked into my parents' room, Dad was snoring audibly, and Mom lay awake, awaiting my visit. I sat down on her side of the bed. "Hi, Mom."

"Hi, honey. Who walked you home?" She knew. I don't know how, but she always knew.

"Buck."

"I thought so. How was it?"

"Kinda awkward."

"Did he say anything about seeing you again?"

"No."

She nodded thoughtfully. "You okay?"

"Yeah, I just have to think about things awhile."

"You'll figure it out. I know you."

I kissed her good night and returned to the solace of my room. I crawled into bed and lay there, questioning if I had done the right thing that night. I clutched my rosary, recalling the day Nana had presented it to me. A gift, purchased when she visited the Vatican.

"The Pope, he blessed it," she told me on my Confirmation day. "Use it, Samantha. And not just when you need something silly. Doesn't work that way. Anyway, the Lord knows."

"Knows what, Nana?"

"Everything."

I pressed the crucifix to my lips and started to pray.

Thirty-nine

I can't see me lovin' nobody but you for all my life

—The Turtles

Buck's intentions were no secret. He was more attentive than ever, behaving as if nothing had happened. He did not allude to his letter or the time we spent apart. It was as if he thought his good behavior would eradicate the pain of the break-up. But the pain still gnawed at me. I never fully understood what had happened to make him push away. What had changed? Doubt haunted me.

My friends and I were sitting in the bleachers in our usual spot. I watched him dribble down the court and remembered when I had occupied the same space as his girlfriend. What was I now?

Earlier that day, he asked if he could walk me home. He knew I was going to the game with the girls. Throughout the first half, my friends pestered me about giving in too quickly. Shelly was keeping track of every move. It was getting old.

"Is he walking you home after the game?" she asked.

"Yes."

"This is the third time this week."

"I know."

"Do you think he'll ask you to go back together tonight?"

"I don't know."

"If he does, will you say yes?"

"I don't know."

"Have you kissed him yet?" She persisted.

"For the love of God! I already told you I haven't, Shelly."

"Don't get bitchy with me! I'm just trying to help. You need to make him pay for what he put you through." Shelly reminded me.

"Porterfield's right, Sam," Annie chimed in. "Has he even said anything about why he broke up with you?"

"No."

"But he seems so lost, like a little puppy when he looks at her," added Darlene.

"Bailey, you're sad!" exclaimed Annie. "Sam, don't listen to Darlene. Go home and read that damn letter again. That'll remind you of what he put you through if we can't."

"You're heartless, Annie," snapped Darlene. "Leave her alone."

"We're just trying to help her, Darlene," interrupted Shelly. "She needs to play it cool for a while before she takes him back."

"But she loves him," Darlene replied. "And he loves her. I was there when he told her the first time, and he meant it."

"That's not enough," Shelly shot back.

Then Annie piped in again. "Sam, here's what you should do . . ."

"Stop! All of you! You're suffocating me. Now watch the damn game, and mind your own business."

A dumbfounded silence prevailed.

* * *

When Buck and I arrived at my house that evening, I invited him in for the first time since the break-up. We were sitting in the living room, making small talk, when he leaned in to kiss me again. And for the third time I dodged him, heeding Shelly's words and remaining wary of sampling a taste of what I couldn't have. The restraint was like putting the brakes on a train that was roaring into the station.

"If you do that one more time, I'm not going to try again." His words flew out defensively, his frustration apparent. His response took me by surprise.

"What?" I said dumbly.

"Pull away from me. You keep pulling away every time I try to kiss you. And if you do it again, I'll stop trying," he announced—and he meant it. "Did the girls tell you not to kiss me?"

I didn't respond, but he read my expression.

"They did, didn't they?" He laughed. "I should have known."

Anger rose. "What makes you think I need them to tell me what to do?" He froze. I could tell he wasn't expecting that kind of comeback. He was anticipating me to cave, kiss him, and fall back in line. But my candor changed the direction of the conversation. "Explain all of this to me, will you? Do you think one little kiss will smooth everything over and make me forget?"

He shrank into the couch. "I was messed up."

"That's it? You were messed up?" My resolve was suddenly stronger than ever.

"Yeah."

"That's not what your letter said. You said we should go out with other people."

"I did think that at first," he admitted.

"But?" I pressed on.

"But then I missed you."

"What about being friends? You said you wanted us to be friends."

"That was a crock. I said that because I was afraid of losing you forever. And I didn't want you to hate me."

"Hate you?"

"I thought you might."

I eyed him suspiciously. "You said something about my being a good girl." *Right! Something about. As if I couldn't recite every damn word.* "What did you mean? Did you break up with me because . . ."

"Sam," he leaned forward, "I don't know what I was thinking. I'm sorry I put you through this. But I don't want to be without you anymore. I'm miserable. I thought . . ."

"You thought what?" My face burned, and resentment escalated faster than I anticipated. I thought having him back would be enough. But suddenly, it wasn't.

"I thought I could move on. I thought I was too young to be tied down," he answered.

"Tied down!" His words slapped my face. "Nobody's holding a gun to your head!" I yanked myself away from him.

"I didn't mean it that way. Wait! Look at me, will you? I meant I was too young to be this serious, to feel this way already with high school and college still ahead."

"So don't be serious! Date all the girls you want. I won't stop you!"

"Shit! This is coming out all wrong. I'm not good without you, Sam. I tried to be, but all I did was think about you all the time and compare everyone to you. I thought I should be dating other girls and playing the field, but . . ."

"Playing the field? Are you kidding me?" I wanted to slap him silly. Nothing would have given me more pleasure at that moment.

"You know what I mean, Sam. Damn it, will you give me a chance?"

"Why should I?"

"Because you have to."

"No, I don't!" I stood up.

"We belong together, and you know it. I don't want anyone else. I want *you*. But I don't want to push you toward something you're not ready for or tie you down. I respect you too much for that. What else do you want me to say?" He lowered his head, now speaking into his hands. "I can't lose you." I couldn't decide what held more despair, his face or his voice.

I can't lose you.

Suddenly I stopped. What exactly was I fighting? Was I just so hurt that I couldn't see straight? What crime had he committed? He hadn't lied or cheated. He told the truth. He was scared and confused. We were definitely young to have such strong feelings. Sometimes it scared me too. The difference between us was I wasn't willing to bail. Was there a law against feeling this way at our age? I never thought it was about age. Maybe it was his unfailing logic that had conquered his emotion, pressing him to separate himself from me. The clock ticked louder than usual, interrupting the heavy silence that hung between us.

"Sam?"

I knew he could read my doubt as well as I could see his pain. Until that moment I hadn't considered that he might be hurting too—after all, he was the one who put us there. What about the endless days and weeks after he left me? I could not endure it again. I wondered which was worse, the torment of not having him or the fear of taking a leap that could be disastrous. I had made it this far. I wondered if his words were enough to make me jump.

"Sam. Say something."

There was a part of me that believed certain things were meant to be. Did I ever have a choice? If I had not run into him that day on his bike, would it have been some other day? "Do you mean it?"

His expression transformed. "You know I mean it."

"Because I can't do this again. If you change your mind and . . ."

"I won't. I swear," he said resolutely.

"How can you be so sure?"

"Because I'm in love with you, Sam." The words popped out of his mouth like a natural reflex. The words that I prayed were still in his heart. "Say something." His body was rigid.

"I'm glad you finally woke up."

All of the air that had tightened his body released in one profound breath. "You're something, DeSantis." He stood up and took my hand. "And?" A hint of uncertainty shaded his face.

"And what?" I felt myself letting go.

"You love me too?" His mouth was so close—I could taste him.

"I do." I fell back into the cool waters, arms wide, perfect ripples circling all around me.

Part Two

1967-1969

One moment in time had changed my life, and I would never be the same. I wondered, was it trust or was it destiny that caused me to take the leap?

In Canto 5 of the *Inferno*, Dante meets lovers who have gone to Hell because of the irresistible force of love. He asks Francesca Malatesta, who fell illicitly for her husband's brother, to describe the moment that she knew it was Paolo, the love of her life. Francesca tells Dante that they were simply reading a book together:

> Sometimes at what we read our glances joined,
> Looking from the book each to the other's eyes,
> And then the color in our faces drained.
>
> But one particular moment alone it was
> Defeated us: *the longed-for smile*, it said,
> *Was kissed by that most noble lover*: at this,
>
> This one, who now will never leave my side,
> Kissed my mouth, trembling.

Was I defeated the moment he rode up to me on his bike? Was he? Had I taken a different route, would the course of my life have been altered? Or would we have found each other anyway? Some people are drawn to each other so naturally that it seems choice is not a factor. I have never believed whole-heartedly in destiny. The idea that everything in the universe is preordained bothers me. A world designed without choice seems pointless. What are we here for if not to fall and get back up again? Is not the journey about the path we choose? Or does destiny plant us in the right place at the right time?

Must choice and fate reside in separate worlds?

Forty

Raindrops keep falling on my head
But that doesn't mean my eyes will soon be turning red
Crying's not for me
Those raindrops keep falling on my head, they keep falling
Because I'm free
Nothing's worrying me.

—BJ Thomas

Rain is magic. I lose myself in the blur and the patter. I am connected to the universe as it falls upon my skin and drizzles down my body. Its scent is life. I look around and see a Monet painting with intricate patterns and soft colors. I step into the painting; I am a part of it. I watch as the rain washes away unwanted remnants and restores life. After a rainfall, the world is new again.

When I was young, my dad would take me out to the sunporch during thunderstorms. I would stand beside him as he pointed to the sky and explained, in intricate detail, the relationship between the speed of light and sound and how they were partners. *They just make their appearances at different times,* he said. My dad had poetry about him. It showed itself in his photography and in his view of life. He loved everything about nature, especially rainstorms, and he taught me to love them too. For as far back as I can remember, rain has fascinated and calmed me. Storms mesmerize me. When the world rumbles and shakes around me, I delight in the enormity of nature, just like my dad. I will always be drawn to rain.

My faith was restored. Buck returned to me with a fervor that I had not yet witnessed in him. The ache that had penetrated my core gradually receded into the memory vault, where I hoped it would remain. There was a change in Buck—no more fear. Maybe he realized what we might lose by not embracing what stood in front of us. And despite our conflicting schedules, which would last only three more months, we were together as much as possible. And then the most extraordinary thing happened: he began composing letters to me.

Every day.

Forty-one

Why don't you write me,
A letter would brighten
My loneliest evening . . .

—Simon and Garfunkel

Is there anything quite as personal as a letter? A handwritten, straight-from-the-heart letter. A sentiment crafted on carefully chosen stationery or a spontaneous note dashed off on the inside of the perfect card? Sadly, such social correspondence seems to be a dying art, yet one that should be resurrected because of its priceless and enduring qualities. Pick up an old letter or note, and it takes you back.

His letters became the third party in our relationship. I loved the way he wrote. I could hear his voice, and I understood his inflection. His words made me smile—well, most of the time. And so our ritual began. He would make the 15-minute trek from my house to his, call me to say good night, and sit down to compose a letter, which I would receive the next day. Some letters were sweet and romantic. Others were silly, marked with his peculiar brand of humor. And some were surprisingly thoughtful and introspective. That was his mix, his mystery.

On this particular day, Buck and I were in front of CHS, standing off to the side of the main entrance away from the mad traffic of teenagers. Whenever sessions changed from morning to afternoon, there was a mob scene. Because the weather was improving, students chose to remain outside longer than they should. Even the familiar warning of the dreaded bell did not deter some kids from stealing an extra moment of freedom.

When Buck saw Darlene approaching us, he handed off the letter surreptitiously.

"Hey, Darlene, how you doing?" His smiles for Darlene were always genuine.

"I'm good." A smirk spread across her face. "What's that you gave Sam? Bet you didn't think I saw," she taunted. Darlene could get away with this kind of repartee. Good nature oozed from her pores.

He grinned, knowingly caught, but chose not to respond. "Gotta go, ladies; math calls. Talk to you later, D." He pointed at me, winked, and skipped up the brick stairway, disappearing through the double doors.

Darlene grabbed my hand. "Let me read that note!"

"Get your paws off! It's private."

"Please, please!" she begged with her entire body.

"No!" I shoved the letter into my pocketbook.

"Oh, come on, just let me read one note," her body folded into a pathetic pile as she tugged at the back of my skirt.

"Stop! Implore no more!" I proclaimed with dramatic flair. "I shall never reveal the contents of my love notes."

"Fine!" Like a petulant child, Darlene shoved her hands into the pockets of her dress and put on a fake pout. I ignored her act. We turned onto Junction Street and crossed the railroad tracks. As we proceeded, Darlene carried on with her ruse in hopes of guilting me into submission. I remained strong. I knew she couldn't keep up her pretense for long. The moment we stopped at the corner to wait for the light to change, she cracked.

"Sam! Just tell me what he says to you!" she screamed as she jumped up and down on the sidewalk.

"Honest to God. Look at you!" I enjoyed my role as "the lucky girl with the good boyfriend who writes letters."

"It's not fair. He writes to you all the time." She spoke more to herself than to me. We had crossed the street and came upon Maria's Italian Bakery, from which emanated the most irresistible smell of freshly baked bread. One whiff and I was a goner.

"Darlene, smell that. I have to go in and get some biscotti." Always a reliable partner in matters gastronomic, she followed without coaxing. We entered the old building, where we were immediately assaulted by the sweet smell of pastries. My knees buckled.

"Oh, man. Look at those éclairs!" I drooled.

"And the Napoleons, Sam. She drizzled the white icing across the top. I love when she does that." Her face was nearly pressed into the glass.

"Hiya, girls. Walking home from school?" greeted Maria. Her head and shoulders just made it above the top of the showcases that held the most delicious Italian pastries in town. She wiped her hands on her checkered apron and pulled back an uncooperative strand of hair, securing it with a bobby pin.

"You wanna a little piece of bread and butter, girls? Justa come outa the oven." We raced toward the wooden table where she sliced the bread and slathered it with butter. *Real* butter. Maria's compact little body shook with silent laughter.

"I guess you hungry, eh?" She handed each of us a piece of crusty Italian bread, literally dripping with butter from the heat. We shoved it into our mouths like there was no tomorrow. Our audible appreciation caused Maria to shake even more vigorously than before. "What else you want, girls?"

We exited with an overstuffed bag and continued our journey toward Darlene's house. And, as if our previous conversation had not been interrupted, Darlene continued.

"So do you write back to him?"

I paused at the ridiculousness of her question. "Are you seriously asking me that?"

"Okay, dumb question. That's so romantic, Sam. Writing love letters to each other. Come on, throw me a bone. Let me read just one. I want to see what he says to you."

"Not your business. Ask Sal to write you a letter."

"Yeah, right! When donkeys fly. It's not his thing. If you were my friend, you'd let me live vicariously for a minute."

"You sound like Shelly," I chided. "I love you, Darlene, but it's *my* letter."

"Well, then read it already. You're making me crazy."

"I'll read it when I get home."

"How can you wait?"

"Waiting makes it better. That's half of the fun."

"You guys are too much."

After a comprehensive algebra review session with Darlene, who excelled at math, I walked the ten blocks to my house, entering through the side door to our kitchen. No one was home except Buffy, who came wagging into the room immediately.

"How's my good doggie?" Her backside swayed enthusiastically.

On the kitchen table was a note from my mother, scribbled on the back of a used legal envelope: *Hi Samantha, call me when you get home. Love, Mom.* I smiled at the predictable omnipresence of my mother and dropped my books on the table beside her note. Then I pulled out Buck's letter.

Dear D,

I'm home. Greg's not here yet, so I am alone in our room. I am restless without you, and the feeling grows more intense all the time.

I dreamt about you last night. I was going to tell you, but I chickened out. We were on your basement couch, only this time your sister wasn't calling us upstairs for dessert. We were making out, and it was so neat. You know that feeling we both say always passes between us? Well, this was definitely it, only stronger than ever. I can feel it now just writing about it. You know how you always say that some dreams are so real they stay with you, and you can't wash the feeling away? That's how this one was. You were letting me closer to you. Then I woke up, and I was so pissed! I tried to fall back to sleep so I could finish the dream, but I couldn't get back to you. Sometimes my gut aches when I am not with you. Is that stupid? Do you ever feel that way? Like it's hard to leave each other?

I never told you this, but it bothers me when you talk to Brian Determan. You keep telling me you two are just friends, and I know you wouldn't lie. But I'm not sure he thinks of you in the same way.

On a lighter note, you know Expo '67 opened in Montreal this month. I heard that Mr. Reardon was going to organize a school bus trip for some upcoming weekend. Supposedly there are over 90 theme pavilions. Sounds pretty cool to me. Maybe we should see if we can go with a bunch of our friends. It's chaperoned and all that good stuff.

I wish you were here. I won't be able to see you after school tomorrow because of practice. So when you go to sleep tomorrow night, think of the Beach Boys singing,

"Wouldn't it be nice if we were older, and we could sleep together."

Wouldn't it? Ponder.

Love,
Me

P.S. Don't show this note to your mom. She'll have a contract on my head!

Forty-two

Darlene's kitchen matched her personality. The sun seemed to shine in perpetually, and the Formica table was always topped with friendly flowers.

"It's almost ready." Darlene was whipping up a batch of her chocolate fudge.

"Oh, good. I've been thinking about it all day." Hers was the best fudge I'd ever had.

"So everything's going good with you and Buck?" She smiled as she stirred.

"Yeah."

"I knew it would." Self-satisfaction crossed her face. "Remember when you were broken up, and everybody was telling you to make him suffer longer 'cause of what he put you through?" I remembered. "Well, I knew you should just get back with him all along."

"You did, huh?"

"Yep!

"Why is that?"

"Cause you're soul mates."

"You think?"

She turned from the stove, and regarded me intently. "I know. You're destined to be together." I laughed. "You are, Sam. It's a powerful thing, you know. Your spirits have probably been circling around each other for centuries. You might have even been married in another life. You have to be together, Sam. And you better hope you end up together in your final lives, or else you can't be together for eternity. Then you'll have no peace."

"What are you talking about? You're Catholic. You don't believe in reincarnation and other lives."

"The nuns don't know everything. Why can't the two philosophies blend?"

"Blend the fudge already. The smell is wafting in my direction."

"Wafting? Who else but you would use a word like that?"

"Buck would."

"See what I mean? I rest my case."

"The fudge! Please. You're killing me."

"You guys are MFEO."

Initials were Darlene's thing, like a secret code. She managed to recruit all of us to use her esoteric language. It was like being part of a clandestine society. I would be walking down the halls at CHS and run into her:

"Hey, S. How's ELT?" *Every little thing.*

"NBAY?" *Not bad and you?*

"JD." Darlene was always *just dandy*. That's why everybody loved her.

"He always knows what you're thinking *and* what you're going to say. Even Sal doesn't do that with me. Now come on, me and Sal? Nobody's like us." She had abandoned the pan, arms flailing about as she spoke. My eyes followed the waving wooden spoon, covered with a thick layer of chocolate.

"No argument here. Best couple at the high school," I affirmed.

"If you two don't end up together, it won't make sense." She finally noticed my concentration on the spoon. "Want to lick the spoon?"

"I thought you'd never ask." I licked the spoon like a dog cleaning a dinner plate. "Oh, man, this tastes so good. Just the right texture."

She poured the hot velvety mixture into a buttered Corningware dish. "When's it going to be ready?" I was salivating.

"Takes about an hour to set up in the fridge," she replied as she swirled the top of the fudge to create a design.

"An hour? Give me the pan."

"Here." She handed me the saucepan, and I scraped the remnants onto my wooden spoon, licking to my heart's content.

"This stuff is sinful."

"I know," she grinned, pleased with her cooking prowess. "Here, have some milk." She began wiping the counter, and then she filled the sink with soapy water. "Give me the pan when you're done."

As she cleaned up, I sat at the table, reflecting on what she had said about Buck and me. Her assertion was not news. I already knew, but the truth of it was huge. We *were* made for each other, but would it work out that way? We were so young. There was much to do between now and whenever I might settle down. And if it didn't work out, what would happen? Would we be circling around, searching for each other in future lives? What if it was just one of us searching for the other? Then what?

Love letters straight from your heart
Keep us so near while apart

—the Lettermen

Dear Sam,

How goes it? Wasn't that an exciting game last night? I saw you in the bleachers, cheering the team on. You were wearing that navy blue sweater I like. Well, I'm not sure if it's the sweater I like so much or the way it hugs your curves. Those are some good-looking curves. Did I ever tell you that you're the best looking of all your girlfriends? Don't blush. It's true. And you're my girl.

I'm in Downey's class right now, and he's babbling on about civil rights, stuff I've heard a hundred times. Well, I exaggerate—for effect, my dear. Anyway, because I feel perfectly well-versed on this subject, I thought I'd take the time to write to my best friend. Admittedly, most people's best friends don't have the same effect on them as you have on me. Guess I'm a lucky guy! I can see your eyes rolling from here. Hey, don't put me down. You asked for a love letter.

So are we going to play miniature golf with Darlene and Sal this weekend? That will be swell! I like doubling with those kids. They're competitive, and that makes the evening more fun. You know how I enjoy making a contest of everything.

Hey, did you hear that Elvis Presley married Priscilla Beaulieu? Swivel hips is off the market! I imagine there are going to be a lot of broken hearts out there.

I know you're going to hate me because I am always telling you that I will write a mushy note, and then I never do because I run out of time, but the bell is going to ring soon, and I have to hightail it to my next class. Later . . .

Love always,
Buck

P. S. Want me to help you with your math tonight?

Forty-three

"Sometimes I see myself as a child in a rainstorm, running around trying to catch all the drops in his mouth. I long for your adventures to be like the raindrops the child saves and not those which crash to the ground."

—Unknown

The change of seasons never grows old, maybe because I grew up with it. Seasonal shifts are a part of who I am. They mark events. They cause me to behave differently. Those who don't experience the change of seasons have been robbed of one of nature's miracles.

That spring saw a deluge of rain, causing everything to awaken from its winter sleep in record speed. One afternoon, lazy and overcast, Buck and I sat on my sunporch, playing Chinese checkers. As usual, he was ahead, which didn't really bother me. It was just a game, and I wasn't particularly competitive. Conversely, when it came to winning, he was single-minded. What's more, he loved rubbing my nose in his victory.

"Do you actually want to finish this game?" he jabbed. "There's no way in hell you can get all of those marbles to the other side."

Until that moment, I had deliberately avoided eye contact, well aware of my dismal chance of winning and of his surly eyes cast upon me. But the taunt was too much. So, as my form of retaliation, I scrambled the marbles all over the board, sending them rolling everywhere. He burst into laughter.

"I'm sick of this stupid game, anyway!" I stood up, feigning bravado. Whenever I knew I wasn't going to win, which was most of the time, I resorted to flippant rants.

"You mean you're sick of losing."

"Don't push it, Kendall." I egged him on.

"What are you going to do about it?"

An unexpected crash of thunder ripped through the sound barrier, and I moved toward the window. The first crash was quickly followed by another as the sky darkened. Within minutes, rain pelted the side of the house in an angular assault. I smiled.

"No smart come-backs, eh, DeSantis?"

I spoke to him without turning around. "Want to run in the rain?"

"What? Now?"

"Right now. No raincoats. Can you handle it, Kendall, or will you get in trouble with your mommy for getting your good clothes all wet?" I goaded.

That was it. He flew out of the chair and raced to the door, where I was already attempting to escape. He tried to pry my hand off the handle, but I managed to open the door and dart down the steps ahead of him. Unfortunately, I slipped as I picked up speed. He took full advantage, pushing past me and tearing off down the path. The raindrops grew fatter and heavier. I caught up to him, and we proceeded to run around, splashing through puddles, circling trees, and pointing our open mouths to the sky. We ran so hard, my sides began to ache.

His tee shirt stuck to him, and his hair was flat and dripping into his eyes. "You do this all the time?" he asked.

"Not *all* the time. I started doing it when I was a kid. Come on . . . this way!"

We ran around until we could run no more. The sky gave no signs of relenting. Out of breath and totally drenched, we retreated to the dry space under my sister's kiddie pool, hanging over the clothesline in the backyard. There was just enough room for both of us to crawl under. I flopped down on my back, my breath still coming in quick bursts. He lay down beside me, and we began to laugh for no particular reason. It felt good to release all that energy.

"I like being out of breath," I panted.

"Why?"

"It's cleansing—like after a belly laugh."

We lay there quietly, staring at the folds inside the plastic pool. The Flintstones stared at us. Fred was chasing Dino down the street. *Yabba dabba doo!* We erupted into laughter again.

"So you like being out of breath," he repeated.

"I do. I feel calm afterward." Our breathing gradually slowed, and we were in that place of communal silence. As I lay beside him, I could feel the warmth emanating from his body. The sensation was peaceful and disquieting at the same time. He took my hand.

"Do you feel calm now?"

"Yeah." I lied.

He peeled back the tee shirt that clung to him. "I'm soaked."

"Me too." I looked down at myself to discover that my shirt was glued to my chest, revealing everything I owned from the waist up. I yanked it away.

"Too late. I already saw."

"Saw what?" I feigned.

"Everything under that shirt."

I could read his thoughts. I folded my arms across my chest, but he rolled over on top of me and pushed them away. Then he brushed the wet strands of hair off my forehead.

"Do you still feel calm?" He buried his face in my neck and slid both hands into the small of my back, lifting me slightly. "'Cause I can fix that."

The rain pelted harder against the exterior of the pool. We remained hidden until the thunder roared no more.

Dearest Samantha,

How's my little sweetheart this evening? I'm sorry that my mom and dad wouldn't let me get my feet wet last night so I could see you. I hope you weren't too upset. I know how you pine away without me (ahem!).

Seriously, I really do miss you tonight. I spent the whole day in the house thinking we'd be together later. It looks like this nasty storm's going to last forever. Did you see the size of the hail stones earlier? Can you believe it? In May! If the weather station wasn't putting out all those damn warnings, we could run in it. But I guess getting hit in the eyeball with a hailstone might hurt. Lake effects. That's what we get for living here.

I hope it's over by tomorrow because I don't think I could go another day without seeing you. It seems I never get to see ENOUGH of you, especially in the winter when you wear all those clothes. That's why I prefer summer. Girls with figures like yours ought to go into math or accounting or something. (Are you laughing yet? I'm working overtime here to entertain you.)

I just started reading The Trial by Franz Kafka. My dad said it's really good. It was on his book shelves in the den. So I picked it up and started reading. Man! It's great. I think the Beatles new album is going to be released soon. It's called Sergeant Pepper's Lonely Hearts Club Band. Neat name, huh?

I have a great idea. Let's have a date at the lighthouse. I was down there with Greg the other day and discovered a couple of secluded little spots. Very romantic. We can sit there and watch the sunset. I'll bring the blanket. You bring the picnic basket. Any chance you could throw some of your mom's cookies in there? What do you say?

Got to go. It's 11:45. Jane told me to go to bed awhile ago. Must be an obedient son. Tomorrow . . .

I love you,
Buck

Forty-four

Tony's oversized pizza oven spit out a ton of heat, the last thing we needed on this evening. Every time Tony opened the door to pull out another pie, the oven blew its hot breath into the room. The fans, blowing in all four corners, were not doing their jobs.

"Want another Coke?"

"Sure."

Buck motioned to the waitress, who nodded and proceeded to the fountain to fetch another glass.

"So, D, what do you want to do for our one-year anniversary?" he asked. We never counted the time we had been apart. Buck said we were still in each other's heads, so that time didn't exist. But it still existed for me.

"I don't have anything in particular in mind. What do you want to do?"

"Well, I was thinking we could go to the steak house in Bay City for dinner."

I was impressed. "That place is fancy. I've never been there."

"Then I'm glad you'll be going with me for the first time. I'll wear a suit, and you can wear one of your sexy, tight dresses."

"I don't have any sexy, tight dresses."

"A boy can dream, can't he?"

"Here you go, kids." Tessa, the only other waitress Tony employed besides Gertie, set down two glasses. "I brought one for you too, Buck. It's on the house. Too hot to worry about payin' today."

"Thanks, Tessa. That's really nice of you. When's your shift end? Aren't you working overtime?"

"Yeah, I'm coverin' for Gertie. She had another house to do, and she makes more money doin' that, so I said I'd pick up her shift. She's gotta pay for them kids of hers to go to college. That ain't cheap, you know."

"I know. Thanks, Tessa."

"You're more than welcome. See you later, kids."

Buck picked up his glass and held it toward me. "Cheers! To our one year."

"Cheers."

He winked. "Gulp it down. I have something I want to show you."

"What?" My clueless expression fed his enjoyment.

"You'll see."

Outside, a heaviness clung to the air, despite the descending darkness. With fingers laced, we headed up the street. "Where are we going?"

"Just wait."

By the time we arrived at our designated spot, stars were beginning to make an appearance.

"St. Patrick's? Why? Are we gonna play hoops?" His abrupt laughter scoffed at me. "What! You think that's so ridiculous?" I was posturing for a heavy comeback.

He choked back amusement. "No. Of course not." He rotated me toward a path, one hand on either shoulder for restraint. Let's face it, I was a force to be reckoned with. "Keep going. Right back there." He escorted me down a gravel walkway that wound around to the back of the old brick building.

"How did you find this spot?"

"I bring all of my girlfriends here." I hip checked him. "Up these steps."

When we reached the top of the short stairway, I discovered a secluded little balcony jutting off the side of one of the classrooms of St. Patrick's School. A wall of red brick, reaching chest high, surrounded us. Crushed pebbles blanketed the floor, and Buck began to brush them aside with his feet, clearing out a place for us to sit.

"This is cozy. How did you find it?"

"I play basketball here, remember? Sit down. I have a surprise for you."

"A surprise?"

"Mm-hmm," he reached into his pockets and then presented me with two closed fists. "Pick one."

I tapped his left hand. When he opened it, the familiar yellow wrapper stared up at me.

"Mallo Cup! I love these. What's in your other hand?"

"My Mallo Cup!" His voice was ten-years-old.

The Mallo cup was a splendid thing: not only was it made of the tastiest chocolate infused with marshmallow and coconut, it contained a coin card that was redeemable for more Mallo Cups. Bonus! The cards ran from five cents to a dollar. This miracle combo was enough to make any kid happy.

"A dollar! I can't believe it. I never get the dollar cards. How much is yours?"

"Ten cents. You hit the jackpot, DeSantis."

We sat there, savoring the chocolate. Then he pointed to the sky. "Stars are popping out, big time." I leaned into him to take in the exquisite transformation. Without warning he shouted, "I claim that one! It looks iridescent."

"Okay," I said with resignation, "if we're choosing, I'll take that one over there."

"That's a decent one too. So what are you going to name it?" he asked.

"Name it?"

"Yeah, you have to give it a name."

"Why?"

"It's the rule."

"Whose rule?" I challenged.

"Mine. Now name it."

"You first," I demanded.

"Not fair," he complained.

"Fair. You claimed the best one without even telling me we were choosing. Unfair advantage! So name it, pal." I figured he'd come up with something clever, if he hadn't already done so prior to his orchestrated surprise.

"Yeah, but what you don't know is I chose it for you," he said in a sweet *Eddie Haskell* voice.

"I'm not buying it, *Eddie*."

"Stop calling me that! You doubt my intentions?"

"I do."

"Okay, I admit that I might have taken an unfair advantage."

"Big of you."

"But seriously, "he said ceremoniously, "I give you my bright, shimmering star." He pointed to the sky with an impressive flourish.

"The name," I reminded him.

"Anne Boleyn," he announced.

"Anne Boleyn! Are you kidding?"

"She was irresistible. Look at the spell she cast on Henry," he explained.

"For the love of God—he beheaded her!" I overdramatized. I was good at it.

"Because he needed someone else to give him an heir. I'll never need anyone else."

"To give you an heir?"

"No," he laughed resignedly.

"Didn't he kill her because he fell in love with Jane Seymour and he was looking for a way out of the marriage? Check your history book."

"Regardless. I'll never need anyone else but you, Samantha."

"The charm's not working." I shook my head, muttering, "Anne Boleyn. Some swell gift."

"Okay. I see your point. Now tell me what you're naming yours."

"Is it my gift to you, or am I naming it for myself?"

"What difference does it make?"

"Makes a huge difference in the selection of the name."

"Whatever you want."

"Okay then. If I'm giving it to you . . ." I paused. "Remind me of those old ladies' names in *Arsenic and Old Lace.* Abby and Martha something?"

"Funny." His impatience was growing.

"Okay. Hemingway."

"Hemingway? You like him that much?"

"Have you read *The Sun Also Rises*?"

"Not yet."

"After you read it, we'll talk. Then you'll understand me better."

"I think I understand you pretty well now." He sidled up to me.

"You do, huh?"

"I am most confident."

"So what am I thinking right now?"

He turned toward me and put his fingers on his temples.

"Hmm . . . Zoltar think that you want the boy to kiss you really badly." I shook my head at his bad accent. "Like he kiss you that day on bluff by lighthouse. Zoltar want to know do you remember that day the boy kiss you on bluff by lighthouse?"

"I remember."

"And Zoltar think," he stalled, "you want to see if boy can one-up that kiss."

I repeated, imitating his accent. "One-up that kiss?"

"Yes. Make better kiss. Bigger kiss." God help me, I was madly in love with him. "Zoltar want to know what to tell boy."

"Tell Zoltar to tell boy that I'd love to be one-upped."

He leaned closer, "Zoltar say practice makes perfect."

I breathed him in as if my life depended on it. "Then let's start practicing, Zoltar."

The sky had become brilliant with stars, illuminating the balcony ever so faintly. And Zoltar was right: practice does make perfect. At least it comes damn close.

Dear Sam,

I hope you're not too bored tonight without me there to comfort you. I had a really swell time with you this afternoon, and it's too bad I couldn't come up tonight too. However, if I had come to visit, there probably wouldn't be much to do because your parents are going out to dinner. They probably would have chained us to chairs in different rooms because of their knowledge of the strong attraction between us. I can't write anything too serious because you let your mother read my last love-packed note. Now, Sam, if your mother wants to read mush like this, she'll just have to tell Nick to get on the stick. I certainly can't do the love writing for both of us. He's a big boy now and should rise to his own obligation.

So I am almost finished reading The Trial. Whoa! I think you'd really like it. Kafka has these men actually accept the warped world they're living in and give up their lives. I'll let you borrow this copy when I'm done.

Hey, I bought the new Beatles album. It's great. We'll have to listen to it together next time you're over. I like it almost as much as I like their last album. Speaking of music, bet you didn't know that Hendrix burned his guitar on stage at the Monterey Pop Festival on Sunday. Ain't that something! Would have loved to see that.

Last week of school. Thank God! I feel pretty prepared for the rest of my finals. How about you? Need any tutoring? I'm here to help. In many ways.

Well, my one and only (yup, it just keeps pouring out!), it's time to sign off for now, but if I get the urge, maybe I'll get around to writing another note. Peace.

Love always,
Buck

P.S. I haven't forgotten about The Sun Also Rises.

Forty-five

Lakeside Haven. Our home away from home. Our entire gang migrated there that summer. First one there saved the prime beach spot, number one priority, and then to the hill to claim a cluster of tables to spread out the food. Radios blared, and Coppertone filled the air.

"Samantha DeSantis!" Sid. Shelly's newest boyfriend, using his "I-didn't-know-you-could-look-that-good" voice. "Wow, the way you look in that bathing suit! I didn't realize all that was under there. Foxy lady!"

I sneered at him because I neither appreciated the nature of his remark, nor was I thrilled that he had made such a comment in front of Buck and Shelly. I knew I was going to pay for his blunder. Buck dropped the beach bag onto the blanket and marched over to Sid.

"What did you just say to her?" His face grew visibly red.

"Don't wig out, pal. I was just giving her a compliment." He laughed at Buck.

"Buck, it's all right. Forget it." I grabbed his forearm, but he shook me off.

"No, it's not all right. And don't call me, pal, asshole." His eyes bore through Sid while Shelly sat, wordless. Then Sid stood up.

"You don't have to get so hot under the collar, man. I didn't mean anything by it." Sid was a decent guy. Just annoying and clueless most of the time.

"It didn't sound that way to me. And stop looking at her like that."

"Like what?"

"Like she's got her clothes off."

"Buck! What are you doing? Come on; let's go." I tried to grab his arm again, but he still wouldn't let me touch him.

"Don't ever speak to her like that again, understand?" The veins in his neck popped out.

Suddenly Shelly stood up, "Sid, you're such a jerk!"

"What's with you?" Like I said, clueless.

"Why did you have to say that anyway? Don't you care about my feelings?"

And now it's about her. Of course!

"What?" Sid was getting hit from every direction. To be sure, Shelly would make his life hell.

"How do you think it makes me feel when you say things like that? And to her! She's my friend." She started to cry, snatched her cover-up, and took off toward the ladies' room.

"Where you goin'?" Confusion covered his face.

I walked up to him. "You know, Sid, you have a big mouth and no manners. Grow up and think before you speak!" I spun on my heels and directed my attention to Buck, "I'm going to the girls' room now to see if Shelly's okay." Grabbing my beach bag, I headed up the hill.

"I'll be at the car." Buck turned toward Sid and gave him the stink eye.

"Jesus! What's wrong with everyone around here?"

"I'd say you're the problem, *pal*." And Buck was off.

I stalled, turning back to see if the tension between Buck and Sid had escalated any further. Buck disappeared while Sid stood, applying more oil to his chest and eying a stacked blonde in a red two-piece as she walked by.

"Man, look at you!" He winked at the girl.

"Skuzzball!" She stuck her nose in the air and picked up her pace.

"I was just bein' friendly!" he yelled. "Jesus, what's wrong with everybody today?"

When I walked into the ladies' room, Shelly was spilling her guts to Gretta Kaplan.

"She ruins everything, Gretta!" Gretta stiffened when she saw me.

"Oh, hi, Sam," Gretta announced for Shelly's benefit. Gretta could be cold and manipulative. I was never sure when she was telling the truth.

"Hi." I dismissed her, directing my attention to my sometimes difficult friend. "Shelly, are you all right?" She turned her back to me and blew her nose. "Shelly?" I pressed.

"What?"

"Why are you acting this way? I didn't do anything."

"Sure." She exchanged a knowing glance with Gretta.

"What's that supposed to mean?"

"Forget it."

Not this time.

"Who ruins everything?" I confronted.

My words startled her. "What?"

"When I walked in here, you said, 'She ruins everything.' Who?"

"I don't know what you're talking about." She sniffled.

"I think you do." Nothing in me said relent.

She whirled around. "Okay, Miss Know-It-All! I'll tell you who. You! You ruin EVERYTHING!" Her anger rose like an unexpected storm.

"Me? What did I do? I think you have things backward."

"You and your goddamn perfect boyfriend! You come waltzing down to the beach, hand in hand, in your new bathing suit, flaunting yourself in front of Sid!"

"Flaunting myself? That's not true, and you know it!" Now I *was* pissed.

"Take it easy, Sam. Can't you see she's upset?" Gretta, who had remained close by to collect all the dirty details, interrupted.

"She's not the only one! And I will not take it easy, Gretta, so stay out of this. This is between Shelly and me."

"Bitch! You're so full of yourself!" She stormed out. One down.

"Okay Shelly, what's going on?"

"It's always about you, isn't it, Sam?"

"On the contrary, I happen to think it's always about *you*. And I have sucked it up more times than I care to count. But I'm not doing it this time. You're mad because your asshole boyfriend looked at someone else. That's what's going on here."

"Gretta's right. You *are* full of yourself! Where do you get off saying that to me?"

"I'm telling the truth. You're pissed because you want Sid to dote on you and pretend no one else exists. Yeah, he's a jerk and says stupid things, but that's not my fault. I didn't come here looking for trouble. I came to have fun and hang around with you. But clearly, that's not going to happen. You know, Shel, you make it really difficult to be your friend sometimes."

"Then don't be! I don't need your shit! And stay away from my boyfriend!" She pushed past me and flew out the door.

When I reached the car, Buck was sitting in the front seat, brooding. I hopped in the driver's seat and peeled out of the parking lot.

"Is everything all right now?" he asked.

"No, everything is not all right! How the hell did all of this happen? Why did you have to react that way to Sid? You should have ignored him. You're better than that."

"I should have ignored him? Are you kidding me? Did you hear what he said to you?"

"I heard him, and I let it go because I know he's an idiot. Plus I can handle myself. You don't need to defend me."

"Oh, sorry! He insulted you, and I didn't hear you putting him in his place. I hate what he said to you, Sam. I hate that . . ."

"*You* hate, *you* think . . . God, Buck! Now I have this whole mess on my hands, and I'm trying to figure out what I did to deserve it." My eyes were fixed on the road ahead. I wanted to retreat from the whole damn business of high school drama.

"Well, I guess you have to deal with a boyfriend who gets pissed off when asshole guys leer at you like you're naked."

"He wasn't leering at me like I was naked. Don't even say something like that. You're overreacting."

"You think I overreacted?" His face twisted. I could feel his eyes burning through me.

"Yes, I do, and sometimes you act like no one else should talk to me."

There! I've said it.

"I do not! If I'd realized that you liked what he said to you, I would have backed off! Did you enjoy that he noticed 'all that was there?'" His agitation escalated.

"That's not what I mean, and you know it. I don't think you're in the right frame of mind for this conversation. You can't be objective when you're this angry."

"Turn here," he blurted.

"Why?"

"I'm going home." He stared at the road.

"Fine with me." I swung the car around the corner and headed straight for his house. It was so like him to withdraw rather than work out the problem.

Forty-six

No true love there can be without Its dread penalty—jealousy.

—Lord Lytton

Jealousy is a cancer. It eats its way slowly, eroding, destabilizing, until it creeps behind your eyes and blurs your vision. Why must it be?

"Sam, are you packed yet?" Her voice traveled from the downstairs foyer.

"Almost, Mom. I just have to throw in a few more things." Clothes were strewn all over my bed. I couldn't decide what to take, not that it mattered. We were just going to be hanging out at my aunt and uncle's camp.

"Snap it up. We're leaving in an hour."

I tossed a couple of books and my diary into my suitcase. His picture stared at me from my dresser. Then the telephone rang.

"Sam, it's Buck."

I hadn't said anything to my mother about our quarrel, but I'm sure she picked up on my tension. She always did. Still raw from yesterday's events, I was tempted not to talk to him. I didn't know exactly what I wanted to say yet. Still, I was always drawn to him. I walked into my parents' bedroom and picked up the phone.

"Hello?"

"Hey, Sam." Contrite.

"Hi."

"You leaving for Maine soon?"

"Yeah, within the hour."

"I see." Silence. "Still pissed at me, aren't you?"

"I don't know what I am." The gentle eyes of the Blessed Virgin Mary watched over the room from my mother's nightstand.

"Listen, I'm sorry I blew up yesterday."

"Yeah, I know." I sat on the bed, instinctively twisting the pearl ring around my finger. "I don't have time to talk now. We're leaving in a minute. We can talk when I get back."

"When's that again?" His restraint was impressive.

"In a week. We're staying at my aunt and uncle's camp on Crystal Lake."

"Yeah, I remember that part. Well, have a good time then."

"I will." I wanted to say more.

"Call me when you get home."

"Okay."

"See you, Sam." His voice held the tones of a concession speech.

"See you, Buck."

I sat in the back seat of the station wagon, trees, farms, and silos whizzing by on our route to the highway. The windows were rolled down, and the pungent smell of cattle assaulted me.

"Let's play silo," announced my mother, always one to get the games rolling. My siblings were more than happy to join in, each poised like a trained dog, ready to sniff out the hidden evidence. I extended the obligatory effort while I contemplated how I could be so in love with a person as complicated as Buckley Kendall.

You never really understand a person until you consider things from his point of view —until you climb into his skin and walk around in it.

—Harper Lee

Time is wisdom. When the dust settles, vision is clearer. Atticus Finch was right. How could I judge the way others behaved if I didn't walk in their shoes? His words gave me pause.

"We're home!" Mom pulled into the driveway, relieved to be finished with the drudgery of the tedious drive from Maine. "Kids, carry your suitcases up to your rooms before you start calling your friends. Ryan, if your dad's not in the house, call him at the store and tell him we're home. And, Lucy, grab that bucket of stones. There's sand all over the floor."

I ran up the stairs and threw my suitcase next to my desk with the intention of unpacking later. My clothes still smelled like suntan oil. I needed a shower. As I assessed my wilted appearance in the mirror, my eyes drifted down to a letter on top of my jewelry box. His handwriting quickened my pulse. I sat on the bed and tore open the envelope.

Dear Samantha,

I hope you had fun in Maine. Lucky you, getting to swim and boat and hang in the sun with your cousins all day. I imagine you're tan. I remain milk-toast white, but oh well. Carlson was a bore without you.

How do I begin to tell you about what occurred last Friday at the lake? I realize that I have a jealous streak in me. It never came out before I met you. Anyway, in retrospect, I recognize that I let it get the best of me. I know I made things worse by reacting the way I did. But when Sid looked at you that way and made that remark about your body, I just went nuts. I know I shouldn't have. After all, he's right. You do know how to fill out a bathing suit (a little levity for the cause).

And by the way, you know what pissed off Shelly. I keep telling you that she's jealous of you, but you don't believe me. It's true. And she hates that our relationship is solid while she keeps going through boyfriends. She still strings Larry along, and that really makes me angry because he still loves her. I think he always will.

Anyway, Sam, I apologize for putting you in an uncomfortable position. If you want me to talk to Sid or Shelly and make things right, I will. For you. Not because I think I owe them anything. Call me when you get home. Maybe I can come over and see your tan lines. Now that's something to look forward to.

Keep the peace.

Love,
Buck

Good to forgive, best to forget.

—Robert Browning

Forgiveness comes in many forms. There is the forgiveness a parent grants his child, knowing that he is still learning. There is the forgiveness an adult child extends to his aging parent, recognizing that the lens of time has blurred his vision. And there is the forgiveness one lover gives to the other, knowing that he acted the only way he knew how.

"Hi, Sam. When did you get back?"

"A few minutes ago. Mom woke us up before the crack of dawn so we could get home at a decent time." A distant strain still hovered between us.

"I'm glad you called right away." Restrained silence. "Will Peg let you go out for a while?"

"I'm sure she will."

"Wanna walk down to the lighthouse and have that date?"

The tension began to lift. "Sure."

The lake was fairly calm, and locals, who loved spending time by the water, lazed on boats of varying sizes. Small crafts were anchored by larger vessels. A couple of visiting yachts had pulled in for an overnight respite as they cruised along the lake.

"Right over here." He pointed to a small, enclosed area amidst the rocks, where the ground was level enough to sit comfortably.

"Oh my God! This spot is perfect."

"Told you."

"It's private and open at the same time."

Large boulders, serving as an extension to the break wall, hugged in on three sides of the hidden space. We sat on the army blanket Buck had brought. The lighthouse, ever steadfast in her duties, blinked at us. For a time we simply sat, listening to the rhythm of the lapping water and the squeal of seagulls dancing overhead.

"Listen, Sam," he began. I knew what was coming, but I wasn't in the mood for a rehashing or a shower of angst. I just wanted to be.

"I read your letter. You don't have to say anything more."

He paused, pensively regarding the water, his arms crossed over his knees. "Forgiven?"

"Forgiven."

Then he reached into his pockets. "I brought Mallo Cups, just in case."

"Bribery?"

"Yeah," he admitted, irresistible as his eyes cast down remorsefully. "I know about your relationship with chocolate. I figured if my apology didn't work, the candy might *sweeten* you up."

"You gotta get some new lines, Kendall. That was weak."

"Yeah, well—this is it." He waved his hands over himself, "That's all there is to me."

"I'll take it." He leaned in to kiss me. "I meant the Mallo Cup. Hand it over."

The lighthouse blinked in our direction.

Forty-seven

Cary Grant, charming man that he was, remained a gentleman, despite the seductive allure that accompanies fame. Although his good looks and charismatic air turned him into one of Hollywood's heavyweights, he continued to treat everyone the same. Coal miner, bellman, Queen of England—each was worthy of respect, a philosophy by which he conducted his life. He impressed me—it seemed he recognized a truth that far too many miss.

Mr. and Mrs. Kendall were Cary Grant kind of people. They made everyone feel special, and when they spoke to you, they looked you directly in the eyes and called you by name. They never forgot a name. They were more concerned about you and what you had to say than sharing stories about themselves.

One Sunday the Kendalls invited me to join their family for brunch at the country club. The day felt breezy and light. The golf course was alive with locals teeing off in front of the big picture window, where our table awaited us.

Buck, his siblings, and I followed Mr. and Mrs. Kendall into the dining room. As we neared our table, his parents stopped to say hello to everyone who spoke to them along the way. As president of the college, Mr. Kendall was acquainted with the majority of people in town, and he always took the time to engage in conversation, as did his gracious wife. We sauntered along behind them, slowing up with each impromptu conversation. Finally Mrs. Kendall recognized that we would probably be more comfortable at the table while they chatted.

"Why don't you kids go ahead and sit down. We'll be right there." Her endearing smile filled me. I loved Mrs. Kendall.

The big table, set spaciously for only eight, wore freshly pressed white linens and held monogrammed china in royal blue and white. Napkins, folded into the shape of flowers, blossomed from each chiseled goblet, and roses sprang from a Waterford vase in the center of the table. Perfection settled all around me. When Buck pulled out my chair, Greg took the opportunity to needle him.

"Oh, Buck, your manners are so impressive. Sam, don't you feel special?" He grinned at his younger brother.

Buck lowered his voice as he leaned toward Greg. "Shut up, Greg. I learned it from you."

"And you learned well, little brother." He slapped Buck on the back, affectionately.

"Greg, why are you so mean to Buckie when Sammy's around? You should give him a break, you know." We cracked up.

"And, you, little sister, seem to know an awful lot about how to behave for a 4-year-old." Greg tousled her hair and put his arm around her fragile shoulders, gently tugging her toward him.

"Catherine, where did you learn that expression—give him a break?" Buck doted on his sister.

"From you, Buckie." She looked very proud of herself.

"Hey, Buck, some girl is staring at you over there." David, the youngest Kendall son, was pointing in her direction.

"Don't point, David. It's not polite," Greg reproached.

"Sorry." He recoiled slightly.

"It's okay, buddy." Greg put his tone in check. "Everybody goofs. Now, what girl are you talking about?"

"The one with the red hair at the corner table under the big mirror," replied David.

"Isn't that Jacquelyn Livingston?' Greg asked. "David's right. She keeps looking over here like she's trying to get your attention." Buck turned in the direction of Greg's nod where Jacquelyn's broad smile and flirtatious wave greeted him.

"Ooh, Buck, she's waving at you," said David. "Better watch out, Sam. She was staring at him when we walked in too." David was a good kid, but at the moment his brand of humor wasn't entertaining me.

"The man-eater." Greg continued to observe Jacquelyn's table, apparently unaware of what he had just called her.

Visibly uncomfortable, Buck switched his attention to check my reaction. Then he turned back to Greg, "She's not a man-eater. Anyway, she's got a boyfriend."

Anyway she's got a boyfriend? What does that mean?

"Who now?" Greg was clueless about any local discomfort.

"Charlie. Isn't it? I think she's still going with him." Buck's voice was flat.

"Charlie Hancock? No! He's going out with Laura Kingsley now. He must have had enough of Jacquelyn."

"Or the other way around."

Now I *was* interested. He was defending her. I had heard other kids say she was a man-eater, but I had no real evidence of its truth. She had recently joined my sorority, but I knew only that she was a sophomore, maintained straight A's, and was an only child. Nothing in her profile violated our code. Spoiled-brat-man-stealer wasn't a deal breaker.

"What do you mean?" Greg's expression changed.

"I think *she* broke up with *him*," Buck clarified with, I must add, irritating emphasis.

"How do you know *that*?" Greg retorted.

"She's in my math class. And we were both freshman representatives for student council last year."

Finally Greg sensed the tension. "Let's order. What do you want, Catherine?"

"She's pretty. I like her red hair." The 4-year-old again.

"Here, Catherine, have one of these crescent rolls. They're the kind you like. Want some butter?"

"Thanks, Greg. I like these rolls. Her dress is pretty too." She took an oversized bite of the roll. "It's pink."

Buck opened his menu. "What do you want to eat, Catherine? Mom and Dad are coming, and it's time to order. They have grilled cheese sandwiches. Your favorite."

Suddenly I felt self-conscious and slightly perturbed. I had no real reason to be—but let's face it, reason has little to do with emotion. I pushed back my chair. "Please excuse me. I'll be right back."

Buck and Greg stood in unison. Well-trained boys. Buck touched my arm lightly. "Are you okay?" Concern framed his face.

"Yeah, I'm fine. If the waiter comes, please order me a cheeseburger."

"Want fries with gravy too? We can share." His solicitous behavior was not endearing.

"Sure, that sounds good. Thanks."

Escape.

* * *

I rotated the porcelain knob on the sink, allowing the cool water to run across my wrists, and examined my reflection in the mirror.

Lipstick. That will help. A veil of discontent descended upon me. *So what if she was staring at him. It didn't really mean anything. From what I hear, she stares at every good-looking guy in the school.* My reflection wasn't convinced, and the lipstick didn't help. The ladies' room door swung open.

"Hi, Sam."

Through the mirror I regarded her perky face. Odd that she should show up at the exact moment of my escape. "Oh, hi, Jacquelyn." As she came closer, I noticed that her hair *was* pretty—prettier than I remembered. And her skin, smooth and creamy, seemed to glow. Instead of going into one of the stalls, she approached the sink next to mine and primped.

"How are you? I didn't expect to see you at the club." She wore an ingratiating smile.

"I'm fine, thanks. How are you?" I closed my tube of lipstick, blotting my lips on a tissue.

"Great." She flipped her copper hair over her shoulders and turned to admire herself in the mirror. "You're with the Kendalls."

No! Really?

"I am."

"How long have you and Buck been going together now?"

None of your damn business.

"A little over a year." I placed the lipstick tube inside my purse.

"You're such a cute couple."

Get me out of here.

"Buck was in my math class, so we got to know each other. He's so smart. Sometimes he helped me because I couldn't always understand the formulas," said the straight-A student. "Are you going to the sorority meeting this week? We'll be talking about rush season." She smiled amicably, not allowing a beat to pass in the conversation.

"Yes. I rarely miss the meetings." I headed toward the door. "I'd better get back to the table. We're about to order."

"See you at the meeting. Say hi to Buck for me," she purred.

I halted. "I will."

When Hell freezes over.

"Bye, Sam."

Grrrrrrrrrrrrrr!

* * *

On the ride home, we drove along the river, which traveled more rapidly than usual. The water level was high, threatening to overflow. I watched the rhythm of the moving waters, rushing over jutting rocks now smoothed by the constant current. I waited for the river to unburden me, but she hurried along, her course clear, and ignored my plea. Like a relentless song lyric, a singular thought stuck inside my head: *Jacquelyn Livingston likes my boyfriend.* I willed the thought away. I had no reason to doubt him. And yet—I never saw it coming the first time. Was I simply blind?

"A penny for your thoughts." The sound of his voice drew me back into the car where my body was stationed.

"Just thinking how considerate it was of your family to invite me today."

"Is that what you were thinking?" he challenged.

"Yes. Why?" I regarded him unflinchingly.

"You just seem sort of preoccupied." Whether he believed me or not, he accepted my words. "Did you have a good time?"

"I did."

"Good. So how come you're sitting so far away? Scoot over here." His expression made me want to abandon my doubts in the river and let them wash away.

"Hey, you two, watch it!" The voice came from our driver. "This is family day."

"You're just jealous that Sharon's not sitting up there with you!" retorted Buck.

"*Nobody*'s sitting up here with me! And you two are cozied up in the back, acting like I'm your chauffeur. Please don't start making out."

"Take us to Sam's house where we won't be interrupted." He returned his concentration to me.

"I wouldn't be so sure about that, little brother. I think Mr. and Mrs. D are on to you."

He ignored the last comment and pulled me closer. I could feel my body relax. *Why am I doing this to myself?* I wondered. *He doesn't care about her.* He put his arm around me and dropped his forehead to mine. "You do know how much I love you, right?"

"Oh, God! It's gettin' thick now. Hang on!" Greg turned up the radio and picked up speed.

*   *   *

Dear D,

I miss you already. I saw this card and couldn't resist buying it for you, even though it cost me $20. Kidding! You're worth it though. I knew it would make you smile.

I've been thinking, how would you like to learn to play golf? I could teach you. Then we could go to the club together on weekends and compete. Now, you might be thinking you don't want to because I have been golfing for years and am experienced, but I'm a really patient teacher. What say you?

My dad told me the news is filled with stories about riots in Detroit. I guess it's really bad. People were killed, and lots of buildings burned. What's wrong with people anyway? It's scary. I can't imagine what it would be like if it were happening here.

You definitely seemed preoccupied on the way home. I hope nothing is bothering you. If so, you know you can always talk to me about it. After all, what are best friends for (rhetorical question). It's my job as your boyfriend to make sure you're happy. Remember that!

Well, my dearest, it's time for me to go to bed. I wish you were here. Voulez-vous se coucher avec moi?

Take care.

Love always,
Buck

Forty-eight

Being good isn't always easy,
No matter how hard I try,
When he started sweet talking to me,
He'd come tell me everything is all right,
He'd kiss and tell me everything is all right

—Hurley and Wilkins

My father was a merchant marine. In truth, he would have been perfectly happy living on the sea for the remainder of his days. But his course was altered the night he met my mother.

One rowdy night while in some nameless port, Dad found himself in the backroom of a questionable bar, from where he emerged with a colorful tattoo of a schooner. It began above his elbow and sprawled all the way to the top of his arm—and there, at the very tip of the craft, a red flag proudly waved. When I was little, Dad would flex his muscles to make the ship sail. I was captivated by its movement as well as Dad's stories. My father's needs were simple. Living in the small quarters of his own boat would have suited him just fine. The fact that we lived in a four-bedroom house with a formal dining room satisfied no need for Dad. "It's all for your mother," he would say.

Dad purchased a 30-foot cabin cruiser that slept four, contained a miniature kitchen in the belly, and had a bow just large enough for me to sunbathe. Every summer Mom and he would spend the majority of their free time relaxing on the boat. They sometimes took short trips to the Thousand Islands area near Alexandria Bay. On weekends our whole family would go out on the boat for dinner and a swim. Those days saw my dad at his finest.

The end of August was a scorcher, the heat killing everybody. On one particularly sticky afternoon, Dad decided, uncharacteristically, to close his shop early and head out on the lake to cool down. Buck joined us.

"Jump!" He was yelling to me from the water. "It feels great!"

"Okay. Here I come! Ready?" Perfect cannon ball!

SPLASH!

My mother howled from the deck. "Very graceful, Sam." She threw in a couple of inner tubes. "You kids might want these."

The water felt cool and silky on my face and immediately extracted the heat from my body. I sprang up to the surface with another splash and doggy-paddled over to Buck, who was treading water while he waited.

"You're a nut, Sam. Why don't you try diving one of these times?"

"'Cause I don't know how." I paddled away, leaving a deliberate spray in my wake.

He wiped his eyes with his one arm while he continued to tread water with the other. "Yes, you do. I've seen you dive before. And stop splashing me in the face!"

"I prefer cannon balls. They've become my signature entrance."

"Indeed, they have." He smirked at me again. "Come over here by me." I paddled over, creating a deliberate water storm. "Knock it off!" he snorted, clearing out his nose.

"What did you say? I can't hear you." I moved toward the closer inner tube.

"You are in so much trouble!" He swam to the tube, where he attempted to pry my hands from their death grip.

"Yeah? What are you going to do?" Although I fought back, I was losing ground fast.

"Make you my prisoner and have my way with you." He was beginning to weaken but would not relent.

"I don't think so. My parents are right there. You'd better stop manhandling me before my father comes after you. Look!" I pointed toward the boat, and he whipped around, inadvertently loosening his grip. I managed to free one arm and attempted to swim away.

"You little brat! He's not on the deck." With that he expended the remainder of his energy on retaliation, draining me of my need to be the victor.

"Enough! You're going to drown me!" I pled.

"You give?" He wouldn't quit until I admitted defeat. "Do you give?" he repeated, pronouncing each word doggedly.

"Yes!"

"Then say uncle!"

"UNCLE!" I screamed. "Bully. Happy now?"

"Yes," he replied smugly. "Let's tread so I can get my breath back."

I glanced toward the boat and saw Dad back on deck. Mom had disappeared into the cabin, probably to make egg salad sandwiches, and my brother and sister were still on the other side of the boat, playing Marco Polo. Dad had taken Mom's place as sentinel; he was sitting back, sipping from a can of Budweiser as he perused the *Carlson Times*.

"You kids want a life jacket?" Dad yelled. Sadly, the lake had seen too many tragedies. He wasn't going to allow either of us to be one of them.

"Sure, Mr. D."

We swam to the stern of the boat, and Dad lowered the life jackets.

"One's good, Dad," I yelled up to him. "We're going to float together, and Buck's going to hold me up."

"Good thing you're in the water, Buck." Dad winked.

"Thanks a lot, Dad!"

"Here you go. One life jacket." He returned to the newspaper, his face registering concern. "Everything all right, Mr. D?"

"Race riots in New Jersey. Paper says they were started because of police brutality." Reality interrupted the lightness of the afternoon, and I found myself at a loss for words.

"Sorry, Dad." I didn't know what else to say. I knew my father took such matters seriously.

"Nothing you can do, kiddo. Go back out and have fun before it's time to eat." He settled into a deck chair. "And be careful."

"We will."

Life jacket secured, we drifted away from the boat, content without words for a time. My legs sliced through the bulk of water, the sensation pure tranquility. My arms hung weightlessly at the surface, fingers filtering through the ripples that our movement had created. Red and orange clung to the horizon, a warning of unwavering heat. It wasn't supposed to break until the weekend. I was grateful to be floating lazily in the lake. We continued to drift, my mind and body in sync, until thoughts of summer's end interrupted my flow.

"It was a good summer, wasn't it?" I reflected.

"The best." He kissed the back of my neck. "And the good part about going back to school this year is we'll be on the same schedule. That will make things a lot easier. Second semester we can both take Mrs. Newton's class. It's open to juniors and seniors. Can you handle a class with me, D?"

"That'll be fun. Our first class together."

"Equal turf. I can whip your butt on the tests." He swirled around, causing the ripples to grow larger.

"Don't be so sure, Kendall."

His left hand drifted down the outside of my leg. I didn't flinch, but my focus began to blur as it always did when he touched me. "You planning to show me up?" As he spoke, his hand detoured toward my inner thigh, fingers tiptoeing softly up the center of me.

"That's the plan." I stared at the horizon, increasingly aware that mind and body were no longer in sync.

"Can't wait to see that." His words exhaled in low tones while he flirted with the top of my suit.

"Buck . . ." His name burst forth like a reflex. "I . . ."

"What?"

"Nothing."

"Are you sure?"

"Yes." I breathed audibly.

He lifted my hand to his mouth and kissed my palm repeatedly. "I love you, Samantha DeSantis. You have no idea," he murmured.

"I think I do." I was losing myself.

His hand traveled down the length of my stomach, halting as it reached the rim of pink ribbon that wove itself in and out of the bottom half of my suit. I swallowed hard. Divergent forces gripped my gut, squeezing tighter. His thumb eased under the lacy rim and slid horizontally, one way, then the other. My legs hung lifelessly.

"You still okay, Sam?" His voice was like silk, while mine was a dying breath.

"Yes."

"You got really quiet all of a sudden; I just want to make sure."

The sun was sinking into the water, falling gradually out of sight. I remember thinking that I would be happy if we could descend together at that very moment, swim along the bottom of the lake, find a cave where we could live and breathe and never surface. Just us. Then his hand ventured down an inch farther, shaking me from my reverie and causing me to pitch ever so slightly.

"Maybe we should head back to the boat now." My words belied my thoughts, my conscience apparently on autopilot.

"If that's what you want," he acquiesced. I rotated and he looked me square in the eyes. "You do realize you're killing me, DeSantis." His levity eased me.

"I'm not trying to. Honest." A residue of concern resurfaced.

"Hey—look at me. I know. No worries." At that moment I couldn't have loved him more.

"You've just spent too much time with those damn nuns."

I smiled inwardly, grateful for this uncommon boy.

"Okay, D, compromise."

"Sure. What?" I asked, wanting nothing more than to devour him too.

"One kiss . . ."

How well I remember,
The look that was in his eyes,
Stealing kisses from me on the sly,
Taking time to make time,
Telling me that he's all mine . . .

Dear Sam,

I had fun on the boat today. Thanks for inviting me. The only problem was I went out for a swim to cool down and got heated up instead. Go figure. You look great in that new two-piece suit. And you gave me a lot to dream about tonight.

Hey, let's play miniature golf tomorrow after we both finish work. We don't have much summer left, and I need to continue my winning streak. (Who said I'm competitive?) We can ask Darlene and Sal to join us. What do you say? I'll call you in the morning before I leave for the golf course.

I'm caddying for two different professors tomorrow. Both of them tip really well. And that's a good thing because my girlfriend really likes to eat when we go out. She's got quite an appetite. But then so do I . . . if you get my drift. And for some reason, I have been extremely hungry lately. I just can't seem to get enough. Yes, I know I'm bad. But it's because I have to look at you all the time.

Guess what? I started reading The Sun Also Rises. You were right about Hemingway. When I finish, we'll talk. And I might even understand you better.

Sleep well, and know that I love you.

Me
XOX

P. S. Did I ever tell you that you're the best person I know? You are.

Forty-nine

Senior year. My life was full. I was class secretary, serving actively on the student council; I wrote for *The Bullet*, our school newspaper; and I was elected sorority historian, a job I was looking forward to. Buck and I followed the same schedule, allowing us considerably more time together. We were both upperclassman now. I think he felt a stronger sense of belonging with our group of friends. While the difference in class years had never bothered me, it was clearly an issue for him, one I never fully understood. Happily, our new schedule eased the edge.

Annie and I were sitting at her kitchen table after school, having just finished our annual drill about classes and classmates.

"So you guys are totally joined at the hip now." Annie shoved a glazed doughnut into her mouth as she spoke.

"How do you mean?" I settled for an apple.

"What do you mean, *how do I mean*? You're together every damn minute now. Same schedule, same breaks . . . we're losing you, Sam."

"You'll never lose me, Annie. Try as you may."

She laughed. "Ah, I love ya, Sammy. You're too good to be off the market and so scheduled all the time."

"I'm not scheduled. I'm here, am I not?"

"Right on. So what's up this weekend, DeSantis?"

"Not much."

"Buck at Varsity practice?"

"Yeah, till God knows when. Then Greg and he always stop for a burger on the way home."

"So are you seeing him tonight?"

"Yeah, he's coming over later."

"See what I mean? Joined at the hip."

"Give it a break, Annie."

"And what's with the apple, by the way?"

"I like apples. They're my favorite fruit. Besides, I want to lose five pounds."

"Why?"

"Because I need to."

"Did Buck tell you that you need to?"

I shot her a look. "No, he did not. He wouldn't dare. And I am offended by that remark."

"Oh, climb off of it. You're not offended."

"Yes, I am!" I stood my ground.

"Why wouldn't he dare? 'Cause he thinks you're so perfect?"

"I didn't say that."

Her expression became contemplative. "But he does." When Annie was serious, you paid attention.

"How's it feel, Sam?"

"What?"

"To have someone be so in love with you." A trace of envy lined her words.

"It feels wonderful, but sometimes it scares me."

"Scares you? Why?"

"Because I think we met too soon."

"Too soon? You mean you wish you had more time to go out with other boys before you met him?"

"No, it's not that. It's never been that."

"Then what?"

"It's just . . . we are so connected. Sometimes it scares me the way I feel about him. I can't imagine being without him."

I paused, deliberating if I should continue. But this was Annie, who perhaps understood me better than any of my friends. She remained quiet, waiting for me to decide.

"This might sound stupid, but sometimes I have these dreams where I'm losing him. He's just slipping away from me. And I try to walk faster to catch up to him, but I'm in slow motion and can't reach him. Then when I try to call out to him, my voice won't come out. It's the worst feeling. My chest starts caving in, and I can't breathe. I wake up, terrified, covered with a sensation I can't shake."

"Like sweat?" she said, straight-faced.

I smacked her on the arm. "No. Not sweat! Like my life is shattered."

Her face grew serious again. "It's just a dream, Sam. That's not going to happen."

"So why do I keep having the same kind of dreams?"

"Who knows?" She thought about it a moment, and I expected her to say something profound. "So stop thinking about it before you go to bed. Just think lovely thoughts. Doughnut?" The girl had perfect timing.

"Okay, Peter. And then will I fly away to Never-Never Land and stay young forever?"

"Yes, with Buck. How's that? And you'll always be in love and feel the way you do right now." She retrieved a bag of pretzels from the cupboard.

"Ah, would that it were so."

"Would that it were so?" she mimicked. "Seriously, DeSantis, nobody talks that way. You sound stupid. Here." She held out the doughnut. "Eat this instead of that damn apple."

"It does look good. Okay, hand it over."

"Now *this* is the girl I love! To junk food!"

"Salute!"

* * *

Love is energy of life.

—Robert Browning

We had no choice but to be together.

I loved his company.
He loved my humor.
I made him laugh.
He made me blush.
We had great conversations.
We talked for hours.
We played duets on the piano.
I was better.
We sang in harmony.
He was better.
I taught him to play Chess.
I usually won.
He taught me to play Pinochle.
I always lost.
I introduced him to Shakespeare.
He introduced me to Heidegger.
We bowled and fished, played badminton and miniature golf.
We practiced French together.
I read to him.
He taught me math.
I loved the multi-facets of his eyes.
He loved the dimples that appeared with my smile.
He melted me.
I drove him crazy.

It became difficult to distinguish where I ended and he began.

Fifty

Every fall, Theta participated in the Greek State Convention, sanctioned by our school district. In 1967 I served as one of the delegates. We traveled to Albany, New York, by bus, leaving on a Thursday evening after school and returning on Sunday afternoon. Three jam-packed days after which my brain turned to mush from all the thinking and debating.

After dinner, Dad drove me to the bus. Buck had eaten with us so he could come along to send me off. The school parking lot was filling up with girls and their baggage.

"Some of these girls have huge suitcases for just one weekend," Buck remarked as he looked out the car window. "I could get along with a duffle bag."

"That's because you're a boy," I replied.

Dad chuckled.

"Girls are too high maintenance," Buck added.

Dad laughed harder. "Okay, Sammy," he interrupted, "I'll see you Sunday." He leaned over and hugged me briefly. "Buck can get your suitcase for you. Got enough money?"

"I'm good, Dad. Thanks."

"Okay, Sam. Have fun."

Buck opened the trunk and grabbed my suitcase. We walked toward the group of travelers.

"You know I'm right. Why do girls have to take so many clothes?"

"This conversation is pointless. You're never going to understand."

"You're right," he conceded. "Beats the heck out of me how you girls prioritize."

"Get a grip, Kendall. We're not talking about brain surgery here. We're talking clothes. It's no big deal."

He seemed amused. "Hey, it'll be weird here without you, D."

"Only three days. You can finish the song you're writing so you can play it for me when I get home."

"I guess I could do that. You sure you don't want to bail and stay home with me?"

"Right!" I replied.

"Ah, I'll be fine. The junior class is sponsoring the dance Saturday. So I'll be busy with that. The officers are setting up about an hour before the doors open."

And Jacquelyn's going to be there, I thought. Amazing how quickly thoughts of her could transform my mood.

"Hey, where'd you go?"

"Just thinking. I'm good."

The bus roared into the lot, and everyone migrated toward it. Buck picked up my suitcase, and we headed toward the line that was forming to stow our bags.

"There's Angie. She's already boarding. Aren't you two rooming together?"

"We are. Angie!" I yelled. "Save my seat."

"Well, I'd better let you shove off," he said.

"Yeah, Angie's waiting for me.

"Have fun, D. Be good."

You too . . .

* * *

The bus trip to Albany took about four hours. After an hour or so, the chatting died down, and night grew darker.

"Sam, I think I'm going to try to sleep for a while. I'm sure we're gonna be up late tonight," said Angie.

"You're right. Good idea."

Angie repositioned herself, placing her pillow under her head. Before I knew it, she was snoring. Lucky her.

I closed my eyes.

The officers are setting up an hour before the doors open. She knows I'll be at the conference.

My eyes popped open. Forget sleep. I pulled out my diary.

September 28
8:15 p.m.

Dear Diary,

I'm on the bus to Albany. I talked to Angie for a while, but then she fell asleep. Normally I would be out cold, but Buck mentioned the junior class dance and now I can't stop thinking about it. Jacquelyn will be there. She'll probably love that! Buck without Sam! I think she has a boyfriend. Maybe he'll be there. Buck better not ask her to dance. No, he won't do that. She'd certainly enjoy it though. Dancing with Buck Kendall while Sam's away.

Man-eater! No, he'll be busy. Presidential responsibilities. I won't like it if he dances with other girls. Unless it's Darlene. Not Shelly. Annie would be okay. He better not dance with Jacquelyn!

Stop!

Stop!

Stop!!!!!!!!

This is ridiculous and sappy! You're not sappy. Pull yourself together.

Okay, so I'm going to this convention and once I get there my mind will be on business. Plus I have to help set up the social for Saturday night. I hope we have a little down time so I can finish my homework. I guess if I don't fit it in at the convention, I can do it on the bus ride home.

I just reread that first paragraph. Why do I do that to myself? I have nothing to fear. Time to sleep.

Dearest Sam,

It's Friday night, and here I lie in on my bed, trying to finish reading Inherit the Wind. Great book. You have to read it.

There's nothing to do here without you. I put on the Beatles, and Can't Buy Me Love is playing. Good lyrics: "I'll give you all I got to give if you say you love me too. I may not have a lot to give, but what I got I'll give to you. I don't care too much for money, money can't buy me love."

My parents are downstairs throwing a big party for some of the professors and their respective wives. They invited me to join them and meet people, but I don't really feel like it, not even for the food. And it was catered by Wellington's! They definitely know how to cook. Now maybe if you were here, we could socialize for a while and grab some good eats. But, alas, you are not. Is the food good there?

Here's some news. I guess Jim Morrison and the Doors were on Ed Sullivan and sang "Light My Fire." Have you every listened to those lyrics?

You know that I would be untrue
You know that I would be a liar
If I didn't say to you
Girl, we couldn't get much higher
Come on, baby, light my fire

The time to hesitate is through
No time to wallow in the mire
Try now we can only lose
And our love become a funeral pyre
Come on, baby, light my fire

Girl we couldn't get much higher

Can you believe that? And we missed it!

Okay, ready for a little Kendall humor? Here goes: I miss the sensation I get when I touch your unshaven legs and the sight of your straight, hard-to-manage hair. (Can you tell I'm bored?) But most of all, Sam, I miss your company. Here I sit, a prisoner in my own room because of a house filled with old people. What a comfort you would be to me. I hope you miss me a little too.

Bonne nuit, ma cherie. Dors bien . . .

Love always,
Buck

P.S. Don't volunteer for the spring convention, okay? Who am I kidding; I know you will. That's my girl, always in the thick of it.

Fifty-one

Absence makes the heart grow fonder . . .

—Thomas Haynes Bayly

The bus ride back to Carlson felt interminable. I had enough of meetings and rah-rah rallies. I was overtired from late nights with all kinds of girls in my room and too fatigued to read my book. So I stared out the window and watched the world pass by, willing sleep to rescue me. The fall colors had already peaked. Most of the trees looked lonely, the streets reaping the benefits of the downfall of fading color. One old house had a huge pile on the front lawn, and kids were jumping into it from the top of an overturned barrel. I caught bits and pieces of muffled squeals. The bus rumbled over a couple of hills and finally sank into a valley where I let myself fall into the blur of vapid orange and copper. I pulled my sweater more tightly around me and started to drift . . .

"I missed you. It's not the same when you're away. Give me a hug. Ah . . . you still smell like you."

He moved on top of me. My lids sank as if tasting the most exquisite fruit, ripe and fresh.

"I love you, Sam. You have no idea." His skin felt damp against my cheek.

"I love you, too." Everything was moving fast . . . faster than I could think . . .

"Let's make love."

I jolted upright and wiped off the drool running down the side of my face. "Let's go, ladies! Make sure you get all your belongings, and don't leave anything on the floor! This is not your bedroom! We'll be at the school in five minutes. Let's go!" Her hands slapped together like an army sergeant's.

"You okay, there, Sam?" Linda smirked. "Need a tissue?"

"Yeah, thanks. Mrs. Betz startled me. I was in a deep sleep."

"She does have a big mouth. Whoops, here she comes! Grab your stuff."

I stuck my head under the seat to gather my belongings.

"I hope my mother's here," I said to Angie. "I need to get home and shower before Buck comes over."

She giggled. "You are head over heels for that boy!"

As the bus lumbered into the lot, I spotted Mom's black Cadillac. And there he stood, leaning against the side of her car, gorgeous and grinning in his letter jacket. I flew off the bus. I couldn't wait to get my hands on him.

His sexy laugh filled the air. "Hey, sweetie. I couldn't wait for you to go home and shower and primp, so I thought I'd surprise you. I don't mind how grubby you are." He sniffed the air around me. "You *did* bathe before you left this morning, didn't you?"

"Smart aleck!" I smacked him on the shoulder.

"Hey! No physical abuse!" He grabbed the suitcase out of my hand.

"Such a gentleman."

"Indeed. And just look at you!" He checked me out from top to bottom. "The woman of many causes," he chuckled. "The streets were dead around here without you."

"So what did you do with yourself these last three days?"

As he spoke, I stared at his face. *So handsome.* I felt like a kid who had been away at camp all summer. Whenever we were separated for any length of time, I reacted the same way.

"Ah, not much. What's in this bag anyway? Bricks?"

"No, cement blocks."

"Quick! Very quick."

"So what's been happening on the home front?" I probed.

"The usual." He threw my suitcase into the trunk.

"How was the dance Saturday?"

"Fine. Kind of boring."

That was all I needed to hear. I jumped in the front seat next to my mother. "Hi, Mom."

"Welcome back, stranger. How was your weekend?"

"Productive, but long."

"Well, it's good to have you home. The house is too quiet without you. What do you kids want for dinner?"

"If it's all right with you, Mrs. D, I was going to take Sam to Tony's for a pizza. But if you'd rather have her stay home, I understand."

"No. That's fine. You kids do what you want. I'll see Sam later."

After pizza we ambled toward his house, content to be together again. "So tell me about the dance." I didn't really care anymore.

"Band was good. We didn't make as much money as I hoped. Larry was plastered."

"No way!"

"Mr. Thompson threw him out and called his parents."

"What was he thinking?"

"He wasn't. He was dogging Shelly. She showed up with her latest."

"Oh, man. What happened?"

"He tried to talk to her, but Sid wouldn't have it."

"Did they get into a fight?"

"They would've if Mr. Thompson hadn't stepped in."

"What did Shelly do?"

"Started crying. Big act."

"Maybe she was really upset." He rolled his eyes. I decided to let it go. "Soooo—did you dance with anybody?" I teased.

"Noooo," he mocked. "I worked the door and the concession stand. You know damn well I wouldn't be dancing with other women while you're away. Don't play coy with me."

"I guess," I added smugly.

"Besides, your girlfriends were there, and I knew they'd sing like canaries."

"You had to get that in, didn't you?"

"It's my job to keep you on your toes."

"Okay. New subject. Our sorority dance is next Saturday night. Did I tell you?"

"You did."

"I'm on the planning committee." I began rattling off the details of the upcoming event and my involvement with decorating the clubhouse dining room. He seemed to be listening—then he stopped abruptly in the middle of the street.

"Come here, DeSantis. I can't stand it anymore." Before I knew what was happening, he kissed me full on. One of those buckle-your-knees-and-please-never-stop kisses. God, he tasted good. "I hate when you're gone. I know you love being a part of this stuff, and I admire you . . ."

"But?" I waited.

My question caused him to shift focus. He stared down the street for the longest moment. I felt as if I were dancing alone in the middle of the floor, my partner having abandoned me. When he centered on me again, his eyes carried a burden. I couldn't imagine what he was about to say—one minute kissing me like there was no tomorrow, the next, struggling to speak.

"I'm empty when you're gone."

A surge of guilt coursed through me. His words resurrected the unfounded doubts I had grappled with on the bus ride to

Albany . . . the foolish diary entry I wrote to eradicate my fears . . . the speculative thoughts that seized me. I was rooted to the spot as he continued.

"I used to be content doing things solo, and I still am when I know you're only a phone call away. But when I know I'm not going to see you for a while, it's different. I can't concentrate. You're always in my head." He stopped himself. "Man, I sound stupid, don't I? Forget it. Let's go to my house." He grabbed my hand.

"No, wait. It's the same for me. There's something about being here without you. I understand that lost sensation. I feel like a part of me is missing. It doesn't bother me when I'm at sorority meetings or out with my friends—'cause I know you're still here."

"Exactly."

Exactly. There was nothing more to say. He yanked my arm and hurried me up the street. "Jane made chocolate cake. Walk faster."

When we arrived, the house was empty. "Where are your parents?"

A devilish smile made its appearance. "Oh, I guess they're out."

"You guess? You knew that when you invited me here, didn't you?"

"Well, actually, I thought this would be a quiet place for us to get reacquainted."

"Reacquainted? I was only gone for three days." I bought into his game.

"Well, that's three days we have to make out . . . er, I mean make up for."

I squelched amusement. "You're right. A lot of making up for lost time."

"Want to play the piano?" Out of nowhere. The black baby grand sat regally in front of the windows overlooking the lake.

"Okay. *Heart and Soul.*" He made a face. "But it's the one I know best."

"We have to learn some new tunes. We're wearing this one out."

"We will. But for now . . ." I pushed him to the left with my hip. "I want to play the top part." His fingers curled gracefully over the keys. We plunged in. "Switch!" I yelled in the middle of the song. Like a Chinese fire drill, we hopped off our end of the bench and scooted around to the other side where we reversed roles, playing another round of "Heart and Soul" followed by three rounds of "Chopsticks."

"Enough! I can't play these songs anymore!" His fingers slid off the keys.

"Okay. Well, let's eat cake then." He was still staring at the keyboard. "That *is* why you brought me here, isn't it?" I expected him to laugh, banter with me. Instead, he turned slowly, deliberately, regarding me with lowered eyes that flickered when they landed on me. His gaze coaxed me to join him.

"What about your parents?"

"They won't be home for two more hours." He was already touching me. His hands trickled down both arms, then hands, then legs. He kissed the bottom of my neck and up the side of my face, crossing both eyelids and traveling back down the other side. He lifted my hand onto his chest. His heart pounded in my open palm.

They say young love won't last, that it's not the real thing. They say first love burns so fiercely because you have never experienced these sensations before. They can say what they want. For me, each time with Buck was a thousand first kisses all over again. More than anything, I wanted this boy, wanted to belong to him and him to me. Would I ever be able to get past the guilt? Was it a sin to go all the way with someone you love? Could I betray myself? I couldn't stop kissing him.

Dear Sam,

I'm glad you're home. Home is a bore without you. I hope you're glad you came up to my abode last night. I certainly am. Things turned out as I hoped they might; well, almost as I hoped. I'll just keep holding out until you're ready. In the meantime, I'll continue to bang my head into the wall after we're together. The pain and swelling make me forget what I was after in the first place (ahem!).

Hey, did I tell you I'm going to be in the vocabulary challenge? Ain't that just grand? You know what a word maven I am, since you are as well, my dear. Didn't you get a 90 percent on our last vocabulary quiz? That's quite respectable. You should have put your name in for the contest too. I'm sure they would have chosen you. But I know you're busy writing articles for the school paper, and that's a very admirable endeavor. By the way, I really liked your last one on the dress code. Nice going.

Okay, I can tell you're sick of listening to me. So I'll see you at school tomorrow. I have to hit the books big time tonight. Carter's gone crazy with testing. Plus I have to start my research paper. But you know how I love that stuff.

Sweet dreams, kiddo.

XOX,
Buck

P.S. I started reading <u>The Adventures of Huck Finn</u>. Twain is brilliant.

Fifty-two

Sororities have been around for a very long time. Their inception dates back to the mid-1800s. Sororities began as secret societies for women and continued to evolve. These days, most college campuses are peppered with sorority houses, havens for sisters to bond and plan and raise a little hell. In Carlson, however, high school sororities had no such places of retreat. Members had to seek more creative ways to gather. It was all we knew.

The country club served as this year's location for Theta's fall dance. On the Friday night prior to the event, a bunch of us trekked up to the club to decorate. The ornate double doors at the main entrance were already festooned with corn stalks and pumpkins, producing a seasonal welcome, a club tradition. Our job was to create a party atmosphere, which began with hanging balloons and streamers from the ceiling and wall posts. We placed jack-o-lanterns everywhere, including the center of each table, with a hidden riddle underneath each pumpkin for door prizes. Candy corn and peanut butter taffy were strewn across the tablecloths, black and orange flashed from every corner, and spider webs and skulls added the finishing touches.

I stood in the middle of the room, appraising our work. Perfect! I was in a grand mood. Anticipation had me bubbling over. My only hope was that reality would match expectation.

* * *

"Wow, Sam, this place looks great! You guys must've worked a long time last night."

"Not too long. It was fun." I adjusted the centerpiece on the entrance table and watched the room fill with Theta girls and their dates. The place was already humming. Most everyone was punctual, and for that, I was grateful, especially since this event was partially my doing. I wanted the evening to go well.

"This punch is yummy. When are they bringing out the food?"

"In about an hour. First we plan to let people mingle and dance awhile. Listen to the band. Aren't they neat?"

"I can't believe you actually signed them for tonight. They're so expensive."

"Yeah, but they're the best in town. The extra fundraisers helped."

I checked out the room, satisfied with the scene that lay before me. Buck caught my eye and headed in my direction. His corduroy jacket and turtleneck gave him a scholarly air, like a professor that all the girls fall for in a movie.

"Wanna dance, or are you too busy being hostess?"

"I can dance." We stepped into the crowd already grooving and singing along to familiar lyrics.

Ain't no mountain high enough
Ain't no valley low enough

When Tammi Terrell and Martin Gaye finished their song, the band mimicked the Monkees with surprising accuracy. Another party-pleasing tune.

Oh, I could hide 'neath the wings
Of the bluebird as she sings
The six oclock alarm would never ring.

I continued to examine the room to ensure that all was well. "Oh, the food's coming out. I'd better go check. Hungry yet?"

"Always," he replied. "Where's the food from?"

"Delcie's Diner."

"I love that place. Did you get any of those mixed sub sandwiches?"

I was about to answer when Jacquelyn and Charlie waltzed in like the King and Queen of England. Their appearance surprised me because the last I heard, they had split up. Distracted from the menu question, I turned to busy myself by attending to the stacks of paper plates and napkins on the buffet table.

"There they are!"

"Who?" I swiveled toward him.

"The sub sandwiches I just asked you about. I better grab one before they're gone." He began filling his plate while I ventured to the other side of the table where Celia was standing.

"Hey, Celia?" I asked in hushed tones. "Are Jacqueline and Charlie back together?"

She leaned in. "So it seems. Guess he couldn't live without her. She looks good, doesn't she?" Celia admitted sourly.

I ignored her comment. "So when did they get back together?"

"Umm, I think only a couple of days ago. She probably lured him so she'd have a date for tonight. You know how she hates to be alone." Jacquelyn irritated most of my sorority sisters. There was something insincere and manipulative that leaked through the sweet exterior. Maybe we were all jealous. Celia and I watched her work the room.

"Always a boy on her arm," added Celia. "See you later, Sam. You and Buck have fun. God he's cute," she drooled.

"Who?"

"Buck, foolish girl. Lucky you. See you later." Celia strolled away.

While I was getting the lowdown, Buck talked with one of the guys on the basketball team. Noting that my conversation with Celia had ended, he walked over to my side of the buffet. "Sam, let's sit down and eat. I'm hungry." A couple of his cronies beckoned us to join them. The conversation turned to sports, so I took the opportunity to check on the status of the food and the band. When I returned, Jacquelyn and Charlie stood next to our table.

"Hi, Sam. You look cute tonight." Her hair kept falling over one eye.

Cute. My favorite word.

"Thanks, Jacquelyn."

"So everything seems to be going great. Good crowd. Almost our whole membership showed up." Every time she moved, her diamond cut chain sparkled. When my gaze fell upon the heart at the end of the necklace, she began twirling the chain and cast her eyes proudly toward Charlie, who clutched her polished fingers as he entertained the boys at our table.

"Charlie gave me this as a getting-back-together gift," she announced. "It's from Tutor Royale. Isn't it pretty?"

A getting-back-together gift? Please. Her affect was nauseating.

"It is." At least it was a response.

She turned toward Buck, flirtatiously brushing back the hair that fell over her eye. "Do you like it, Buck?"

"Sorry, what did you say?" He looked up from his seat, regarding her as if she were a waiter asking if everything was all right. Her reaction revealed embarrassment and a trace of shock that she wasn't the center of attention.

"I just told Sam that Charlie gave me this necklace as a getting-back-together gift. Don't you think that's sweet?"

"I never knew there was such a thing." I had to look away because I thought I was going to start laughing. Then he tapped Charlie's shoulder. "Good-going, pal. You're smoother than you look."

Jacquelyn's disappointment was visible. And now the light shone on Charlie instead of her.

"Thanks, Buckaroo," replied Charlie as he man-slapped him on the back. "Anything for my gorgeous girl here." He leaned over and lavished her with a big, wet, open-mouthed kiss.

"Get a room!" shouted one of the guys at the table.

"Charlie, not in front of everybody!" She feigned embarrassment while she lapped up the attention. And just when she was back in the spotlight, the band broke into their rendition of "Something Good."

"Herman's Hermits, Sam. Dance with me?" Buck took my hand and led me away. End of Round One.

I walked her home and she held my hand
I knew it couldn't be just a one-night stand
So I asked to see her next week and she told me I could.
Something tells me I'm into something good

From across the noisy space between us, I shouted to Buck, "Carole King wrote these lyrics."

"Leave it to you, D."

Across the room Charlie was in signature motion, arms flailing about. He managed to produce some combination of the Freddy, the Monkey, and the Jerk. I must admit that he was entertaining; however, Jacquelyn didn't seem to think so. Her face was that of a mother whose child was throwing a tantrum in public. Until she saw me looking. Then she transformed, delighted by her boyfriend's comedic moves and demonstrative display of affection. I almost felt sorry for her.

"You okay?" Buck never missed a trick.

"I'm great."

"Did I tell you that you look really nice tonight?" he yelled across the floor.

"No."

"You look *really* nice!" He grabbed my hands and swung me around. The remainder of the evening was smooth.

* * *

The temperature drop caused me to shiver. Smoke poured out of the fireplace, tempting me back inside where I could curl up in one of those comfy chairs and feel the heat radiating on my face. The shivering escalated.

"Who's picking us up?"

"Greg's got the wheels tonight. He should be here in a minute." He rubbed my shoulders while remaining on the look-out for his brother. Even he began to shift around for warmth.

The dance was a hit. I was happy for the success but relieved to shed my responsibilities. Fortunately, the clean-up committee took over, and I was free to leave. Most everyone had exited as soon as the band stopped playing. The parking lot was emptying while the circular drive filled with parents serving as chauffeurs. Kids were piling into cars and making plans about where they were going next. It was, after all, Saturday night.

Buck snuggled up tighter for warmth. "Damn, it's cold."

"The dance was good, wasn't it?"

"A success! Congratulations." He kissed the back of my head, nestling his face in my hair. "You smell good. Ambush?" I nodded, pleased that he had noticed. Then he turned me around.

There are far too many kisses to remember; they blend together in a haze of memory. But then there are some . . . what is it? The moment, the surroundings, the sensation . . . all join to form that particular kiss. And that's the one that haunts you. This was possibly the most tender touch we had ever shared.

"Warmer?"

"Much." My heart was full.

Suddenly I was aware that we were not alone. Jacquelyn Livingston's flamboyant giggle filled the space between us. Charlie was planting another sloppy man kiss on her while he dipped her backward. "God, Charlie! You're so rough!"

When I glanced over Buck's shoulder, she rolled her eyes as if she just couldn't keep him off her because she was so irresistible. She smiled when she saw me looking.

"Hey, forget them." Grateful for the intervention, I folded back into him. "There's Greg coming up the driveway. Let's go." He grabbed my hand, and we ran to the car.

"Hey, kids, how was the dance?" Greg's arm hung out the window.

"Fun," Buck answered. "Sam did a great job."

"Hop in the back."

Sharon was pressed against him. "Roll up the window! I'm freezing." He did as he was told.

"Let's go to the house and play *Jeopardy!*. Or are you afraid to get your ass whooped?" His good mood was contagious.

"Let the games begin!" announced Buck. Knowing him, we *would* win—with little help from me, unless, of course, the categories were about language or theater. My areas of expertise were admittedly narrow.

The car took off around the wide circular drive, and from my window, I could see Jacqueline staring at us as she pushed Charlie away.

Fifty-three

Trust is the lifeblood of a relationship. Without trust we wither and seek other sources of nourishment. But sometimes we simply fail to see the certainty that has been there all along.

It was the Thursday after the Theta dance and my turn to host the weekly meeting. Over fifty girls filtered through my living room and into the kitchen, socializing before the meeting. Mom loved having the girls around. She said the presence of youth added energy to the house. Earlier that day, she had baked a ton of cookies and arranged an attractive spread on the kitchen table. The household was happy as everyone milled about.

Enter Jacquelyn.

I felt my body stiffen, remembering the way she had watched Buck and me at the club. I knew I was going to see her on that evening but wasn't prepared for the physical reaction that buckled me. I deliberately busied myself as hostess, trying my best to be where she wasn't.

Thwarted.

"Hi, Sam." She was standing beside me. "Your house is cute."

Cute again.

"Thanks. Brownie?" I held out the plate.

"No thanks. You did a great job on the dance," she fawned.

"I didn't do it alone. I was just on the committee. Potato chips?" I picked up the bowl from the table.

"Oh, no thanks. Well, you all did a good job. It was fun."

"Thanks. Oatmeal cookie?" The plate was back in my hand.

Shove it in your mouth and stop talking!

"No thanks. I'm watching what I eat."

Of course you are.

"Well, make yourself comfortable. The meeting is about to start." I had almost made a clean get-away when, without transition, her words stopped me in my tracks.

"You and Buck are such a cute couple." Her voice held longing. Had my reflexes been quicker, I would have reacted as if this were a compliment. But there was something about the way she said the words that halted me.

"And he kisses you so nice."

FREEZE!

She talked more to herself than to me. "So gentle. Not like Charlie. He just grabs me and throws me back. Not exactly romantic. But you guys . . . you're different." When she looked up again, her eyes registered shock, as if I had read her diary.

"You watched him kiss me?" I couldn't move beyond that idea.

"I couldn't help it." She shifted position. I had never seen her when her defenses were down. She always appeared overly confident, comfortable to jump into any conversation, whether she was invited or not. "You were right next to us. You didn't hear us when we first walked out. Not until I started laughing and you turned around."

A disturbing awareness crept though me. It was one thing to admire a couple or want to have what they had. But that was not what she wanted. An awkward stillness held both of us in position.

"Sam! The meeting's about to start. We need you over here." The president's voice traveled across the room.

Thank God.

"I'll be right there, Maureen." I didn't want to look at Jacqueline again, but I sucked it up. "Sorry. Duty calls."

"Oh, I understand."

Did she?

I sat in the middle of the floor amongst my sorority sisters, doing my best to concentrate on the business at hand. But fundraisers and parliamentary procedure took a back seat to the conversation repeating itself in my head, to the envy in her eyes, to the seed that had taken root deep inside me. I don't know why it weighed on me so heavily. I trusted Buck. This had nothing to do with him.

He kisses you so nice . . . she watched us kiss . . .

"Sam?"

"Sam! The dance report." The room chuckled.

I trust him.

Fifty-four

I am a fool for traditions. One of mine is watching *White Christmas* every holiday season. Yes, I am one of those people who watch movies over and over, ad nauseum. So shoot me. Some stories just make me happy. *White Christmas* is one.

We were sitting by the tree, and Bing Crosby was trying to figure out why Rosemary Clooney's character had suddenly pushed him away. That part always frustrates the hell out of me. I want to scream at the TV and tell Rosemary that it was the Busy Body's fault.

"That woman irritates me so much! She screwed up everything!"

"Sam, you know how it turns out." Buck threw more popcorn in his mouth.

"But why does she do that? She's such a busy body!"

"M-O-V-I-E." He spelled the word with deliberation. "Not real. How can you get so involved with this story that you have seen a hundred times?"

"It's like visiting old friends," I explained.

It was our second Christmas. Earlier that day we had exchanged gifts. He gave me a gold heart-shaped locket with a custom inscription inside: our initials, with the **S** over the **B**, a symbol we had created during our profusion of letters to each other. One word appeared below the symbol, engraved in French script: *Forever.*

I opened the box and caught my breath. "It's beautiful." The necklace twinkled as I lifted it from the box.

"Do you like it?" he asked timidly.

"It's beautiful. You had our symbol inscribed inside. I can't believe it. Those aren't real diamonds are they?"

"Really *tiny* diamonds. One for you and one for me. But you're the keeper. Here, turn around, and I'll put it on for you." He guided me to the hall mirror and hooked the chain around my neck. "What do you think?"

"I think I'll wear it always." As I admired the sparking reflection in the mirror, I imagined him going to the jewelry store and selecting my gift. What made him choose this particular one? What was going through his mind when he decided on the inscription? *Forever.*

"Okay, are you ready for one more?" He looked exceptionally pleased with himself.

"What?" My eyes scolded. "You didn't stick to the deal. You went over the budget."

"What budget?" He walked to the chair where he had tossed his coat and dug underneath, retrieving another package. "Here. And you can close your mouth now."

"You weren't supposed to do this."

"Just open it."

We sat down on the rug, and I tore off the paper like a five-year-old. I lifted the box top and pushed back the tissue paper. Gold initials stared up at me: *SLD* on a leather-bound journal. I ran my fingers along the supple leather cover and gold-tipped linen pages. A silk ribbon slid through the pages. I glanced up from the book.

"So, do you like it?"

It was moments like this one that I felt the purity of his love, the thoughtfulness of his gestures. "I couldn't love anything more."

"Not even me?" I covered him with kisses. "Sam, you're a great writer, and I want you to have a special place to collect your ideas. Mrs. Newton is right about you. You must write."

I turned to the page held by the silk marker.

Dearest Samantha,

"Real writers are those who want to write, need to write, have to write."

—Robert Penn Warren

That's you, Sam, Use your talents. You have to. Merry Christmas . . .

All my love,
Buck

"You *will* write, won't you?"

"That's a silly question."

"Even if I'm not around?"

Ah . . . and there we were. He spoke a truth I was not prepared for. "Why? Where are you going?" I teased. It was all I could muster.

"You know what I mean." His eyes narrowed. "When you're at college, and I'm not . . . not there to bug you." He sighed heavily with the admission of his words. It no longer felt like Christmas. It was the unexpected night I sat in the waiting room at St. Joseph's Hospital, watching the minute hand crawl while my mother's younger brother lay cut open on the operating table. While I pushed back my anxiety. While I watched my mother's expressionless face as she paced around the room, willing him to be all right with the fidelity of her steps. Knowing he wouldn't be.

I shook myself loose.

"When have you ever had to bug me to write?" My eyes fell back upon the journal that I cradled. He knew what I was thinking.

"Promise you'll write?" he asked.

"Promise. Not to mention all those long letters I'm planning to write to you."

His vulnerability quickened my heart. I slid my hand through his hair, breathing in the here and now.

"This is the best gift ever."

"Even better than the locket?"

"Yeah, even better."

Fifty-five

The New Year's celebration is the oldest of all holidays. First observed about 4000 years ago in ancient Babylon, the celebration lasted for eleven days. Modern New Year's Eve festivities pale in comparison, yet people have high expectations. They dress up, attend elaborate parties, and kiss whoever happens to be standing nearest at the stroke of midnight. Then everyone breaks in to a chorus of "Auld Lang Syne," even though most people have no clue what the words really mean. They stay up all night in the name of ringing in the New Year. They make resolutions to be better humans next year. Out with the old and in with the new. New Year's Eve. *Should* old acquaintances be forgot and never brought to mind?

"So after the movie, do you want to go back to your house? Your parents are having a party, aren't they?" Buck looked really handsome in his camel hair coat. It was a gorgeous winter evening, so we decided to walk to the movie theater. Why waste such a night inside a car.

"Yep, and we're invited," I said.

"So let's do that. Peg and Nick's parties are always fun."

When we returned to my house after the movie, the celebration was in full swing.

"Kids! Come in and join the party!" said Mom.

My mother wore a shimmery gold dress with matching drop ball earrings that swayed from side to side when she moved. She looked beautiful and, as usual, was the life of the party. She managed to get everyone to twist to Chubby Checker at the same time and later to play Charades. Mom always said that games brought people together.

"Go in the dining room and get something to eat. Lots of food! How was the movie?" She was on a roll, as usual.

The spread of food included Mom's famous liverwurst pate, tiny meatballs in sauce, a plate of little sandwiches, two of her pies, lemon and chocolate. The Christmas tree shone happily in the living room and lights flickered from every corner of the house. As midnight neared, Mom assembled everyone in front of the television in the living room where she distributed hats, noise makers, and streamers.

"Okay, everyone. It's almost time. Find your spot!"

My brother and sister appeared and plopped themselves in front of the television. Mom had made them her helpers. Throughout the evening, they carried trays, serving hors d'oeuvres, and kept the ice bucket filled.

As Mr. New Year's Eve, Guy Lombardo, and his Royal Canadians played to a full house in a ballroom in Manhattan, excitement filled Times Square. Thousands of bundled onlookers crowded the streets, cheering loudly in anticipation of the moment when the famous twinkling ball would descend at One Times Square. I love those last moments before midnight, especially the stroke of midnight when time stands still for a spectacular second. I wait for that perfect moment when everyone screams "Happy New Year" and sparks of colors sprinkle down on jubilant faces.

"Happy New Year, Sam," Buck kissed me softly.

"Happy New Year." I burrowed into his neck, pressing my lips into his sweet, salty flesh.

"Would anyone miss us if we slipped away and went downstairs to have our own party?" he asked.

"No one will miss us."

I took his hand, and we headed down the basement stairs. The wrought iron banister was swathed in cedar roping mixed with holly and colored lights. A second tree stood at the foot of the stairs, and it winked at us as we descended. Mom had turned on the Ben Franklin stove in case anyone ventured to the lower level. We walked over to the bar area next to the sliding glass door. Heavy flakes danced around the lamp posts, eventually landing and adding to the hills of white.

I picked up two flutes and poured an inch of champagne. "To what shall we toast?"

"To the beginning of another year together. To having found the one who understands you."

"Salute."

We took a sip and settled into the couch. Holiday music filtered through the speakers. Andy Williams, Mom's favorite. The familiar lyrics filled me with a sense of well-being. Lights twinkled around us, inside and out. Everywhere I looked Mom's touch had remade a space that would otherwise have been just a basement. I knew I was lucky to have been born into this family who reveled in the joy of ordinary moments.

He nudged me. "You're smiling. What are you thinking about?"

"Just happy."

"You're always happy, DeSantis. You're the happiest person I know." He kissed me. "By the way, do you like this champagne?"

"Not at all."

"Well, we were grown-ups for a minute. Give me your glass." He placed both glasses on the bar top and grabbed the plate of biscotti cookies that were begging to be eaten. "These are more our style."

"I agree. But we had to have our toast."

"Indeed." He shoved half of the cookie in his mouth. "These things are sinful. Your mom can cook." He grabbed a second cookie. "I could scarf down the whole plateful." Crumbs fell from the corners of his mouth. "We need milk!"

"There's some in the refrig behind the bar. I'll get it." Milk in hand, I returned to our spot under the stairs and took my seat beside him.

He downed the entire glass. "Ah! Now this is more like it."

So often we retreated to this space. It belonged to us. It was quiet and familiar. It held no expectations. No eyes invaded our sanctuary. It occurred to me that we were completely ourselves whenever we were alone . . . on the bluff overlooking the lake . . . on the balcony off the side of the school . . . snuggled together under the basement stairs. I knew I was going to miss these moments and the easy access we had to slip away. I could feel him looking at me.

"What am I going to do without you, Sam?"

I had pushed that thought so far back that the reality was miles away. I could only picture now. But that reality loomed above us, a hovering reminder that life goes on and nothing remains the same.

"It'll be the same for me, only you'll still have your buddies here. Your life will be pretty much the same."

"No, it won't. It'll be like eating pizza without cheese."

I liked when he made light of things. That was not always the case. "So I'm the cheese now?"

"Hey, the cheese is the best part. And it's a staple in France and Italy, your favorite countries."

"Let's make a New Year's resolution."

"Okay."

"We won't talk about being separated anymore. We'll focus on now."

"Deal. Let's lie down and watch the snow fall. It's really coming down. Look at your backyard." It was like looking into a snow globe.

"It's mesmerizing." I could feel myself sinking.

"Snow or rain?" he asked.

"They're different."

"Snow or rain?" he insisted.

"Rain."

"Hemingway or Twain?"

"Hemingway. For sentimental reasons."

"No clarification, please. Just answer," he added. "*Bonnie and Clyde* or *The Graduate*?"

"*The Graduate*."

"Dustin Hoffman or Warren Beatty?"

"For acting or looks?" I demanded.

"Just pick!"

"Hoffman for acting. Beatty for looks."

"You're not playing by the rules!"

"Screw the rules!"

My head was on his chest, which gently rose and fell with laughter. Without decision, we settled into the tranquility of our surroundings, the hypnotic movement of the flakes lulling me. I willed myself to stay awake.

"Tired?" he asked.

"I am. Sorry I'm being a party pooper."

"It's fine."

There was comfort in the weight of his arm across my body, the softness of his sweater on the side of my face, the feel of his hand wrapped around mine. I felt his body relax, and I curled into him more tightly. Against my will, I drifted between intermittent bursts of consciousness. Later he told me that the rhythm of my breathing put him to sleep too. Such peace. Too bad these euphoric moments can't be bottled so you can swallow a spoonful whenever life becomes too much.

It was 1968, the year I would turn eighteen, graduate from high school, and move away from home. My life would change far more than I knew. But in the first hour of that year, I remained in my life as I knew it, ignorant of the unavoidable complications waiting around the corner. That night was the first time Buck and

I had ever fallen asleep together. It seemed so natural, the way I had always imagined it.

"Happy New Year, Sam," he whispered. His voice traveled into fading awareness. I felt him pull me closer. That's the last thing I remembered until my mother woke us up.

My dreams were sweet that night.

Fifty-six

The snow just kept on coming. Each day saw a steady fall that began to feel endless. Piles of white mounted so high on the street corners that making a turn without smashing into another car was a delicate dance. Red warning flags waved on the antennae of most vehicles. It was going to be a long winter.

"Happy New Year, everyone. I trust your holidays were festive and fulfilling and that you received everything on your list. It's good to see you all looking so rested." Mrs. Newton stood in front of the classroom. She looked happy to be there. She may have been the only one who felt that way.

"Why, Mrs. Newton? Could it be that we're going to need our strength because of the rigorous mental workouts you have planned for us?"

"However did you know, Buckley? I've always said you were an intuitive young man." Her smile revealed fondness.

"Now, I do have an announcement to make."

"Here we go . . ." Chad Donaldson. Last row, last seat, corner. Always hiding from responsibility.

"No worries, Chad. It doesn't concern you today," assured Mrs. Newton.

"Thank God!"

Everyone loved Mrs. Newton's class. She was exuberant, she was there for her students, and she inspired us.

"No, this is not about missing assignments, Chad." She eyed him good-humoredly.

"Come on, Mrs. Newton, cut me a break. It's Monday."

"Seriously, everyone. I do have an announcement. There's a writing contest that features young authors and helps substantially with promoting new voices. It's sponsored by The Wordwall Company, and both scholarships and publishing opportunities are available for the winners. They are choosing a first, second, and third place writer."

"And you want me to submit my last paper, right, Mrs. Newton?" Chad continued. The class cracked up. Everyone counted on him for comic relief.

"Chad, while yours is a generous offer and delights me to no end, I will spare you the revision time. Sporting activities are your arena."

"Good one, Mrs. N."

"Actually, I was thinking of Samantha DeSantis and Buckley Kendall, two outstanding and original writers."

"So that's what they see in each other. Now I get it. They can write back and forth, and they don't have to talk." Chad again.

In the midst of my classmates' amusement, I sat, stunned.

"What do you say, kids? Are you up for the challenge?"

* * *

Is competition healthy? I'm on the fence. Invariably, a cutting edge surfaces and disappointment follows. But is there any way around it? We live in a competitive world. Can we learn to compete graciously? Must we in order to survive?

I never thought I had the competitive gene. Expending my energy to beat out others was not on my list of things to do before I die. Doing my personal best was. Call me Pollyanna. Buck, on the other hand, loved the adversarial role. There was no question that he was more intelligent than I, in the cognitive sense. My strength lay in emotional intelligence. Buck was quick and witty, and he could spit out facts about anything. He earned A's on everything he wrote, and I teased him that his teachers graded him before they even read the damn papers.

Oh, it's Buckley Kendall's paper. Heaven! It's surely a top-notch piece.

They were right. He could produce remarkable papers, quite different in style from mine. This writing competition presented an unusual situation for us. As we walked out of Mrs. Newton's class, Buck seemed preoccupied with the contest, as he had since Mrs. Newton made her announcement.

"So what do you think, D? You planning to submit something?"

"Are you?"

"I asked first."

"I might as well. If Mrs. Newton hadn't asked me, I wouldn't have sought out a contest. But since she brought it up, I think *yes.*" I waited.

"You can probably just whip out one of those articles you already wrote for the newspaper and edit it to fit."

"Funny. And you?"

"Definitely." The overconfident smile.

"You can probably just polish up one of those old "A" compositions. You do have a file, right?" And I walked, quite proud of myself, I must say.

"Touché.

I kept walking.

He caught up. "So we're in competition, eh, babe?"

"Yep, along with thousands of other writers across the United States. This isn't going to create any friction, is it?"

"Of course not. You know how I savor healthy competition. Besides, you have no chance."

"You're arrogant, Kendall."

"And you, Miss DeSantis, better sharpen your pencil."

"So who's going to edit your paper? It would be a conflict of interest for me." I smirked.

"So you're holding out on that? Really?"

"Just this time."

"I'm going to remind you that you said that, DeSantis. No more holding out."

"Double entendre? Clever."

I walked away thinking that he would probably win.

Fifty-seven

There are many legends about St. Valentine. One claims that a man with this name sent the first "valentine" greeting while he was in prison. He fell in love with a young girl who visited him during his imprisonment. Before he died, he supposedly wrote her a letter and signed it "from your Valentine." Who knows if this story is true, but its appeal is romantic. Forbidden love. The bad boy behind bars and the innocent girl who falls in love with—the idea of the best version of him, most probably. Selfish. She probably pined away for him for the remainder of her years.

"It's just a money-making day created by Hallmark," he declared.

"It is not! St. Valentine existed long before Hallmark was ever heard of."

"You just ended a sentence in a preposition, DeSantis."

"What are you talking about?"

"And there it is again!"

"Yuck it up. You're just trying to change the subject because you know you're wrong. And for your information, prepositions *are* used at the ends of sentences in colloquial language." My hands were on my hips.

"Stop talking and come here."

"I'm willing to accommodate that request if you'll admit you are wrong." I walked toward him with deliberation and slid my hands up his legs to his hips. He lifted my hands, pulling them around his neck.

"Say it."

"I was wrong," he admitted.

"That's all I wanted to hear." I pulled away and headed toward the refrigerator.

"You little brat! You think you're smart, don't you?"

"I do. Pepsi?" I filled two glasses with ice.

"Okay, so what do you want to do for Valentine's Day, my little trickster?"

"Be with you. I'm easy."

"No, DeSantis, you are definitely not easy. You're a lot of work sometimes."

"Okay, I'll cooperate. Let's just go to a movie. That's not much work."

"We do that all the time. There's nothing special about that. Don't you want to do something special for Valentine's?"

"I know!"

"Why do I think I should be worried?" His brow was furrowed.

"Let's go to CSU to see *Romeo and Juliet*. It just opened, and the Performing Arts Department has a great production company. I've seen their plays before." The words sped out of me.

"But *Romeo and Juliet?*" He spoke as if a judge had just handed him an unfair sentence.

"Can you think of anything more romantic?"

"I can't." I could see that he was trying to be a good loser. "Fine."

"I love you for this, Kendall!"

"I'll keep telling myself that's why I'm doing it."

"You'll love it. I promise."

* * *

The red rose. Elegant, timeless, an enduring symbol of love. According to Greek mythology, Aphrodite, the goddess of love, created the rose as she ran to her dying lover, Adonis, but was inadvertently scratched by a thorn. The scratch drew blood, and the drops landed on the white rose, turning it red. On the other hand, Roman mythology maintains that Venus, the Roman name for Aphrodite, created the red rose when her tears for the dying Adonis fell upon the rose. Blood or tears, it's a beautiful myth. The red rose sends the strongest message of love.

"A rose! Oh, Buck, thank you!"

"I know it's corny, but I couldn't help myself." He was standing in the foyer as he presented me with a rose in perfect bloom.

"Come in and say hi to Mom." I held onto the rose as if it were the Hope diamond.

"Hi, Buckley." Mom walked toward him.

"Happy Valentine's, Mrs. D." He kissed her cheek.

"A rose! That is so sweet," she gushed. I'm not sure who was more pleased about his gift, Mom or me.

"Thanks, Mrs. D. I figured it was fitting since we're going to see *Romeo and Juliet*. You know, *a rose by any other name* and all that good stuff.

"Well, that's just so thoughtful," added Mom.

"So, is Mr. D. taking you out on the town tonight?" Buck asked, expecting that this was the norm for them.

"No, we're staying in. Having dinner at home tonight."

I chimed in immediately, not wanting her to feel bad because she wasn't going out to dinner. "But Dad always gives her a romantic card and gift, right Mom?"

"He does." She smiled reflectively at the thought. "So, *Romeo and Juliet*. Have you read it, Buck?"

"Nah, but I'm sure I will." He shot me a side glance.

"Well, you'll enjoy the performance."

"Hopefully. That's what my girl here wants to do, so that's what we're doing."

"And you're all dressed up. I don't get to see you like this very often. You both look so nice," she admired.

"Thanks, Mrs. D."

I'm sure she was still smiling long after we left.

*   *   *

The Play's the Thing . . .

Two households, both alike in dignity . . . in fair Verona, where we lay our scene . . . from forth the fatal loins of these two foes . . . a pair of star-cross'd lovers take their life . . . is now the two hours' traffic of our stage . . . O! she doth teach the torches to burn bright . . . let lips do what hands do . . . my only love sprung from my only hate . . . my ears have not yet drunk a hundred words of that tongue's utterance, yet I know the sound . . . parting is such sweet sorrow . . . there stays a husband to make you a wife . . . wisely and slow; they stumble that run fast . . . these violent delights have violent ends and in their triumph die, like fire and powder, which as they kiss consume . . . I have more care to stay than will to go . . . O think'st thou we shall ever meet again? . . . then I defy you stars! . . . tempt not a desperate man . . . thus with a kiss I die . . . thy lips are warm . . . for never was a story of more woe than this of Juliet and her Romeo.

Romeo and Juliet
—William Shakespeare

When I get inside a story, it's difficult to remove myself. The sensation is akin to the dreams I cannot shake. And like my dreams, the feeling changes something inside of me.

The cast was taking final bows.

"Are you all right, Sam?'

"I just need a minute." His handkerchief was still balled in my palm. I sat there, my heart aching for Romeo and Juliet. People filed out of the auditorium, and an occasional passerby would glance at me empathically.

"My romantic." Buck sat patiently, waiting for me to collect myself.

"Wasn't it beautiful?" I was still lost inside the two anguished souls.

"It was. I enjoyed the production more than I expected. Will's a pretty clever guy."

"A pretty clever guy? For the love of God, he's Shakespeare! A little reverence for the bard, please."

"I'm messing with you." I stood up in response. "And you're such an easy target.

I blew my nose again.

"So was it everything you'd hoped it would be?" he asked.

"I loved it. Thank you for bringing me here."

"It was worth it to watch your face during the performance. Are you composed enough to exit yet?"

"How are my eyes?"

"Red. Puffy. Need more time?"

"No thanks. I will proudly display my torment," I said dramatically.

"You're too much, Sam."

"I know. It's my flaw."

As we exited, we ran into Jacquelyn Livingston, wouldn't you know. She wasn't with Charlie. She must have moved on. Naturally, she spotted us immediately.

"Hi, Buck. Sam. This is Kenny." The guys shook hands. "Wasn't the play great?" She didn't wait for a response. "Romeo was so cute, wasn't he? Sam, your eyes are swollen."

Thanks for pointing that out.

"You must have really liked it if it made you cry. Some girls cry easily."

Buck rested his hand on my shoulder. "Sam's sentimental. It's one of the things I love most about her." Then he kissed me right in front of her, as if it were the most normal thing in the world. His behavior shocked me. "Happy Valentine's you two. Sam and I have plans." He nodded politely and escorted me toward the parking lot.

"Hey, love, would you like to grab a bite to eat, or would you rather watch the submarine races?" His eyebrows shifted up and down. "It is Valentine's Day, after all."

"You did that on purpose," I stared at him. "You kissed me in front of her on purpose, didn't you?"

He paused. "Any doubts about where my loyalties reside?"

I wish I could have said I had none.

Fifty-eight

We were sitting in the living room, eating toasted tuna sandwiches and watching *Jeopardy!*. One of our routines.

"Oh, no! These categories are the worst!" Buck was immersed in the game. He could have been a *Jeopardy!* contestant.

"Afraid you're not going to win this time, Kendall?"

"I highly doubt that's going to happen."

"Oh, I know this one; I know this! What is St. Petersburg! Ha!" I jumped up and began dancing around the room.

"How the hell did you know that?" He looked stunned.

"Because I've been there with my parents. So there!"

"It's a riot playing this game with you, Sam. You get yourself all worked up every time you get a correct answer."

"Are you insinuating that the instances of my success are few?"

"I would never say something as insulting as that." He cupped both of his hands over his mouth in the pretense of hiding his mockery.

"Shut up!"

"I'm just kidding. Come back." I sat next to him on the couch and continued eating.

"Here, have some chips with your sandwich." I pushed the bowl his way and returned my focus to the game. Even though there wasn't a chance in Hell that I would win, I loved competing with him.

"God, I'm going to miss you." Out of nowhere. "I can't believe you're graduating in less than three months. What am I going to do without you, DeSantis?"

What am I going to do without you?

My leaving was a cloud that spread wider each day. I was about to embark on a journey filled with new experiences—without him. He was remaining behind, surrounded by friends and familiarity—without me. We would be in separate worlds, each trying to belong there. Whether we spoke of it or not, we were thinking the same thing.

"Who is Joyce Kilmer?" I ignored him.

"Did you hear what I said?"

"Yes. What about our New Year's resolution?" I reminded.

"Screw the resolution!"

"Buck, we'll be fine." I paused, doubting the conviction of my words.

"How will we be fine if you're there and I'm here? Architecture? I hate this category!"

"We'll have some weekends. I can come home, and you can visit me. If your parents will let you."

"And you think that will be enough . . . history! Yes! Much better category."

"Enough?"

"To sustain us." He turned from the television, fixing total attention on me.

It was apparent that what would sustain us was different. I was sure of my feelings for him. I knew that making time to see each other was going to be a challenge, but I also knew it could work. It was only for one year. Then he, too, would be immersed in college. A wave of excitement traveled through me when I pictured myself going to school in NYC. I could tell he was bothered by staying back, remaining in high school, and I knew his friends would harass him about his "older girlfriend" hanging with college men.

But that was the way it was. There were some things that simply could not be altered. I was willing to work around the limitations of our circumstances.

"To sustain us?" I repeated his words, reflectively. "Well, it will be different, but we can manage. And we'll have our letters." That brought a smile to his face.

"We will, indeed, have our letters. That is if you're not too busy with your classes."

"I'll never be too busy for you, Kendall."

"What is the Treaty of Versailles?" he yelled, almost knocking my plate off my lap. "Tie score! Take that, DeSantis!" He laughed like a maniac.

"You took advantage of me. We were talking, and I wasn't paying attention to the television. And listen to yourself! You're the one who gets carried away with these games, not me."

His braying escalated. "Here comes your category, Sam. Better pay attention." Before I had a chance to finish reading the question, his words sprayed into the air. "What is iambic pentameter? Right!" He stood up and began his own victory dance around the living room. I tried not to give him the satisfaction of laughing at his antics. "My score just surpassed yours, Miss English expert!"

I shook my head scornfully. "This shameless self-adulation is not attractive."

After his celebration played itself out, he faced me, fully returning to the gravity of our previous conversation. And as if my words had just left my mouth, he said, "You sure about that?"

"About what?"

"That you'll never be too busy for me?"

"Will you be too busy for me?"

"A question for a question?" he challenged.

"Answer."

"Never. Of that you can be sure, Sam."

"Ditto." I needed to drain some of the heaviness out of the conversation. "Want a cupcake?"

"Sounds good. Plus it's time to hit the books. I'll help you with your math homework.

"I hate math." I whined.

"That's why I'm helping you."

We settled at the kitchen table, where the environment would be all academic. I told myself that things would be fine.

Fifty-nine

Can men and women be *just* friends? It's rare to find that one person who can be a true friend without sexual attraction getting in the way. Many people maintain that this kind of friendship cannot work, that on some level an attraction exists. I think otherwise. You just have to find the right friend.

"Sammy girl, I never see you anymore! Come over here and give me a hug."

Brian and I had seen each other very little since our junior year began. We had no classes together, he was involved in every after-school sport imaginable, and I spent the majority of my free time with Buck. Somewhere along the way, Buck had developed a dislike for Brian, which irked me because it was unwarranted. I'm not sure his objection was directed as much at Brian as it was toward me for the attention I gave my friend. Buck's irritation began as an insignificant sliver sliding unmenacingly under his skin, but it gradually worked its way deeper until it festered into full-blown jealousy.

I loved spending time with Brian. There was no girl drama, and we could just be ourselves. It was pure. Before I met Buck, I never had to justify the time I spent with Brian. Things were different now, and I resented it. Sometimes I just missed Brian, his joie de vivre and his simple view of the world. Plus he understood me. I could talk with him about Buck when things went wrong, and unlike my girlfriends, he listened with an objective ear. He offered a calm male perspective.

"Brian! How are you?" I threw my arms around his neck, and he squeezed me in a bear hug. Because of his height, my feet came off the floor, causing them to dangle. Kids passing by stared.

"I'm great, but I miss you, Sammy. I know you're in love and all that good stuff, but we never get together anymore. I miss my friend."

"I know. I miss you too."

"And look at you! *You* are a very attractive woman, Samantha DeSantis. That Buck's a lucky guy. I certainly hope he appreciates what he's got." A deep chuckle.

"You wouldn't be biased, now, would you?"

"No! I see what I see, and that's the way I call it. So, what's the story? How's your family? I haven't seen Nick and Peg in a dog's age."

"They're good; you should come by sometime to see them—and me."

"Name the day. You don't have to ask me twice. Any chance of stopping by when I can get some of your mom's home cooking?"

"A very good chance. She loves you—and your dad. She always talks about what a nice man he is. So what about tomorrow after practice? Can you come over then?"

"That'll work for me, but what about Buck?" He eyed me cautiously.

"What about him?"

"Won't you be with him then?"

"No, not tomorrow. He's busy with school stuff."

"And he'll be okay with it?"

"Why wouldn't he be?" I knew exactly why he was concerned. I just didn't like to think about it.

"Just a feeling I get when I see him. He knows we're only friends, right?"

"Yes, he does. I clarified that point."

"Clarified? So my instincts are not totally off." Brian could always see right through me.

"He knows we're just friends, Brian. If he's bothered about anything, it's probably because you're so good looking!" I teased.

The big laugh again. "Sammy girl, you little charmer. Way to redirect the conversation. So what time tomorrow?"

"Come over right after practice."

"Perfect!" He winked at me. "Later, Sammy." He pointed at me and clicked his tongue. Such a great guy.

The next day, the doorbell rang at the appointed time. There stood Brian, freshly showered and beaming. In his hands he held a bunch of flowers. He nodded toward the bouquet. "For your mom." He was like a little boy presenting his handmade gift.

At the sound of his voice, my mother came through the foyer. "Well, Brian Determan! How are you?" She took a shine to him the first time he'd come to our house in ninth grade.

"Mrs. D!" Brian had a unique way of laughing his words. The sound was not only melodic, but joyful and contagious. "Long time, no see. These are for you."

"Oh, my goodness. You didn't have to do that. Thank you."

"It's the least I can do for an invite to dinner."

"Well, Brian, we're happy to have you. When Sam told me you were coming for dinner tonight, I was really pleased. How's your dad doing these days?"

"He's just swell, Mrs. D. I told him I was visiting the DeSantis family after practice tonight, and he said to send his regards."

"Well, please extend ours to him too. And your mom?"

"She's good. All's well in the Determan household."

"Come on in, hon. Make yourself at home. We're having meatloaf and mashed potatoes."

"Music to my ears, Mrs. D. Nobody makes comfort food like you."

I rolled my eyes. "Mom, are you sure you made enough? Look at the size of him. And he just came from practice. He'll probably scarf down everything in his sight." I loved messing with Brian.

"You're a gas, DeSantis." He threw his arm around me, and we headed to the kitchen.

The meatloaf and the visit were both delicious.

* * *

Doubts are more cruel than the worst of truths.

—Molière

There's a fine line between truth and the whole truth. Does the omission make the admission a lie? Are we responsible to tell *all*, even if we know that the *all* might hurt? *Do you swear to tell the truth, the whole truth, and nothing but the truth so help you God?* What's the penalty if I tell the truth minus a couple of details? *Cuff her, boys, and take her away.* But I didn't lie!

"Sam, I called you last night, and your brother said Brian was there for dinner." Shelly was attempting to catch up to me in the hallway.

Since the New Year, Shelly and I had drifted apart. I attributed the change mainly to the fact that I spent my free time with Buck. Also, Buck and I really liked hanging out with Darlene and Sal, so we opted to go out with them more and more frequently. Without conscious decision, I was spending less time with the girls.

I stopped when she reached me. "Ryan didn't tell me you called." Shelly was looking down the corridor, preoccupied. "Who are you looking for?" I peered down the hallway in the direction of her gaze.

"Larry."

"Larry?" Her response took me by surprise.

"Yeah. I figured your brother would forget to tell you. So why was Brian over?"

"For dinner. And to visit. Why are you looking for Larry?"

"He said he has something to give me." She pressed the palest shade of pink lipstick across her bottom lip and smacked the top and bottom together.

"When did you talk to him?"

"Last night. He called."

"To say he had to give you something?" My suspicion grew.

"Yeah. Does my hair look all right?" She pulled out her compact to check her appearance in the tiny mirror.

"It looks fine. So what's going on with Larry? Does George know you talked to him?"

"Does Buck know Brian was at your house last night?" She stared at me defiantly.

"That's different, and you know it."

"How?"

"We're just friends. You and Larry used to go out. He's still in love with you."

"How do you know that? And how do you know that Buck accepts that you and Brian are just friends? I think it bugs him when you talk to Brian."

"Brian and I have been friends for a long time. Longer than Buck and I have been together. He knows! All right?"

"So you think that excuses it?"

"Excuses what?" She was seriously pissing me off.

"Being with him."

"I wasn't *with* him! We were visiting. At my house with my entire family present. We ate meatloaf, for God's sake. It is different from what you're doing with Larry!"

"Oh, don't act all high and mighty." Then she shifted her attention. "Here he comes. Look at him. He's still cute, isn't he? And Buck's with him." She preened like a cat.

I knew the remnants of my irritation were still all over me when Buck and Larry walked up to us. Buck smiled seductively, bumping into me on purpose.

Larry spoke first. "Hey there, Sam. How you been?" He wore the look that told me he was up to no good.

"Fine. You?" I barely tolerated him.

"Just swell now that I'm standing in the radiating beauty of Shelly Porterfield." He gave her the once over.

Shelly's attempt to act embarrassed was beyond weak. She was lapping up every bit of the attention. Then she turned to Buck.

"Hi Buck." The sing-song voice.

"Hey, Shelly. What's up?" Buck's exchanges with her were limited to niceties for my sake.

"Just meeting Larry 'cuz he said he's got something for me." Her sickening sweet nauseated me.

"I do. Come over here where we can have a little privacy and I can give it to you." Then came the demonic laugh.

God, he's revolting sometimes.

As I watched them walk away, I realized Buck was right. Larry was still in love with her. Would every guy feel that way after she broke up with him? Would she have the mercy in her heart to release any of them?

"She's still messing with him, Sam." Buck's annoyance mounted.

"Well, she said he called her. That's not her fault."

"Yeah, after she interrogated his brother about him for so long that he went home and reported to Larry. She staged that one."

From down the hall, I heard Larry's voice. "Ooh, Buck won't like that shit!" He guffawed obnoxiously.

Unfortunately, Buck heard him too. "Won't like what? What's he talking about?" He looked to me for some clue.

"Larry!" Shelly's voice was considerably louder. She turned her back on us as she scolded him. "I told you not to say anything."

My chest tightened. Not because I'd done anything wrong. Brian was my friend. But now, thanks to Shelly's big mouth, things were going to be messy.

"I'm not exactly sure, but I have a pretty good idea." I took a deep breath.

"What?"

I plunged in. "Brian came over to my house for dinner last night."

He stared, nodding to himself. "Brian." The pronouncement was controlled, intense. "Why didn't you tell me?"

"Because it was no big deal. We hadn't seen each other in a while, so he came over to visit."

"If it was no big deal, then why didn't you mention it? I'd tell you if I were having some girl to my house for dinner."

"But he's not just some boy . . ."

"He's not? What is he then?" His body clenched.

"He's my friend. Why are you acting like this? You know we've been friends since Pioneer. *And* he's friends with my family."

"You should have told me, Sam. Those two," he pointed at Shelly and Larry, "knew before I did. How do you think that makes me feel?"

"You're making more out of this than it is." My emotions ran between indignation and regret.

"Am I? How about you reverse the situation. How would you feel if you accidentally found out that some girl came to my house for dinner? In front of your friends. Tell me how that would sit with you."

"That's not fair. Brian's not just anybody."

"Right. So should I invite Jacquelyn Livingston to my house for dinner?"

Low blow. My whole system registered shock.

"What are you talking about? Why would you bring her up? You are not friends with her. You're classmates. There's a difference. Brian and I have been friends since Pioneer Park. Before you and I ever met."

"It doesn't feel so good to be on the other side, does it, Sam?"

"But it's not the same," I insisted.

"Isn't it? We're both jealous. You know how I feel about you spending time with him."

"I'm not jealous of Jacquelyn," I denied.

"No? You sure about that?" he retorted.

"Yes! I just don't trust her. There's a difference." I stared him down. "Unless there's something you're not telling me?" My voice oozed anger.

"Don't be ridiculous. And don't try to turn this thing around. You're the one who keeps secrets." He stopped looking at me.

"Secrets? You're unbelievable!"

Our voices had escalated noticeably, and we were still standing in the hall, where kids passed all around us on their way to classes. Suddenly Sal appeared.

"Hey, kids . . . what's the problem?" He placed one hand on Buck's shoulder and the other on mine.

"Ask *her*!" He stormed away.

Sal looked from Buck to me in confusion. "What's going on, Sam? Are you all right?"

Tears spilled down my cheeks. "Damn it!" I have always hated my lack of control when it comes to crying. But I've never had a choice.

Sal put his arm around me. "How can I help, Sam?"

"You can't. Thanks, Sal. I've got to get to class."

When I walked away, I noticed that Shelly and Larry had conveniently disappeared.

Cowards!

* * *

Most fights arise out of festering resentments and impulsive reactions. I am always amazed by how quickly things can escalate. Worthless issues, most of the time. But they chip away, bit by bit, and filling the holes is not always possible.

I wondered whether he was angrier about my spending time with Brian or being humiliated in front of Larry. Probably equal tugs on his pride. I questioned myself. Was I required to report everything to him? *No.* Then again, if the situation were reversed, I wouldn't react well, particularly if the person in question happened to be Jacquelyn Livingston. Still, Brian and I were just friends, and Buck knew it. Wasn't that different?

He didn't call that night. But Shelly did.

"Hi, Sam. Are you still speaking to me?" Her obsequious voice ignited a resurgence of annoyance. I wasn't buying it.

"You put me in a really bad position today, Shel."

"I didn't mean to."

"Why did you tell Larry?"

"I never should have. He's got such a big mouth."

"*He's* got a big mouth?" I wanted to climb through the telephone line and choke her.

"What do you mean?" Her defenses were up.

"You know exactly what I mean. You're the one who opened your mouth. If you hadn't said anything, Larry wouldn't have been able to either." I simply could not hold myself back any longer.

"Well, you're the one who was with Brian behind Buck's back! Don't blame this on me."

"Don't try to turn the tables, Shelly. Why did you really call me, anyway?" I demanded.

"To tell you I'm sorry that you and Buck had a fight."

I wanted to scream. "Let me get this straight. *You're* sorry that we had a fight, not that *you* had any part in causing it? For the love of God! You lit the freakin' dynamite! Wake up!"

"I can't believe you're talking to me this way!" Shelly was not accustomed to anyone speaking to her with such raw candor because no one ever dared. She had created an air that told everyone she was special and should be treated with kid gloves. And it worked. How do some people just get away with those things?

"Well, I am! Everybody tiptoes around you and lets you get away with murder. I'm really tired of this shit!" I slammed down the phone.

* * *

Love isn't easy. It's complicated and messy. It changes its mind. It is restless and it is content. It overflows and it dries up. It morphs into multitudes of shapes. Love is a sky dive. The first time the chute actually opens, you float through the air in disbelief and wonder; you can't wait to experience the exhilaration again. Eventually the thrill wanes when the fear of plunging becomes more reality than possibility.

The next day I walked into Mrs. Newton's empty classroom. In the solace of the room, I mulled over all that had transpired as a result of an innocent visit with a friend. As bothered as I was by the repercussions of my get-together with Brian, I maintained that I had done nothing wrong. As I sifted through the debris of events, my eyes wandered around Mrs. Newton's room. Her walls displayed memorabilia from her travels. Among her treasures were posters of the Coliseum in Rome and the Parthenon in Athens; a Monet print from Giverny; and a bust of Shakespeare from London. I smiled as I recalled the stories attached to each purchase. Someday I would travel and experience the cultures that I only knew through the words of great writers.

"Good morning, Samantha. How are you today?" She was her usual perky self.

"I'm fine thanks, Mrs. Newton," I pulled out my copy of *Great Expectations* and proceeded to read. Normally I relished moments alone with her, and she knew it. I could feel her studying my odd behavior.

"Not convincing, Sam. What's going on? Buck?"

"How'd you know?"

She sat in the desk across from me. "It doesn't take a brain surgeon. You two are rather transparent. Strong energy going on there."

"Yeah." I could feel my shoulders hunch in confirmation.

"Quarrel?"

"Sort of."

"Does it have anything to do with your going off to college this fall?" she probed.

"No. Although that has been presenting a problem too."

"I figured it would. You know, Sam, I think it really bothers Buck that you're moving on before him. You two have become quite the couple. This is going to be a tricky balance for both of you." I nodded to her accuracy. She shifted position. "Well, time to face the music, Sam."

"What?" I regarded her quizzically. She motioned toward the door. My heart thumped when I saw him standing there.

"A word of advice," she added softly, "Don't mess with love, Sam. Tell it like it is." She patted my hand and stood up. "Good morning, Mr. Kendall. I'm on my way to grab a cup of coffee before everyone arrives. See you kids in a minute." She left—but her words didn't.

Don't mess with love, Sam.

I could feel his every step in my direction. He took the seat that Mrs. Newton had occupied. When I looked at him, I felt apprehension and relief battling for control. I had know idea what to expect.

"Hi." There was an edge to his voice.

Don't mess with love, Sam.

I plunged in. "I didn't tell you Brian was coming over because I knew you'd get mad. I thought I'd save us both the trouble. I'm sorry. It wasn't my intention to be deceitful. I figured there was nothing wrong with seeing a friend . . ."

"Who just happens to be male and a heartthrob to half of the girls at Carlson," he added flatly.

"Buck . . ."

He plowed through my interruption. "And who doesn't have a girlfriend of his own but likes hanging out with mine."

"You don't trust me."

Say you do.

He stopped tracing the crevices of his palm. His eyes swam in pain. "I do trust you, Samantha. That's the problem."

"I don't understand."

"It's other people I don't trust. You just go along being you, friendly with everyone. People are naturally drawn to you. You don't see the way kids look at you—with admiration and envy."

"Envy?"

"You have all these amazing qualities, Sam. You're funny and approachable. You understand people. You're considerate."

"And why is that a problem?"

"It's not a problem for you. It's a problem for me. You see the world in a different way from me. You're trusting and innocent. That's what makes you such an easy target."

"A target?" I bristled.

"You're an easy mark to let other people in."

"I disagree. I'm not a target, and that's insulting."

"I didn't mean it in an insulting way," he pled with a conviction that made me believe him.

We studied each other for a while, searching for safe ground. And then I spoke. "You said we see the world differently. How do you see it?"

"I'm more of a cynic. I don't trust that everyone's actions are genuine or what they seem on the surface."

"But what does this have to do with Brian coming over?"

"I'm always afraid I'm going to lose you to someone . . . why not him? He's a great guy, and you like him."

"As a friend. Are you hearing me?"

"I hear you, Sam."

He looked torn. I sat there wondering how this sort of thing could happen. How did we get to this place where we caused each other unintentional pain? We'd been together for two years, and still there were insecurities, question marks—on both sides.

"You are not going to lose me."

"Are you sure about that, Sam?" he confronted.

"Not unless you're the one who does it." That clearly pissed him off.

"I told you *that* was never going to happen again." His jaw tightened.

"Are *you* sure about that, Buck?" I was too spent to be anything but direct. If honesty meant we were stepping into dangerous territory, so be it.

"What's that supposed to mean?" His tone was hateful. I had never heard it before. Not directed at me, anyway. But I wasn't about to back down.

"It means that it sounds like you're the one who can't handle things. You say you trust me, but you don't act like you do. You say you're afraid you are going to lose me, but I have told you over and over again that's not going to happen. It doesn't matter how friendly I am to other people. I love *you*. And you know it. Sometimes I think that you're looking for excuses to doubt me—to start fights."

"Why would I want to do that?" he defied angrily.

"I don't know. You tell me. Maybe it's because everything has to go your way."

"Where's this coming from, Sam?" His face flushed. I couldn't tell if it was from anger or fear.

An explosion was balling together inside me, threatening to blast. Some days his attitude was too much for me. "From here, Buck," I pointed to my gut. "From way down deep where I store everything so as not to upset the delicate balance. From the same place I have stored it ever since last January when you broke up with me because of what *you* needed. Because things weren't the way *you* thought they should be. So that *you* could date other girls. Remember?"

His eyes were fixed, his expression unfamiliar.

"And then, when things didn't work out the way you had hoped they would, back to good old Sam. That's when you decided you couldn't live without me, isn't it?" Even though I knew that last statement was unfair, momentum propelled me.

"Are you serious?" He regarded me as if I were a stranger. "First of all, you know that was a mistake. You know I meant it when I said I compared everyone to you. And you know goddamn well that I'm in love with you! That's what causes all these flare-ups. If I didn't love you, I wouldn't give a shit! And that was over a year ago! Why are you bringing this up now?"

"Why are you telling me you don't trust me now?" I pressed on.

"I never said that!"

How can so much rest on the pinnacle of a moment? On the right words? On the omission? "Maybe not with words. But you scream it with your actions."

"Where are you going with this, Sam?" He faltered.

I didn't know. I just knew that Mrs. Newton had told me not to mess with love. So I spilled my guts. What I hadn't anticipated was the geyser that would bubble over inside me. It had been waiting a long time. "I don't know. But I do know that everything can't always go your way. I'm tired of tiptoeing around so you don't fall into one of your funks and brood like a spoiled child. You need to trust me."

"And you need to trust me." The fire in his eyes spit at me.

Oddly enough, I wanted to kiss him. I wanted him to touch me. I wanted everything to be better. But I was spent, and I didn't know what to do. Love aside, I knew something was wrong.

The door opened to the turn of a key, and Mrs. Newton entered, followed by a collection of students who had been waiting in the hall. I didn't realize she had locked us in. But that was just like her. Our classmates filed in around us, oblivious to our predicament. But Mrs. Newton wasn't.

"You two okay?" I figured our voices might have carried through the door, and I was certain that neither of us looked happy.

I turned to face Mrs. Newton directly; she read my face. Words weren't necessary. "May I be excused, Mrs. Newton?"

"Sure, Sam," she sighed. She wrote the pass and handed it to me, empathy filling her eyes.

"Okay, everybody. Let's get started."

I picked up my books and headed toward the door. Buck stood in the aisle. As I walked away, I heard the hushed tone of his voice. "Sam . . ."

I walked into the nurse's office.

"You don't have cramps again, do you, Samantha?" Her eyes accused.

"No, I don't. But I want to go home. Please."

"What's going on?"

"I'm upset. I can't deal with being here right now. I'm sorry, but that's the truth." I braced myself for a lecture, but her expression changed, and I realized she was regarding me as a human being instead of a student.

"Okay." She wrote the pass. I couldn't believe it. "Going to your grandmother's house?"

"Yes. How did you know?" Her behavior baffled me.

"I remembered. Your place of solace." She was kinder than I had realized.

* * *

"Samantha! Il mio dio, bambino! What's wrong?" Nana shut the screen door to the front porch after I entered.

"I don't know, Nana. Everything feels wrong."

She put her arm around my waist. "Come in. I'll make you some hot tea. Is it school?"

"No."

"Buck?"

I sat down at the kitchen table while she turned on the flame under the tea kettle.

"Yes."

"What's up now? He jealous?"

Her words took me by surprise. "What made you say *that*?"

"I watch. I see. It's in him, the jealousy." She shook her head from side to side as if she felt sorry for him.

"What?" I wanted her to explain.

"It's a hard thing to be jealous. It eats you up. He's to be pitied."

"Pitied? Are you kidding me, Nana? What about me?"

"You?" she smiled lovingly. "You're strong, la mia bellezza. You don't get eaten up by the ugly beast. He does."

"But I love him just as much as he loves me. Sometimes I think more. And it bothers me when I think he's flirting with other girls. A lot! Doesn't that count?"

"*Bothers* is different from *consumes*," she explained.

"But Nana, don't you remember when he broke up with me last year? I was eaten alive with the idea that he would meet someone else and start dating her."

"I remember," she nodded. "You anguished deeply."

"Doesn't that count?" I demanded. I would never forget the horror of that time.

"Of course it counts. But you survived."

"But that's because we got back together."

"Yes and no."

"What do you mean?"

"Down the road, you would have been all right, if the two of you hadn't mended things. Ah, of course you were deeply wounded. And *that,* you'll never forget. I know. It stays here," she pointed to her heart. "But you would have survived, Samantha. I know this about you."

I sipped my tea, feeling sorry for myself. How was it that he got to be angry and jealous and still be pitied? The hot liquid soothed as it trickled down my throat. I felt my chest begin to relax. Odd that I didn't feel like crying. I sipped more tea and tried to focus on nothing other than the sweet sensation in my mouth and the healing power of my nana's voice.

"Biscotti?" She handed me the sweet toast. "I just made them yesterday. Perfect with the tea."

She sat down next to me, indulging in her own cup as she nibbled at the biscuit. "Your uncle, you know, went through this. I watched it."

"Uncle Danny?"

"Si, Daniel. He was head over heels for the girl. Every time he brought her here, I could see it. And she was crazy about him too. They were always making goo-goo eyes at each other."

I laughed. She was such a storyteller.

"Then the beast paid a visit. Ah! The quarrels, then the tears. Caro dio! *Dear God!* It was a rough time there for a while." She returned to her teacup.

"Really? I never knew that." She had my attention.

"You think you are the first one to fall so deeply in love that it tears you?" She shook her head from side to side.

"Well, no. Of course not."

"Love has been around a long, long time. Man and woman still play the same games, make the same mistakes. It's a hard game. Some make it; some don't."

I nodded in agreement. "So what happened to the girl?"

"Well, la mia nipote," *my granddaughter*, "they worked it out."

"But what happened to her? Did she move away?" I was confused.

"Quite the opposite. She married Uncle Daniel." Nana's expression resonated with satisfaction.

"Aunt Bette?"

"Si, Aunt Bette." She placed her hands in her lap.

Uncle Danny and Aunt Bette. I'll be damned! I couldn't believe it. Her story gave no hint. "So, it worked out for them," I mused.

"So, you see, my sweetheart. You have choices to make. Which road you gonna choose—that's up to you." Nana had an uncanny knack for getting to the heart of things.

"You want to lie down, take a nap?" She stood up and straightened her apron.

"No, I think I'll have another cup of tea and go back to school. You made me feel better, Nana. Thanks." I hugged her. "Mmm . . . . you smell like garlic."

"The meatballs. I rolled them this morning. Sente l'odore di buon." *Smells good.* She sniffed the scent from her hands.

"I love you, Nana."

She chuckled joyfully as only she could. "E ti amo anche." *I love you too.*

*   *   *

When I walked out of French class later that morning, he was waiting. The power of his presence always surprised me.

His face looked older. "You came back."

"How'd you know I'd be here?"

"I didn't. I've just been walking by after each of your classes in case you did. Did you go to your grandmother's?"

"I did." He knew me well.

"Does she hate me?"

"No, of course not."

"How 'bout you?"

"Me?"

He literally held his breath.

"I already told you. I'm in love with you, Buck."

He reached for my hand. "I'm sorry I was such a jerk."

"I'm sorry too," I admitted.

"That I'm a jerk?"

"No." His humor somehow came at the right moments. "For not telling you Brian was coming to my house in the first place. For the angry words we exchanged. But *not* for telling the truth. I'm not sorry about that."

He tugged on my hand tenaciously. "Come on."

"Where are we going? I'll be late for class," I objected.

"Skipping last period."

"Skipping? I can't skip."

"Yes you can."

"Where are we going?"

"My house."

"Why?"

"No one's home."

*   *   *

His room was quiet, lazy, unkempt.
He took off his jacket and threw it on the unmade bed.
The note I had written last week curled open on the nightstand.
He turned on the radio.
Aretha Franklin.
Oh, baby what you've done to me.
He pulled down the blinds and came to me.
I slid my arms out of my jacket.
It fell on the floor.
You make me feel so good inside.
"Wanna dance?"
We turned slowly, my picture smiling down from his dresser.
And I just wanna be . . .
He kissed me.
. . . close to you.
His mouth was warm.
You make me feel so alive.
So alive
So alive
He kissed me again.
And again.
And again.
And again.
And again . . .

You make me feel like a natural woman.

* * *

She crossed her hands and placed them on her lap. "You have choices to make. Which way you gonna go?"

"There's only one way to go."

"What makes you speak with such certainty?"

"I don't think I have a choice. Ever since I first saw him."

"Yes, you do, my naïve one. You haven't experienced enough of life to know."

"To know what?"

"You think because you love this boy, you can never love another with the same ardor."

"Ardor?"

"With the same fullness in your heart."

"I can't. What we have is real."

"You feel that way now, I know."

"What do you mean *now*? I'll always feel this way."

"Sometimes life holds a different plan."

"Why are you telling me this?"

"I want you to have the strength ready if God unfolds a different plan."

"Why would He do that? If there's a God, He knows how I feel."

"He knows."

"Then I have nothing to worry about."

"He also knows *you*, heart and soul, and He knows the best path for you."

"I'm on the right path."

"You are on a good road—with a fine companion."

"So why would He alter it?"

"To help you fulfill yourself."

"I don't understand."

"Ah. That is because it's too early to understand."

"Too early? Why did you come here?"

"I am your protector. A protector tells the truth so you recognize it when it comes to you."

"What truth?" She stood, turning her back to me. "Stop! What truth?"

"Ti amo." She disappeared.

"Come back! What truth!" I screamed.

"Sam, wake up. You're dreaming again."

"What truth?" I repeated quietly.

Sixty

The weather was finally warming. We had managed the winter with school dances, basketball games, bowling . . . inside activities that were now growing old. And for as much as I wanted time to slow, it was time to breathe fresh air again.

"Only two more days till your seventeenth birthday."

"Then we'll be the same age." He grinned.

"For two months," I added. "Then I'll be 18."

"Too old for me, man," he needled.

I smacked his arm in retaliation. "Have you heard anything about the young author's contest?"

"Not a word. You?" I could see his interest pique.

"No, Mrs. Newton hasn't said anything. But all submissions were due at the end of January, so I'm thinking pretty soon."

"You never told me what you submitted." His curiosity was evident, but this was the first time he had broached the subject.

"That depends on if you're going to do the same."

"Fair enough."

"My story is about a woman who was trapped in a marriage and wouldn't leave because of her children."

"Trapped? Did she love someone else?"

"No. But she didn't love her husband. Ever."

"So why'd she marry him?"

"She was pregnant and thought it was the right thing to do."

"Heavy stuff. Pathos. Morals. Appeals to readers. Good going. So how does it turn out?"

"You'll have to read it if you want to find out how it ends," I smirked.

"Listen to you. Do I sense a little attitude?"

"Your turn," I smiled patronizingly.

"War story. Well, more about the internal conflict of the protagonist during war. He was only eighteen."

"Was? Did he die?"

"Well, now, you'll just have to read it to find out, won't you?" Smart ass.

"So, is it like *All Quiet on the Western Front*?"

"All I'll tell you is it's original."

"I have no doubt. And I'm betting it's good."

"Thanks, Sam. Ditto."

"We have very different writing styles." For a moment we were no longer Sam and Buck. We were comrades discussing our art. "You're cerebral. Your voice is satirical, witty, and certainly more subtle than in the notes you write to me."

He laughed at himself. "Thanks. And you are more poetic than I am. There's something very personal about the way you write. You get inside your characters' heads with such intimacy."

"Well, aren't we just the pair. You're wonderful. No, you are. No, really, you are." I mocked the oddity of the situation.

"Yeah, enough of this. So have you heard anything from NYU?"

"Not yet."

"You will. You're not worried are you?"

"Sort of."

"You'll be accepted. Have faith."

I have faith in a lot of things. I just hope my faith doesn't fail me.

"So tell me what color dress you're wearing to the prom."

"You don't really want to hear about this, do you? It'll just bore you."

"Is it supposed to be a surprise?"

"No."

"Then tell me. What color? I have to order flowers to match it anyway."

"Not for another month."

"Tell me, DeSantis." He would not be deterred.

"Yellow."

"Yellow? That doesn't sound like you. What made you choose yellow?"

"It's springy."

"As good a rationale as any, I guess."

"I told you this was a boring topic."

"Hey, let's walk to my house instead of yours. I can play my guitar for you. I've been playing around with it a lot lately, but I still need more practice. You can critique me. And we can harmonize while I pluck away. Sound good?"

He positioned the guitar in front of him, head bent over the strings. His fingers curled gracefully, and he strummed with ease, all the while staring at an invisible target as if the notes were suspended there. His mouth opened and closed, moving in sync with his fingers, one seemingly controlling the other. His whole body was working together, the guitar an extension of his hands. He was beautiful, like an exquisite piece of art, a sculpture in motion.

"That sounds good. When did you learn that song?"

"Greg taught me last week. I just keep playing it over and over so I can master it. Guess what else I learned to play?" His eyes twinkled with self-satisfaction.

"Must I?" I feigned impatience.

"Come on, humor me."

"Give me a clue."

"Three people harmonizing."

"Not Peter, Paul, and Mary!" He nodded, pleased with my reaction. "Do you have any idea how much I love that song?"

"That's why I learned it. I've heard you singing it."

"Play it!"
"Okay, but it's not that good yet. No making fun."

All my bags are packed; I'm ready to go
I'm standing here outside your door
I hate to wake you up to say goodbye
But the dawn is breakin, it's early morn
The taxi's waiting, he's blowin' his horn
Already I'm so lonesome I could cry.

So kiss me and smile for me
Tell me that you'll wait for me
Hold me like you'll never let me go.

Sixty-one

Disappointments are to the soul what a thunder storm is to the air.

—Friedrich von Schiller

Most people are not good with disappointment, no matter what kind. Logic would dictate that the degree of discontent should be proportionate to the significance of the event over which the disappointment arose. But logic and emotion are not often companions.

"Sam, may I speak with you for a moment in my room?" Mrs. Newton took me off guard. I was headed to French class when she spotted me in the hall. Her expression was odd.

"Sure, Mrs. Newton," I smiled as she stood at her door, waiting. "Oh. You mean now?"

"Yes. I can write you a pass to your next class. This is my planning period, so it's a good time for me to meet with you."

"Sure." Trepidation filled me. I immediately thought about the most recent paper I had written. Admittedly, I had not put forth as much effort as I normally did. I was preoccupied with a culminating school year and my upcoming graduation. Not to mention that I still hadn't heard from NYU. *Could my paper have been that bad*? I recalled the day she had hauled me into the library and made me write an essay in front of her. My punishment for not being prepared that day. She sat across from me, pressing me to the task.

"Write it now," she said and proceeded to correct papers. No teacher had ever put me on the spot like that. So I wrote.

When I slid my paper in her direction, disbelief marked her face. "You're finished?"

"Yes." While my voice held conviction, I suddenly doubted myself. Was her reaction because I had crafted my response so quickly? Was that wrong? Sometimes I produced my best work when I didn't think too long or play around with the words ad nauseum. Gut responses were authentic.

She read it in front of me. I wondered what she was thinking. The product was an extension of me. Critique the words, criticize me. It was much easier when she returned my papers in class where I wasn't witness to every rise in her eyebrow, each twitch in her face, the subtle hint of a smile in the corners of her mouth. I waited, never taking my eyes off her. Then she looked up, amazed. She set the paper in front of her and marked something on the top.

"See you in class tomorrow. No more late work." She handed me the paper and left. I didn't even have time to thank her. I picked up the composition I had just created. Beautiful! A-

I walked into her room, feeling as if I were about to be lectured. She closed the door, motioning for me to sit across from her. My stomach tightened. *It must be bad.*

"Samantha," she said with deliberation. Then her face cracked out of its uncharacteristic shell. "You won the contest."

"What?" My brain had not yet transitioned from *what was wrong with my paper*?

"You were Wordwall's first choice!" She stood up and put her arms around me. "Samantha, I couldn't be prouder. I'm so pleased that they recognized your talent." I gaped at her as if someone had just told me I won the Miss America contest. Definite stretch. She chuckled. "Say something."

"They picked *me*?"

More chuckling. "Yes, my dear, they chose *you*."

"Are you sure?" My mouth was moving, but I was numb.

"I'm sure," she laughed. "This may seem like an insignificant contest, but Wordwall is highly regarded. This achievement, and hopefully subsequent pieces that you will submit to other competitions, will help to launch you, Sam."

"I don't think it's insignificant. I know it's an honor. I'm just in shock."

"Sam, I know you have not fully realized your potential, but you have the makings of a writer whom people will believe. They'll read your stories and find themselves in some small part. Word mavens will appreciate the delicate balance of your words, the juxtaposition of your ideas. Your heart opens on the page."

"Thank you, Mrs. Newton." Then, without warning, I broke open and cried.

"I hope those are happy tears."

I could only nod.

* * *

I sat in French class, stunned. *I won the writing contest.*

"Mademoiselle DeSantis, comment dit-on en français *consider the source*? S'il vous plait." *How do you say "consider the source" in French, please?* I stared at the kind and understanding face of Madame Passant as she awaited my response.

"Oh, I'm sorry, Mrs. Passant," I began.

"En français, s'il vous plait," interrupted Madame Passant.

"Naturellement. On dit considérez l'origine." *Of course. It is considérez l'origine.*

"Très bien, Mademoiselle DeSantis." *Very good, Miss DeSantis.* "Bon. Conjugez le verbe prendre a l'imparfait. Ensemble. En haute voix, s'il vous plait." *Good. Everyone, let's conjugate the verb prendre in the imparfait. Together. Aloud, please.*

Je prenais	Nous prenions
Tu prenais	Vous preniez
Il/Elle prenait	Ils/Elles prenaient

After we conjugated the verb "to take" in unison, we practiced several others that required review before the quiz. My focus was compromised. Thank God I already knew those words.

I won the writing contest. Holy shit!

I couldn't stop ginning.

Buck was waiting outside the door.

"Bonjour, ma belle!" *Hello, beautiful.* "How was French class?"

"Formidable! Merci," I replied. *It was great, thanks.*

"Where were you after second hour, Sam? I waited by the water fountain." We were walking toward the southern stairwell when he asked the question. The weight of the news about the contest pressed on me.

"Sorry. Hey, did you talk with Mrs. Newton about the writing contest yet?"

I hope, I hope, I hope.

"The writing contest? No, why?" He regarded me suspiciously. I might as well have just spit out the news. He knew me too well.

"Just wondered." I could feel myself chickening out. "Hey, there's Darlene. Let's catch up with her." He wasn't buying it.

"Oh, no, no, no. Finish what you were saying about the contest." He stopped walking. An odd nervousness crept over me. *Why should I be nervous to tell him my good news? If he had won, I'd be happy.* But when I met his eyes, I realized I wanted to deliver a different outcome.

"Well, that's where I was. With Mrs. Newton. She asked me to come to her room so we could talk, and then . . ." I trailed off and looked at my loafers. The penny was gone from the right shoe. "Damn!"

"What?" He looked down.

"The penny must have fallen out of my new shoe. And it was so shiny!" I knew I couldn't buy much more time.

"Sam—finish what you were saying," he insisted. "I'll get you a new penny after school."

"Mrs. Newton wanted to talk about the writing contest—you know, you really should talk to her about this." My eyes wandered back to my loafer.

"Maybe. But I'm talking to you." His voice had softened. He knew. "And I think I'd rather hear the news now, considering I think I already know the outcome."

"You sure? She's the person who should give you the official word."

"I'm sure." His face was somber.

I stared at him, the seconds stretching on. "I won the contest." The words just hung in the air. I wondered why this felt wrong. Sure, he was a great writer. But he was great at everything. And it was only one contest. Perhaps if we had submitted different stories from the ones we actually handed in, the results would have been different. There was no saying what might have happened.

"Congratulations, Sam." He leaned forward and kissed my cheek.

"No PDAs!" shouted Sal from the stairwell above us. "If the principal sees you, you're in trouble!"

Normally, Buck would have had a clever retort, but he simply waved Sal off and turned back to me. "I'm really proud of you, Sam. You deserve this."

"Thanks." *I think.*

"Listen, I'll see you after school, okay? I gotta get to class."

"Okay, see you then."

I headed upstairs; he headed down. When I peeked over the railing, he was gone.

Sixty-two

Two Weeks Later

"So guess what?" His eyes danced.

"I can't imagine." We were sitting at my kitchen table, doing homework.

"I got my letter from Boys State."

"You did? Oh, Buck, congratulations!"

Founded in 1935, American Legion Boys State is a prestigious program of government instruction for high school juniors. This program focuses on the structure of city, county, and state governments. The selected candidates participate in such activities as legislative sessions and court proceedings, among others. And it's a very big deal for those chosen. This letter couldn't have arrived at a better time.

"I knew you'd get in!"

"You had that much faith in me, huh?"

"Of course. So when do you leave?"

"It's scheduled for the second week in July."

"A whole week?"

He laughed. "Can you handle it?"

"I can handle it; I just don't like it. I'll miss you."

"Then you can appreciate how I'll feel when you go away to school."

He had me there. I never actually turned the situation around. Him—gone. Me—home. Granted, I had nothing to worry about with Boys State, but that wasn't the point. "I guess I can," I replied meekly.

"Ah, look at it this way—I'll write to you every day."

Sixty-three

We're captive on the carousel of time
We can't return we can only look behind . . .

—Joni Mitchell

A rite of passage marks a significant change in a person's life. While it focuses on the celebratory aspect of an entrance through a new door, its life implications reach far deeper. Rites of passage come in the form of ceremonies or milestones . . . baptisms, coming of age celebrations, graduation, weddings. Some are more significant than others. Rites of passage can fall into three categories: separation, transition, and incorporation. I was caught between two doors and didn't know which way to turn.

Senior prom. The last time Buck and I would have formal photographs taken on my parents' staircase. The last time we would sit in a transformed gym with high school friends. The last time we would take the dance floor as a high school couple. I wore out my camera trying to capture every moment. I scanned the room, attempting to imprint each detail inside me: Darlene's laugh, Sal's bad jokes, the magically transformed gym, the smell of my bouquet. I even tried to embrace the irritating photographer taking our picture in front of the trellis, stuffed with crepe paper flowers. I stayed until the very end—I wasn't going to miss a thing.

When the band launched into their closing number, we joined a cluster of kids, locked in their last song. I was flooded with the flight of time. Everything sped by me like the landscape through a car window. I'd driven by these fields many times before but never fully paused to take in the beauty. Instead, I counted on the next time.

First the tide rushes in, plants a kiss on the shore

"You're a die-hard, Sam," declared Buck.

Then rolls out to sea, and the sea is very still once more

"I know, but this is our last prom dance," I whispered. He pulled me closer.

So I rush to your side like the oncoming tide

"And a romantic," he added.

With one burning thought: will your arms open wide?

We moved through the room, familiar faces passing by.

At last we're face to face, and as we kiss through an embrace, I can tell, I can feel you are love, you are real

Darlene and Sal were making out at the table. Shelly was crying again, fighting with George—her latest.

Really mine in the rain

Annie's laughter cut through the music.

In the dark, in the sun

Brian and his date danced nearby; he winked when we made eye contact.

Like the tide at its ebb, I'm at peace in the web of your arms

The irritating photographer was still taking pictures, random shots of the thinning crowd. The collective voices of the band swelled.

Ebb tide!!

"Sam, you can let go now." His words were hushed.

I can't let go.

I stalled in the doorway when we were about to leave.

"I have to go back to the table. I forgot something," I lied.

"What'd you forget? I'll get it for you."

"It's okay. I'll be right back."

He shrugged his shoulders. "I'll wait outside the door then." He exited with Sal and Darlene. They were discussing Greta's party and whether we should go.

I made my way back to our table, assaulted by the wilting vision of broken streamers and stain-filled tablecloths. The janitors were already picking up after the careless teenagers who had celebrated mindlessly. I wondered what they thought of us. I snapped another picture.

"Where did the time go?"

"Forget something, miss?"

"Oh, I . . ." I figured he had heard me talking to myself. "I think I left my lipstick on the table."

"Go ahead and check. We're just startin' the clean-up. Looks like you kids had a good time."

"We did. Thanks."

When I reached our table, I noticed a bunch of leftover napkins. "Good reason to come back. A napkin for my scrapbook."

"You talkin' to me, miss?"

"No, sorry," I smiled weakly. "Just myself again," I mumbled.

"What?"

"I'm good! Thanks again."

When I reached toward the pile in the center of the table, I spotted a crumbled-up napkin that had started to unfold as if it had a secret to share. There was scribbling inside; I picked it up and instantly recognized the signature doodling. I smoothed it open. Within a mass of caricatures and random symbols stood the words . . . *don't go, don't go, don't go.*

My hand began to shake.

* * *

Gretta Kaplan invited the entire senior class, and then some, to her house after the prom. The first person I saw was Shelly Porterfield. Ever since the "Brian" incident, she had been cool to me, and we continued to drift apart. To add to that tension, we were in completely different corners of our senior year. Hers was about raising hell and drinking until she threw up. Mine was about spending time with Buck and maintaining a decent average. My choices edged me out of the "girl circle" most of the time. So there we were. Awkward. But that's the way things sometimes go. Friends today . . . then there's tomorrow.

"Hi, Sam. I never see you anymore. How are you?" Shelly spoke in a more restrained fashion than I was used to.

"I'm good. You look pretty in that dress, Shelly." I meant it.

"Thanks." She perked up. "You look good too. Yellow is a nice color on you. Where'd you buy your dress?"

"In Watertown."

"I figured." She nodded. "So, did you guys drive here with Darlene and Sal?"

"Yes."

"I see." She strained slightly. "Where's Buck?"

"In the living room, talking with his brother."

"Oh, yeah. I see him." She turned back to me with a complete change in tone. "Why don't you call me anymore?"

I hesitated—then met her eyes. "I think we both know the answer to that question. Same reason you don't call me. Works both ways."

She nodded at the floor. "I guess that's true."

Awkward silence. I waited for the backlash, but it didn't come. I had to give the girl credit.

"So have you heard from any colleges yet?" Impressive.

"A couple."

"Which ones?"

"Michigan State and Albany."

"Those are good schools. But you're holding out for New York, aren't you?" Her voice began to sound more like the one I knew.

"I am. And you? Heard from anywhere yet?"

"Yeah, I think I'm going to Shillington Community College and then transferring to a four-year school later."

"Sounds like a good plan. How about George? Where's he going?"

"Ohio State."

Her response took me by surprise. "I thought he wasn't going out of state."

"Changed his mind."

"Doesn't that bother you? It's a lot farther away."

"No, not really. We'll still see each other every now and then." Her blasé attitude baffled me. "So how's Buck handling the fact that you're leaving him?" Dagger!

"I'm not leaving him. I'm going away to school." The hair on the back of my neck stood up.

"Same difference."

"No, it's not." Defiance swam in my throat.

"You're still going to be away from each other. How's that's gonna work out?"

"It'll work out." I wanted her to shut up, but the girl was a steamroller for details.

"How?"

"Some weekends and over school breaks. We'll be fine."

"You think?" He eyes flashed defiantly. "And you're not gonna go out with other people?"

"No."

"Why not?"

How hard is your head? "I told you. I don't want to go out with anybody else." I inspected the room in an attempt to divert my attention from her annoying face. *Jacquelyn Livingston. What is she doing here?*

"Sam, this is college. Time to spread your wings." Her voice dug into me and crawled under my skin, scraping the final remnants of my patience.

"Spread yours then." I turned away from her. "I'm hungry."

She flinched, her mouth poised in retaliation, but nothing came out. I started toward the food table, even though hunger was not my problem. The red-head sidling up to my boyfriend was.

But before my escape, Shelly discovered what I'd already seen.

"Sam, look who Buck's talking to. Check out the way she's acting. That girl is something. I've noticed them talking before. You better watch her. Get over there and protect your territory."

Her words were like a fist in my gut. I turned back to her, wondering where my friend had gone. "Thanks, Shel. I appreciate your concern."

She walked away.

I slid in next to Buck, weaving my fingers through his. "Hey, handsome, want to get something to eat and sit on the porch?" *Coquette* was definitely not in my profile. But I could work it up when I needed to.

Jacquelyn's smile dissolved, the spell broken. "Hi, Sam. You look cute."

Buck chuckled audibly at her choice of words.

Will that damn word follow me forever?

"Thanks, you too." That was all I could muster. I tucked into my boyfriend a little closer for good measure. "They have pizza." I smiled at him possessively.

"Pizza," he smirked. "Well, then let's eat. See you, Jacquelyn." He slid his hand around my waist, escorting me to the table.

"So what were you guys talking about?" My attempt at nonchalance was transparent.

"The student council meeting. We're on the same committee, remember?" I could feel him side-eying me. "Sam, what was that all about?"

"What?" I feigned innocence.

"That little demonstration in front of Jacquelyn?"

"Nothing. Want some salad to go with your pizza?"

He shook his head. "Foolish girl. Don't you get it? You're it." And then it struck me—*that is the crux of our discontent, isn't it?*

"Come on, Buck. Get your plate, and let's eat on the porch."

Sitting in the fresh air was exactly what I needed. I had had enough of the women in the house. I needed to breathe and relax. Life was changing so much. Every day marked something significant. How had the pace of my life accelerated so dramatically? It no longer felt simple. I worried that I was leaving simple behind.

"So, did you have fun at your senior prom?"

"I did. But it's kind of sad—last prom and all."

"Last prom that belongs to *you*. Next prom belongs to *me*."

Next prom belongs to me.

A foreign melancholy grabbed hold of me. I wanted to stop time.

"Whatcha thinking?" He was watching me closely.

"It's all so fast. One minute I'm dressing for my senior prom, and the next minute it's over."

"Yeah, the end is fast, isn't it?"

I stood up, escape on my mind. "Let's get out of here."

"Sounds good to me. I'll get Darlene and Sal. They'll be glad to leave."

Sal's oversized clunker, a '58 Chevy, inched through the thicket of trees, branches scraping across the windows. The Delfonics crooned *la la la la la la la la la means I love you.*

As soon as the car stopped, Sal and Darlene wrapped around each other and disappeared in the front seat.

"I better roll this window down a little so the whole car doesn't steam up," Sal announced as he leaned across Darlene to crack the window.

Darlene giggled. "Sal! Shh!"

In the back of the car, the energy was decidedly different.

"Last prom," he said.

"Last prom," I repeated.

"You look really good tonight. When you told me the color of your dress, I didn't know if I'd like it. Mellow yellow, huh, DeSantis? You make every color look good."

"I think I'm gonna puke!" screamed Sal.

"Then mind your own business, Ucci!"

"Sal," Darlene whispered, "leave them alone."

Buck motioned to me, mouthing—*watch this*. Then he began to recite. "She walks in beauty, like the night of cloudless climes and starry skies . . ."

"Oh, shit! Listen to that!! Buck's reciting poetry. Who you quoting, Kendall—Shelley or Keats?" I could barely contain myself.

"As a matter of fact, it's Lord Byron, smart ass!"

"Oh, sorry, Mr. 99.9 percent! Well, here's a poem for you!" Sal yelled.

Roses are red
Sam's dress is yellow
My advice for Buck is
SHUT THE HELL UP, FELLOW!

"What the hell was that?" Buck leaned over the front seat and smacked Sal on the back of the head.

"Sal, you're so dumb! That didn't even make any sense."

The amusement in Darlene's voice was an elixir. The car rocked with laughter. Finally, we all managed to calm down, but every now and then one of us would think about Sal's creative verse and lose control. Contagion followed. It was hard to be serious around Sal.

For weeks I had thought about prom night—the dresses and tuxedoes, the moment we'd walk through the door, the excitement in the room. And now here I was in the undergrowth of maples and oaks, curls falling out of my hair, make-up sucked away by the evening. Suddenly I realized—*this* is the best part. Just the four of us. And I wondered, *What am I going to do without these kids?*

Sixty-four

Graduation is such a common rite of passage that many people take it for granted, perhaps because they have already been there. It is, after all, a part of the normal course of life. These factors, however, do not diminish its power or the emotional upheaval that, for many, is overwhelming. Off to college, away from home, fend for yourself. Yet for some, graduation marks a time of longed-for freedom, a liberation from rules. The life implications are a very big deal when you're living through it—and only eighteen.

I found myself more sentimental than expected. When I reminisced about the last few years, I could only remember the good.

Shelly. Good old Shelly Porterfield. She taught me about the art of style, which may seem of lesser importance on the scale of life lessons, but she executed her knowledge with such panache and sincerity that she drew me in and nurtured my girly side. While she had the ability to infuriate me like no other, I was drawn to her vulnerable side, the part that longed to be embraced but was too proud to ask. Although that facet of her personality hid behind a tough and confident exterior, it was, for me, her redeeming grace.

Annie fed my soul with laughter and wit, woke me up to the harshness of reality, wrapped a sheltering arm around me and extracted my pain. Her honesty was brutal, but her smile lit up the room. I often thought I'd like to come back as Annie in another life and view the world through her bohemian eyes. Would I be happier, or was I simply destined to be who I am? There was no one quite like Annie.

Darlene. A breath of fresh air among the catty and dramatic. Darlene was pure. In my life, few people have come along who are as genuinely good as she. Being around Darlene made me feel like a better person. She had a capacity for understanding people on a higher plane than most kids her age. There was something extraordinary about her spirit. And she lived for the "fun factor." Darlene enriched my life.

My girls.

Brian Determan. Ah, yes . . . how lucky was I to have a guy for a friend? Brian offered me the male perspective, the down and dirty, no bullshit. I liked that about him. He said what was on his mind, and that was that. For as gruff as he could sometimes be with his words, he handled me like a fragile piece of crystal, gentle and appreciative. If the stars had been aligned in our favor, we would have fallen in love. But that was never meant to be. Our love was on a different level.

And then there was Buck. The boy who, with one look, stole my heart. The boy who showed me a side of joy I had never known. He watched me cross one threshold after another, each one before him. And despite the most painful thorn, his inability to walk through those doors by my side, he celebrated my milestones. I could feel his eyes on me as I crossed the stage of Carlson High School to receive my diploma, as I stood in the shower of graduation caps that rained down on the class of '68. He smiled, all the while the thorn lodged deeper inside him.

* * *

After the ceremony, my entire family—grandparents, aunts, uncles—went to our favorite Italian restaurant. Buck couldn't join us because he was with his own family, celebrating with Greg.

Our plan was to meet up before the graduation picnic at the lake. The day was bittersweet, from start to finish.

"To Samantha." At the sound of my father's voice, my family raised their glasses. All eyes were on me, but mine rested on Lucy, holding her goblet high and smiling from ear to ear.

"Tell 'em your news, Sam," prodded Dad proudly.

I could feel my entire being swell. "I was finally accepted to NYU." My family broke into applause, and the people at surrounding tables turned to check out the source of the cheering. They smiled along with us. The whole restaurant was in a good mood. It was graduation day in Carlson. Congratulations traveled from the tables next to us. I was on top of the world.

"I'm proud of you, Sam." The lake glistened, sun reflecting on the still, flat sheet of water. We sat in his car next to the fish fry stand, overlooking Lake Ontario. The place was jammed, exploding with celebration.

"Yeah? You mean because you never thought I'd graduate?"

"Yeah, that's it." He took my hand. "You worked hard, and you were accepted to the college of your dreams."

"NYU, baby!" I screamed out the car window.

"You're a crazy girl. You know that?"

"I do!" I laughed at myself, drunk with lightheartedness. "And you're lovin' me right now, aren't you, Kendall?" I leaned across the seat and kissed him straight on the mouth, and he took that kiss adeptly.

"I am," he crooned. "I *am* lovin' you now." He reached across me and opened the glove compartment. "I have a graduation gift for you."

"You do?" I emitted coyly, as if I didn't already know. "Good hiding place, Kendall. I would *never* think to look there."

"Keep it up and you won't get it!" He clung to the gift.

"Ooh, it's little," I delighted.

"Yeah? So what does that mean?"

"Good things come in small packages!" I oozed.

"Open it." He handed me the gift.

Normally I prefer to draw out the process of unwrapping gifts. But on this day, all I wanted to do was celebrate. I ripped off the wrapping and pulled off the top of the box. Inside lay a silver charm to add to my bracelet. The thick silver jewel took the shape of an open book, a tiny pearl-tipped bookmark hanging fancifully across the curved page. Imitation words scrawled over the surface. I lifted the charm from the box and turned it over to reveal the front, which was fashioned in the form of a hardcover book. There, emblazoned in gracefully crafted letters was the title of my short story:

Her Unintentional Life
by
Samantha DeSantis

Over the years he had given me charms to add to my bracelet: a camera, a treble clef, the Empire State Building, each symbolizing some interest in my life. He knew my goal was to fill every link, to create a collage of my high school years. I half expected that his gift would be a charm. I guessed he might choose something along the lines of a heart with our names inscribed, our anniversary date, a sentiment that would remind me of him as it dangled and twirled at the end of my wrist. Instead he chose to celebrate my story, the story that had beaten out his. The airiness that had filled the day evaporated with the intake of a single breath.

"I can't believe you did this. It's . . ."

A multitude of inconsequential seconds come and go, filling the space between the significant moments of our lives. For most, the majority of life is spent between those moments, in the habitual, the ordinary progression of a day. But when those moments come, they burst through all that is common and seep inside so deeply that we are somehow changed. And all that makes us who we are is altered to some new way of thinking and seeing.

And this is how we grow and learn to sift through the minutiae of our existence.

Something profound happened in that instant. I looked at his face and understood everything inside of him, his doubts and fears. We belonged to each other. The night of August 16th was no accident.

"It's what?" A loving pain flickered in his eye.

"It's perfect. Just when I think I have you all figured out, you sneak up on me."

"You've always had me figured out; you just don't trust it yet. I'm not that complicated, Sam."

"Oh, but you are."

Sixty-five

July 1968

Dearest Sam,

How's everything in Hometown USA? Things here are going well. However, my roommate wouldn't say the same. He just got knocked silly playing basketball, and he went down hard. He's still in the infirmary. They're making sure he doesn't have a concussion. Looks like I might be sleeping alone tonight. Life's tough. Wish you were here (Yuk, yuk)! Actually, no yuks. I mean it.

I seem to have a lot of free time. Not that I don't like writing to you. Hope you don't get bored with my small talk. Speaking of small, I must say the kid I rode down here with, about four foot ten by my estimations, is a royal pain in the ass. Luckily I only have to put up with him for FIVE MORE DAYS! Who's counting, eh?

Some of these guys THINK they are real politicians. They act like they're in D.C. I've met this one guy four times already. He's obviously running for some office, but he forgets everyone he meets. We call him Mr. Gladhand. Sad story is he'll probably be in Washington someday. Okay,

I'll finish this letter after dinner. Can't wait to see what hash they're serving tonight.

I'm back. Beef stew and mashed potatoes. Acceptable. My roommate returned. He's pretty much out of it. I think they must have given him some pain killers. I could use some of those drugs for the next time I'm around Gladhand. Maybe they would dull my senses.

By the way, what book are you reading now? I brought East of Eden. One of Steinbeck's best. Well, it's almost 10:00 p.m. That means "time for lights out, gentlemen." So, until the official announcement, I'll keep telling you what's in my heart.

I love you + I miss you.
I love you + I miss you.
I love you + I miss you.
I love you + I miss you.
I love you + I miss you.
I love you + I miss you.
I love you + I miss you.
I love you + I miss you.
I love you + I miss you.
I love you + I miss you.
I love you + I miss you.
I love you + I miss you.
I love you + I miss you.

And there it is! The official directive. See you Saturday.

Love ya always,
Buck

Sixty-six

After graduation, I chose to let go of the hard feelings that had wedged between Shelly and me. Sentiment makes me soft. She readily accepted my overtures toward mending, noting that she may *possibly* have behaved badly herself, but she *"forgave me."* The restraint I exercised after she exonerated me took much more strength than my initial approach to let bygones be bygones.

We walked into her house, which smelled great, as usual. Her mom had made a fresh batch of brownies and left them on a plate in the kitchen. I was demolishing my third with an ice-cold glass of milk when Shelly's lecture began.

"Are you going to spend every waking moment with Buck this summer? We only have about five weeks before we leave for school."

"Exactly. We only have about five weeks, and I want to be with him as much as I can. What difference does it make to you anyway? You have tons of people to hang out with. You have George."

"Yeah, but I told him we have to see other people when we go away."

"I thought you really loved him."

"I do. But I'm only 18, and I need to sow my wild oats."

"Why do you have to sow any oats? You sowed plenty during high school." She didn't flinch. Could it be she was getting used to my digs?

"I just know that's the course of my life. We'll both go away to college. Date whoever we want. But we'll be together every time we come home. Then after that we can get married."

"You already know you want to marry him?"

"Yeah."

"Why?"

"Good sex."

"You're having sex with him! As in actual intercourse?"

"Sam, grow up. Honest to God, sometimes you're such a drag. Lots of people are doin' it. They just don't tell you 'cause they know you're a prude." She splashed another inch of milk into her glass and grabbed a brownie.

Prude remark aside, I pressed on. "How can you know you're going to marry him and be *doing it* with him—and then go off to college and date other people?"

"That's what everybody does. It's no big deal."

"It *is* a big deal! Next you're going to tell me that you're going to *do it* with other people too."

"Probably."

I almost fell off the chair. "Probably! I didn't ask you if want another gulp of milk. I'm talking about sex!"

"I know. And, by the way, you *are* going to tell Buck that you guys should date other kids when you go away to school, right?" She poured another inch of milk into her glass.

I was exasperated and in no mood for this conversation with the girl with sliding morals. What made her think college changed everything? I could feel the tightening in my chest as she swallowed the remains of her milk. She waited for my response.

"Shelly, we already had this conversation at Gretta's house. You know how I feel."

"Well, I thought you might have wised up by now. Seriously, you're not going to make him stay here and wait for you while you're off at college meeting new guys, are you? That wouldn't be fair to him. It's his senior year. You should give him his senior year."

"Don't you listen? I told you I don't want to date other people."

"You will though. Just wait. This is what you get for falling for a younger man. If he was going away to college, too, you'd feel different about everything."

"How? We'd still be in separate places."

"Yeah, but you'd both be in college. Then it's accepted that you both go out with other people and see each other when you come home for holidays and stuff."

"That doesn't make any sense."

"Don't get mad at me. I'm not the one who made the rules."

"Who made them then?" I challenged. She blatantly dismissed me and sauntered to the refrigerator to pour another "last sip" of cold milk, an odd habit of continually doling out one mouthful at a time rather than filling her glass. "Why don't you just fill the whole damn glass so you don't have to keep pouring more?"

"Because the last drop tastes the best."

Of course it does!

"So . . . when are you gonna tell him?" She pushed on.

"I'm not."

"What?"

"I'm not telling him to date other people. I don't want to."

"You're really selfish."

"Why? Because I love him, and I want to stay with him? He doesn't want to see other people either. And it's only one year that he'll be here without me. Then we'll both be in college, and Cornell is not that far from NYU." That outlook made perfect sense to me.

"No, that's not why. It's because you're not giving him the freedom to live his life and have a normal senior year. Because you're afraid that's exactly what he'd like to do. Have you ever actually asked him if he wanted to date other people when you're away?"

"No." I felt like a child whose mother had just questioned her about sharing her candy.

"Well, you should at least give him the choice."

"Why, because you gave George the choice and he ran with it?"

"You know I set that up so he'd say yes and be okay with it. I want to be able to meet new boys at school." She had to win. Failure was a wretched punishment.

"Well, I don't. And why does that bother you so much anyway? Clearly, we are very different, Shelly." My remark offended her. Maybe because I had the nerve to actually say those words. She was completely aware of the differences between us.

"I don't really care what you do! I just think you're afraid Buck might want to date other girls and that's why you're not asking him."

"I'm not afraid. I know how he feels."

Then ask him," she dared. "If he really loves you, it'll work out for you in the end. He's only seventeen. Don't be so selfish, Sam."

Don't be so selfish, Sam.

I began to think there might be some truth to what she said. Was I being selfish? Was this the natural course of things, to move on from your high school sweetheart and date new people in college? But what if you had already met the one you wanted to be with forever?

* * *

The shelves in the den held enormous numbers of books, old, new, and collectors' items. I loved the musty scent in that room. The pages, worn by the constant touch of fingertips, emitted a smell like the backstage of an old theater. Inhaling that smell made me feel as if I was standing exactly where I belonged. It was a good room for a serious conversation. I took a deep breath.

"Shelly said we should date other people when I go to college. She said I'm selfish if I don't give you the chance to have your senior year." I experienced a certain sense of relief in finally saying the words but almost instantly wanted to take them back. Why was I listening to Shelly? Was it guilt? I couldn't read his face. "Did you hear me?"

"I heard you." His tone was flat, like his expression.

"So what do you think?"

"Is this what you want or what Shelly wants?" he asked pointedly.

"I'm just asking." Why, I had no clue. *This* was not what I wanted.

He stared at me, eyes wide and challenging. "Is this what *you* want, Samantha?" He rarely called me by my full name.

"I mean, you'll be here, and I'll be there. And I'm willing to talk about it if you think you might want more freedom during your senior year." The muscles in the side of his face pulsed. I misinterpreted his silence. Panic swept through me, so I blurted out my worst fear. "Do you want to break up completely?"

"No!" he shot back.

"Well, what?" My heart was beating out of my chest.

"Sam, you don't understand. I don't want to break up at all. And I don't want to date other people. Is this really just from Shelly, or are you having second thoughts about going away to school and being tied to a high school boy?"

Now it was my turn to stare. I had not anticipated that response, but I should have. My feelings for him were so unconditional that insignificant factors such as age and distance didn't stand in my way. "You know it's not that. It's just that when Shelly started talking about letting you have some freedom, I wondered if she was right. If I was being selfish and tying you down."

"Shelly is just filling your head with shit because she's jealous. She and George broke up, and you and I are going strong."

"She said they're going to see each other when they come home from school. She wants to marry him."

"Why did she break up with him if she wants to marry him? I'll believe that when I see it."

"I don't know, Buck." I felt helpless.

"She's always been jealous of us, Sam. And *you* for that matter. She's insecure, and she can't stand to see anybody do better than she does. You know how much she pisses me off when it comes to us. She's always telling you that you spend too much time with me and trying to make you feel guilty that you're not with the girls. And then she punishes you by excluding you from the "girl plans." His fingers formed quotation marks in the air. "And she makes damn sure to tell you how much fun they all had. She's manipulative. She's the one who's selfish. You just don't see it. And now you're going away to college, and she's continuing to fill your head with crap because she's single and on the prowl and you're not! That girl gets on my goddamn nerves!"

"I'm sorry. I don't know why I ever listened to her. You're right. So you're sure about this?"

"You really don't get it, do you? I don't want to break up at all. I just want you, Sam. But if that's what you want, to date other kids, then I'll accept it."

We had been in perfect sync for two years, except for that one little blip. Besides my family, he was the one sure thing in my life. Why, then, was I doing this? What was my doubt? Or was this simply payback for the time he had broken up with me? *No.* For the remainder of that summer, we operated as one and ignored the looming presence of the fall of 1968.

Sixty-seven

The best laid plans of mice and men . . . .

—Robert Burns

Hard as you may try, you cannot really prepare yourself for a separation of the heart. You have no idea what it will feel like until you are on the other side. You have to live through it to know what you'll do. Buck and I planned to stay together. We just had to weather this one year. I was sure we could handle it.

My parents drove me to New York City. Ever since the first time I had flown there with my dad for the March of Dimes convention and met Dr. Salk at the Aster Hotel, I was enchanted with New York. Going to NYU *was* a dream come true, and I sometimes had to pinch myself to realize my good fortune.

Mom sat in the front seat, wearing sunglasses and staring straight ahead. Earlier that morning, I had walked into the kitchen to find her frying bacon and eggs in the dark glasses, a sure sign that she had been crying. The day was bittersweet. As proud as she was that I was launching my college career at NYU, she knew life would never be the same in the DeSantis household.

Buck and I sat in the back seat, pretending everything was going to be the same. But the simple entrance into a new city marked a significant change. I glanced down where his hand cradled mine, a frenzy of emotion seizing me. We loved each other; that was a fact. I told myself that people who felt this way could make it. While the distance would add a strain, I knew we were strong enough to make it. Once he was in college, things would be different. We would both be immersed in the same pursuit.

After the fifth haul to my room, comforter, clothes, photo albums all thrown on my bed, there was nothing more to transport. The trunk was empty. I stood by the side of the Lincoln, hugging my parents and assuring them that I would be fine. Mom couldn't let go. While this experience was exactly what she wanted for me, particularly because she never had this opportunity, she understood the implications.

"Sam?" I could tell Mom had something big on her mind.

"What, Mom?"

"Honey, be careful with all these anti-war protests. I worry."

"You? Worry?" I kidded. "No!" She laughed. Exactly what I was going for. "Mom, I'll be fine." I remember feeling embarrassed by her effusive show of emotion.

"Make sure you write and let us know how everything is going."

"I will, Mom; don't worry."

"Ah, she'll be fine, Peg. Our girl is strong. She'll probably be heading up some of those protest committees," Dad hugged me.

"Nick!" scolded my mother.

"I'm kidding, Peggy." Then he turned to me. "Need anything before we go, honey?"

"No, Dad; I'm good."

"Money? You have enough?"

"Yes, Dad, I'm fine." I smiled at my father's predictable comments.

"Okay, Buck, it's your turn," directed my mother. "We'll wait here in the car."

Walking back to the dorm was awkward and unfamiliar. We didn't know how to behave in this world. We seemed to know how to do everything else, but this . . .

"Well, I guess this is where I take off, D." My gut ached. "Be good, and write to me."

"I will. And I'll see you at Homecoming. That's not so long from now."

We had never been away from each other for longer than a week. And we had never been in this odd space before. It was like creeping though a dark labyrinth.

"No, not too bad." He hugged me, his face in my hair. "Learn a lot here, Sam. Be good, and remember us."

Remember us?

"You sound as if we will never see each other again."

"That's not what I meant. It's just that things are not going to be the same anymore."

No, they're not. I closed my eyes, breathing him in as I swallowed the lump in my throat.

"I'd better go." He broke away. "Your parents are waiting." Then he left, head down, and he didn't look back.

The Big City surrounded me. Suddenly, I felt inconsequential and alone.

* * *

The first few weeks at NYU were hectic. Navigating the campus proved challenging. Meeting new people every day was something I looked forward to, but it definitely required a certain level of stamina and balance. I was used to knowing everyone and feeling at home. Nonetheless, I embraced the change. My courses were rigorous, and I knew I had to throw myself into them to succeed. Majoring in English was a natural choice for me, and I loved studying French as my minor. My plan was to go to Paris after I graduated and then come back to New York to write.

Buck and I began our correspondence right away. He wrote as soon as he arrived home that first day. Besides my studies and a few trips to the off-off-Broadway plays I could afford, I dedicated myself to our communication. Mail was a major event in my life, and I looked forward to the daily delivery. When I spotted the familiar handwriting with its fancy cursive twists, I would rip open the envelope, and his voice would fill the room. We shared the love of language, and writing was an outlet for both of us. His words made me feel as if he were there, and his humor, sometimes cerebral and sometimes purposely corny, amused me.

My first read-through was a fast search. Once devoured, I would sit on my bed and reread, lingering on each word and analyzing the meaning between every line.

Dearest Sam,

How's the big city? You're probably living like a queen, with filet mignon every night. Isn't that what you ate at the Astor? Don't worry about those calories though, because with your figure, you don't have to think about what you eat.

Maybe if I can scrape up a little extra coin, I'll be able to phone you this week. You know with all the dates I've had lately, money's getting scarce. Not really. You know I'm only kidding, don't you? But then again, you don't know, do you? You'll just have to take my word for it.

I sent for my applications yesterday. I wrote to Cornell, Boston College, and big Harvard, just for fun. I will probably send out more. This is just a start.

School is the same. The senior class raked in a whopping $26 profit on our overly planned dance. Mr. Olsen was quite perturbed and gave hell to the seniors. Your handsome boyfriend conducted an unusually orderly meeting today. Who said I was scared? Actually, I was a little. Tell no one. I must maintain the mystique.

Well, my love, it probably doesn't look like much, but I write small. I realize that I am verbose in person, but truly, there lies a quieter side, as you know. Write back or I won't write any more. Be good.

Love always,
B R K

P. S. I miss the way you jump up and down when you answer a Jeopardy question. I miss watching crumbs fall on your clothes every time you eat a cookie. But most of all, I miss you. See you soon—I hope.

After a thorough read, I would select the perfect stationery from the hoard of designs in my trunk. Choosing the right stationery has always given me pleasure. The choice generally reflects my mood. For me, composing alone in a room is a religious experience. With no one to interrupt, no distractions—words fall out honestly. My ritual involved placing his letter on the left side of my desk so I could refer and respond to each paragraph in order. It made our communication more like a conversation. Replying to each sentiment, I would often write four pages to his two. Even when I write, I have a lot to say. Licked and stamped, my letters hurried into the mouth of the closest mailbox. Expeditious delivery—prompt response.

And thus our custom of writing continued.

* * *

New York City was still unfamiliar to me, and I was eager to get to know it. I didn't have the money to take advantage of its many cultural opportunities or city tours that would help to unlock some of the mystery. So I did a lot of walking. One sure way to get to know a place is to wander around on foot. You grasp a feel for the lay of the land and its people. And the people, especially unaware, speak multitudes about the culture.

I frequented Central Park, the area closest to the Plaza Hotel and FAO Schwartz, where horses and carts waited for tourists who couldn't resist. I sat and read, worked on homework, or sometimes just people-watched. Tons of people flocked to New York from absolutely everywhere. I kept a journal with me so I could jot down the details I knew I would forget.

In addition, I took advantage of the museums and became especially fond of The Metropolitan Museum of Art and the Museum of Modern Art. The Impressionists were my favorite; I fell in love with Monet and his water lilies and dreamed of seeing the gardens at Giverny. But for the time being, I settled for sitting on a bench and allowing my focus to blur into the art. It made me happy, which I've always been about.

One night some of the girls from my dorm and I went to the top of the Empire State Building, which may sound cliché and touristy, but the experience was spectacular. From this pinnacle I had a panoramic view of the city. Lights flickered everywhere. Cabs crawled up and down the streets like yellow bugs. Broadway's angular path cut through Manhattan, intersecting uptown and downtown. As I stood there, high above everything I'd dreamed about, something inside came alive. The city's pulse crawled inside me, and I knew, as I had somehow known ever since my father whisked me away for my first visit, that I was in the right place. New York worked its way into my blood—and my heart.

Sixty-nine

There is just something about home. It stays inside you. No matter where you venture, home travels with you.

Each time I walk into my bedroom on Sunset Terrace, familiar voices greet me. I sit on my bed and run my fingers across the knots of the white chenille spread. My eyes wander over the same old pieces of furniture from the desk in front of the window to the dresser on which my jewelry box still remains. Those walls were privy to so much; they heard my innermost thoughts and held my secrets. And now they speak to me in faded tones upon my return. In my room I become the girl I once was. I like her, and sometimes I miss her.

I hadn't been away from home for very long, but it sure felt that way. Maybe because I was finding my way down an unfamiliar path all by myself. Sure, I had met a few people in passing, one who even qualified as a potential friend. But my daily routine was solitary. Solitary time is easily twice as long as time spent in the familiarity of home, where the hands on the clock seem to run between habitual undertakings. I missed my family and the space they had filled in my day. So when I finally arrived at my front door, I barged through, announcing my return.

"I'm home!"

Mom came running into the living room from the kitchen.

"Hi, honey! Look at you! Give me a kiss." Mom was so excited to see me; you would have thought I had been gone for months rather than weeks.

"Nick, Sam's home! Come in and say hello to your daughter."

"Hi, Sammy," Lucy ran to me and wrapped her arms around my waist. "I miss you."

"Hey, Luce!" She buried her head in my chest. "You look taller."

"Really?" Her face shone.

"Really. Just look at you! Here, I brought you a present." I knelt down to retrieve the bag.

"Open it. I bought it in New York. See, the bag says The Empire State."

"It's a diary. Like yours!" Her face continued to light up.

"It is. Now you can start writing in it every day like I do. And there's a key, see? Lock it so no one else can read it."

"Thanks, Sammy. I just love it." Her demeanor spoke of birthday parties and balloons.

"SAMANTHA!" Dad came waltzing in from the kitchen, singing my name. Dad sang everything.

"Daddy!" I wrapped myself around him.

"Good to see you, daughter. How's school?"

"I like it a lot. But I miss home more than I thought I would."

"Ah, you'll get over that. Did you hear the Soviets sent a man around the moon, big college student?" Dad and his tidbits.

"I did. One of my professors talked about it in class."

"It's a big deal, you know." Such things always fascinated my father.

"I know, Dad." I walked toward the kitchen. "Where's my brother?"

"He went to a movie with his friends. He said to tell you hello and not to touch anything in his room."

The words assaulted me, partially by disbelief and partially by the possibility that my brother may have said just that. "He did not!"

"Dad's only kidding, Sammy." Lucy to the rescue.

Dad laughed at his own joke.

"Dad!" I rebuked.

"Nick, don't say that to your daughter. She just got home. Sam, Buck called and said he'd be here by 5:30. I have pizza. You want some now, or do you want to wait for him?"

The mention of his name never failed to cause a reaction in me. "I'll wait, Mom. I'm just going to take these things up to my room and change." Halfway up the stairs, I looked back to see my little sister staring at me longingly. I halted mid-step. "Luce, do you want to help me carry this stuff to my room?"

"Sure, I'll help!" In moments she was on the step behind me, hauling my bag.

* * *

When the doorbell rang, my pulse quickened.

"It's probably Buck, Sammy. Want me to go downstairs and answer it?"

"Would you, Lucy?" She bounded down the stairs and yanked open the front door.

"Hey, Lucy! Look at you. You look older since the last time I saw you. How are you, kiddo?" He gave her a hug, which sometimes embarrassed her, but mostly she wallowed in his attention.

"I'm nine now."

"Nine! When I first met you, you were only six. Just this high. So where's your sister hiding?"

"She's upstairs."

"Well, tell her to get down here! I miss her, and I want to give her a hug too."

I abandoned any notion of looking calm and college-like and bolted down the stairs. The interminable bus ride had been trying enough. With each step, a little more of his body revealed itself until he finally leaned down to peek up the stairwell at me.

"There's my girl!" He met me at the bottom stair and flung his arms around me, hanging on tightly and kissing the top of my head. I couldn't wait to get him alone.

"Hello, Buckley. It's good to see you." In walked Mom.

"Hey, Mrs. D. Long time, no see."

Greetings continued, Mom served pizza, and everyone caught up on the local news. I remember the way Buck kept looking at me. It was making me crazy. As soon as we could escape, we tore out the door. The second we slid into the car, we were on each other. The familiarity of his touch was absolute. I was definitely home.

"Let's go." He pulled the car out of the driveway and drove down the street, heading toward the lake.

"You're going the wrong way. I thought we were going to the pep rally."

"Screw that noise!"

"Where are we going then?"

He hit the gas and turned up the radio. "You'll see."

* * *

He parked the car and smiled. "Remember?"

"I do." I loved him for giving me that moment, for the tenderness in his eyes. "We're going to freeze, you know."

"Got it covered." He reached into the back and grabbed the army blanket that always traveled with us. "Come on." He pulled me toward him, and we slid out the driver's side.

The distant sound of the high school band carried through the air. We ran down the slope toward the break wall. The summer crafts were gone, and the lake seemed lonely, except for the lighthouse and its friendly wink. We found the familiar shelter amidst the rocks, and he spread out the blanket. Harbor lights reflected across the water, accentuating gentle ripples. It smelled like fall. A shiver traveled through me.

"Cold?"

"A little."

"Here. Take a sip." He produced a flask from his jacket.

"Where did you get that?" I laughed.

"It's Greg's. I borrowed it."

"Borrowed, huh?"

"Maybe a loose interpretation." He opened the flask and took a slug. "It'll warm you up."

"What is it?"

"Brandy." He took another hearty pull before handing me the flask.

"You're not legal yet, Kendall," I teased.

He flinched only briefly. "So. Who's gonna catch me in this hideaway? Besides, eighteen's just around the corner, love. Drink up."

I took a sip. "You *do* have all the details covered tonight, don't you, Kendall? Blanket, brandy, romantic spot." The warmth began to filter through me.

"Yup!" He laughed. "And my best girl."

"I love that you did all this. And I love it here." I lifted the flask to my mouth, craving more of the liquid heat. A trail leaked down my cheek.

"You like that, don't you?" He slapped his leg and laughed while I wiped my mouth and returned to the flask. I took another generous sip. His cheeks were growing ruddy from the brandy and the nippy air, and his eyes pooled with intoxication. When I looked at his face, he was once again the boy I had met on the bike, the boy who stopped to talk to me, the boy who changed my life. He wore no creases of worry, no tension, no doubt. He looked at me the same way he did that night, abandon guiding him. And in that moment, I could tell he was reading my thoughts.

"Come here."

The days and weeks we had spent apart only made me want him more. Intimacy had always been a big deal to me, but with Buck, everything felt right. Ours was an oddly familiar dance from the moment we had stepped onto the floor. He was the one who trained my feet to follow. In a sense, we grew up together. Now, without conscious decision, I wanted more of him.

He leaned forward, covering me with hot kisses. I couldn't get enough. "Jesus, Sam. Why did you have to pick a school so far away? This is insane."

"Stop talking." I said. With that, he pushed me down on the blanket and pulled off his jacket.

"Take this off."

I ripped off my peacoat and flung it against the wall of rock.

"This too," he said. My sweater landed next to the jacket. He slid on top of me. "You're so damn pretty." He brushed my hair back from my face with both hands. "I miss you, Sam."

"Me too. Me too," was all I could muster. I was lost in my body.

His forehead dampened. He sat upright, yanking off his sweater and added it to the pile. "Take this off too," he told me. I followed orders as he watched intently. "God, you're beautiful." His hands were on me. They seemed to be everywhere at once. I loved the feel of his skin on mine.

"Do you really need those jeans?" He managed a smile.

"No. Do you need yours?"

"Race ya." His voice was a whisper. I felt my entire being shudder.

The pile grew.

"And those?" He pointed.

"Turn around."

"Are you serious?"

"Turn around!"

"Okay, but you're killing me here."

"And take yours off too. I'm not doing this alone."

"Wow! You are a bold girl!"

"All right. I'm good."

He turned around. Nothing stood between us. He looked down the length of my body. I began to shiver, so he wrapped the blanket around my shoulders and folded me into him, our bodies a faultless fit. I was home.

"You're mine, Samantha DeSantis. This body is mine." He ran both hands over me. "God you feel good."

"So do you," I managed.

His face wore the urgency of one who has waited patiently, only to be issued another delay. His were the eyes that had watched me turn sixteen and seventeen and eighteen, the eyes that loved me and wanted me with all my imperfections.

"I love you," he blurted in a foreign spasm. The water splashed lightly against the rocks.

"Sam, let's make love. Tell me it's okay."

When does it become okay? Everything in me said yes. How much more proof did I need to follow my heart and still know I was a good person? Sex before marriage in 1968 was a sin for a Catholic girl—or so I had been told. Was I brainwashed? And what if we didn't end up together? Used goods?

No! That won't happen to us.

I wanted him more than I had ever wanted anything.

The lighthouse continued to blink.

Seventy

On the way home we stopped at his house to grab a bite, some of Jane's left-over lasagna. The driveway was unusually dark. We walked the path to the front door of the stately home.

"Looks like nobody's here," observed Buck.

"It does. That's odd. Did your parents go out to dinner?"

"Yeah, but I thought they'd be back by now. Hey, I've got an idea. We can walk around the back and sneak into my room. Pick up where we left off. No one will even know we're there." He started kissing me again. Suddenly, the spotlights were on us.

"Ha!! Psyched you two out!" Greg's laugh filled the air.

"You asshole! You scared the shit out of us!" Buck was half laughing and half shaking as he spoke.

"You should see your faces!" Greg pointed at us.

"Greg! One of these days . . . I swear!"

"Yeah, what?" He grinned at his brother.

"Payback!" Buck ran toward Greg and punched him in the gut. "What are you doing home, big brother? I thought you and Sharon were going to the bar after the pep rally."

"Sharon's mother said she had to make it a short evening because her grandparents were stopping by for an early visit in the morning. Where were you two kids?"

"Out."

"Out where?" No response. "Ooh! Hot and heavy after being away from each other for a few weeks, huh?" He began making smooching noises.

"It's none of your damn business!" Buck threw his arm around my shoulder protectively.

"Yeah, like I can't tell from your faces. Look at Sam's cheeks! They're all chafed."

My embarrassment was minimal because Greg had become my friend. "I keep telling him that he needs to shave."

"We're here to eat lasagna," announced Buck. "Want to hang with us?"

"Why not? Then I can ride you two some more. You're such easy targets."

"Shut up, Greg." More punching.

We entered the spacious kitchen and started pulling food out of the fridge.

"You're going to the game tomorrow to see your man, here, aren't you Sam?"

"Of course. Wouldn't miss it." We sat at the rectangular table in front of the window overlooking the lake. The moonlight created an illusion of glass on the surface of the water.

"Kaplan's having a big party at her place tomorrow night after the game. Everyone's going to be there. You guys are going, right?"

"Right." For me it was an automatic response because all of my friends would be there. It was Homecoming weekend, after all. I glanced at Buck and noticed a distant expression. "We're going, aren't we?"

"If you want." Discomfort traced his face momentarily but then dissolved as Greg pushed a plate of chocolate cake toward him.

"Have some." Greg read people so well and was consistently the one to play peacemaker.

Without warning, Mrs. Kendall waltzed into the kitchen, softly stepping in her fluffy slippers and wrapped in the warmth of her robe. "Hi, kids," her voice oozed like liquid gold, elegant and timeless.

"Hi, Mrs. Kendall," I stood up to give her a hug.

"Sam," she issued my name as if I were a long-lost friend. "How are you? I miss you and your darling smile. How's school going?" Her gaze spread upon me like the Pope's blessing.

"It's good. Demanding, but I really like it there."

"Yes, Buck's been keeping me updated." She leaned her head close to mine. "He's one lonely boy without you."

"Mommm," Buck groaned.

"Well, you are, my son." Then she leaned closer to me and placed her hand on my shoulder. "He just doesn't want you to know how much he misses you. You know how stoic he can be." She smiled affectionately at her son.

"Stoic?" piped Greg, "Don't you mean tormented?"

"That's it, Greg!" Buck launched toward his brother. In seconds they were swinging and scuffling, while Skippy, their Golden Retriever, circled them, barking protectively. The more the dog barked, the more the brothers horsed around.

"Stop it, you two. You'll wake your brother and sister." Her words said one thing, her expression, another.

"Only 'cause you said so, Mom. Otherwise he'd be a dead man!" boasted Buck.

"Right! You and your false bravado." Greg lived to get a rise out of his brother.

Mrs. Kendall shook her head. "I'm going back to bed now. Don't stay up too late, boys. Night, Sam. Good to see you, sweetheart. I expect we'll see you the next time you're in town." I loved Mrs. Kendall. She always said I was the only person who truly understood her son.

The three of us clustered at one end of the table, talking and eating, content to be together. Yes, everything seemed so much the same.

Seventy-one

I never understood much about the rules of football, nor did I care. For me it was all about the ambiance, the people around me, and hanging with my friends in crowded bleachers full of screaming fans. Winning the game was a bonus.

There was a bite to the air, just enough to make us huddle a little tighter. The game was one of those matches that keep you on the edge of your seat. The crowd roared when we advanced and booed when the opposing team made a touchdown. Larry stumbled into the bleachers, stinking of alcohol, and sat in the row behind me. His friends all smelled the same. Pre-parties were everywhere. The whole town celebrated Homecoming.

Buck played exceptionally well that day. When Carlson's victory was apparent, he beamed triumphantly from the field. I figured a major part of his joy was tied to the fact that his brother was watching. Instead of playing together to carry the team to a win, Buck had done it without him. That in itself was a personal victory.

When the final whistle blew, the atmosphere grew chaotic. All around me kids were jumping up and down, hugging, cheering—just like we used to. It made me smile reminiscently. Something felt different, however. How could I be gone such a short time and already experience a noticeable disconnect? I had a foot in both worlds—Buck's and mine. I was discovering that the balance was, indeed, tricky.

Down on the field, Buck swam in victory. Watching him, I felt an awkward detachment. Circled around him were his friends, and although I recognized some of the guys, I didn't know many of them. I headed down the stairs to congratulate him, and he looked up, sensing my presence, and winked at me from amidst the mass of players and cheerleaders. I stopped at the railing above the field.

"Hey, gorgeous, what do you think?" He was a ball of dirt.

"Great game, Buck. You played really well. Better than I've ever seen you play."

"Thanks." He climbed up to my level on the bleachers and gave me a sweaty kiss. I didn't mind at all. His breathing was still erratic from the game.

"So you're heading out now?" He bent down to loosen his cleats.

"Yeah, unless you want me to stick around to drive you home."

"No, I'm good. Greg's still here, and we're going to get something to eat after I shower."

"So I'll see you later at my house?" I questioned.

"Definitely." Another quick, salty kiss. "You smell good, Sam."

"You don't." I pinched my nose in exaggeration.

His eyes crinkled. "Yeah, well, the stink goes with the territory."

"Later then . . ." I waved as I walked toward the parking lot. When I reached my car, I glanced back to catch another glimpse of him in his uniform, all dirty and sexy. That's when I saw Jacquelyn Livingston making a beeline for him. She had waited until she thought I wasn't around. He met her halfway, and they began to talk. I willed myself to look away to prevent this image from haunting me.

He loves you, Sam. He's entitled to talk to other people. "But she's not other people."

The kid in the car next to mine looked around and then regarded me quizzically. Old habits die hard—or maybe they never die. I smiled dismissively.

Buck held his helmet under one arm, and Jacquelyn was in total motion, grinning and swaying as she stole a precious bit of conversation. Their profile, there on the deserted field in front of empty bleachers, resembled a photograph, one that would be shot in black and white. One that tells a story. Only the wrong girl was in the picture.

Finally, he headed toward the locker room while she hung back a moment before walking away. My stomach hurt. I hopped in the car and drove to the restaurant where I was meeting up with some of my sorority sisters. The bubble I'd been in from the previous night burst.

* * *

"You clean up well."

He wore his letter jacket and a pair of jeans. His hair looked darker than usual, the golden threads camouflaged by dampness. Every year he got better looking, the remnants of adolescence fading.

"Ready to go?" His smiled was forced.

"I am." I slipped my arm through his, hoping the touch would soften his mood. Wrong. He barely said a word on the drive to Kaplan's party. The silence was getting to me.

"Are you sure you want to go?"

"No, but you do," he continued to memorize the road.

"I just want to be together," I said.

Nothing.

The lake beckoned me through the passenger window. I stared at the water, shimmery still.

"We don't have to stay long."

"Whatever you want, Sam. You haven't seen your friends in a while."

I nodded, grateful for the compromise, but somehow, the evening was losing its luster.

We parked behind a long line of vehicles on the dirt road. As soon as I opened the car door, I heard noise emanating from the kitchen. Then I saw Annie and ran up to the house.

"Sam!" Annie raced down the porch steps and threw her arms around me.

"Annie!"

"How are you? You look so great! How's NYU?"

"I love it. I miss you, Annie. When are you coming to visit?"

"Maybe toward the end of October. I need to see this city you're so fond of."

"You haven't lived until you've experienced the City."

My former classmates bustled around me. Standing among them made me realize how much I had missed them. I wanted to hear their stories, trade mine. Transitioning from high school to college is huge, and only those who actually experience this passage understand its complexity.

"Sam, I'm going to get a Coke. You want anything?" He was heading away from the college conversations.

"Yeah, I'll have a beer." In my elated state, I didn't consider that my having a beer might bother him. He was still seventeen. Suddenly this, too, added to the growing chasm.

"Have Darlene and Sal been here yet?" I craned my neck to find them, certain they must have already arrived.

"Not yet. Greg said they're with Sal's family for a while. Then they're coming out. And Darlene said they were going to the bar with us later."

"Good! I can't wait to see those crazy kids."

Buck had drifted over to his brother and looked fairly comfortable, so I continued my catch-up conversations. At about 10:30 p.m. Shelly made her entrance with George. So typical. She looked really good in her tight jeans and striped V-neck sweater. Everyone flocked over to her.

"All hail the Queen," said Annie.

"You're bad, Annie." We laughed to ourselves, but apparently not as subtly as we thought, because Shelly stared in our direction. She didn't miss much.

"Hi, Sam. Hi, Annie," she sang out, waving, while she wallowed in the attention of the assembly surrounding her.

"She should be gracing us with her presence any minute now." Annie's tone was icy.

"Annie, don't you like her anymore? What happened?"

"Her attitude bugs the shit out of me. Ever since this summer she's been hard to take." She paused. "Look out. Here she comes."

I turned, and there she was. "So how are you guys doing?" Shelly asked, her head alternating mechanically from Annie to me.

"I'll go first. I'm just wonderful, and how are you?" Annie's mockery hung in the air.

Here we go!

Shelly stiffened. "What's wrong with you? Are you in a bad mood or something?"

"Sorry. Just being a smart ass. You know me."

"How are you, Sam?"

"Good, Shel." I hugged her for good measure. "You look nice."

"Thanks." Her shoulders relaxed slightly. "You too. I like your shirt." Same old, same old.

I spent the majority of the evening on the other side of the room from Buck. He either migrated toward the current seniors at CHS, who were few in attendance, or kept to himself, which somehow irritated me. Why couldn't he branch out? He knew these kids. Why was he so stubborn about mixing with this crowd? He was a football hero today. He should have accepted the pats on the back instead of retreating. When I wasn't checking the status of his social endurance, I totally enjoyed catching up with my former classmates. Unfortunately, that portion of the evening ended abruptly.

"Sam, you ready? I have to get going." Buck had drifted back to my corner of the ring. It was 11 o'clock. The party was in full swing.

"Sure." A compromise was a compromise. Besides, leaving would put me out of some of my misery too. The weight of my concern for his well-being grew heavy.

"Sam, you guys *have to* come with us to the bar," Annie pleaded. "Darlene and Sal are going to be there. Remember?"

I was tempted to try to persuade Buck to go to the bar, but his body held the rigidity of a guest who had walked into the wrong party. "Nah, I'd better get going. I have a bus to catch tomorrow, and I still need to do some laundry," I answered.

Annie saw my turmoil and let me off the hook. "Okay," she resigned. "But pick a date when I can come to visit you. And write me. I'll be there." We hugged.

"Done. See you soon."

As Buck and I drew near the door, Shelly yelled from across the room. "Call me, Sam!" I nodded, more to indicate that I had heard her than to confirm.

On our way out the door, it seemed everyone stopped me to talk. It took us another excruciating twenty minutes to escape. Actually, it was Buck's escape. The delay was fine with me, but I sensed I was going to pay. Sure enough, the ride home felt like a punishment. His petulance settled between us, tension oozing from his body.

"You could have gone to the bar, you know." He spoke to the white line down the center of the road.

"I know. But I'd rather spend time with you." If I was forced to make a choice, he was it.

"Did you have fun?" He released his words as if he only had a few to spare.

"Yeah, it was great seeing everyone. How about you?"

"I don't know as many of those people as you."

"What are you talking about? These are all kids who went to high school with us."

"With *you*. And now they're all in college."

I didn't know what he wanted me to say. It was what it was. The remainder of the drive was a torturous silence. He pulled into my driveway and put the car in park, resting both arms over the wheel. The engine idled ominously. I knew he wasn't getting out of the car.

Damn him!

"You're not coming in?"

My question should have been an accusation. I was leaving in the morning, so why weren't we spending every waking moment together? What had changed since Friday night?

"No. I'm tired from today's game." His tone was brittle.

"Okay." I could see no point in fighting it, so I opened the passenger door.

"Want me to drive you to the bus station tomorrow?" His words were meant to stay my movement.

"Yes, that'd be good." I watched him nod, but he was far away. I waited for him to say something, anything to cut the thickness in the air.

Now's your chance. Be the man.

I don't do well with ill-tempered silences. I had suffered through a bumpy bus ride home from New York City to be with him, and he was behaving as if I had all the time in the world to humor him. I threw one leg out of the car before he grabbed my arm.

"Sam."

"What?" The word accosted him.

"I *do* love you, Samantha," he held me with sad, tender eyes. Tears stung me as I sat, perched on the edge of the seat, trying to figure him out.

"What's wrong, Buck? You've been so distant all night." I implored the truth.

"It's nothing," he released my arm and turned away again. "I'm sorry, Sam. I didn't mean to ruin your night with your friends."

"Is there something you want to talk about?"

He stared straight ahead, his profile unyielding. Silence spoke for him. I gave up and turned away to get out of the car when he clutched the sleeve of my jacket and pulled me to him, crushing me with his mouth.

There was more we should have said, but a dark stubbornness had settled on him. Sometimes the truth is simply too much to face. What a peculiar weekend. I wanted Friday back.

I slumped into my room, crawled under the covers, and cried myself to sleep.

Seventy-two

The guilty one is not he who commits the sin,
but the one who causes the darkness.

—Victor Hugo

The tone of his letters began to change. They became more newsy, less personal. He cataloged the events of his daily life. He reported on fundraisers for the senior class, his grades, and the student council. He reminded me that it was difficult to write about much else because he was a "recluse these days." Distance was a higher hurdle than I'd realized.

I was inundated with papers and French interpretations, and I had limited time to do much else. On top of academic pressures, the girls in my dorm hounded me to join them at Friday night beer parties and mid-week social gatherings. As much as I wanted to partake in all of the fun, I had to be selective with my time. School first, social life second. And then there was sleep, blessed sleep.

Somewhere in the mix of my life, guilt seeped in and ate at me. I revisited what Shelly had said about Buck having his senior year. She kept up the theme whenever we had contact. Maybe she was right. Was I selfish? He said he had become a recluse, and he sounded sad all the time. I didn't want that. It hurt me to think of him that way. But he had made it clear that he was not interested in seeing other people, at least not then. Maybe things had changed.

Should I ask him again? Will he think I don't love him anymore? If we decide to try dating other people, then what? I couldn't stand the idea of his being with someone else.

"Let him have his senior year, Sam."

"But I don't want to."

"You're selfish."

"No, it's not that. It's because I love him. He doesn't want to either."

"If you really love each other, things will work out?"

"How?"

"Let him have his senior year, Sam."

"You're not listening to me!"

"I am. *You* are not listening to *me*."

"Why are you here? To make me miserable again?"

"To tell you how selfish you are."

I lurched up, sweat running between my breasts.

I looked at the clock. Two a.m.

Dear Sam,

How are you? Sounds like your classes are keeping you busy. Things have been hectic around here too; it's getting me down. I probably won't have much time for this letter either. Sorry.

In your letter you sounded pretty determined that I should go out and enjoy my senior year. Well, don't worry about me, Sam. I'm fine. It sounds to me like you're not getting out as much as you should either. Where's that social girl I know? Listen, Sam, here's some advice: don't go through college without having fun and meeting new people.

I went to the counselor's office to find my rank in class yesterday. As of now, there are 225 seniors, and I stand second from the top. Report cards come out this Friday, and I don't think I'll make high honor this time. I might get an 88 in Chemistry. I think my average in math is 100, 98 in French, 95 in English, and 95 in government.

Well, I told you I wouldn't have much time. I have to leave for a Chamber meeting now. See you soon.

Love always,
Buck

P.S. I miss kissing you.

Seventy-three

My family celebrated Thanksgiving in a big way. Mom laid out the good china and crystal. She roasted a huge turkey stuffed with Nana's dressing. We had every kind of accompaniment imaginable: mashed potatoes, the world's best gravy, peas and carrots . . . and the pies! Pumpkin, apple, and chocolate cream. Nana made her traditional Gentlemen salad, with green Jell-O, cottage cheese, and maraschino cherries; everyone looked forward to Nana's green Thanksgiving tradition. But the best part was having the family together.

After grace, we'd toast with our tiny glasses of tomato juice, "Alla famiglia!" Then the feast—amidst boisterous conversation and beautiful confusion.

Mom was serving dessert when the doorbell rang. Lucy ran to the door.

"Hi, Buck. Happy Thanksgiving."

"Same to you, Luce."

"Good timing. Mommy's just getting dessert out. Apple pie, your favorite. Sammy! Buck's here again!"

"Apple pie? You wouldn't be toying with me now, would you?"

"No. Mom likes to make your favorites, Buck, but don't tell her I told you."

"I'll keep it under my hat."

His laugh sang through the room, revealing that everything was all right in his world. He seemed himself again. Thank God. His last couple of letters had worried me.

* * *

The previous night when I stepped off the bus, I scanned the terminal in search of my dad. When I didn't see him, I started to worry. Dad was always on time. I dropped my suitcase and just stood there, waiting. Time was a lengthy penance. During the long bus ride from New York, I had plenty of time to think about how Buck might behave when I saw him. My stress level accelerated.

Where's Dad?

I was just about to hunt down a pay phone when I spotted Buck. He stood across the way from the bus, one hand tucked behind his back. He broke into a wide grin when he saw me.

"Get over here."

The seduction in his voice swallowed me. Suddenly, it was the summer of '66 again, and he was riding toward me on his bike. The same helplessness washed over me. As I drew closer, he pulled his hand from behind his back to reveal a bunch of flowers. I stood in front of him, immobile. He pulled me to him, and I was sixteen again. *We were on Shelly's couch, and my heart was pounding. Without warning, he kissed me. Time and space slipped away. Sounds dissolved into a dull echo. Intermittent chatter and laughter drifted through in waves until a veil of peace enveloped me.* No one else was in the depot. The smell of warm Jade East surrounded me

* * *

Now, in my living room, he was once again presenting his charming side, the side everyone loved.

"Hey, Sam. You look good, babe. Nice sweater. New?"

"Yep."

"Did Peg spring, or did you buy it in the Big City?" He knew my mother's habits.

"It's from Mom. A Thanksgiving gift."

"I wasn't aware there was such a thing."

"You know my mom."

"Indeed. So, are you ready to go?" His face, light and happy, held a secret.

"Well, first I have to help with the dishes. Why?" I regarded him quizzically.

"No, honey," came the voice from the kitchen. "You aren't home for that long. You two go and have fun."

"Are you sure, Mom? There are a lot of dirty pots and pans out there."

"I can help, Mrs. D," he crooned, fawning deliberately.

"Oh, Buckley, that's sweet, but I can handle it. Thank you." Even Mom's words smiled.

I shook my head in mock reproach. "I swear, you're such a brown nose, Kendall."

"What?" he pled.

"Listen to you. You know what. Let's go." I grabbed my peacoat from the chair.

"Where's your other jacket?"

"I'm wearing this one."

"I think you should wear something warmer. It's cold. And bring your scarf and mittens."

"Why? I thought we were just going to your house to visit your family."

"Later."

"Where are we going now?"

"You'll see. Grab your other jacket."

I could tell he was up to something. "It's too cold for the lake!"

"We're not going to the lake."

"Where then? Tell me."

"Just wait," He smirked.

His renewed attitude was almost as good as finding a lost piece of chocolate buried in Easter grass. As we drew near our destination, I figured out his plan. "We're going to freeze here! It's November!"

"Have you forgotten about the trusty army blanket so soon? I'm disappointed in you, Sam."

"We're still gonna freeze."

He parked the car, opened the trunk, and held up the blanket. "Where's your sense of adventure?"

"In a warmer place."

"Ah, come on. I'll keep you warm." He threw his arm around my shoulder, and we climbed the familiar steps on the side of the school.

"So you remember this place, huh, big college girl?"

"Of course I do. It's in the vault."

He smiled, grateful for the shared memory, and then spread the blanket on the floor of the balcony. I nestled in front of him, between his legs. He wrapped his arms around me, tucking me into him. Gloved hands covered mittened hands, and we sat quietly for a time. The cold felt good on my face. Each time I exhaled, my breath swirled upward and then dissipated. As I leaned against him, I thought about the times we had retreated to this place. The first time was right before our one-year anniversary.

He broke my reverie. "When will you be home for Christmas?"

"My last class is on December 13 in the afternoon. So I'll catch the bus on Saturday morning."

"I see." I heard disappointment.

"What?"

"The Christmas formal is that night. I thought maybe you'd be home in time to go."

"I'd love to if I were able to be home."

"Why can't you be? It's just one day early. Couldn't you skip that day?"

"I can't. Final exam day."

"Couldn't you ask your teacher to take it early?"

"No. I can't do that."

"Why?" he pressed.

"Because. I don't even know the professor that well. It's not like high school where . . ." As soon as the words were out of my mouth, I knew I was in trouble.

"Where what?" He tensed.

"Where you get to know your teachers better."

"Than your *professors?*" he emphasized.

"You know what I meant." Now I was the one tensing.

"Yeah." He lowered his head. "College and high school are a lot different, aren't they?"

"Not that different."

"Forget it. I just won't go this year."

"Are you even supposed to be there? Is this a big deal?"

"Senior class president. Kind of expected." His tone held an edge.

"But it's a sorority-sponsored dance—not a school dance."

"Everyone from CHS goes, so I should be there. You know that, Sam." I didn't know what to say. "And maybe I want to go." His words sliced the air.

"I see." But I didn't. And I didn't like any of it—his mood, his attitude. "Fair enough. Is there someone you could go with?" I hated saying those words.

"What do you mean? I don't want to go with anyone else."

"Then what do want me to do?"

The enormity of our situation seized me. It wasn't just this dance. There would be another event and another and another. He wasn't good with these things, and I could feel his angst permeating my own body.

"I didn't think it was going to be this hard, Sam."

"It doesn't have to be." As I heard myself speak, I recognized that it wasn't as hard for me. The real problem was *his* unhappiness. I was content to study at school and be with him whenever I went home. It was only one year. "Next year you'll be away at college, too, and it won't feel as weird."

"Why? We'll still be apart," he added unflinchingly.

"I know, but there's something different about . . ."

His head sprang up, and he cut me off. "What? Not being left behind? In a world where we existed as a couple, but we no longer do?"

"Is that really how you feel?"

"Yes, it's really how I feel, and I hate it! You don't know what it's like, Sam. You're off doing your thing. I'm still here."

"Doing my thing? I go to school. I study all the damn time. What can I do about it?"

"Nothing. This! We do this. We spend time together when you're home. It's the in-between shit that kills me and makes me feel left out. I'm in this vacuum, Sam. I feel like I don't belong anywhere, and it's wearing me down." Raw candor stabbed me in the gut. *Am I so ensconced in New York that I've lost my perspective? My ability to judge his pain?*

"What do you want to do then?" I could feel the direction in which we were headed, and the old fear arose inside me.

"I don't have an answer," he exhaled audibly, as if he'd been holding all of this inside for too long.

I braved it. "Do you want to start seeing other kids so you don't feel left out?" The words hung in the air before I could swallow them. He clenched. When he didn't respond, my concern escalated. "Is there someone you want to ask out?" My gut knotted tighter.

"No!" The word snapped into the air. He sounded pissed.

"Would you tell me if there were?" I pressed on, despite the prevailing uneasiness.

"Yes." Suddenly, his voice became flat. "Would *you* tell *me* if you wanted to go out with someone?"

"Yes, of course." I paused, waiting for the right moment to crack through the spiraling intensity. "As long as you didn't flip out on me." A hint of a smile flickered on his face. "But for me it would just be a casual thing. I'm not looking for anything else."

"Me either." His shoulders relented in relief or defeat, I couldn't tell which.

"Hey," I nudged him, and it seemed to shake loose everything inside of him. He leaned forward, pressing his forehead onto mine.

"I miss you."

"I miss you too. But look—it's already November. The year will go by faster than you think."

He laughed. "You're such a Pollyanna. You'll never change."

"Probably not."

"I don't mean to be a downer. I just feel like I have lost who I once was. I don't know where I belong. My mother was right—I'm lost without you, Sam. I love you, but I'm lost." A cold wind blew, and I pulled closer. "What are we going to do?"

* * *

What are we going to do?

For me, it was simple. We were going forward. But for him . . . I tried to focus on my book, but the movement of the bus and the words in my head sabotaged concentration. I reread the words for the third time.

"**A** SATURDAY afternoon in November was approaching the time of twilight, and the vast tract of unenclosed wild known as Egdon Heath embrowned itself moment by moment. Overhead the hollow stretch of whitish cloud shutting out the sky was as a tent which had the whole heath for its floor."

Beautiful words. I love Thomas Hardy. But what was I thinking, starting this book now?

" . . . darkness had to a great extent arrived hereon, while day stood distinct in the sky."

I have lost who I once was. The muscles in my stomach squeezed tighter. How did this happen? How did we get to this place? I closed the book and tore a sheet of paper from my notebook.

Dear Buck,

I keep trying to read The Return of the Native, but I can't concentrate. I know. I love Hardy. But instead of his words, I hear yours in my head and . . .

I reread my letter. Then I read it again.

Am I doing the right thing?

The next day, on the way to psych class, I mailed it.

Seventy-four

It took me by surprise I must say,
When I found out yesterday . . .
I heard it though the grapevine

—Marvin Gaye

New York may be the most beautiful city in the world at Christmastime. I have visited a lot of amazing places, but there's nothing like the feel of New York in December. Walk down Fifth Avenue and witness the holiday splendor in every shop window, one more elaborate than the next. Stroll around Times Square and blend in with the throngs of people, bustling in and out of theaters and restaurants at the crossroads of the world. Linger a moment in Rockefeller Center and take in the majesty of the giant tree as it watches over skaters and tourists. There's nothing like New York at this time of year.

On the day before my departure for Christmas break, I received a long-distance call from Shelly. Our friendship had taken a nose dive since our senior year, particularly after she informed me that I was selfish if I didn't break up with Buck. Now she was calling me out of the blue.

"Hi, Sam. How are you?"

"Shelly?" I was taken aback. "I'm good. I can't believe you're calling me."

Awkwardness hung on the line.

"Yeah, I was wondering how you're doing in the *Big City*." She said the words as if I'd received a coveted invitation to a gala from which she had been excluded. She was probably perturbed that I hadn't extended a personal invitation for her to visit.

"Relieved. I just finished finals today. You?"

"Done. I've been home for a week."

"You're home already? Lucky you."

"So I was wondering. When are you coming home?" Her voice was up to something.

"Tomorrow. Why?"

"Oh, just wondering."

Odd.

"How's Buck? Do you still talk to him much?" she asked.

Is she living in a cave?

"Yes, of course I do. We're together all the time when I go home. Don't you remember seeing us over Thanksgiving break at Beekers?"

"That's right." She laughed at herself. "I was plastered that night. I forgot a lot of stuff."

"Yeah, you were pretty lit."

"So did you ever talk to him about going out with other kids?"

"Yes . . . we talked."

Is she going to push this shit again? The girl has a one-track mind.

"Oh, good! I just wanted to be sure 'cause you said you weren't going to before. But I figured you must have changed your mind after you talked to me because he went on a date with Jacquelyn Livingston. But you probably know that already."

Jacquelyn Livingston. Her name strangled me.

"My cousin told me. He said he saw them walking to the movies the other night."

Tighter . . .

"He said they were holding hands and laughing."

He held her hand . . .

"I guess they've been out a couple of times now. But you probably know that too if you guys talked about dating other people."

I'm lost without you, Sam.

"But here's the part you need to know, Sam. My cousin said they act like they really like each other, and that people are starting to talk about them like they're already a couple. It's probably just *her*. You know how *she* is. Remember the way she was always looking at him and talking to him? I'll bet . . ."

Her voice faded.

I love you, Sam. I'm lost . . .

Louisa Verdile, my roommate, walked by in the direction of the snack machines. She smiled but gave me privacy, unlike some girls who hung around the phone, waiting for their turn. Louisa came from upstate New York not knowing anyone at NYU, so we both went into the dorms blind. Thankfully, we hit it off immediately, and our friendship blossomed without intention. She was unusually considerate, and I loved spending time with her. I knew, without question, we would be life-long friends.

" . . . such a man-eater. That's what everybody always said about her, and now I can see what they're talking about. Sam? Did you hear me?"

I'm lost.

"Sam, want me to get some peanut butter crackers for us? There's cold milk in the fridge, too." Louisa's smile dissolved. "Oh, my God, what's wrong?" I'll never forget her expression.

"Sam? Are you still on the phone? I can hear people in the background. Say something. Sam!" Shelly's impatience spilled through the line.

Louisa's hand touched my shoulder. "You look awful. Did you get bad news?"

"Sam!" Shelly yelled into the phone. I summoned up my voice.

"Yeah, I'm here." At least my body was.

"Jeez! I thought you hung up or something. Anyway, I just thought you'd want to know before you come home."

"Yeah . . ."

"I'd want to know if it was me. You know I'm not trying to hurt your feelings, right? I would never do that."

Right.

"But it's best to deal with the truth. That's what you've always told me. I guess you just didn't expect him to like somebody so soon, though, huh?"

A jagged knife tore my gut.

"Especially not Jacquelyn Livingston," she continued.

It ripped upward, threatening to tear into my heart.

"Sam, did you hear me?"

"Yes. I . . . no . . . I didn't expect that."

The razor-sharp tip caught the edge . . . I started to bleed out.

"Sam, when you come home, you should show him that it doesn't bother you."

The loss of blood made me weak.

"You're with college guys now. That'll make him jealous." Her voice streamed through a tunnel, bellowing and receding. "And it's normal for all of this stuff to happen, you know. Especially because you're older than him and he's still home and in high school. I know things have gotten strained between us. But I didn't want you to go home and have everyone know except you. That's the worst! So I called you so you'd be prepared. You understand that, right?"

Right.

"By the way, are you dating anyone yet? You should, you know. I bet there are a lot of cute guys in New York."

"I have to go." Sandpaper lined my mouth.

"Already? You're not mad are you? You guys will get back together someday. You're meant to be together. Everybody knows that. This is just probably a little break. Wait till he goes to college too."

"I have to go," I repeated.

"Well, call me when you get home, okay? And don't be mad. I'm just the messenger. We can plan things, and I can help you make him jealous. Just like in the old days."

The phone slid out of my hand and swung from the wall. Back and forth, back and forth, like a toy that had been wound too tightly and finally lost its momentum.

"I've got it, Sam." Louisa replaced the phone on the cradle.

This is just a dream. I'll wake up soon. Like I always do.

"What happened?" Her arm was around my shoulder, supporting me. "Is it your parents?"

I shook my head. "I think I'm going to be sick."

My mind raced.

What have I done?

A thousand thoughts pummeled my head.

What should I do?

My chest was caving. I couldn't get air.

"Sam? Sam, answer me," Louisa continued.

Did I sabotage myself? I didn't mean it!

"I was so brave behind that cursed pen," I blurted.

"What?"

"I let him think I was okay with the idea of seeing other people. But I wasn't!"

"Sam, sit down. Let me get you a glass of water."

"He probably thinks I'm having a grand old time in New York." I put my head between my legs. Louisa rubbed my back.

"You'll straighten it out when you go home tomorrow. It's easy to imagine all sorts of things when you're not there."

"He's walking around Carlson holding hands with Jacquelyn Livingston. You don't hold hands with someone unless there's some emotion between you. Have you ever had a boy try to hold your hand when you don't like him? It feels awful."

"You don't know exactly what happened, Sam. And from what you've told me about Shelly, she probably exaggerated to make herself feel better. You never hear from her, and suddenly she's your friend again. Wait till you get home and let him explain. It was probably nothing."

"No! No! You don't understand, Louisa. He wouldn't bother with triflings. It's not his style. He must like her." The realization caught in my throat.

"You don't know that. Maybe he was just flattered by the attention. You know how guys are. But she can't replace what he has with you. He said he was lost without you, remember?"

"Maybe her attention did make him feel good. Made him feel like he belonged. She has flirted with him since forever. He must know she likes him. Everybody else does."

"That's not the way I meant it. I meant his ego."

The room swam, and a swell of vomit rose in my throat. I ran into the bathroom. I stood over the toilet, retching, holding back my hair with one hand. Everything whirled sideways. I returned to the day when I had asked Buck if he wanted to see other people and replayed the conversation. His eyes were vacant when he looked back at me. I misread him, thought he didn't care, and thought maybe he was okay with dating other people.

No, you don't understand, Sam. I don't want to break up at all. I just want you.

Swishing water in my mouth, I lifted my head over the sink and gazed at my hollow reflection. Voices inhabited my head.

This is harder than I thought it would be.
They were holding hands and laughing . . .
Couldn't you skip that day?
They act like they really like each other . . .

"Sam, how can I help?" Louisa's voice held restrained panic.

"I have to fix this, Louisa. I have to fix this. I have to fix this." I brushed by her and pulled my suitcase from under the bed. I began throwing things in randomly. She looked bewildered.

"What are you doing? You're not going home today? You're too upset. Sam, let me help."

"You can't help. I have to do this."

"But you're in no shape. You're scaring me."

"I'm fine." I wasn't. I just propelled myself forward because I didn't know what else to do. I thought if I kept moving, kept going, I would be all right.

"No you're not. Sam, I know you don't want to hear this, but you gave him permission to go out with someone in that letter."

The sweater in my hand slid to the floor. I turned back to Louisa. "To go out if he needed a partner! Not to date! Why did I send that goddamn letter? He said he only wanted *me*."

"You sent it because you were trying to do the right thing. You were trying to be fair to him. And, Sam, just because he went out with someone doesn't mean he stopped caring about you. It was just a date."

"But they were holding hands! I went to a movie with a guy in my class, and we didn't hold hands. We watched the stupid movie! And we discussed it afterward. And we drank coffee and went home. It wasn't a *date*!"

"Sam, you need to calm down and think rationally. You can't go home."

"I have to. I know you don't understand, Louisa, but I have to fix this before it goes any further."

The last thing I remember before boarding the bus was dissolving into a heap of tears in Louisa's arms. Everything after that became robotic.

* * *

The rhythm of the bus betrayed me. I tried to sleep, but every time I closed my eyes I saw him, touching her, holding her hand, and my eyes would fly open to escape the painful imagery. The bus rolled on and on, and intermittently, exhaustion would pull me under. But the moments of repose were few. Haunting images assaulted me again and again, and I'd awaken to a pain I'd never experienced. I couldn't stop crying; it sucked my energy.

The woman across the aisle watched me, concern narrowing her eyes. She looked like such a nice lady. Normally, I would have talked to her and enjoyed myself. Instead, I turned my back and balled up against the window. When I closed my eyes, I saw us the last time we were together.

How could he say all of those things to me and then do this?
He made a mistake—that's all.
Everyone makes mistakes.
When he sees me, he'll change his mind.
But he held her hand.
I don't think I can do this again.

Halfway home the sky darkened, and it started to pour.

Rain in December?

It rained with such a force that I could barely see out the window.

* * *

Home. Solace. *Let me crawl inside this womb and find myself again. Lift this burden from my chest.*

I walked into the kitchen. "Sam! Dear God! You scared me. You didn't tell me you were coming today." Seeing my mother put me over the edge, and I broke open again.

"What's wrong? Are you sick?" She approached me with alarm. I shook my head. "Then what? Is it Buck?" I pressed my face into her shoulder and let her arms surround me. "Did you have a fight?"

"He's going out with Jacquelyn Livingston, Mom," I blurted.

She relaxed momentarily, relieved that I wasn't returning home with some dreaded disease. But mine was a deeper malady for which there was no medicine.

"How do you know he's going out with her?"

"Shelly called and told me."

"Of course she did." As I said, never a fan.

"Did you and Buck ever talk about going out with other people before you went away to school?"

"Yes."

Her eyes widened. "Who initiated the conversation?"

"Me."

"Why?"

"Shelly said I was being selfish if I didn't give him some freedom his senior year. So I talked to him about it, even though it wasn't what I wanted."

"And you listened to her? Sam, you should know better." I had no response. "What did you say to him?"

"I asked if he wanted to date other people. He said no and that he didn't want to break up at all."

"And that's how you left it?" I could see her trying to figure it out.

"Pretty much."

"And since then?"

"Since then everything's been fine. Well, mostly. I mean it's a little strained because we're away from each other. But he asked me to go to the Christmas formal when I was home for Thanksgiving."

"Well, that's a good sign."

"But I told him I couldn't go because of exams."

"What did he say?"

"He wasn't happy. So I asked him if there was someone else he could go with."

"You did?" She added another piece to the puzzle.

"Only because he said he should be going because he's president."

"Have you dated other boys at school?"

"Not dated. Just went to a movie at the Rathskeller once. It was nothing."

"Did you tell Buck?" she asked.

"Yes. I tell him everything."

"I see." Her pause was contemplative. "Well, it must be hard on Buck that you went away to college and he's left behind. I always had a feeling that was going to bother him. He doesn't deal well with separation, does he?" She didn't wait for an answer. "He's very attached to you, Sam."

And I'm attached to him, I thought.

"I have to go to his house and talk to him."

"Now?" Her face contorted. "I don't think that's a good idea. You're too upset. Wait till the morning."

"I can't wait till the morning. I have to talk to him now." I walked over to the wicker basket that held all the keys. "Is it all right if I take your car, Mom?"

"Honey, it would be smarter to wait and think about this before you say something you might regret. Besides, it's late," she urged.

"Mom, I can't wait." And that time she got it.

"Be careful, Sam."

Fueled with a pernicious combination of anger and pain, I drove faster than I should have. When I pulled into his driveway, I saw a light in the living room. *He's probably still up*. I ran up the steps and knocked on the front door, my heart pounding wildly. When the door swung open, I hoped to see his face. Instead, I saw Mrs. Kendall.

"Well, hello, Sam! Come in. What a nice surprise!" She hugged me immediately. When she pulled back and saw my face, her expression changed. "Is everything all right, Sam? You look upset."

"I'm fine," I lied.

"What brings you here? Buck will be so happy to see you." She leaned in as if she were telling me a secret. "He really misses you. I don't think he's quite the same without you." She chuckled. Her words told me that she was in the dark about the Jacquelyn thing.

"I'm sorry it's so late, Mrs. Kendall. I just really need to talk to Buck for a minute."

The words were barely out of my mouth when he walked around the corner, entering the foyer like a timid child. The sight of him jolted me. God he was beautiful!

"Look who's here, Buckley. Your favorite college student. Do you kids want a snack?"

"No thank you, Mrs. Kendall. I'm fine." *Right.*

"Okay, I'll leave you two alone. Good to see you, Sam. It must be glorious in New York this time of year."

"Yes, it is."

"Well, I'm sure I'll see you again soon." She winked and walked away.

We stood like statues in the foyer. I wanted to run to him so badly, throw my arms around his neck and bury myself in him. Restraining myself at that moment was one of the hardest things I have ever had to do. I sensed that he felt the same but was following my lead. Pride can be a foolish thing.

I stared at the boy I loved with my heart and soul and knew, inexorably, something had changed between us. I wanted to tell him how all of this nonsense about seeing other people had been a mistake. How the conversations had escalated into something I didn't intend. How the dominoes had just fallen, one against the other, toppling so fast I couldn't reverse what I had begun with one simple touch. But I was so hurt. I kept picturing him walking around our town, holding her hand, touching her. I simply could not get past it.

"Hi, Sam. I thought you weren't coming home until tomorrow." He leaned against the wall, hands buried deep in his pockets as if to protect himself. His voice sounded vulnerable, broken.

Instead of throwing my arms around him as I wanted to, I went for total confrontation.

"How's Jacquelyn?"

And there it was—the words just bursting forth like hot lava. Shock crossed his face. He barely regained his composure before responding, his expression continuing to contort. I thought I saw pain flicker in his eyes.

"She's good."

In a million years, I could not have anticipated that response. I tried to mask the shock my system withstood as he spit acid into my face, my eyes, my soul. I began to shake inside but willed my voice not to give me away. "Well, that's just fine. When were you planning on telling me?"

"Sam, you didn't give me a chance."

"There's always a chance to tell the truth." My eyes bore through him. "And by the way, what about all that stuff you said to me the last time we were together? Was that all just a crock?" I could feel myself losing it again, but I held tight to control.

"No, I . . ."

"You know what?" I held up the palm of my hand. I couldn't handle anymore. "I don't care. You can have her. I hope you're happy." His eyes widened at the calm in my voice.

Where did that come from? I wondered. I didn't mean it—but I had to say it. I spun on my heels and headed for the car, reeling.

"Samantha, wait!" He followed me out the door.

I swung around, ripped the chain from my neck, and threw it at him. "Too bad the initials don't match. You could reuse it. Like your hands and your mouth and your heart!" I couldn't stop myself. It felt good to hurt him.

She's good.

I lost all focus.

She's good. She's good. Like a broken record in my head.

My hands shook uncontrollably, but I managed to shove the key into the ignition and peel out of the driveway. I didn't want him to see me cry. My heart was breaking.

I expected him to call that night.

He didn't.

My world was collapsing around me. I wept, silent sobs controlling my body. My mother walked into my room and sat on the side of my bed. "Sam?"

"I don't think I can live without him, Mom." I felt as if someone had died.

Seventy-five

January 1969

Objects move past me.
I stand still.

Professor Rickman speaks.
He is brilliant.
I love American literature.
I take copious notes.
I keep writing, recording his brilliant words for fear of missing even one.
I listen intently as he speaks, breathing in every word.
I write.
He fills my lungs with his words.
I keep writing.

"Jay Gatsby," he says.

His name strikes a familiar chord in me.
I know Jay Gatsby.
His heart was broken.
He tried desperately to fix it.

Daisy didn't deserve him.
He deluded himself that he could fix it.
Daisy didn't deserve him.
There's no going back.

"Not just a love story," says Professor Rickman.
"Much more."

Much more . . .

I returned to my notes.
Someone had scribbled in the margins.

The Great Gatsby
Notes

Narrated by Nick Carroway. West Egg, East Egg. Jay Gatsby lives in a mansion. He threw parties hoping to see Daisy. Her voice was like money.

Buck *The decline of the American Dream. Tom treated her badly . . . treated her badly . . . treated her badly.*

& *He was selfish and careless.*

Sam *Not just a love story. Much more. The 1920s. Nick and Gatsby fought in WWI.*

I *Social climbers. Old money, new money. Her voice was like money.*

LOVE *Gatsby's dream of loving Daisy. His old love. They should have been together.*

YOU *They loved each other once. Gatsby's dream is ruined. Tell him you never loved him, Daisy.*

So

what! *Daisy. Old aristocracy. Southern belle. Strong need to be loved.*

I

love *Tom Buchanan cheats with Myrtle. Her husband idolizes her.*

Buck *Tom has been unfaithful before. Cheater, cheater, cheater! Myrtle's breast, ripped open by Daisy's selfishness.*

Jordan is dishonest, cheats and lies. Romantic connection between her and Nick.

Buck *I don't like her. Phony!*

Kendall *Gatz. Changes his name. Changes himself for Daisy. Part of his greatness?*

Buckley *What's so great about that? He shouldn't change himself for her. She's not worth it. He* just thinks she is. He loves what he remembers. He loves an old version of Daisy. Can never go back. It just doesn't work.

Take that!

We're going to be writing a paper. A paper. Let me write what I want. I know it's about more than the love story, but I like the love story. Let me write what I want. Please!

Why?

Why? Tragic ending. Very tragic ending. Was she worth it? She walked away. No remorse.

Nevermore

Tom broke Myrtle's nose. Break his nose. Don't take it!

NOT AGAIN

so, so Old sport, odd expression. Myrtle's death was awful. Her breasts ripped open.

so, so Keep reading. I am, professor. This is not my first time. I've met Jay Gatsby before.

SO When is the paper due? One week. Good. One week.

THERE

love = Careless people . . . such careless people.

pain DON'T YOU SEE!

January 30, 1969

Dear Sam,

I have been meaning to say some things for a long time, and I'm really sorry I haven't. I don't know where to begin explaining, but I will try.

I think things started this summer when we talked about going out with other kids when you went away to school. Hearing you say that really bothered me and made me wonder about our future and what you wanted. Then you went away to college and seemed to be doing just fine. Things became strained between us, even though it felt like "us" again whenever you came home. But then you'd return to your world, and I was home without you.

When you came back for Homecoming, and we went to the party at Greta's, it all went really wrong. For the first time in the two years we have been together, I felt so out of place. Everyone was home from school and talking about all the fun they were having at college. I felt like a sixth grader that night. And when your friends wanted to go to the bar, I know you said you wanted to be with me, but I felt as though I was keeping you away from where you belonged. This is when I realized what a difference one year in our ages could make. I suddenly saw all the things I kept <u>you</u> from doing. Sure, you said it didn't matter as long as we were together, but it really does matter.

Recently you mentioned dating other kids again—asking me if I was still okay with the way things were. I wondered where that was coming from. I thought maybe you wanted more freedom, but I didn't think it was what I really wanted. Then I thought maybe Shelly had been talking to you again. When you came home for Thanksgiving, I was sure you'd be excited about the Christmas dance. That's why I took you to the balcony. Instead you said you couldn't come home and we got into that whole conversation. It bothered me because I thought you knew me and how I felt. Then your letter came. The one you wrote on the bus. I don't know, maybe you were feeling guilty, but I didn't know what to think. So I got a date. This resulted in your coming home, driving to my house late at night, and greeting me with, "How's Jacquelyn?" And when you threw your necklace at me, it was as if I didn't know who you were. That was when I knew that things had really changed.

I hope you can understand how I feel. It just seems to me that we're living in two different worlds right now. Sure, you can come home some weekends for two days, but there are five days in between. In your letter you said that you didn't want to "tie me down" my senior year. This made me think how much I was tying you down, not only your senior year, but your freshman year in college.

I'm sorry if I've hurt you or if this letter is painful for you to read, but I had to explain why I acted the way I did and why I haven't been in touch with you lately. I only hope that you can understand and that all I have said was not in vain. You know how I feel about you, Sam. That will never change.

Take care of yourself, and let me know how things are going at school. Write whenever you're ready.

Love always,
Buck

Seventy-six

Time heals all wounds. Bullshit. We just learn to deal with it, work around it. And when the hole in your heart finally closes enough to stop oozing, fresh blood begins to pump again.

"Are you going to write back to him?" Louisa asked.

She walked over to my side of the room and sat next to me on my bed, wrapping an afghan around her. I set down my book and stared out the window. The sounds of the city, dependably deafening, became the white noise that drowned out the repetitive thoughts drumming inside my head. Thankfully, Louisa didn't mind leaving the window cracked open, despite the frosty air. Losing myself in the metropolitan symphony was a welcomed anesthesia.

"I don't know." My voice felt flat—like my emotions. I still didn't feel like me.

"Maybe at some point you'll be ready."

"I saw him with her on Christmas Eve."

"You didn't tell me that!" She sat upright.

"At my church. Midnight mass. He was with her family."

Louisa inched closer to me and brushed my arm. She sat silently, allowing me to spill the painful details, the poison that coursed through me every time I pictured them together. Every time I saw his face. Every time I closed my eyes.

"I always go to midnight mass with my family. Mom likes to sit in the front, so we get there early. It's really beautiful with all of the trees they bring in to place around the altar. Bare trees, smelling of pine. The wise men have reached Mary and Joseph and baby Jesus with their gifts. The choir sings from up in the balcony. We have an amazing choir. My dad is one of the members. During one song he had a solo. His voice is something. They were singing *Ave Maria*, and I started to cry. I turned around to look up at him."

I could feel my stomach clench. Louisa touched my arm again.

"That's when I saw them. Her whole family. And Buck. They had just arrived and were sitting down in a pew in the back. Jacquelyn was flitting around like the belle of the ball. She knew I'd be there. So did he. And it's not even his church. Throughout the mass, all I could think about was them, together in my church. My mother knew. She put her hand on my shoulder and brushed it softly. I couldn't look at her. It was hard to hold back the tears, but I'd be damned if I would give in to them. The worst part was Communion, when they walked past me to receive. I could feel them. For a moment I couldn't tell if I was still breathing. I stared at the floor so I wouldn't have to see them when they walked back to their seats. But I still felt them. I knew the exact moment he passed by."

"Oh, Sam."

"After church I ran into Shelly. She said she was sitting in the back, behind Jacquelyn's family. 'They looked pretty cozy,' she said. 'Buck said hi to me. He was holding her hand. Oh, I'm sorry, Sam. But you'll get over him. You'll probably meet some dreamy boy in New York.'"

"I remember thinking *shut up, you stupid, stupid bitch!* She wasn't sorry. I wanted to slap her face and hurt her the way she hurt me. But then I realized that she doesn't know any better. She can't help herself. 'By the way,' she added, 'My brother said they started seeing each other in November, before Thanksgiving. I just thought you should know that.'"

Louisa's eyes bulged. "Do you believe her?"

"I don't know what to believe. He's the one I should have slapped. For leading me to believe he only wanted me. For waiting so long to explain how he really felt."

"My God, Sam. What are you going to do?"

I remember thinking there was nothing left in me to *do* anything. I was going to breathe and study and work on erasing the images from my mind. When I didn't respond, she tried another tactic. "Hey, let's go to Harry's and have a beer. Hell, let's get drunk!"

"No thanks. Beer hasn't been tasting very good to me lately."

Her shoulders drooped. "But you love Harry's! And getting out will be good for you."

Harry's. With its colored lights draping the booths and its wide, pockmarked mahogany bar. I loved running into the Wednesday regulars who sat in the same spots, eating chicken wings and drinking draft beer at ten cents a mug. Harry's smelled happy. I even loved Harry, the proprietor who took pride in serving his customers himself. Walking into Harry's was like going home. But not that night.

"What are you thinking about?"

I turned to my friend. "How do I fill this hole in my heart?"

"I don't know, Sam. But I know you'll be okay."

"You sound so sure. What if I never get over him?" I stared into her eyes, imploring her to lift the suffocating burden from my chest.

"You will, Sam. You just have to give yourself time. You were in love with him, and it was real. That doesn't go away quickly."

"It's never going away. This wasn't supposed to happen to us. He told me if we ever broke up, it wouldn't be him because he loved me too much."

"You really should talk with him again. Get the whole truth. Besides, you don't know if it's over for good. Maybe now is just not the right time. People break up and get back together all the time."

"You didn't see the way he looked at me that night, Louisa. I kept expecting him to walk over to me, tell me it was nothing. But he didn't. He let me go. He's never treated me like that before."

"Sometimes guys are so stupid. They don't know what's good for them when it's staring them in the face."

I turned toward the window. Cold air seeped through the crack. "You know, every time I close my eyes, I can see him touching her."

"Oh, Sam."

"It's always about some other girl, isn't it? Some new conquest. Another pair of breasts to unwrap. I never thought he would be a cliché. I thought he was better than that."

Louisa looked as if she were trying to absorb my pain. "Hey, I have chocolate—want some?" She jumped up and ran to her desk.

"Maybe one piece."

"Come on, let's go sit in the stairwell and look outside. We can count yellow cabs."

She handed me the box. "Godiva! Are you kidding me? Where did you get these?"

"Macy's." She looked pleased. "I figured if anything could wrestle a smile out of you, it was Godiva chocolate."

"But they're so expensive."

"You're worth it, roomie."

"You are so sweet."

We sat in the stairwell, looking out the long rectangular window. The city twinkled; cabs raced by the dorms like ants toward a sugar lump. We savored the chocolate. Louisa rarely ate candy, but tonight she indulged, even though she was trying to lose five more pounds. The mantra of the young woman—just five more.

Like the first suture in a gaping cut, that moment on the stairs somehow made me start to heal. At least I could breathe and swallow.

"Sam, you're eating. That's so good!"

"It's Godiva . . . what did you expect?" I smirked.

She moved closer and nudged me with her shoulder on which I promptly rested my head. Then, from a place deep within, I broke open and cried so hard I could barely catch my breath. All the while Louisa remained a quiet, consoling presence. When she finally spoke, her tone was soft, motherly. "I know you're hurting, and you didn't ever expect this, but it will turn out the way it's supposed to, Sam."

My mind and body, exhausted from the purging and the tears, struggled to process her words. *It will turn out the way it's supposed to* . . . I heard myself release a heavy sigh, as if there were some other person in the room, releasing her pain. Where was the anger? I longed for rage to propel me into the rant that would cleanse me, make my pulse beat again.

"Sam, I know you said the things you did because you were tying to be fair to him and because Shelly said you should let him have some freedom. And maybe you're regretting that now, but obviously something inside told you to give him that leeway. From what you've told me, I think he was very lonesome. You said he was always a little lost when you went out of town, even when you lived at home."

I couldn't summon the energy to nod. But I continued to listen.

"People don't always break apart because they stop loving each other. There are so many other factors. And maybe he's not like you."

"What do you mean?"

"You're strong. I could see it the moment I met you. You don't even realize it. I've watched how you operate these last few months. I admire your energy and your ability to tackle anything. I admire your resilience."

I looked at her as if she were describing some other person. "*My* resilience?"

"Give it time. You'll be fine. And, if you and Buck are meant to be together, you will be. It'll work out the way it's supposed to."

Louisa always told me the truth. Others said what they thought I wanted to hear, either believing their own empty words or content that their little white lies helped to console me. But no comfort resides in falsehood. Louisa never offered false hopes, just hope for a better tomorrow. Her honesty nourished me; her friendship became the crutch that supported me until I could walk on my own again. But the process required time. And I had plenty of that. Time sprawled before me, with its lengthy hours and interminable minutes.

I could feel Louisa's eyes on me. "How you doing, Sam?"

I lifted my head and looked out the window again. I loved New York. It just kept going, no matter what. There is a kind of dying that happens when love meets its end. And just when the welcomed numbness penetrates nearly every pore, a burning begins again, ignited by some hidden ember. It rages with furious consumption, burning until every single ember breathes with shallow intake. Once again, life is barely visible.

The light inside me dimmed. I had no choice but to adjust to the dark until I could find my way once again.

Part Three

1969-1979

Seventy-seven

July 1972

Sometimes dreams come true. Louisa and I backpacked throughout Europe that summer, staying in hostels and cheap hotels. The sleeping arrangements were far from perfect, but the glory of each day overshadowed minor inconveniences.

I walked through the Vatican Museums to the Sistine Chapel and cried when I gazed upon Michelangelo's work of art . . . I climbed the Acropolis to the Parthenon, towering over the Plaka in Athens, and I marveled at the city's textbook view . . . I walked under the Lion's Gate in Mycenae, home of Agamemnon, and the stories of the Cyclopes came alive before me . . . I visited Shakespeare's home in Stratford-on-Avon and breathed the air that once filled the lungs of the great bard . . . I witnessed the running of the bulls in Pamplona and imagined that I was walking in footprints that Hemingway had once pressed into the ground . . . I climbed the many, many stairs to Sacre Coeur atop Montmartre and sat alone in a pew to say a prayer . . . I experienced the splendor of Versailles and beheld the opulence of Marie Antoinette's life . . . I drank French beer in the Latin Quarter and strolled along the Left Bank of the Seine where artists sell their wares . . . Paris became my second favorite city.

New York City became my home.

* * *

September 1972

"So you want to be a writer, eh, Ms. DeSantis?"

"I *am* a writer."

He smiled.

"So you are. I've read some of your work. You're good. Could be a little edgier, but that will come."

"And from where will that come, Mr. Hopper?" In retrospect, I was probably a tad too cocky. Ah, youth!

He sat back in his chair. "Well, if you've got the chops and can handle the criticism, I think right here."

"Here? In this building? Overlooking the river?"

"Overlooking implies a window, Ms. DeSantis."

"Did you say a window? By the way, please call me Samantha."

He laughed. "Pay starts low."

"That's not a problem. Just as long as I can cover the rent."

"Where you living?"

"What are you paying?"

I ran to the closest phone booth. "Mom! I got the job!" There was so much noise on the other end of the line, I couldn't understand a word. I stood on the corner of 54th and 6th—Avenue of the Americas to tourists—breathing in the possibilities in front of me while my family screamed into the telephone.

Seventy-eight

December 22, 1979

The Christmas tree in Rockefeller Center is an elegant Norway spruce, towering 65 feet into the winter sky. Year after year it lures thousands upon thousands of tourists who have heard the stories of its majesty. It winks at me as I walk by, beckons me to linger awhile. My arms are laden with purchases from a nearby deli: sopresata, pungent cheese, crusty Italian bread. I'm in a hurry to drop them off. I try to ignore the temptation to stop, but the tree calls to me like the Sirens.

Okay, you win.

I sit on a bench next to an elderly couple who smile at me. It's good to sit for a while.

"The tree is magnificent, isn't it?" I say. The strangers nod. I'm not sure they understand me.

I lose myself in the hum of the city that surrounds me. I inhale the electric air. People scurry everywhere, bundled to protect themselves from the cold. Gloved hands tote shopping bags with famous logos—last minute gifts that cost far too much. Skaters brave the rink below me, despite the bite in the air. Smiles emerge amongst strangers. It's Christmas.

The man and woman beside me stand up, gathering their packages. They smile at me again and nod. The woman pats my hand, which instinctively rests across the expanse of my belly.

"When?" she manages.

"Soon," I say. "Merry Christmas." I point to the big, decorated tree, the universal symbol. "Merry Christmas," I repeat, louder than I need to.

They both nod. "Ah, Wesołych Świąt!" *Merry Christmas.* They walk away, hand in hand.

I decide to sit awhile longer to watch the people. A girl with long frosted hair and burgundy bell-bottoms runs by. Maybe she's late for the theater. Her platform shoes slow her. She looks frustrated. A man in a colorful 3-piece suit, which seems to match his personality, lights a cigarette and throws the match to the ground. His stance is arrogant, and he gazes around as if he owns the city. An attractive woman, maybe in her late 40s, pulls her fur coat tighter to keep warm. She looks expensive. Her high heels match the skirt that keeps peeking out. An Annie Hall look-alike in a brown tweed jacket runs up to a handsome man and kisses him. They look happy. I smile.

"Mama!"

I look up in surprise to see my rosy-cheeked daughter running toward me. She wears a dark green velvet coat with a matching hat tied under her chin. The sight of her reminds me why I am alive.

"See my baby!" She cradles the doll in her arms like a little mother. When she reaches me, she hands me her doll and rests her head on my belly. Her small arms stretch around the expanse of me.

"Oh, Lila! She's beautiful. Did Daddy buy her for you?"

"Uh-huh." She turns and smiles up at her father. "At Foe Switz."

I laugh at her pronunciation. "You went to FAO Swartz! Did you see the big bear?"

"Uh-huh. And the candy. Kiss my baby, Mama."

"What's her name?"

"Heidi," she tells me proudly.

"Heidi. Well, I just love that name."

My husband towers above us, wearing his camel hair coat and killer smile. "Hey, babe. How you feeling?" He looks proud of himself for finding me.

"What are you doing here? I can't believe you found me."

"You're easy, Sam." He points at the tree. "Big Christmas tree, skaters, decorations in every window."

I smile at my husband's sixth sense when it comes to me. "I was on my way back to the apartment, but the tree tempted me."

"Isn't Rockefeller Center a little out of the way?" he says sarcastically.

I am predictable. "So."

"Come on, I'll carry those bags for you. The deli again, huh?" He smirks as he relieves me of my burden.

"I could smell it when I walked by."

"Mama," Lila reached her arms up to me. "Hold me."

"Mama can't pick you up, Squirt. The baby's too big," says her dad.

"That baby *is* gettin' big." She pats my belly.

"Daddy will carry you." He whisks her up. Her head drops on his shoulder like a sinker. "You're not tired now, are you, little one? We still have to go to the Christmas show later this afternoon."

Her eyes brighten. "The pretty ladies?"

"Yes," I add, "the pretty ladies."

"And Santa?" she asks.

"Do you think Santa's going to be there, Squirt?" His voice is pure when he talks to our daughter.

"Yes," she says weakly. Her lids drop over her eyes.

"Let's get you and Mommy home. We still have a couple of hours before the show. My girls can take a nap."

I rub my daughter's back and then attend to my own.

"How's my big girl doing? Baby pulling on your back?" His arms are too full to touch me, but his eyes tell me he wants to. I loop my arm through his, close to our daughter.

"Yeah. I'm ready for him to be here."

"Him?" His eyebrows arch.

"Yeah, I figure if I keep saying *him*, we might get our boy."

He laughs. "Okay, Pollyanna. That would be perfect."

"Don't call me that!" I feel him smiling on me, even though I look in the other direction. "Let's stop a minute and look at the tree some more. And don't make fun of me!"

"I'd never do that." He clears his throat to hide his amusement.

A man wrapped in colored lights skates around the perimeter of the rink below us. He grins at the crowd as the lights blink on and off. His goofy charm seduces passers-by.

"Sam, look at that guy down there! What a riot!"

I look at my husband and remember.

Harry's was wall-to-wall people. Colored lights blinked at the patrons, as usual. Off-tune singing emanated from a happy group at the bar. *Oh there's no place like home for the holidays.* I stood in the third tier of college students surrounding the bar, desperately trying to order a beer. He stared at me. He was wearing a Santa hat with a big ball on the top. He smiled, his face covered with mischief.

"You want me to order you a beer? You're drowning back there."

"Sure," I shouted over the noise.

"I'm Rick. This one's on me."

"That's okay. I can pay for my own."

"Aw, come on. Give a guy a break. It's not often I run into such a pretty girl."

"Does that line work for you often?"

"Ninety-eight percent return." He grinned. The white ball on the top of his hat bobbed when he spoke. I shook my head. "Hey, give a guy a break. It's my birthday, after all."

"Is it really? Or is that another line?"

His held up his hand. "Scout's honor. Come on, one beer."

"You don't even know my name," I shot back.

"What's your name?"

"Samantha DeSantis."

"See, I got you to tell me your name," he announced proudly.

"Are you drunk?"

"No! Just buzzed. It's my birthday."

"Yeah, you already said that."

"So? You gonna have a beer with me, Samantha DeSantis?" I had wiggled my way closer to the bar, money in hand.

"I already said I can pay myself."

"Aw, you're no fun!" He slugged his beer and slammed it down on the bar.

"I am too!"

"Yeah? Prove it!" The grin emerged, its effect contagious.

"Take off your glasses," I told him.

"Why?"

"I want to see your eyes."

"Okay, Samantha DeSantis." He whipped off the thick, unstylish frames. Big, sexy blue eyes stared at me. I couldn't look away.

"Um . . . you have . . . kind eyes," I told him.

"What kind is that?" His grin widened again.

"That's not even funny. You're a smart ass."

"So they tell me."

"Okay, one drink," I slid my money back into the pocket of my jeans.

"You won't be sorry."

"What makes you so sure?"

"You'll see."

"I'll see what?"

"I'm gonna marry you, Samantha DeSantis. But not before you fall in love with me."

"You must be drunk, pal, cause I'm not gonna marry anybody."

The skater with the blinking lights turns on a hidden microphone and starts singing along with the music that is piped into the rink.

"This guy's a hoot!"

"What?" I realize I am lost in thought.

"Look at him down there, Sam. He's either an NBC plant, or he went to some great length to entertain the crowd." The square is jammed with people, hanging over the rails to watch the skater's antics. "We better go, babe. She's out cold," he shifts his weight as he readjusts Lila in his arms.

I look at my husband and fall in love again, like I do every day. "Rick?"

"Yeah?" He looks alarmed when I don't answer. "What? Are you having contractions again? Is this it?" His eyes are hopeful.

I chuckle. "No. Not yet."

"What then?"

"Nothing. Merry Christmas."

He leans over and kisses the top of my head. "Merry Christmas, babe." He examines my face again. "You sure you're all right?"

"Yeah," I reassure him. "Time to get the pregnant lady home. She needs to elevate her fat feet."

"And finish her manuscript," he reminds. "Your editor called again this morning."

"So what's new? Any by the way, Scrooge, stop cracking the whip! It's Christmas."

"Yeah, well, you've got a deadline. First of the year, remember?"

I rub my back. "Deadlines, due dates . . ." I hear myself exhale.

"Yeah, but look at the results. Come on, I'll take care of everything. I'll put Lila down and make you some tea. Let's go home, Sam."

Epilogue

Buck was accepted by all of the colleges to which he applied—except for Harvard. He chose Cornell. He wrote to tell me of his acceptance. I didn't respond. He broke up with Jacquelyn at the end of his first semester. She didn't take it well. I guess she really loved him. I later learned that he told her he was still in love with me. He wrote to me again during his second semester and filled me in on his course of studies. Law. No surprise there. I didn't respond. He continued to write, despite the absence of response. One day he called. I almost didn't answer. His voice was haunting, stirring me inside. He said he wanted to see me. I was reluctant. We had been apart for over a year and a half. I guess I had to see what would happen. I agreed.

It was summer. We decided to meet for lunch. When I walked into the club dining room, he stood up. He took my breath away. I could tell I took his too. It was awkward at first. Stolen looks, nervous smiles, small talk. Thank you for coming, he said. God, you're gorgeous, Sam. I could tell he meant it. Your hair is longer, and it looks like you've been spending some time in the sun, he said. We talked about college, our classes, our families. It was so familiar.

I never stopped loving you, he blurted in sudden courage. He reached for my hand. I let him take it. He felt so good. Sam, do you think there's a chance? he asked. My heart pounded harder.

I still loved him. Would always love him. We grew up together. Now he was speaking the words I lived for. The words I believed I would never hear again. Louisa told me it would work out the way it was supposed to. She was right.

It's too late, I told him. I watched the color drain from his face. I told him this was hard for me. That I loved him too. Always would. But I could not go back. So that's it? he said. I heard the pain. I felt my eyes filling up, threatening to spill over. I blinked and blinked and blinked, trying to make it go away. The waitress returned. Have you decided yet? she asked. He looked at me, his stunning eyes suspended in hope. I'm sorry, I told her, but I think we've changed our minds.

He walked me to my car. I could tell he wanted to kiss me. I wanted the same. He came close to me, his breath on my face. Asked if he could continue to write. I wanted him to. So much. I don't think that's a good idea, I said. You mean we're never going to talk to each other again? The impact of his words resurrected a deep pain. I could feel my eyes filling again, my heart breaking open. I could not bear it. Sam? His voice tugged at me. I wanted him to stop saying my name. I have to go now, I said. He grabbed me. Kissed me hard. I kissed him back. I almost lost myself. And then I pulled away.

I returned to NYC for the remainder of that summer. I fed my soul with books and theater and the simple pleasures that take one's thoughts away. I wrote some of my best work that summer. Angst—great fodder for stories, especially when it's real.

He eventually stopped writing, and I cried. I kept expecting another letter. I reached way back into my mailbox, but it was empty, day after day. He finally let me go. I guess it is choice that triumphs after all.

I dream of him sometimes. In my dreams he is young again. And I am sixteen. But sixteen is gone—sixteen breathes only in memory. In a recessed corner of my heart, resides the shadow of a boy who awakened me first and loved me well.

It was our hour.